Dear Reader,

Harlequin has been a longtime supporter of women's causes. The Harlequin More Than Words program is Harlequin's primary philanthropic initiative and is dedicated to celebrating and rewarding ordinary women who make extraordinary contributions in their community.

We always knew that Harlequin readers cared for those around them, but this was proven over and over again when we launched the More Than Words program last year. Readers turned out in each city to support our first five More Than Words award recipients, and in this our second year, nominations streamed in from all over North America. Now, with our second annual More Than Words award winners chosen, we are proud to share stories of these women with you by asking five of our most acclaimed authors to write these wonderful fictional stories inspired by the lives of our award winners. Debbie Macomber, Sharon Sala, Jasmine Cresswell, Beverly Barton and Julie Elizabeth Leto all gave their time and energy to create stories that we know will entertain and inspire you. All of the proceeds from this book will be reinvested in the More Than Words program, further supporting causes that are of concern to women.

Please visit www.HarlequinMoreThanWords.com for more information, or to submit a nominee for next year's book. Together we can make a difference.

Sincerely,

Donna Hayes
Publisher and CEO
Harlequin Enterprises

DEBBIE
MACOMBER

SHARON
SALA

JASMINE
CRESSWELL

BEVERLY
BARTON

JULIE ELIZABETH
LETO

VOLUME 2

More Than Words

HARLEQUIN®

TORONTO • NEW YORK • LONDON
AMSTERDAM • PARIS • SYDNEY • HAMBURG
STOCKHOLM • ATHENS • TOKYO • MILAN • MADRID
PRAGUE • WARSAW • BUDAPEST • AUCKLAND

ISBN 0-373-83580-9

MORE THAN WORDS

CONTENTS

TEENS LIVING WITH CANCER
LAUREN SPIKER

Lauren Spiker's daughter Melissa was a typical high school senior preparing for her prom and graduation, excited about attending university in the fall to study nursing. And then Melissa was diagnosed with a rare bone marrow cancer. In June 2000, after two courageous years, Melissa lost her battle with the disease. She was nineteen years old. But before Melissa died she asked a promise of her mother. "If you have learned anything from me through all of this, do something with it to make a difference—to make things better."

Lauren kept her promise, establishing Melissa's Living Legacy, a foundation dedicated to helping teens with cancer meet their life challenges in productive, creative and satisfying ways. In June 2002, the foundation implemented Teens Living with Cancer (www.teenslivingwithcancer.org), a Web site committed to "making things better" for teens with cancer by providing on-line resources to support teens, their families and friends. Teens Living with Cancer is cosponsored by The Children's Oncology Group, the premier pediatric cooperative oncology research group in

North America, creating the most comprehensive Web-based resource available for teens with cancer.

Motivated by the special needs of teens

Melissa received excellent medical care, but Lauren was struck by the limited focus on the issues faced by teens with cancer, as well as the absence of helpful resources. Information in books and on the Net was either filled with complicated medical jargon or too simplified and geared toward children. Through Teens Living with Cancer, Lauren strives to fill this gap. The Web site provides information about the various forms of cancer and describes treatments and their effects on the body in "teen-friendly" terms and based on the real-life experiences of teens with cancer. The site, which gets about 50,000 hits a week, upholds and fosters basic values of honesty, compassion, self-determination, courage and perseverance. A focus on quality of life is promoted throughout all stages of the disease, from diagnosis through treatment and remission and, if necessary, when facing death.

Teens Living with Cancer is also an online community, offering a forum for teens struggling with the disease to meet online and share their experiences. It's an opportunity to connect, interact and encourage each other, bridging emotional gaps with an understanding the teens can't truly get from people who aren't living with cancer.

Nearly 15,000 teens are in active treatment for cancer each year, and the unique challenges confronting *all* teens are magnified in those with this disease. Teens with cancer must face physical changes and/or disfigurement at a time when appearance is a paramount concern, loss of peer groups and acceptance when inclusion is a primary need, and reproductive challenges and sexual dilemmas at a time of emerging sexuality. They also must deal with unwanted dependence at a time of newfound independence, and a loss of control when new boundaries are just being tested.

It's important to Lauren that Teens Living with Cancer be sensitive to these issues. The Web site offers information and advice that is medically sound *and* nonjudgmental—answering important questions that teens may be hesitant to ask their parents or medical team. The goal is to empower young people to make the best decisions for themselves, both physically and emotionally. Teens want to have a voice in what happens with their care but often feel they have no spokesperson. Teens Living with Cancer encourages them to be their own advocates. Lauren herself is committed to motivating teens with cancer to live to the fullest, just as her daughter Melissa did—to have a sense of their own ability to influence their situations and lead meaningful, productive lives.

Support for families and friends

Teens Living with Cancer also addresses issues relevant to the families and friends of teens living with the disease, providing information as well as stories from family members and friends of teenage cancer patients. So often friends and loved ones want to be helpful, but they aren't sure what to say or do. Through Teens Living with Cancer, family and friends find ways to provide help and understanding—even if they can't take away a friend or relative's suffering.

The Teens Living with Cancer Web site connects groups and individuals with ways to volunteer and participate in fund-raising for the cause. Lauren especially encourages teens who want to help other teens, and works with groups of young people on fund-raisers, giving them the chance to feel they are doing something concrete and productive to help their peers who are living with cancer. Lauren has recruited people in all walks of life to use their individual talents—from music to juggling to gardening—to come up with imaginative ways to participate.

Lauren also works closely with the medical community to involve them in new projects and, with their approval, helps raise money for endeavors that will benefit hundreds of teens with cancer. Doctors and nurses are not immune from human emotions when treating teens with this disease. Each day they face their teen patients with a warm smile on their faces and deep pain in their hearts. Lauren says that words cannot adequately express her gratitude for their efforts.

A commitment...for life

In addition to having a full-time job running her management training company, Lauren continues to devote countless hours as executive director of Melissa's Living Legacy, trying to help the foundation reach its goals. These include the creation of adolescent oncology centers of excellence where teens have access to age-appropriate programs and services, and the development of innovative educational resources for health care professionals. With three grown sons, two stepdaughters, and in recent years her first grandchildren, Lauren tirelessly balances family and work with traveling on the foundation's behalf, speaking at conferences as an advocate for teens with cancer and heading charitable events that raise funds and awareness for the cause. The subject matter is an emotional one, and some of her speaking engagements are difficult, but Lauren never shrinks from the opportunity to help others dealing with cancer.

Lauren Spiker continues to be motivated by her daughter Melissa's extraordinary spirit for life and by the promise Lauren made to her daughter—to make things better for teens with cancer. Today Teens Living with Cancer is helping to support and celebrate the courageous journeys of thousands of other teenagers... just like Melissa.

More Than Words

DEBBIE MACOMBER

WHAT
AMANDA
WANTS

DEBBIE MACOMBER

One of America's most popular novelists, *New York Times* best-selling author Debbie Macomber has more than 60 million copies of her books in print. In 1982 she became the first series romance author ever to be reviewed by the prestigious trade publication *Publishers Weekly,* and shortly thereafter was featured in *Newsweek.* Debbie was recently asked to become one of the first board members for Warm Up America! This charity organization asks knitters and crocheters to make 7" x 9" squares that can be joined into blankets and donated to the needy. Debbie and Wayne, who are the proud grandparents of seven grandchildren, live in the state of Washington and winter in Florida.

CHAPTER ONE

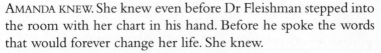

AMANDA KNEW. She knew even before Dr Fleishman stepped into the room with her chart in his hand. Before he spoke the words that would forever change her life. She knew.

The cancer was back.

She'd always realized that it might return, but she'd been cancer-free for almost eight years. An intellectual understanding of something wasn't the same as an emotional acceptance. Perhaps she'd grown complacent, convinced that after all this time she was cured. As a childhood-cancer survivor, perhaps she'd come to believe she was invincible.

The silence that followed his announcement reminded her of the eerie lack of sound before a storm. Before the thunder and lightning and torrential rain.

"Amanda," Dr. Fleishman said, breaking into her thoughts.

He wanted her attention, but she couldn't give it to him. Instead, she continued to stare at the floor. She didn't look up. She couldn't. Not just then. It would take a few minutes for the news to settle, a few minutes before she could face him.

It was the same with her mother. Joan Jennings sat in the chair next to Amanda's and it seemed as if all the life had drained out of her. Suddenly, after that long, awkward silence, Amanda's mother started to weep.

"I'm so sorry," Dr. Fleishman said softly.

Amanda nodded. Needing to hold on to something, she reached for her mother's hand. "It'll be all right, Mom," she whispered. She didn't know where that encouragement came from because she didn't feel it. Her entire world was about to implode.

"I guess this means I won't be cheerleading at the pep rally, doesn't it?" She tried hard to make a joke of it. She failed miserably; she didn't even sound like herself.

"Not this year," Dr. Fleishman murmured in reply.

She honestly hadn't expected an answer. He seemed so calm about it, but why shouldn't he be? It wasn't *his* life that was taking a nosedive. Anyway, the cheerleading thing was minor. More importantly, the Junior/Senior Prom was in May. By then her hair would've fallen out and Lance… She couldn't do that to him, couldn't embarrass him that way. The dress she loved, and had saved countless months for, would languish in her closet. Maybe she could be buried in it. Funny, the idea of dying didn't immediately upset her. She noticed then that her mother and Dr. Fleishman were carrying on a conversation.

Amanda sat there, half listening while they exchanged questions and answers. When he saw that he finally had Amanda's attention, Dr. Fleishman outlined a treatment schedule.

Amanda tried to take it all in but she couldn't. By the time they left the office, her mother had stopped crying. She clutched a wet tissue in her hand, and Amanda was afraid she'd dissolve into heart-wrenching sobs once again. Maybe in public.

"I don't want anyone to know," Amanda insisted as they walked toward the parking complex.

"We're going to do whatever it takes," her mother said with a grim set to her mouth. "I don't care what it costs. I don't care how much the insurance company fights us—I'll fight harder."

Her mother hadn't even heard her.

"You weren't listening to me," Amanda said. All her mother

could think about was the money and how much these treatments were going to cost and struggling with the insurance company. Amanda wanted an iPod and her mother had claimed it wasn't in the budget. But chemo, radiation, a bone-marrow transplant would cost a whole lot more.

"What did you say?" her mother asked.

"When?"

"You said I wasn't listening. Tell me what you said."

"Annie," she whispered. "I'll tell Annie." Annie was one of her best friends, and Amanda wouldn't be able to keep this news from her. Besides, when she didn't show up for the pep rally rehearsal, Annie would know something was wrong. So would Laurie, another of her good friends.

"I blame this on that party job," her mother said angrily.

"What?" Amanda stared at her in shocked disbelief. She worked with Annie and her mother on their birthday party business. Almost every weekend, Bethanne organized a number of birthday parties for youngsters, and she paid both Annie and Amanda to help. At first Amanda had tagged along...just because. She soon discovered it was a lot of fun; she liked helping kids celebrate their birthdays in a creative way. Annie's mother was really good at this. The money was a bonus, and Amanda had used it to save up for her prom dress.

"Those kids exposed you to all their germs," her mother snapped. "Those birthday parties are breeding grounds for—"

"I didn't get cancer at a birthday party."

Amanda could see it already. Her mother was going to smother her. In a misguided effort to protect her from harm, Joan would make everything worse. It'd been bad enough when Amanda was eight and nine. She couldn't even *imagine* what her mother would be like now. Amanda figured she'd be lucky to step inside a movie theater again—the germs floating around in places like that. And if her mother had anything to say about it, she'd be banned from shopping, too. How ridiculous was that! Amanda sighed heavily. Even if she survived, she'd be doomed to her mother's heavy-handed protection for the rest of her life.

And that remark about the birthday parties! It was as though her mother would feel better if she had someone or something to blame. Amanda didn't understand why. It wouldn't make the cancer magically disappear. And it didn't benefit anyone, except maybe her mom. That kind of thinking would drive Amanda crazy.

Neither spoke on the ride home. The minute she got out of the car, Amanda went straight to her room and shut the door. Once inside the relative privacy of her bedroom, she placed headphones over her ears and immersed herself in music.

Someone—obviously her mother—knocked loudly on her door, but Amanda ignored it. She didn't know if Joan came in to check on her, because she kept her eyes closed.

For whatever reason, the cancer was back and Amanda would be the one dealing with it. This wasn't a trig problem she could pass off to Lance in study hall to solve for her. Her parents couldn't help her, either. She was alone, and that was the most frightening thing of all.

Ten minutes later, the phone rang. Even with the music turned up full blast, Amanda could hear it. She ignored that, too. When her mother came into her room, Amanda reluctantly removed the headphones. "What?" she demanded.

Her mother's eyes filled with tears. "That was Annie."

"I don't want to talk right now." She was seventeen and she was dying and if she didn't want to answer the phone she shouldn't have to.

"I called your father…."

Amanda closed her eyes again. She didn't want to hear it. "Mom, please, give me a few minutes by myself. Just a few minutes." She didn't know why her mother was doing this. A little time alone shouldn't be that much to ask.

"I can't," her mother sobbed. Joan sank onto the edge of the bed, covered her face with both hands and began to cry.

Amanda bit her lower lip and knelt on the carpet at her mother's feet. After a moment she laid her head in her mother's lap. It occurred to her then that this diagnosis wasn't only about her. Her cancer affected everyone in her life.

Slowly Amanda's arms went around her mother's waist and she straightened. Her mother clung to her, burying her face in Amanda's shoulder, still sobbing.

Surprisingly, Amanda shed no tears. The emotion was there, just beneath the surface, pounding, throbbing, pulsing. What shocked Amanda, what threw her completely off guard, was her mother's reaction. This was the second time she'd faced cancer, the second time for her *and* her parents. You'd think her mom would know how to cope. Or maybe it was the exact opposite; maybe knowing what to expect made it worse.

"I'm going to be fine," Amanda cooed softly.

"I know."

Amanda had been too young the first time to remember how her mother and father had dealt with everything. Certain memories were strong: the pain, throwing up, losing her hair—and her mother at her side. Other memories had faded. The one constant had been her mother's devotion. She'd desperately needed it then and Amanda knew she'd need it now.

"I'm…sorry," her mother whispered. "I didn't mean to do this. You need me—but I'm so frightened. I can't bear to see you go through this again."

Amanda gently kissed the top of her mother's head. "It's all right, Mom. It's all right."

"I should be the strong one."

"You are." In the months to come, Amanda would need to lean on her mother's strength. Her mother would be her advocate, her nurse, her coach and her friend.

CHAPTER TWO

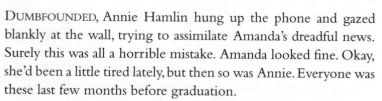

DUMBFOUNDED, Annie Hamlin hung up the phone and gazed blankly at the wall, trying to assimilate Amanda's dreadful news. Surely this was all a horrible mistake. Amanda looked fine. Okay, she'd been a little tired lately, but then so was Annie. Everyone was these last few months before graduation.

Her mother walked into the kitchen, humming "Home on the Range." That meant Bethanne was getting ready for a Wild West Birthday Extravaganza. This particular party involved a cookout over a campfire, plus a bale of hay where Annie sat strumming a guitar and singing cattle-drive favorites. Little boys loved this theme because they got to wear cowboy hats and sheriff's badges, and the villain was quickly found out when the cake was sliced. Her mother dropped a black jellybean into the batter and whoever got that slice was declared the bad guy.

Bethanne walked past her, paused and then glanced back. "What's wrong? You look like you've lost your best friend."

At those words involuntary tears welled in Annie's eyes. "Amanda just phoned. She had a doctor's appointment this afternoon."

"I remember. You were upset because she was supposed to go shopping with you."

Annie nodded, hardly able to believe she could've been angry with her friend over something so meaningless. "Mom, she told me..." She blinked hard and tried again. Even saying the words caused her pain. "Amanda has cancer."

Her mother stared at her. "Cancer?" she repeated slowly.

"It's leukemia."

Her mother pulled out a chair and sat down at the table next to Annie. "How long has she known?"

"She just found out."

"I'm so sorry." Her mother frowned. "Has anyone in her family ever had cancer?"

"Yes." Annie swallowed. "Amanda has. Don't you remember me telling you she had leukemia when she was in second grade?"

Her mother wrinkled her brow, suggesting that if Annie had mentioned it, she'd forgotten. "Her poor mother," she said.

Annie wasn't sure what Amanda's mother had to do with it, but she didn't ask. "The cancer's back and according to the doctor, it's worse than before."

"Oh dear." Her mother's eyes met hers.

"You know what's really sad?" Annie whispered, glancing away from her mother. It was embarrassing to confess this, even to her own mother.

"What?" Bethanne asked.

Annie felt horrible. Her friend had cancer and might not survive and when Amanda had told her, all Annie could think about was herself. "My first thought—my very first thought—was that I'd have to find someone else to double with for prom night." She paused and waited for her mother to berate her. Bethanne didn't.

"It was...so unexpected," Annie continued, as the beginnings of this new reality settled in the pit of her stomach. "I didn't know what to say and neither did Amanda. Then she started to cry and asked if I thought she should tell Lance so he could ask someone else to the prom."

"What did you say?"

"I didn't say much of anything. I just muttered something and she seemed to think I said yes. But I didn't... If I were her I wouldn't know what to do, either. I feel awful, like I'm going to throw up." Annie almost wished her mother would chastise her for being so self-absorbed.

"Amanda's still in shock."

Annie knew that had to be true.

One of her dearest friends was desperately sick, and she had no idea how to help her.

"What'll happen now?" Bethanne murmured.

"I asked Amanda that." Well, it was one point in Annie's favor. "She said there'd be a series of chemotherapy sessions and she'd lose her hair and then she'd have to go through a bone-marrow transplant."

"There's a good donor in her family?"

"I hope so," Annie said, wishing she'd asked more intelligent questions. "The thing is, Amanda doesn't want anyone other than me to know."

"People will find out. That's unavoidable, don't you think?"

Annie agreed. News like this would spread in about five minutes once Amanda stopped attending classes. Everyone would want to know where she was and why. Annie couldn't understand Amanda's reasons for not telling her friends.

"She wanted me to lie to Lance for her."

Bethanne's eyes widened. "Did you say you would?"

"No way."

Her mother nodded approvingly. "Good."

Refusing Amanda had been difficult. Still, Annie didn't feel she could lie to Lance. He genuinely cared for Amanda and in Annie's opinion, Lance was entitled to the truth.

"She's afraid, you know," her mother said.

"Of cancer?" Annie asked and then answered her own question. "I would be, too."

Bethanne shook her head. "The cancer's scary enough. But I was talking about everything else."

"What do you mean?"

"Other people's reactions." Bethanne took a deep breath. "After your father moved out," she said, "I was afraid to leave the house."

"But why? You didn't do anything."

"I didn't want people to know Grant had left. For the first couple of months, I pretended he was away on an extended business trip. If anyone asked, I made up this elaborate story about Grant's heavy traveling schedule. I even invented a date when he was supposed to return."

This was all news to Annie.

"In my mind, I actually came to believe that within that time frame, your father would realize what he was doing and move back home. After two months, I was forced to admit that Grant meant what he said. He wanted out of the marriage."

Bethanne so rarely mentioned the divorce, Annie actually felt privileged that her mother had shared this with her.

"In some ways," Bethanne continued, "I think Amanda is afraid of people talking about her and pitying her, just like I was. It's difficult enough to accept devastating news, but then you have to handle everyone else's feelings about it, as well."

Annie frowned in puzzlement. Some of this made sense to her, but part of it didn't.

"When people hear bad news, their first reaction is usually shock and sadness. Sometimes curiosity. And sometimes they think they can fix it."

Then Annie understood. She hadn't even disconnected from her conversation with Amanda when she'd begun making plans. She'd get all their friends together and they'd make a huge get-well card and fill a basket with gifts and… It was an automatic response. Looking for an easy fix. She was still trying to figure out how to deal with this shock.

"Other people aren't as kind," her mother said. "They want to find a way to blame you. One friend suggested…" She paused. "Never mind, that isn't important now. My point is that once the news is out, Amanda will be confronted with everyone's reactions—family, friends, teachers—not just her own."

Annie had a renewed respect for her mother's insight. "That's deep."

Bethanne laughed softly. "Are you making fun of me?"

"No," Annie said. "I meant it. You're so right, Mom. About people's reactions. All I could think about when Amanda phoned was what her cancer would mean to our friendship."

"That's perfectly understandable." Her mother stood and checked her watch. "If you need to talk more about this, let me know."

"I will. Thanks, Mom."

Her mother went to open the kitchen cupboard. After shuffling several things around, she asked, "Do you remember if I used the last of the liquid smoke?"

"No, you didn't." Annie's mind was back on Amanda and how she could best be a friend to her. Not a fixer or a comforter. Not a weeper or a gawker. Just a friend.

"Just a minute," Bethanne said, whirling around. "You know who you should talk to?" Before Annie could answer, she said, "Lydia Hoffman."

"The lady who owns the knitting shop—A Good Yarn?"

Her mother nodded enthusiastically. "Lydia had cancer as a teenager, too."

Annie vaguely remembered her mother mentioning that.

"She's been through this herself. Twice, in fact. She was only sixteen when she was first diagnosed."

"Did she have leukemia, too?"

"Brain tumor."

"And she survived…" Knowing that her mother's friend had come through this encouraged Annie.

"Yes, and she didn't have an easy time of it, either. She's never said much about it to me. Margaret's the one who let certain details slip."

"Who's Margaret?"

"Oh, sorry, her sister. She works at the shop, too."

Annie thought she might've seen her once.

"Lydia's just the person who could help you be Amanda's friend."

"I'll call her, Mom. Thanks."

She might have faltered when she'd first heard the news about Amanda's cancer, but Annie was determined that wouldn't happen again.

CHAPTER THREE

LYDIA HOFFMAN GOETZ

I'VE KNOWN ANNIE HAMLIN for over a year and I've never seen her looking this serious. Or this sad. She phoned me earlier in the afternoon and asked if she could come and visit after school. The request surprised me. Annie is the daughter of one of my customers and friends, Bethanne. I've often chatted with Annie but always on a casual basis.

She arrived at the store just before five. I needed to finish up with a couple of customers, so Annie waited for me. She strolled through the shop, studying the hand-knit socks and sweaters on display, and leafed through a pattern book. After I rang up the last sale of the day, I locked the front door and turned over the sign to read Closed. I was now free to talk to my friend's daughter.

"How about a cup of tea?" I said.

"Sure." Annie followed me into my small office. There really wasn't room for us to chat comfortably, so once I'd made the tea I carried two cups out to the table where I teach my knitting

classes. I'd met Annie's mother in a sock-knitting class. Bethanne was an emotional wreck at the time, her self-esteem in the gutter after her divorce. Annie had experienced her share of emotional trauma, too. I was proud of the turnaround in both their lives.

"What can I do for you?" I asked.

Annie set her cup carefully back in the saucer. "Mom suggested I talk to you about my friend Amanda. She's one of my best friends and, Lydia…" Her voice shook, and she paused long enough to regain her composure. "Amanda just learned she has cancer."

So that was what had upset Annie so much. It also explained why she'd come to me. I'm a two-time cancer survivor. When I went into remission after the second bout, I opened A Good Yarn. You see, this store is an affirmation for me—an affirmation of life.

"The thing is," Annie went on, "Amanda had cancer when she was eight."

"So this is her second time facing the beast."

Annie nodded expectantly. I wished I knew what to say. "How can I help?" I asked.

"Amanda didn't want to tell anyone, not even me. One reason she did was because we were supposed to double-date on prom night."

"She can't go now?"

"She didn't seem to think so. This hit her out of nowhere."

That I understood. I'd been sixteen when the first brain tumor was discovered and in my early twenties the second time around. The second diagnosis was the hardest to accept; it blindsided me and my family. I think that's partly because I was sure I'd triumphed over cancer, and it seemed so *unfair* to go through it again. To this day, I believe it was my second bout with cancer that killed my father. The death certificate says it was a heart attack. Medically that's accurate, but I'm positive the underlying cause was dealing with my cancer. I could well understand Amanda's shock and horror at learning the disease had returned.

"Did she tell you what kind of cancer she has?"

"She had a technical name that I couldn't repeat if I tried. She

explained it's a rare form of leukemia." Her gaze held mine. "She's acting all weird. Like I said, Amanda doesn't want anyone to know—not even Lance, and he's her boyfriend."

"Give her some time to adjust to the news," I advised.

"That's what Mom said I should do, and I'm trying." Annie didn't seem satisfied with that, however. "She's reeling from this. I want to be a good friend." Annie leaned toward me as if I had secrets to share. "I want to say the right things. I don't want to…to be insensitive, but I don't want to act like I pity her, either. Do you know what I mean?"

I nodded. "Amanda's fortunate to have you for a friend," I said, searching for suggestions that would help Annie feel she was contributing in an appropriate way. "It might not seem like she wants her friends around just now, but in a little while that'll change. She's going to need you."

"I haven't said a word to anyone at school."

I realized it must've been hard on Annie to keep this to herself.

"Lance is pestering me to tell him what's up. I told him he should talk to Amanda."

"Has she been to classes?"

Annie shook her head. "Her mom's homeschooling her for the rest of the year. She did say she wants to graduate with our class, but she doesn't know if that'll be possible now."

I knew that keeping Annie's friend away from school protected her from any unnecessary exposure while her immune system was compromised. At the same time, I was aware that Amanda was now isolated from everything familiar. The same thing had happened to me. I couldn't attend classes, either. My friends had stuck around for a while. But later, as my treatment wore on, they lost interest. There wasn't much entertainment in a cancer ward. It was awkward, too, because my life in the hospital was so completely unlike their carefree times.

When I was a teenager I was first put in a pediatric ward, along with the little kids. I didn't appreciate visits from clowns who thought their antics would amuse me; I felt humiliated when my

friends showed up to find some ridiculous-looking character at my bedside, blowing up a balloon for me. Nor did I appreciate the Sesame Street drawings on the wall. I was a teenager, and everyone treated me like I was a three-year-old.

"Amanda said she won't go to the dance but I know that deep down she really wants to."

"Of course she does." I understood that, too. "When I first found out I had cancer, I'd just turned sixteen." I'd gone in a for a routine eye exam and that was when it all began. Soon afterward, the brain tumor was discovered. I paused to sip my tea. "As crazy as it sounds, one of the first things I did after I was diagnosed—" I hesitated to tell Annie this because it embarrassed me "—I...I cut up my driver's license."

"Why?"

Even after all these years I couldn't exactly say. "I don't know. I guess it was because I felt that every good thing in my life was about to be destroyed, so why not that, too? It doesn't make any sense, I know. I can't explain what came over me. I took a pair of scissors and cut my brand-new license into tiny pieces."

"Did you...do you drive now?"

"Yes." I smiled. "I realize it was rather melodramatic of me. I wish I could explain it better."

Annie grew thoughtful. "I think I understand. Amanda's rejecting the things that used to matter to her. She's pushing all her friends away from her, too."

"So did I, at first. I tried to close everyone out." I took another sip of tea. "That didn't last long, though. I got lonely and bored, and I missed my friends."

"Lance needs to know. He's driving me crazy."

My smile was sad as I recalled my relationship difficulties. "It's up to Amanda to tell him. She'll do that when she's ready."

"Can you give me any other advice?"

Annie was so sincere that I reached across the table and gripped her hand. "Amanda needs you more than ever now. Be her friend."

"That's what I want to do, but I'm still not sure I know how."

"She's going through a hard time emotionally. It might sound like a cliché—but just be there for her. In time, she'll want to discuss uncomfortable subjects. Don't let that frighten you. Hear her out."

"Do you mean she'll want to discuss…dying?"

"Probably." I watched Annie and was pleased that she didn't flinch. When you're dealing with cancer, the threat of death is a constant presence. In the beginning I ignored it. Later, the sicker I became, the more at ease I got to be with it. Death became a very real companion and the fear and mystery of it vanished.

"Okay," Annie said. "I won't let talk of death upset me."

"Good. She might mention her treatment and how sick she feels. Don't let that gross you out, okay?"

"All right." Annie finished her tea.

"Don't wait to hear from her, either. Take responsibility for maintaining the friendship."

Annie nodded. "Thank you, Lydia."

"You're welcome. If there's anything more I can do, please give me a call."

We both stood at the same time and then Annie did something unexpected. She hugged me. I hugged her back and wished her friend the very best.

AMANDA WATCHED her mother as she slipped away from the darkened bedroom doorway. In the silent stillness of dawn, Amanda could hear her weeping. She hated this, hated the way her mother reacted to the slightest sigh or moan. It was just as she'd expected. Her mother was suffocating her. Twice before, Amanda had awakened in the middle of the night to find Joan standing inside the bedroom, watching her. She hated feeling smothered, but most of all she hated causing her mother so much grief.

This morning, Amanda would begin what Dr. Fleishman had termed aggressive chemotherapy, followed by total body radiation. Although she'd only been eight when cancer struck the first time, Amanda remembered the hellish side effects of those treatments. The nausea had been the worst—until she'd suffered brain seizures.

Back then, Amanda had been mostly out of it. She remembered how sick she'd felt and asking God to let her die.

She was older now, more experienced in life, and she knew the horrors she faced. Her parents did, too, and her older brother, as well. Joe hadn't said much. He was at Washington State University in Pullman and had called her as soon as he heard the news. Like her friend Annie, Amanda's brother had been at a loss as to what to say. He wanted to help, but didn't know how. She sensed he was grateful to be away at school and frankly she didn't blame him. If their situations were reversed, Amanda figured she'd feel the same way. Finally, after several awkward minutes, he managed to croak out that if she needed anything, all she had to do was ask.

What she needed was a life. A real life. Her biggest fear wasn't the treatment, which she already knew wasn't going to be any picnic. No, top on her priority list was graduating with her friends. It wasn't so much to ask, was it? Graduation was six weeks away. Six weeks wasn't that long. She'd wear a wig for the ceremony. Apparently there were some really good ones.

At six her mother came into her bedroom to wake her. "Rise and shine," Joan said, wearing a bright smile.

Amanda saw through her facade immediately. This false cheer was hard to swallow. "Mom," she said, sitting up in bed. She patted the space next to her. "I have something I want to tell you and Dad."

"Leon," her mother shouted over her shoulder. "Amanda wants to talk to us."

Her father stepped into the bedroom, dressed and ready to leave for his job at Boeing as a control systems analyst. "What is it, pumpkin?"

Amanda smiled. She was close to her father; her mother, too, only it was different with her dad. They were more alike, and they had a similar sense of humor.

She released a pent-up sigh. "I don't want to sound like a drama queen, but you need to know I've reached an important decision."

Both her parents stared at her. There wasn't any reason to keep them in suspense. "I know I might die. Cancer is serious, and I'm going through it for the second time. Dr. Fleishman didn't say it, but he didn't have to—I could see it in his eyes."

"Now, pumpkin, don't talk like that. You're going to lick this."

"Dad," she said, meeting his gaze without flinching. "You were the one who said 'prepare for the worst and hope for the best.' That's all I'm doing."

Her mother's eyes filled with tears. "I want you to think about living, not dying."

"I am. I will."

Her mother sobbed again.

"Mom," Amanda shouted, losing patience with her. "Stop crying! I can't stand seeing you cry all the time. Get a grip. I've got enough on my plate without having to worry about you." She sounded harsher than she meant to, but it had to be said.

"I'm sorry." Her mother's voice quavered.

Amanda's father placed a protective arm around his wife's shoulders. "There's no need to snap at your mother, pumpkin. She loves you. We both do."

"I know, I know."

"You w-wanted to say something?" her mother asked, her resolve clear.

Amanda nodded. "Let's try this again." She took a deep breath. "I know I could die and I want you to know I'm fine with that."

Her mother crumpled emotionally and couldn't suppress a protesting sob. "You're giving up, aren't you?"

"No way." This was the really important part. "The thing is, I'm willing to do everything necessary to get well. I know it isn't going to be easy. I accept that from this point forward, my life will change. It sucks, but I don't have many options. I'll fight the disease with everything in me."

"But?" her father pressed. He knew there was one coming.

Amanda let her love for them show in her eyes. "But I won't fight death."

Tears rolled down her mother's pale cheeks and she started to shake her head; if Amanda wasn't going to fight death, she seemed to say, then she'd do it for her. Somehow, some way, regardless of the cost, Joan Jennings would hold back the Grim Reaper.

"I was thinking about it this morning lying in bed," Amanda explained, eager to share this new insight with her parents. "It was because of something Annie said." She had her parents' attention. "When I told her about the cancer, she didn't know what to say at first. The next day she phoned back, and the two of us talked for a long time."

"Annie's a good friend," her mother whispered.

Amanda agreed. She hadn't realized how good a friend until now. It felt good to discuss what was happening to her with someone her own age. "Annie said she was afraid for me, afraid I might die."

Her mother covered her mouth as if to hide her fear. But it was unmistakable. Her eyes were ablaze with it. Amanda wanted to cry out that she needed her mother to be strong, that she'd have to lean on her, especially during the chemo. It would take everything she had to get through this, and she didn't have the strength to support anyone else.

"What was it Annie said that you found so enlightening?" her father asked.

Amanda loved the way he always got right to the point. "When she talked about how I might die, it occurred to me that eventually everyone dies. I will. So will you, Mom. You, too, Dad. Just like Grandpa did. I remember his funeral. I was really little when he died. What was I, six or seven?"

"Six," her mother said.

All Amanda remembered was that she'd barely started second grade when her wonderful grandfather died of a heart attack. Everyone had been sad and crying and upset. There were lots of people at the service. "When we went to the funeral home and saw Grandpa resting so peacefully, I thought dying mustn't be so bad, especially if you weren't afraid. And I'm not." She meant that. Death wasn't an alien darkness one struggled against. She no longer considered death the end of everything; it was a new beginning.

When you saw it that way, the meaning of death changed. She couldn't explain that to her parents—it would freak them out.

For the first time since entering her bedroom, her father smiled. "When did you get to be so smart?" he asked.

Although Amanda shrugged, she was pleased by her dad's praise. "I didn't know I was."

"You're going to make it," her mother insisted.

"If that's what God wills." Amanda didn't explain her feelings about God to her parents, either. She wasn't sure they'd understand. For now, it was enough that they know and accept her feelings about the cancer. Although her illness affected them, too, it was hers and hers alone, and she was the one who'd have to deal with it.

Her father glanced at his watch. "I have to get to work."

"It's all right, Dad. Go. I've said everything I have to say."

He leaned forward and kissed Amanda's cheek before leaving the room. Her mother walked out with him.

By herself again, Amanda threw aside the comforter and sat on the edge of her bed. It was about to start. This morning her mother would take her to the oncology center, and by noon she'd be heaving her guts out. Annie had promised to stop by after school. Amanda would look forward to that—the one bright spot in what was going to be a hell of a day.

CHAPTER FOUR

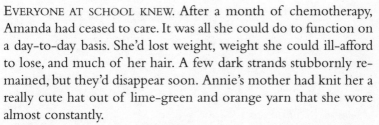

EVERYONE AT SCHOOL KNEW. After a month of chemotherapy, Amanda had ceased to care. It was all she could do to function on a day-to-day basis. She'd lost weight, weight she could ill-afford to lose, and much of her hair. A few dark strands stubbornly remained, but they'd disappear soon. Annie's mother had knit her a really cute hat out of lime-green and orange yarn that she wore almost constantly.

What had once seemed important, joining her high school class for graduation, no longer concerned her. Amanda didn't possess the energy to stand for even brief periods of time. The chemo had been worse than she'd expected, and the doctors were now giving her morphine, which helped with the pain. Because of her weakened condition, she'd been hospitalized shortly after prom night.

Fortunately, she had a private room, even if it *was* on the pediatric floor. That way she and Annie could visit. Laurie would come by later, too. Her friends always closed the door, and Amanda didn't have to worry about a roommate.

Propped up against pillows, Amanda looked over at the clock

on the wall and realized school was out for the day. Annie had been her only really faithful friend. She came at least three times a week, and often four and five times. Annie was her link with her other friends, with school activities and the world she'd once known. Laurie didn't visit as often, but at least she stopped by every week or so, which was more than most of her other friends did.

Someone tapped lightly at the door. Amanda rolled her head to one side and smiled when she saw Lance. He'd brought a single long-stemmed red rose and a card. It'd been ten days since his last visit.

"Hi," she said and wished he'd let her know he was coming. Amanda would've put on makeup and her knit hat. She hated that he was seeing her almost completely bald. On his last visit, she'd had a respectable amount of hair left. She self-consciously placed her hand on her bald head.

"Hi, yourself." Lance cautiously stepped farther into the room. "How are you?"

Amanda didn't understand why anyone would ask a cancer patient that question. She was irritated because it should be fairly obvious that she felt like crap. She looked like crap, too, and everyone pretended not to notice.

He didn't meet her eyes but gazed past her to the window. It was a lovely day and the sun was shining. This was the first time Amanda had noticed.

"I'm okay. How about you?" she said, deciding to fall into a meaningless exchange of pleasantries.

Lance set the rose and envelope on the nightstand and approached the other side of her bed, facing the hallway. "I'm sorry I haven't been by lately."

"You're busy. I understand." Amanda was willing to offer him excuses. It was hard not to stare at him—he just looked so good. She'd had the biggest crush on Lance for two years. It'd taken him almost eighteen of those twenty-four months to even notice her. He played defensive back for the football team. He was tall and dark-haired, with strong features and an endearing smile. He didn't kiss her or reach for her hand the way he had on his last visit.

He shuffled his feet and slid the tips of his fingers into the back pockets of his jeans, as if he wasn't sure what to do with his hands.

"How is everyone?" she asked, wanting him to talk because carrying a conversation drained her of the little energy she still had.

"Okay."

This wasn't working. "Something on your mind?" Amanda asked. She knew what was coming, could feel it, and in fact she'd sensed it the instant she saw him standing in the doorway.

"You've been out of school a whole month now."

Like he needed to tell her how long she'd been sick! Yeah, well, he had it wrong. She'd been puking up her guts, literally pulling out her hair, for exactly thirty-two days, fifteen hours and ten minutes.

"Everyone's been real worried."

That was a joke, too. Her first week in the hospital she'd had visitors every day. Her bedroom had been crowded with friends until her mother had to usher everyone out. The second week, a few had stopped by and five or six had phoned. At the end of the third week, there were only Annie, Laurie and Lance. Her so-called boyfriend had made a couple of token visits; he never stayed long. The funny part was, she didn't expect him to.

"Tell everyone I'm thinking of them."

"Jake and Kristen came up to see you, right?" He seemed grateful to have a question to ask.

Amanda knew they hadn't. "I must've been asleep."

"Yeah," he said, animated now. "That's what it was. They came and you were sleeping. More people would come but everyone's busy with graduation and all." He frowned as if he'd said something he wasn't supposed to say. "You aren't upset about not attending the ceremony, are you? I mean, you'll have your diploma and everything, so it doesn't really matter."

In spite of what she'd told herself, it mattered a lot. This was one more thing to add to the list of what cancer had stolen from her.

"Thank Jake and Kristen for me." She ignored his question and did her best to keep the sarcasm out of her voice.

Lance stared down at the floor. "I will."

Suddenly she was overwhelmingly tired. Her eyes closed and she struggled not to drift off. Amanda always welcomed sleep. It was an escape.

"Have you listened to the new U2 CD?" Lance asked.

Amanda shook her head.

"Ellie and I—" He stopped abruptly in midsentence, faltered a moment and tried again. "I bought it the day it came out," he finished lamely.

Apparently Amanda wasn't supposed to be aware of his slip. At first she'd pretended not to hear. Only she had, and she knew. This small revelation didn't surprise her. She opened her eyes.

"I like Ellie," Amanda murmured. Her voice was weak now, partly due to her exhaustion and partly to the lump forming in her throat. Amanda did like Ellie Logan; she'd never believed Ellie would sink so low as to steal her boyfriend.

Lance shrugged, guilt written plain as a warning label across his face. "She's okay."

His effort to conceal his betrayal failed miserably. Amanda knew she had every right to scratch his eyes out. Her first thought was that she wanted him to hurt the same way she did, but a moment later, she decided she didn't care anymore. She didn't have the energy.

The best thing to do was make this breakup as easy for him as possible. "Lance, would you like your ring back?" He'd bought her a sterling silver promise ring at Christmastime. She'd worn it every day since.

Now the question was out in the open, and she waited for him to respond. She didn't want to delay this any longer than necessary. He'd already hung around two weeks more than she'd figured he would.

"I…I said I'd be there for you, remember?" His husky voice was low and timorous.

Amanda did. Annie had convinced her to tell Lance she had cancer. He'd been terribly sympathetic and concerned, and to his credit, he'd spent prom night with her at the house. Her mother had cooked a wonderful meal just for her and Lance. Afterward her parents had left them alone to dance in the dimly lit living room. The evening had been sweet and romantic. For as long as she lived, Amanda would treasure that one night with Lance.

"I can't walk out on you now." His protest sounded weak. A self-deception.

He wanted out so bad she could feel it. Amanda wasn't sure which of them he was trying to convince.

"I'm not a good bet, Lance."

"Don't say that!" he barked angrily.

"Don't say what—that I could die?" She relaxed against the pillow, closed her eyes again and smiled. "The thing is, there's a very good likelihood I might. Did I tell you there's only a twenty-percent survival rate with the form of cancer I have? In other words, there's an eighty-percent chance I'll kick the bucket. Deal with it, Lance. I have."

He backed away from her as if she'd scorched him with a live wire. "Don't talk like that—like you've given up."

"Lance, listen," she said, mustering her strength to rise up and lean on one elbow. "It's all right about you and Ellie. I understand. I want you to know I don't hold any ill will toward either of you."

"I…I can't walk out on you when you need me most."

Amanda did her best to comfort him. "You aren't. So don't worry, okay?"

"I am worried."

"Lance, please." She didn't have the energy to argue anymore. Her head fell back to the pillow as she slipped the ring from her finger and handed it to him.

It was a long time before he reached for it. "I feel like I'm letting you down."

She didn't answer; she couldn't.

"I wrote you a letter," he said. He sounded perfectly miserable now. "I explained everything about how it happened with Ellie and me."

She nodded, letting him know she'd read it later. Right now, she wasn't in the mood.

"Are you going to cry?" he asked. "I couldn't stand it if you started to cry. I don't know what I'd do."

Despite herself, Amanda nearly burst into peals of laughter. Her lips trembled and it took all her restraint to keep a straight face. "No, Lance, I'm not going to cry."

"We didn't mean to hurt you."

"I know… I'm very tired. I don't mean to be rude, but I think you should leave now."

The look on his face was almost grateful as he moved away from her bed. "Annie's kept me updated…. She's been a really good friend, hasn't she?"

"Compared to you, you mean?" It wasn't fair to say that, but Amanda couldn't help it.

"Yeah," he said and he seemed genuinely regretful. "I thought I could handle this, you know? I couldn't. I'm sorry, Amanda, sorrier than you'll ever know."

"It's all right, Lance. Don't worry," she said again.

He left, and Amanda suspected Ellie was sitting in the waiting room, anxious for him to return.

Amanda slept then, and when she woke, she found Annie by her bedside, knitting.

"So you're awake," her friend said as she put down her knitting needles and yarn.

"What are you making?" Maybe she'd learn herself one day. Knitting appealed to her. When the chemo was finished, perhaps…

Annie glanced at her knitting bag on the floor. "Leg warmers."

"Cool."

She smiled and picked up the needles again. "They're for you."

"Really?" This was an unexpected surprise.

"Yeah. You might need something extra to keep your legs warm."

Annie completed a row in silence, then noticed the red rose and unopened envelope. She stood so they could talk at eye level. "Lance was here?"

Amanda's pleasure slowly faded. "He stopped by right after school. Did you know about him and Ellie?"

Annie's shoulders rose with her sigh and she nodded. "Are you upset?"

"Should I be?"

"No," was her adamant response. "He isn't worth the energy."

That had been Amanda's thought, too. "It's funny, you know?"

"What is?"

Amanda hesitated and wondered if she dared mention this. It might freak Annie out, and friends were in short supply these days. "I knew the minute he walked in the door. Do you think people who are close to dying develop ESP? I mean, I literally knew when Lance showed up with the flower and the card that he'd come to break up with me."

Annie's eyes widened but she didn't comment right away. "I suppose it's possible. When my mother's aunt Paula died, she saw angels. To this day, my mother believes that, and so do I. So if you've developed a sixth sense or whatever they call it, then it's a gift. Accept it."

Annie's response assured her she could share even her most unconventional feelings with her friend. It felt good to know that. Although Amanda wasn't so sure she wanted this so-called gift.

"You didn't answer my question," Annie said. "Are you upset? Because you don't seem to be, and that kind of surprises me."

Amanda shrugged. "I thought I should be, but I wasn't. Not really. The thing is, Lance and I don't have that much in common anymore. I'm wondering if I'll live long enough to spend Christmas with my parents, and his biggest concern is which college to choose." She grinned then, because she did feel bad about what she'd said to Lance.

"What's so funny?"

"You won't believe what I told him. I made up some gruesome statistic about only having a twenty-percent chance of surviving."

Annie's eyes grew huge. "You *wanted* him to think you were dying?"

Amanda laughed out loud. It was wonderful, truly wonderful,

to find humor in this situation. "It was all I could do not to place my hand over my heart and call out to St. Peter to take my soul."

Annie had the giggles now, too. "You're kidding."

"I'm not," Amanda said. "I guess I should feel a lot worse about losing the love of my life. Oh, well. To quote my uncle Mortie, 'C'est la vie.' Ellie's welcome to him."

"Are you holding out on me?" Annie asked, hands on her hips. "Have you met someone else?"

"Holding out on you? Where am I going to meet any guys?" She was certainly in no condition to attract one.

"Doctors," Annie said. "I've seen dozens of really cute residents on every floor. This is a teaching hospital, you know."

Amanda arched her brows—or what was left of them—and decided her friend was right. Hey, if she attracted a handsome resident, there might be a medical discount in it for her mom and dad.

CHAPTER FIVE

LYDIA HOFFMAN GOETZ

IT WAS A COUPLE of weeks since Annie had told me about her friend Amanda, and I hadn't been able to stop thinking about her. I was going into my junior year in high school when I was diagnosed with cancer. I remember it so well; it feels like only yesterday that I sat in Dr. Wilson's office that first time. Now it was happening to another girl, not unlike me. I'd asked Bethanne about Amanda's progress several times and she'd filled me in, but I still couldn't stop wondering about this young girl.

"You're looking thoughtful," Margaret said as I sat knitting furiously, which is something I do whenever I'm troubled. My sister works for me, and during the last couple of years we've grown close—closer than we've ever been. I blame my cancer for the disjointed relationship we had. It's a disease that ravages more than your body; it ravages relationships, families and lives.

Margaret seemed to think I wanted those brain tumors because of all the attention I got from being sick. I found the idea so offensive and ridiculous that I dismissed it entirely. What I didn't realize until this past year was that while I hated being sick, there were—in more ways than I'm comfortable admitting—certain advantages to being coddled by those I loved. I got used to being looked after and having decisions made for me. Not until I lost my father did I take my first bold step out into the real world.

I'd assumed that Margaret was jealous and if she were to examine her feelings, she'd discover that I'm at least partially right. But I guess it doesn't matter anymore. Over the last two years we've learned valuable lessons from each other. We remain about as different as two sisters can be, but since I opened the yarn shop, our differences are less important than our similarities. We don't act or think alike, and yet the bond we share is stronger now than ever.

"I did mention Annie's friend, didn't I?" I asked, looking up from my knitting. The store would open in a few minutes.

"You did," Margaret returned in that gruff way of hers. "She's the reason you've been spending so much time on the Internet, isn't she?"

My sister has the uncanny ability to predict what I'm going to do in certain situations. I nodded. "I keep thinking about her."

"You can't save her, you know."

"Now, Margaret…"

"I know you," my sister cut in sternly. "You've got a soft heart and you've decided there's something you might be able to do for her. Think, Lydia," she ordered, frowning now. "Think of all the responsibilities you already have and then ask yourself just how much energy can you afford to give anyone else."

I knew she was right, but I couldn't get Amanda out of my mind because I understood exactly what she was going through.

"I suppose you want to go to the hospital to visit her yourself." Apparently Margaret wasn't finished yet.

I had thought about doing exactly that, but Annie hadn't told me where she was and besides, I didn't want to interfere. Amanda didn't know me, and I wasn't sure how she'd feel about getting a visit from a stranger. There might be restrictions on visitors, too, depending on what stage of treatment she was entering. My main purpose would be to tell her about a link I'd found on the Internet that might help her and her family. Still, I felt uneasy about involving myself in someone else's business.

"I remember what it was like," I reminded my sister as I set aside my knitting. Now that I owned the shop, I had less and less time for my personal projects. I walked over to the front door and switched the sign to Open.

"You have a husband and a son," Margaret said unnecessarily.

It was during moments like this that I had to bite my tongue. She was only being protective, but I find her meddling a bit annoying. I know she does it because she cares about me, so I do my best to let such comments slide. She was right about my responsibilities, of course. I'd recently married Brad Goetz and I was now stepmother to nine-year-old Cody. His dog, Chase, and my cat, Whiskers, were cohabiting for the first time, too. We were learning to be one cohesive family. We'd had only a few minor dissensions, and all in all, things were going well.

"Did you say anything about this girl to Brad?" Margaret asked, continuing with her interrogation.

Thankfully I had, otherwise Margaret would have leaped on that like Whiskers on his catnip mouse. "Yes. In fact, Brad was the one who helped me find the Web site."

Margaret looked puzzled. "Which Web site is that?"

I was about to answer when the door opened and in walked my first customer of the day. The woman wasn't familiar, otherwise I would've greeted her by name.

"Hello," I said as I walked toward her. "I'm Lydia Goetz. Welcome to A Good Yarn."

"Thank you." She stood there awkwardly, just a few steps past the door, as if she wasn't sure she'd come to the right place. "My name is Joan Jennings."

"Do you knit, Joan?" I asked.

She shook her head. "I've never even been inside a yarn store…. It's a bit intimidating."

"Oh, please don't let it be. How can I help you? Are you interested in taking a beginners' knitting class—because we're about to start one and we'd love to have you."

She shook her head again. "I...I don't think so, but thanks."

I backed away, not wanting to hover as she slowly ventured forward. She stopped at a display of pattern books and reached for an *Easy Knitting* magazine. I went behind the counter and turned the page on my day-by-day knitting calendar. Each day featured a new pattern. The one for today's date was a lacy bookmark with a heart design in the middle.

Joan returned the magazine to the rack, then wandered over to the shelf where I displayed the worsted weight yarn. She ran her fingertips over a skein. "It's very soft, isn't it?"

I nodded, realizing that Margaret was in our small office making a pot of coffee.

"I assumed a knitted sweater would be that scratchy wool most people find so irritating."

"Oh, not at all," I was quick to assure her.

Joan glanced down at the floor and then back up at me. "Actually, your name was given to me by a friend, Bethanne Hamlin."

"Bethanne," I repeated enthusiastically. "She's one of my dearest friends."

"That's what she said." Joan approached the counter, biting her lower lip. "Her daughter, Annie, is a good friend of my daughter's."

"Annie's a sweetheart."

"She's been wonderful with Amanda," Joan said, and her voice shook with emotion.

"You're Amanda's mother?" I asked, astonished that this woman had walked into my shop at the very moment her daughter had weighed so heavily on my mind. I didn't remember whether Annie had given me Amanda's surname and, even if she had, I'm not sure I would've made the connection. "How is Amanda?" I asked, almost fearing what Joan was about to tell me.

She shrugged as if it was hard to explain. "She's doing about as well as can be expected. The physicians are optimistic, but they're in and out of her room. They don't spend the time with her that

I do. They don't see how sick she is and how she struggles each and every day." Tears glistened in Joan's eyes. "I'm the one at Amanda's bedside, the one who sees what it's really like for her. She hides it from everyone else, even her friends."

"I remember," I said and gently placed my hand over hers. It was my father who'd sat at my bedside and, in some ways, I think the emotional agony he endured watching over me was more painful than the physical ordeal I went through myself.

"Bethanne said you had cancer as a teenager." Joan lifted her gaze until it met mine.

"I did. The first time at sixteen and then later at twenty-four."

"Twice?"

I nodded.

"This is Amanda's second bout, too. She's been in remission for so long we'd all believed—we'd all hoped—that the cancer was completely gone. I blame myself.... If I'd been paying better attention, if I hadn't been so wrapped up in my own life, then I might have recognized the signs. I should've—"

"That's not true." I didn't mean to be rude by cutting her off. But I'd heard my parents discussing this very topic, looking for blame when there was none to be found. It was a frustrating, pointless exercise.

I motioned for Joan to sit down. The door opened again and the bell chimed. Margaret had obviously overheard part of our conversation because she stepped out from the office and hurried over to assist the customer.

"Would you care for some coffee?" I asked.

Joan hesitated. "I don't want to take you away from your store."

"It'll be fine. My sister, Margaret, is here." I could tell she wanted to chat; at the same time, I was grateful because I had information to impart. "How do you like your coffee?"

"Black, please."

I went into the office and filled two mugs, then carried them to the table at the back of the store. Joan had already taken a seat, and I sat across from her.

"I can't tell you how much I appreciate this. When Bethanne

said she knew a cancer survivor, I felt the strongest urge to talk to you. I don't know why or what you could possibly tell me, but something or rather Someone urged me to seek you out." She lowered her head as though a bit embarrassed. "I've been doing a lot of talking to God lately."

"I did, too, and I know my parents also prayed a great deal when I was sick. Believe it or not, I consider that closeness to God one of the benefits of cancer. It shoves everything else aside and forces us to focus on our priorities."

Joan held my gaze an extra-long moment. "Priorities," she murmured. "Cancer sets those straight, all right."

"Tell me more about how Amanda's doing."

She nodded and then released a deep sigh. "Medically, she's on schedule, according to the physicians. We won't know anything, really, until after the bone-marrow transplant."

"You have a donor?"

Again Joan nodded. "Her brother is a match, thank God."

I wasn't all that familiar with leukemia, although I was better informed than some registered nurses when it came to malignant brain tumors. I knew more than I'd ever wanted to about those. However, I lacked knowledge of other cancers.

"How's she doing emotionally?"

The dark circles beneath Joan's eyes seemed more pronounced. "Her boyfriend broke up with her last month."

"How did she handle it?" I remembered how I'd felt. I'd gone through several stages when Roger and I broke up. I started off angry and then I'd wrapped myself in self-pity and wept for days on end. It was a long while before I could look at the relationship with any perspective. In retrospect I realized that, although it had been difficult at the time, ultimately it was for the best.

Amanda's mother managed a half smile, her first since entering the shop. "I'm surprised by how well Amanda took it. I thought, you know, that she'd be really upset. She seemed to like him so much. He gave up prom night to be with her." Joan shrugged as if she couldn't understand her daughter's reaction even now.

"Amanda has more important things on her mind," I said.

A weary sadness came over Joan. "Amanda didn't attend her graduation, either, and I know she wanted to. From the minute she heard the cancer had returned, she said she had every intention of graduating with her class, but when the time came she was just too weak."

I could almost feel Joan's disappointment for her daughter.

"My husband and I were going to take her in a wheelchair so she could at least be with her friends, but Amanda said no, she'd rather not." Joan's eyes moistened and she bit her lower lip hard enough to make me wince.

"Just before you dropped by, I was talking to my sister about Amanda."

"You were?"

I smiled. "Annie came to see me a few weeks ago, when she found out about Amanda's illness, and we had a long talk. There are plenty of support groups that offer emotional encouragement for parents. I hope you and your husband have been able to avail yourselves of those, because it's important for your marriage and your own emotional health."

"We have."

"Good." I hadn't taken a sip of coffee yet and paused to do so. "Have you heard of Melissa's Living Legacy Foundation?" I asked next.

Joan shook her head.

"I discovered this site on the Internet and I think it would be worth looking at—for both you and Amanda. Melissa Sengbusch was a teenage girl who died of cancer in 2000. Her mother founded the organization to help other teenagers experiencing the same things her daughter did. I was deeply impressed when I read Melissa's story. She lived an inspiring life and her mother's working hard to give other teenagers hope. Teenagers with cancer have special needs."

"I didn't know such an organization existed. You're right. Teenagers are different. My husband and I were just discussing this the other day—how we can let Amanda be Amanda, especially while she's in the hospital. She feels she's too old to be on the pediatric ward, but we don't feel right having her in the adult ward, either."

"This is one of the very issues the Web site addresses. Promise me you'll check it out."

"I will. Oh, Lydia, I feel so much better just talking to you."

Margaret approached the table then. I knew she'd been listening in on the conversation, but it didn't bother me.

"Are there other children?" she asked.

Joan reached for a tissue and dabbed her eyes. "We have a son, too."

"How's he dealing with all this?"

"Joe's been great. He said he'd be willing to do whatever he could to help his sister, and he has."

Margaret crossed her arms. "Try to be aware of his needs, too. Make sure they don't get ignored. It's easy to let it happen, you know. He might not feel comfortable coming to you when you're already burdened with everything Amanda's going through."

Joan looked at me and then back at Margaret. "I'll do my best to see that doesn't happen," she said quietly.

The bell chimed and another customer entered the shop.

Margaret seemed relieved to have an excuse to abandon us.

The bell chimed again and Joan stood. "I've taken enough of your time. I'm so grateful to you, Lydia. And I'll check out that Web site you mentioned right away."

I watched as Joan left and hoped she followed through on that.

After logging onto Melissa's Living Legacy, I knew there was something else I could do. This was important, and I was sure that once I told Brad and Margaret, they'd both agree.

CHAPTER SIX

THE REGIMEN OF CHEMOTHERAPY was finished now. It'd been so hellish, Amanda sometimes thought the cure was worse than the disease. She'd lost weight and all her hair, but she'd slowly begun to regain her strength. The hospital was preparing her for the second stage of this healing process.

Funny, when she was eight years old and had cancer she'd never really thought she would die. She knew she was sick and that her mother cried a lot, but the possibility of dying hadn't even entered her mind. It did now. People died every day. People her age. She could be one of them.

When the cancer came back, it'd been a shock—to everyone. The difference this time was that Amanda knew what she faced. Although she was only a kid before, she'd learned a lot more about the disease than she'd realized. This second bout was more serious than the first, and chemo and radiation weren't enough. The treatment was more intense, lengthier, scarier.

Closing her eyes, Amanda tried to think positive thoughts. She'd made that big announcement to her parents early on, about fighting the cancer but not fighting death. She'd meant every word and she *was* fighting, harder than she'd dreamed possible. What she hadn't recognized at the time was how badly she wanted to live. Even though her friends had dwindled down to relatively few, and Lance, her bastard boyfriend, had walked out on her. Okay, she'd given him permission, but what other choice did she have? Her feelings toward him weren't nearly as gracious these days. If he'd had the slightest idea of what love was about, he wouldn't have taken up with Ellie. Instead, he'd be with her, lending her his strength, encouraging her, loving her. But he was gone, like so many others.

Annie claimed Lance wasn't worth the emotion. Not that she had much emotion to spare. Isolated as she was, Amanda had come to know herself well. She wanted to leave this hospital one day in the future and live a relatively normal life.

What was normal, anyway? Amanda no longer had any idea. She'd taken so much for granted. Until a few months ago, she'd been normal, lived a normal life, but she hadn't appreciated it. Someone with cancer took very little for granted.

Here it was, the middle of summer and the sun was shining and she was stuck in a hospital room by herself. Her steroid treatments had started and soon her face would swell up, become moon-shaped, grotesque. The thought of anyone seeing her with her features all distorted appalled her. This was so much worse than she'd expected. She hadn't known until she saw the others. They looked gross.

There was another problem. Amanda's parents were almost constantly at her side. If Amanda so much as hinted that she wanted a milkshake or a book or the latest CD, her mother or father made it happen. That cloying attention drove her to distraction. Amanda had sent her mother out of the room this afternoon, pleading with her to go home and make dinner. She also called her father and asked him not to visit her that evening, claiming exhaustion. She wanted her parents to have a normal night together. Her dad usually arrived at the hospital after work and spent a few hours; Amanda couldn't remember the last time her parents had actually left her before eight or nine in the evening. They liked to be available, they said, to make sure she ate everything in order to keep up her strength.

Now that her mother had gone home, the peace was wonderful, but at the same time, Amanda felt terribly, terribly alone. She wanted Annie. And although she'd never openly admit it, she wanted Lance back, too. She hated the thought of him with Ellie. They'd been the perfect couple, Amanda and Lance. Everyone had said so; and now everyone had forgotten her.

A nurse entered the room. It was Wendy, her favorite, who didn't seem that much older than Amanda. Wendy was old in cancer years, though; she'd seen it all before. Amanda figured that was why Wendy so often knew what she was feeling.

"Hello, Amanda," Wendy said as she approached her bed and checked the IV tube. It was hooked to a monitoring machine— this was something new since her last visit at age eight. Three bags hung from the contraption, and each was connected to a digital monitor. She wasn't sure what all those numbers meant, nor did she care.

"Hi," she mumbled back, turning her head so she wouldn't have to see what Wendy was planning to subject her to next.

"Hey, what's that glum face all about?"

"Want to trade places?" Amanda asked sarcastically.

Wendy didn't respond immediately. "Not today."

"That's what I thought."

Wendy moved to the other side of the bed. "Do you want to talk about it?" she asked in a gentle, concerned way.

Amanda clenched her teeth and shook her head.

"It might help."

"No, thanks."

Wendy hesitated. "I saw Annie get off the elevator a few minutes ago."

Amanda's mood instantly brightened, but then she remembered Annie's last visit. It'd been humiliating. Bad enough that she'd finally caught on to the fact that Annie and her parents coordinated their visits. Annie only came by when Amanda's mother wasn't there. Even worse, though, was the incident with the CD Annie had brought.

"Do you know how mortified I was the other day?" she asked the nurse. "My friend's visiting me, and then some old biddy comes rushing into the room and tells me I've got to turn down the music? I felt like I was back in grade school."

"I'm sorry, Amanda, but you're not the only patient on this ward."

"The music wasn't that loud," Amanda protested. "I suppose if I'd been listening to Frank Sinatra, it would've been perfectly fine."

"Well, there *are* a number of older patients here." Wendy patted her hand. "Anyway, you told me you didn't like being on the pediatric ward."

"I didn't. I'm not a kid who appreciates being serenaded by a troop of Boy Scouts. I know they meant well, and the other kids really enjoyed it, but I'm almost eighteen years old—an adult."

"Which is why we moved you to the adult ward," Wendy reminded her.

"I know." Amanda had asked, pleaded actually, to be transferred shortly after the clown had come to her room. He'd done some stupid tricks, and then, to add insult to injury, he'd twisted pink and purple balloons into the shape of a French poodle in her honor. She was supposed to wear that idiotic thing on her bald head. *Very* funny.

Wendy seemed to have trouble holding back a smile. "As I recall, you described that nice clown as a form of cruel and unusual punishment, and you asked what you'd done to deserve it."

Amanda almost smiled herself. "You're right, I did."

"So we transferred you. It might not seem like it, but we really do want you to feel as comfortable and relaxed as possible."

Amanda felt bad about her grumpy mood. "I know."

"Chin up," Wendy said, encouraging her with a warm smile. "It's practically over and then you'll be home with your family and friends. All of this will be behind you."

Amanda nodded, although she understood it wasn't that simple. From this point onward, everything would be different. Any hope of living a completely normal life was forever gone. The long-term effects of the chemotherapy were depressing, and there'd be drugs to take for the rest of her life. She couldn't allow herself to think about it, otherwise she'd want to give up, and she was determined to fight this disease and win.

No sooner had Wendy left the room than Annie walked in. Amanda had never had a friend as good as Annie. Two years ago they'd barely known each other, even though they were in the same year. That was the period Annie referred to as the Dark Years, shortly after her parents' divorce. Annie had been furious with her father and tried to destroy everything that was positive in her life. She'd dropped out of the swim team and started hanging with a questionable group at school.

Something happened over that summer, Amanda was never sure exactly what. When Annie returned for their junior year, she was almost back to her old self. She'd become friends with a new girl in school named Courtney, who was in the senior class. Amanda didn't remember her last name. She recalled that Courtney and Annie's older brother had been an item. They'd both graduated since and gone to different schools. She should ask Annie if they were still involved.

Then in the last trimester of their junior year, Amanda and Annie were in earth sciences together and were also chosen to be part of the yearbook staff.

They'd met after school a few times and Amanda had volunteered to help Annie and her mother with the party business. That had been a lot of fun. All through senior year, they'd remained friends. Even now...

Amanda closed her eyes again, mentally readying herself for this next confrontation. She didn't want to do it, but she just couldn't let anyone—well, other than her parents—see her once she started to look like a...a gargoyle or something during the next stage of treatment. And that included Annie. She heard her friend enter the room and considered pretending she was asleep. She couldn't do that, though.

When she opened her eyes, Annie had made herself comfortable in the bedside chair, flipping through a magazine. She smiled and stood the moment she saw that Amanda was awake.

"How's it going?" she asked. She was wearing a bright pink summer dress with big white flowers and matching pink sandals.

Amanda stared past her. "All right, I guess. Why do people always ask that?" she demanded. "How do you *think* it's going? I'm in the hospital. I'm about to have a bone-marrow transplant and get stuck in an isolation chamber for God knows how long."

Annie raised her eyebrows. "My, my, aren't we in a testy mood this afternoon."

"Out in the sunshine, were you?"

Annie nodded. "I was working a birthday party with Mom. It was a ten-year-old girl and she wanted a Bratz theme."

Amanda knew the teenage dolls were popular with the younger set. Annie's mother had at least a dozen inventive party themes; Amanda's favorite was the Alice in Wonderland tea party.

"I had sixteen ten-year-olds screaming in my ear all afternoon, so don't you start," Annie joked.

With an effort, Amanda sent her friend a weak smile. "Listen, I've been thinking that you're probably getting really busy, with work and all."

"It's been like that for a while," Annie said. "No big deal."

Amanda briefly looked away. "You should have a life."

"I do."

Annie wasn't making this easy. "When's the last time you went out with friends?"

"Saturday night. Why?"

"Because."

Annie's eyes narrowed as if she'd suddenly caught Amanda's drift. "Are you trying to get rid of me?"

Finally. "Not exactly," Amanda said, being careful not to hurt her friend's feelings.

"What is that supposed to mean?"

"It means," Amanda elaborated, "that things are changing for me."

"In what way?"

"Steroids."

Annie stared at Amanda, her gaze blank. She made a circular motion with her hand. "And?"

"You don't know?" Amanda hated having to spell it out. "My face is going to swell up to gigantic proportions. In a little while, a few days, I don't know how long, I'm going to look like a freak."

"I see. And that's supposed to frighten me off?"

"No," Amanda cried. "Why are you making this so hard?"

Annie seemed utterly baffled.

"Don't you understand?" She was struggling not to cry. "I don't want you to see me like that…. I don't want *anyone* to see me. It's going to be horrible and then later…later I'll be in isolation."

"I've already talked to the nurse about that," Annie said. "I can still visit but you'll be behind this glass and—"

"It'll be like visiting someone in prison."

"No, it won't," Annie insisted. "I'll be coming to see my dearest and best friend. You've been through so much already," she said. "You're the bravest person I've ever known."

"Don't say that," Amanda pleaded, her voice quaking. She was afraid she really would break into tears.

"I mean it. You can make a big fuss, say whatever you want, but it isn't going to make any difference to me. You're my friend, and I'm not leaving. I need you."

"No, you don't."

Annie shook her head. "Don't argue with me. I want you to be in my wedding and I plan on being in yours. You're a friend for life, so just accept it."

Amanda covered her face with both hands. "Go away."

"Sorry, did you say something? Because I can't hear you." Annie sank down in the chair next to Amanda's bed and reached for the magazine, which she opened and resumed reading. It was one of the teen magazines, filled with the latest celebrity gossip they loved to read.

Amanda ignored her, although she was dying to get her hands on this issue.

"Oh, my goodness, you won't believe it," Annie gasped. She uncrossed her legs and leaned forward as if in shock. "Madonna's pregnant again—with Britney Spears's baby."

"What?" Amanda's jaw dropped open.

Annie waved her index finger. "Gotcha."

Amanda wanted to be mad, but she laughed instead. "That was ridiculous."

"It got your attention, didn't it?"

Amanda had to admit it did.

Annie's eyes sobered as she put down the magazine. "Amanda, I'm serious. It doesn't matter to me what you look like when the steroids kick in. I'm not that kind of friend and you aren't, either. If I was the one going through this, you'd be here for me."

Amanda sighed. "I don't know," she whispered, being as honest as she could.

"What do you mean?"

"Just what I said," she returned, her voice gaining strength. "I thought Heather and Jenna were my friends, too, but they're gone. Lance is gone. You and Laurie are the only ones who even make the effort to come and see me anymore."

"We're your true friends," Annie said.

"I just wonder if I'd be as good to you as you've been to me."

"You would," Annie said without a hint of doubt. "Besides, the worst is over." She got up and hopped onto the edge of Amanda's bed. "It's going to be clear sailing from here on out."

"Well, I don't know…" But now that Amanda had completed her chemotherapy, she'd begun to feel a tiny, new sense of hope. "I don't really think it could get much worse than it's already been."

"It won't." Annie sounded so positive, Amanda could almost believe her.

CHAPTER SEVEN

LYDIA HOFFMAN GOETZ

I'D SPENT SO MANY HOURS in front of the computer Sunday evening that my vision had started to blur. I felt Brad's hand on my shoulder. Covering it with my own, I looked up at him.

"What time is it?" I asked. My husband tended to be the night owl, not me. He often stayed up to watch the news and Jay Leno. I tried to join him but was usually too tired.

"Almost eleven-thirty," he said and yawned. "I've got work in the morning. Are you ready for bed?"

I was and I wasn't. I'd logged onto the computer right after Cody had gone to bed around nine, and those two and a half hours had passed in the blink of an eye. "I've been on discussion boards," I explained, twisting around in order to talk to him. "Oh, Brad, I just felt I had to give these teens some hope." I'd typed so fast my hands ached and my fingers could barely keep up with my thoughts. Many of the teens I'd met on the boards were in a state of despair. I heard the fear and anxiety in their messages.

"Where are these discussion boards?" he asked.

"On that Web site I mentioned—*teenslivingwithcancer.org.* It's part of Melissa's Living Legacy. She's the teenage girl I told you about who died a few years back. Melissa asked her mother to help other teenagers who were going through cancer. She wanted to make a difference, and she left this request with her mother, who took on the task and did a magnificent job. Because of Melissa, a lot of kids now have a voice. They're able to connect with one another and become their own support group."

"You're really passionate about this, aren't you?" Brad said, and he gave me the sweetest smile, as if he knew something I didn't.

"What?" I asked, not knowing what he meant.

"You," he said, his face alive with love. "I wish I had a mirror so I could show you to yourself. Your eyes are bright and intense, and I think, my dear wife, that you've just stumbled on something that's going to change your life."

I hadn't realized it until just that moment, but Brad was right. "I want to be a positive influence for these teens. I was one of them. I understand what they're enduring. I've suffered the same way they're suffering now, and I can give them hope. I can encourage them."

Brad leaned toward me. "Then do it." He yawned a second time, hiding his mouth. "Ready for bed?" he asked again.

I nodded and shut down the computer, but my mind was racing, with ideas and memories and hopes. "All these years," I mumbled, unaware I'd spoken aloud.

"All these years what?" Brad slipped his arm around my waist as I stood up and we headed toward our bedroom.

I hesitated as I considered my reply, and he stopped, too. I was slightly uncomfortable with this confession. "I used to hate telling anyone I had cancer. I didn't want people to know unless it was absolutely necessary."

Brad's soft laugh followed my painful admission. "Tell me about it! I remember when you told me that first time. Your body language said *warning, danger, stay away,* I've had cancer, so beware—don't get too close."

"It did not!" I said, laughing at my husband's exaggeration.

The smile left his eyes. "Lydia, you did. It was as if you assumed that because you'd had cancer—twice—you weren't entitled to a real life. You pushed me away with both hands. Lucky for you, I don't take rejection personally. I wanted to get to know you and eventually I wore you down."

I was grateful for that. Still, what he'd said gave me pause. Because of my medical history, I'd lived a sheltered life. No one could blame me for being cautious; if you've fallen through the ice not once but twice, you don't step onto a frozen lake without trepidation. That was how it was for me. I was cautious, afraid...and then my father died.

Without Dad standing guard over me, I felt unsteady. But I knew I had to step out of my small, protected world and live, really live. As I've often said, opening my yarn store was an affirmation of life. I wanted to stand on the street corner and shout, "I'm alive! Come and look at me. I'm a normal person with dreams and aspirations." That's what A Good Yarn was all about. Brad's words confused me.

"I wasn't *ashamed* of my cancer," I insisted after a moment. "All I ever wanted was to be normal." The teens I'd met that evening felt the same way. I read that again and again on the discussion boards. These kids were describing exactly what I'd felt when I was their age. To be different, to have this disease, set us apart. Like me, they were overwhelmed by the consequences of their illness.

Many of them were wise beyond their years. The things they'd written had deeply touched me, and I knew I wanted to help. I *needed* to help. Like Melissa, I, too, wanted to make a difference.

Wearing my nightgown, I sat down on the side of the bed and tried to explain. "After each remission, especially the second, I made an effort to put the cancer out of my mind entirely," I said to Brad. "I longed to pretend it had never happened, although that wasn't easy. I told myself I'd move forward with my life and not look back."

"And you feel differently now?" Brad asked as he climbed into bed.

"Now…now I understand how wrong that thinking was. I feel I have something to offer and that I'd miss out on a wonderful blessing if I ignored it."

I climbed under the sheets, too, and nestled against my husband. When Brad had turned off the light, he wrapped his arm around me. "You're making progress in stepping out of your comfort zone—although I guess it was more of a *discomfort* zone. You married me, didn't you?" He kissed my temple and then settled back in bed.

With my head on his shoulder, I closed my eyes and smiled, awash with contentment. Brad was a very special man, who loved me despite my fears and flaws. I realized while we were dating that it was my fears that held back the relationship. I'd given up counting the number of times Brad wanted to talk about marriage. I was the one who'd balked, continually putting him off.

Oh, there'd been a brief period when his ex-wife had re-entered the picture and I thought I'd lost him. Thankfully, nothing had come of it. That period had been difficult for both of us because Brad loved me and I loved him—so much that it frightened me. When I believed I was on the verge of losing him, I'd experienced a whole new kind of fear. It was as if life was about to cheat me again.

In that time of emotional turmoil, I made a mistake. When I was faced with the challenge presented by his ex-wife, I'd walked away. With the clarity of hindsight, I knew I should have fought for my husband and son. Without a doubt, I would now.

In a few minutes, Brad's breathing evened out and I could tell he'd fallen into a fast and peaceful sleep. Although I was physically tired, my mind remained wide-awake, popping with ideas. I'd occasionally wondered about visiting oncology centers and teaching knitting. It was while receiving lengthy chemo treatments myself that I'd first learned to knit. I began to think about that again.

A new world of possibilities had opened up to me since Annie had talked about her friend. I don't think anything happens by accident. Some greater power had sent Annie to me that day. The timing was right; I was at a point in my life where I could make a difference to these kids, and I was determined to do so.

In the morning, when the alarm rang at seven, I groaned, reluctant to get out of bed. Brad threw aside the covers and went to the kitchen to start the coffee. A few minutes later, Chase, my stepson's dog, skidded enthusiastically into our room. At Brad and Cody's urging, Chase hopped onto the bed next to me. My two men found it downright funny when Chase decided to lick my face. Apparently even the dog couldn't stand the sight of me lazing away in bed. There are advantages and disadvantages to living in an all-male household. One of the disadvantages is the way they find amusement in the most unlikely situations. I've concluded that there's something unremittingly juvenile about most male humor.

"Are you ready to get up yet, or do I need to get Whiskers, too?" Brad asked, hands on his hips.

"Very funny." I shoved Chase away and rolled onto my back. It helped that the sun was shining; when the sun's out in the Pacific Northwest, there's no place lovelier on earth.

"I'm up, I'm up," I muttered.

"I've got camp today," Cody reminded me. This was a compromise for our son, who felt, at age ten, that he was way too old to go to day care during the summer months. Brad and I had found a day camp that offered a variety of activities we knew Cody would enjoy. Although it was early August, Cody was still excited about going off to camp every morning. If this continued, heading back to school in a few weeks would be a major disappointment.

"What are your plans for the day?" Brad asked as he brought me a cup of coffee and set it on my nightstand.

Oh, how my men spoil me. There might be disadvantages in being the only woman in a household of men but there are significant advantages, too. I sat up in bed, reached for the cup and leaned against the headboard. I sipped my coffee, listening to the classical music playing softly on the clock radio, luxuriating in my morning ritual. Because my yarn store is open on Saturdays, I close on Sundays and Mondays. "I'm going into the shop. I have a lot of paperwork to catch up on this morning," I said.

"I'll probably have a delivery to make on Blossom Street around midmorning," Brad said. He was already dressed for work. We took turns dropping Cody off at camp, and it was my turn.

"Come in for a coffee," I invited. While we were dating, Brad often stopped by for coffee. I'd go into the office to pour him a cup and he'd follow me—to steal a kiss. Marriage hadn't changed his habit of visiting me at work, and I was glad.

"This afternoon I thought I'd walk over to the hospital," I said, watching for his reaction.

"Which hospital?" Brad asked.

"The one where Annie's friend is having her treatments."

Brad grinned as if he'd known what I planned to say.

The instant Cody heard the word hospital, he flew into the room. "Mom's going to the hospital?"

"To ask if I can volunteer and to visit a friend," I said. Amanda wasn't a friend yet, but she soon would be. I knew she'd undergone the bone-marrow transplant; Bethanne had told me. I also knew that Annie had taken my advice and stayed in close contact with Amanda. She and another girl were the only two who'd stood by Amanda's side throughout the whole ordeal. I was proud of Annie, and Bethanne was, too. This was exactly what Melissa's Living Legacy meant—teens helping other teens.

Brad didn't seem surprised by my decision to volunteer. I could see from the look in his eyes that he approved.

"You aren't going to have a baby?" Cody asked. His face fell with disappointment.

"Cody," Brad chastised and the two of us exchanged a mournful glance.

This was one sad effect of my cancer—and the treatments that had cured me. *Saved* me. There would be no babies for Brad and me. Brad and I had discussed adopting, but because we were still newlyweds, the agency wanted to be sure the relationship was stable before they considered us as candidates. I'm in my thirties now, and so is Brad. If they do decide to let us have a child, it won't be for several years.

Infertility was just one more factor these teenage girls faced. And many of the boys, too. It wasn't anything they needed to concern themselves with yet. I know they're thinking about it, though. I can't really speak for the boys, but I can imagine their emotions about this. I am, of course, familiar with what a girl would feel. It's disquieting to any woman, no matter what her age, to know she might never have the choice to be a mother.

I'd only recently learned I was infertile. All along, I'd suspected the chemotherapy had destroyed my chances of having a family. It was another thing cancer had stolen from me, and I'd taken the news hard. I'm just grateful to have a wonderful husband who comforted me. He suggested adoption, and we're going to pursue it. But if we're not successful, I won't let it ruin my life.

We'd put the matter in God's hands and were prepared to accept His decision.

"What are you volunteering for at the hospital?" Cody asked. "I know what that word means," he added proudly.

I smiled at him. "I'm hoping to help teenagers who have cancer."

"But what can you do?" He frowned a little, as if this worried him.

Brad kissed me on the cheek, rubbed the top of his son's head and said, "Gotta go."

"Bye, Dad." Cody sounded a bit distracted.

"Bye, Cody."

Our eyes met, and my husband whispered, "See you later, Beautiful." He gave me a little wave and left the bedroom. I heard him walking down the hall.

Cody returned his attention to me. "But how are you going to help teenagers?" he asked.

"I'm working on that," I told him. "I want to encourage them and be there for them." I'd e-mailed Melissa's Living Legacy Foundation to find out exactly what I could do. I'd explained that I understood the problems of being a teenager with cancer because

I'd been one. Perhaps I could help educate health care profession-als, too.

Cody gave me a quirky look. "I know why my dad loves you so much," he said, his face thoughtful.

"Why is that?" I asked.

"Because you have a really big heart."

I hugged my stepson. "That's so I can love *you* so much," I told him.

CHAPTER EIGHT

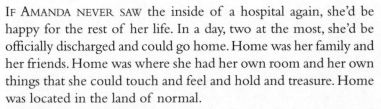

IF AMANDA NEVER SAW the inside of a hospital again, she'd be happy for the rest of her life. In a day, two at the most, she'd be officially discharged and could go home. Home was her family and her friends. Home was where she had her own room and her own things that she could touch and feel and hold and treasure. Home was located in the land of normal.

If she died—if the cancer got her despite all the chemo and the steroids and the bone-marrow transplant—Amanda wanted her family to understand that she refused to die here in this sterile environment. It was her highest and most important goal. She wanted to leave this hospital and never come back. It didn't matter how cute the doctors were. Not a single one of them was worth stepping foot inside this place again.

The nurses and other staff were great. Amanda's feelings weren't personal. It was the disease itself that had driven her to think this way. She would always associate the hospital with cancer, and it was an association she desperately wanted to break.

No matter what was happening to her blood, she told herself

she was better. She prayed with everything in her that her body would accept Joe's bone marrow. So far it looked promising. She knew that simply from what she saw on the physicians' faces as they read her charts.

As for feeling stronger and having more energy, Amanda *thought* she did but she wasn't sure. Funny how easily your brain could fool you. She'd been fooled before. She was trying not to set herself up for disappointment, so she didn't demand answers from any of the doctors. She left that to her parents. She didn't ask them questions, either; she was afraid they'd only tell her what she wanted to hear.

Annie would be coming later in the day and although it was only midmorning, Amanda was already looking forward to seeing her. She owed Annie so much; Annie had taught her what it meant to be a friend. On her last visit they'd had a blast. Through her mother's party business, Annie had gotten wigs in every color and style. There must have been twenty of them. Together they'd tried them all on and laughed themselves silly.

Amanda had found it difficult to keep the wigs on her head. Being bald was a real detriment there. The wig would slip to one side and then forward until it reached the bridge of her nose. They'd laugh and laugh and giggle some more. Amanda had lost count of the number of times the nurses had come into the room and asked them to keep the noise down. They'd honestly tried, but to no avail.

Amanda had forgotten how good it felt to laugh. Someone wise—she thought it was a man called Norman Cousins—had written a book about the healing properties of laughter. After Annie's visit, she believed that. For the first time since she'd been admitted, she'd slept through the entire night. Laughing had worn her out. It'd been a delicious feeling and so…she'd almost come to hate this word…so normal.

A quiet knock sounded at her door and Amanda turned to discover a petite woman with shoulder-length dark hair and brown eyes standing just inside her doorway. She didn't recognize her but felt that perhaps she should.

"Are you Amanda Jennings?" the other woman asked.

Amanda nodded. "Should I know you?"

The other woman's smile drew her into a warm embrace. "There's no reason you should. My name is Lydia Goetz."

The name wasn't familiar to Amanda.

"I own a yarn store in Blossom Street."

"Oh, yes," Amanda breathed, as everything clicked into place. "My friend Annie went to talk to you because you had cancer as a teenager, too." Amanda gestured for her to come into the room.

"You look good."

Amanda dismissed the compliment and rested one hand on her bald head. "I look better with hair."

Lydia agreed with a slight smile. "Most of us do. I was referring to the color in your cheeks."

Amanda avoided mirrors whenever she could. The wig session with Annie had been the one exception to that. As soon as she'd started taking the steroids and the swelling had begun, Amanda decided it was better for her own peace of mind to remain as uninformed as possible about her appearance.

"At least you didn't ask how I'm feeling," Amanda said, then made a face. "Sorry, that's a pet peeve of mine."

"Don't you *hate* that?" Lydia cried. "You'd think people would get a clue. You're in the hospital and you're afraid you've already got one foot in the grave and someone bebops into your room like it's a garden party and asks you a stupid question like that."

This was exactly how Amanda felt and she was delighted to have her sentiments echoed by someone else. Someone who'd been there… "They did that to you, too?"

"Oh, yes." Lydia set down her purse and knitting bag. "Even worse is when a friend sits at your bedside and complains because she's broken a fingernail."

Amanda rolled her eyes. "People can be *so* insensitive."

"They mean well," Lydia reminded her, "it's just that they don't have any idea. A broken fingernail isn't a disaster. It isn't going to tear your life apart."

Amanda nodded. "Cancer does that."

"Yes, it does. It tore mine apart twice."

"Twice." Amanda paid close attention now.

"Yup, I'm a two-time winner," Lydia said, "and so are you."

Amanda wasn't so sure about that, but… "How old are you?" she asked.

"Thirty-four."

"Wow."

Lydia was smiling. "Is that old?"

"In cancer years, you bet." Amanda had gotten curious and done a little research one day, using some medical periodicals from the hospital library. What she'd learned depressed her. "The first time I had cancer I was eight."

"That's young."

Far too young, Amanda agreed, but she'd known children who'd had it much younger. "I remember the names of some of the other kids I was in the hospital with. I used to get together with a couple of the girls for our birthdays and stuff, and then we stopped meeting. I recently found out why." A lump formed in her throat and she swallowed hard. "They both died, and my mother never told me."

"I'm sorry," Lydia whispered gently. Tears gathered in her eyes.

"Why them and not me?" It was a question that had gone repeatedly through her mind.

Lydia shook her head. "I can't answer that any more than you can."

"I'm probably going to die, too." She might as well accept the truth of that now. The likelihood of surviving another five years wasn't good.

To Amanda's surprise, Lydia nodded. "There's about a one-hundred percent chance that you're right. The thing is, we all die."

"You know what I mean."

"I do," Lydia said, "but what makes you assume it'll be anytime soon?"

"I'm looking at my odds compared to other people with this kind of cancer, and I can see that—"

"Looking at your odds is a bad idea," Lydia said, cutting her off. "It'll drive you nuts. If so and so had cancer twice by age eighteen, then died at twenty-two, I should live another sixteen months, and so on and so on. I've played that game and, trust me, it goes nowhere. Take my advice and don't do it."

"You did that, too?" No matter how many times she tried to avoid it, she found herself making those comparisons. Amanda had thought she was the only one. No one needed to tell her it was a stupid thing to do, but she couldn't stop. Whenever she came across statistics or heard about someone else's survival, she automatically started calculating her chances of having a *normal* life after this— there was that word again. *Normal*. For someone with cancer, nothing was ever normal again.

Lydia's sigh was deep enough to raise her shoulders. "Everyone does. I forced myself to stop, and look at me—I'm thirty-four. Furthermore, I have my own business."

"You're married, too." Amanda had noticed the ring.

"Married with children," Lydia boasted proudly. "Or rather, child."

This was beyond anything Amanda had hoped for. "You had a baby?"

"I have a stepson who's as much a part of me as if I'd given birth to him. I'm his mother. Yes, he has a biological mother, but she's rarely around." She paused. "Cody knows how much I love him."

Amanda hadn't dared to dream she could ever have that much. Still, she wasn't completely convinced. After two bouts with cancer, the future didn't seem that promising. It remained cloudy. Dark. Uncertain.

"I don't know if I'll make it to thirty-four," she said and meant it. This wasn't a ploy so Lydia would quickly dismiss the notion. This was the naked-as-her-bald-head truth.

"Who knows?" Lydia asked without a qualm. "We might both make it to eighty. Or older."

That would be a miracle of biblical magnitude, as far as Amanda was concerned.

"On the other hand, I could get run over by a taxi on my way out the door. Life doesn't have any guarantees. If you're looking for one, then shop at Sears. For me, it's a day at a time. Yes, the cancer might come back. I had a scare a couple of years ago when another tumor was detected."

"What happened?" Amanda whispered.

"It was benign."

"What if it hadn't been?"

Lydia didn't hesitate. "Then I'd be dead now." Surprisingly, she smiled. "But I would've gone knowing I'd done something I'd always wanted to do, which was to open a yarn store. I'd fallen in love, too."

"You knew your husband then?"

"We'd met and dated a few times, and I loved him, really loved him. These feelings were a lot more intense than anything I'd experienced with anyone else."

Amanda didn't want to ask this question, but she needed to know. "If…if the tumors had been cancerous would he…this man you loved and married, would he have stayed with you?"

Lydia's face relaxed into a soft smile. "His name is Brad, and yes, I believe he would have." The smile went away. "I take it your boyfriend broke up with you?"

Amanda stared down at her hands and nodded. Her feelings toward Lance were mixed. She'd been hurt and disappointed by him. It was crazy; the last thing she wanted was for Lance to see her like this, bloated and bald, yet she wished he'd come back. She missed him and loved him. Half the time she referred to him as the bastard and the other half she dreamed he'd return to her and beg her forgiveness.

"There's someone out there who's going to love you, Amanda."

She started to argue, but Lydia stopped her.

"I speak from experience on this one. I lost two loves-of-my-life and was convinced it would never happen for me."

Amanda would believe it when it happened for her; until then she was reserving judgment. Despite enjoying Lydia's visit, she yawned, drained of energy.

"I never did tell you the reason I came," Lydia said. "Let me do that, and then I'll go."

Amanda nodded sleepily.

"I talked to the hospital staff and described Melissa's Living Legacy Foundation. I think your mom told you about it?" When Amanda nodded again, Lydia continued. "I'm going to help raise money so the hospital can provide teenagers who can't afford them with laptops. That way they can log onto the message boards. Communication will help."

"You mean I'd be able to link up with other teenagers who have cancer and talk to them about…anything?"

"Absolutely."

Amanda was thrilled. "That would be great!"

"The head of oncology thought so, too." Lydia beamed.

"Wow!" Lydia had already been hard at work. "Yeah," she added, "my mom did tell me about Melissa. I was planning to check it out when I got home. But it'd be even better if kids could do it while they're still in the hospital."

Lydia agreed. "At some point in the future I'm going to be talking with staff here about the special needs of adolescents with cancer. My hope is that they'll set aside an area for teenagers to meet their friends and chat, play music, whatever."

"You mean taking us out of the pediatric ward *and* the adult ward?" That would be perfect.

"I might need a bit of help convincing the powers-that-be that this is necessary. This is where you come in."

Amanda didn't need to think about it. "I'll do whatever I can, and I know a few other kids who'll volunteer, too."

"Wonderful." Lydia looked really pleased. "Rest now, and I'll be in touch. We'll talk more later."

"Okay. Only…" She hesitated, not sure how to ask. "Why are you doing this? I mean, it's really cool and everything, but why now? You're not a teenager anymore."

"Far from it," Lydia said readily. "Why am I doing this?" she repeated. Her eyes grew serious. "I'm doing it to help a mother keep a promise to her daughter. A very special daughter and an equally special mother."

That was a good enough reason for Amanda. She wanted to be part of it, too.

CHAPTER NINE

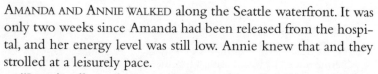

AMANDA AND ANNIE WALKED along the Seattle waterfront. It was only two weeks since Amanda had been released from the hospital, and her energy level was still low. Annie knew that and they strolled at a leisurely pace.

"I can't tell you how good the sunshine feels," Amanda said, pausing to gaze up at the sky. "Let's sit for a while," she suggested.

"Sure." Sensitive to her friend's needs, Annie was immediately prepared to stop.

They found a bench and sat facing the dark green waters of Elliott Bay in Puget Sound. The breeze off the water had a briny scent, and the sky was as blue as Annie had ever seen it. A white-and-green Washington State ferry glided toward the end of the pier; there was a long line of vehicles waiting to board for the next sailing.

"Tell me when you're feeling tired," Annie said urgently.

Amanda smiled, and again turned her face skyward, letting the sun bathe her in warmth and light. Annie closed her eyes and did the same thing. Amanda wore the hat Bethanne had knit for her, and it nearly slipped from her head.

Annie knew that beneath the lime-green hat, Amanda's hair resembled peach fuzz. It was already apparent that when it did grow back, it would be in tight curls. That was kind of funny, since Amanda's hair had always been straight as a broomstick. Apparently one of the side effects of chemotherapy was that when hair returned, it was often completely different from the way it had been before.

"Want to go to a movie?" Annie asked.

Amanda took a long time to consider that suggestion. "I hope you won't mind if I say no. I feel like I've been in a dark place for so long, I want to soak up as much of this fresh air and sunshine as I possibly can."

Annie didn't mind at all. The only reason she'd suggested it was that sitting in a theatre wouldn't drain her friend's energy. "I want to do whatever you want," Annie assured her. This was one of Amanda's first times out, and Annie was trying not to overtax her.

"I don't need to *do* anything," Amanda explained.

"That's okay, too."

"Is it?" Amanda asked. "I mean, before I was always the one who wanted to go and see and do. I thrived on being in the middle of the action. I don't feel like that anymore."

"I'm comfortable doing absolutely nothing, if you are."

"It's what I want for now."

Annie didn't fully understand this change of attitude in her friend. Amanda was different. She'd noticed that before her release from the hospital. She wasn't sure exactly why, but the friend who'd been admitted to the cancer ward wasn't the same girl who sat next to her now. Amanda had changed, and Annie guessed that in the process of being her friend, she had, too.

"The things that used to seem important don't anymore," Amanda admitted with a thoughtful frown.

"Give me an example."

"Well, Lance. I mean, okay, yeah, he broke up with me. It hurt at the time—it still kind of hurts—but my mother called it a blessing in disguise, and she was right. Naturally, I didn't see that, but now I understand what she said. Before I discovered the leukemia was back, it was just so important to have a boy in my life. It…sort of defined me. I wasn't just Amanda, I was Amanda-and-Lance. And that's wrong."

Annie knew a lot of girls felt the same way. Having a boyfriend was ultra-important, as if their identity was linked to their ability to attract someone of the opposite sex. She wasn't like that herself, although she dated lots of guys.

"Lance disappointed me," Amanda said, "yet at the same time, I didn't blame him."

Annie wasn't so willing to forgive Lance—or his new girlfriend. "I was even more upset with Ellie." By graduation, Annie could hardly keep from glaring at the other girl. She found it impossible to believe that Ellie could live with herself after what she'd done. Ellie was supposed to have been Amanda's friend. One of her best.

Amanda shook her head. "I didn't mean to get sidetracked by rehashing all the he-done-me-wrong stuff, because breaking up with Lance isn't the point." She paused as if to consider what she'd discovered about herself in the process of the breakup.

When she spoke again, her voice had gained conviction. "I'm content being who I am, cancer and all. I don't need validation from the opposite sex, and for me that's personal growth."

Annie nodded vigorously. "I know what you mean."

"I know you do," Amanda told her softly.

There was a long blast from the ferry, and a line of bicyclists boarded the vessel, pedalling onto the long ramp.

"Do you remember the summer between our sophomore and junior years?" Annie asked her. "That was a year after my dad left us and moved in with his girlfriend."

"Of course I remember."

It had been hellish for Annie and her mother. "I was furious with my father, and I blamed my mother for being such a wimp. I thought she should've done something to get him back— anything. All I wanted was my life the way it used to be." Annie didn't care if her parents still loved each other or not. She just wanted her mother and father in one place, because even if they didn't love each other, they at least loved her.

"It was a hard time for you," Amanda sympathized.

"For my entire family. The only one who seemed exempt from all the grief was my dad. He bought himself a new Cadillac and took trips to Vegas with *her*. What's funny is that now Mom, Andrew and I are the ones who are doing well." She grinned. "Hey, did I tell you my brother might get to play first string quarterback at Washington State University this fall?"

"That's fabulous!" Amanda sounded genuinely pleased.

Annie couldn't resist bragging about her brother. "He's doing great." She smiled again. "He's still in touch with Courtney. You remember her, don't you?" She didn't wait for a response. "They're really close, even though Court's in Chicago."

Last year Annie and her mother had attended every home game and cheered for Andrew. Her dad was probably somewhere in the stadium, too, Annie assumed, although she didn't know where and neither did Andrew, who had limited contact with his father.

"My mom's business has really become a success," she added.

"I think her party business was such a clever idea," Amanda said.

"It was." Annie frowned darkly. "When my dad left, he assumed Mom would get some minimum-wage job and live a dull existence without him. Dad was the center of her world, and his leaving hit her hard. She might never have regrouped if it wasn't for her Blossom Street friends."

"I really admire her."

"Mom found her niche and I'm going to tell you something that won't be announced publicly for another week." Annie had been dying to let someone know.

"About your mom?" Amanda asked.

"It's just so exciting I can hardly keep still. Mom is starting a party franchise. So many other people wanted to copy her ideas that she saw an attorney and set everything in motion. Some good friends Mom met through her knitting group are helping her with the finances, and it feels like things are really going to take off. The lawyer figures that within the next five to ten years, Mom's party franchise will be all over the country. Is that exciting or what?"

"That's wonderful!" Amanda squealed. "Just *wonderful.*"

Smiling, Annie shrugged. "I shouldn't brag about my mom, but I can't help it."

"And your dad? What's your relationship with him these days?"

That was more difficult to explain. "Okay, I guess. Dad got passed over for a big promotion at his company and that set him off, so he quit and went to work for another company. The new job didn't turn out to be everything he thought it would. He isn't happy, and I don't think he and *Tiff* are getting along."

"Tiff's the woman he left your mother for, right?"

"Yeah, and it wouldn't surprise me if they ended up getting divorced, too. It's sad, you know. I think Dad had all these expectations when he left. He was going to start his life over with this younger woman and leave all his responsibilities behind." Annie gazed at the ferry, which was just pulling out. "I have this feeling he was trying to stay young, if you know what I mean."

Amanda nodded. "Do you and Andrew see him?"

"On occasion. I was supposed to spend every other weekend with him until I turned eighteen. I didn't. Tiff and I never saw eye to eye—although a lot of that was my fault. I gave her plenty of reason to dislike me. That was because I blamed her for stealing my father. My dad seems to think Mom turned Andrew and me against him. She didn't. What he doesn't get is that *he* was the one who turned against us." Annie sighed. "I don't mean to talk about my own family so much."

"No, I'm glad you did. It helps me understand why we're such good friends."

"It does?"

"We're honest with each other. We can say all kinds of things, whatever we feel, and know it's okay." Amanda threw her a quick grin. "Even before the cancer, I admired you." She looked away suddenly, as though embarrassed to be admitting this. "You just seemed to have it all together."

"Oh, hardly," Annie muttered.

"No, I mean it. You didn't let stuff bother you like I did. You just sort of let it go. I understand that now, and I think in some ways I've reached the same place."

"Really?" Annie said, nearly blushing at her friend's praise.

"Yes. You're content with yourself. It's more than just being content with who you are. There's an inner peace about you. I think it comes when you've had to walk through a hard stretch of your life. For you it was when your parents split. It must've seemed like a betrayal, so you reacted with anger. You lashed out." Amanda turned away. "When I heard I had cancer again, I did, too. But my anger didn't last long. It couldn't, because I was immediately thrust into the medical world and they took over my life. I had no choice but to submit."

"You're not the same person you were six months ago."

"You're right. I don't want to be, either. Even if I could change the last six months, I wouldn't. It wasn't easy, and yet I feel as if what I've learned about myself, my family and my friends—" she glanced significantly at Annie "—my very *good* friends, made all that suffering worth it."

By unspoken agreement they stood and began walking again, enjoying the lovely afternoon. Soon the October rains would arrive and this afternoon's azure skies would turn gray.

"I was upset with my mother when I was first diagnosed," Amanda continued. "All she seemed to do was weep, and I hated that. In the middle of the night I'd find her standing in my doorway, crying and crying."

"She hated to see you go through this."

"I know," Amanda whispered. "I feel differently about my mom now, and my dad, too. Mom fought for me. She stood up to that insurance company and demanded I get the treatment I needed. Dad had to work in order to support the family, but he came to see me almost every day, no matter how late he'd worked. It was Mom who took on the insurance people and the doctors and everyone else. Nobody did a thing to me until she understood why it was necessary, the pros and cons of the procedure, long-term effects—everything. She was a medical warrior for me. Mom wasn't the emotional wreck I assumed she was in those first few weeks. She's been my advocate, and I needed her."

"Our moms are incredible," Annie said. She'd seen her own mother in an entirely different light since that summer she'd mentioned to Amanda. Her respect for Bethanne had grown a hundredfold.

"As for friends," Amanda told her, "I know who my true friends are. They're the ones who stuck by me through all of this." She paused for a moment. "Ruth phoned me not long ago when she heard I'd been released from the hospital. She wanted to chat, and I was glad to hear from her. Sure, I was disappointed that she'd wandered away when things got really tough for me, but I was willing to overlook that."

Again Annie wasn't so sure she'd be as willing and applauded Amanda for her forgiveness.

"Then Ruth started in about getting charged too much for a skirt she bought and went on and on about this buck ninety-nine she overpaid." Amanda shook her head as if astounded even now, repeating the story.

Annie knew Ruth and it sounded just like her.

"I don't have the patience for that anymore. My mom says I have a low threshold for unimportant concerns." She laughed as she said it.

Annie smiled.

"You're my friend, Annie, a true friend. I don't know if I can ever find the words to thank you for being there for me."

"You're my friend, too," Annie told her, and it was the truth. As Amanda had said, they could tell each other anything. She didn't have a sister, but she felt Amanda was the sister of her heart.

"You introduced me to Lydia, too," Amanda reminded her.

"Lydia's the one who advised me how best to be your friend."

"She's just so impressive with everything she's doing," Amanda said. "I don't think the hospital knew what hit them. Lydia's energy has turned that entire place upside down."

Annie couldn't keep from laughing. "She's a ball of fire, all right."

"A woman with a mission." Amanda glanced at her shyly. "I'm going to be working with her, you know."

Annie was exceptionally proud of that. "My mom told me."

"We're going to make a difference."

Annie breathed in the fresh warmth of the day. "I believe you already have."

CHAPTER TEN

One year later

"HELLO," AMANDA SAID as she stepped into the hospital room. "I'm Amanda."

The sickly pale teenager who stared back at her with blank eyes didn't immediately acknowledge her. After a moment, he said, "So?"

Amanda moved closer to his bedside. "So a year ago I was in this same room. I had leukemia."

Her announcement was followed by stark silence. "I've got it now. Do I have you to thank?"

It was a weak attempt at humor, and Amanda rewarded him with a warm smile. "You can thank me later."

"Thank you?" He wasn't amused by her response and then, as if he'd suddenly understood, he added, "Oh, you're one of those Pollyanna types who want to play the glad game. Well, if you're here to tell me everything'll be better in a few weeks, then you should leave now. I don't want to hear it."

"I don't have much in common with Pollyanna," Amanda told

him, "although I saw the Disney movie when I was a kid. As for everything getting better in a few weeks, it might not." She wasn't going to lie to him.

"In other words, I could be dead."

She nodded. "You could. I was one of the lucky ones. The survival rate gets better every year with medical advancements, but there aren't any guarantees."

"Yeah, right," he said with a snicker.

Amanda set the laptop computer on his nightstand and removed it from the case.

"What's that for?"

"Tell me your name first."

"Derek."

"Hi, Derek."

He offered her what could best be termed a half smile. "Hi—what was your name again?"

"Amanda."

"What's the computer for? If you think I want to catch up on homework, think again."

Homework had been the last thing on her mind while she was hospitalized, too. She shook her head, wanting to reassure him that wasn't the reason for her visit. "I'm here to help you get through this."

"Why do you care?"

"Because I've been where you are. I know what chemotherapy is like and what it means to feel the way you're feeling right now. I hated it, and I hated the whole world. Nothing seemed fair, and I wanted to know why this was happening to me. I can help."

Derek didn't bat an eyelash; of course, he didn't have any to bat, but Amanda understood that, too. "The laptop is so you can connect with *teenslivingwithcancer.org*. It's a Web site where you can chat with other kids going through this at the same time as you."

His eyes remained focused straight ahead and, for a moment, it seemed he hadn't heard her. "Why won't the pain stop?" he asked instead. "It just won't go away, and I don't think I can handle it anymore."

"It's like that for everyone in the beginning," Amanda told him gently.

"My ears hurt, my teeth, my head. I can't stand this. It's unbearable."

"Yes, it is. I cried and screamed, but it didn't make any difference. I couldn't stop begging for someone to take the pain away. That's the main reason I ended up in the hospital. They had to give me morphine."

"Me, too," Derek confessed, sounding embarrassed, as if he considered himself weak for not tolerating the pain without drugs.

"You've had how many days of chemo?" she asked.

"Four."

Amanda reached for his hand. She remembered how hard it was; no one who hadn't experienced it could appreciate the pain.

"So you're in remission." When she nodded he said, "I still don't get why you're here. Once I'm out of this place, I'm gone."

"I used to feel the same way," she explained, "but I'm here because of Melissa."

He stared back at her, frowning, and Amanda smiled. "You'll read about her once you get online. Like us, she was a teenager with cancer. She wanted to help other teenagers with cancer, and she has in a big way."

"She died?"

"But I'm still kicking."

"You gonna live to see thirty?"

"Maybe." She laughed. "As a good friend of mine says, if you want a guarantee, shop at Sears."

"Interesting company you keep."

"The best." She gave his hand a small squeeze. "I'll be back later to see how you're doing. Once you're through with the chemo, everything else will seem like a party."

He frowned again. "This is the worst of it?"

"It was for me."

She turned to leave, but Derek called her back. "Hey, Amanda," he said, his voice shaky but with more energy than before. "Thanks for coming."

"Be kind to this room."

He gave her a thumbs-up, and she returned the gesture.

At the end of the hallway, Lydia was waiting for her. She stood and smiled as Amanda approached. "Did you give out all the laptops?"

"I did. I think that connection with other teens will help." She thought about Derek, and her heart went out to him because she knew so well what he was enduring. He wasn't in good shape, but she hoped he'd be better once he went on the message boards.

"I know it'll help," Lydia agreed. "I spoke with the nursing staff at the oncology center here, and they want me to give a presentation at a series of hospitals in the area."

"That's wonderful, Lydia!"

"I'd like you to join me."

"Me?" The invitation flustered Amanda. She was happy to visit other teenagers and talk to them about Melissa's Living Legacy Foundation. Speaking in front of a bunch of physicians and nurses and hospital staff was a different story altogether.

"Yes, you," Lydia reiterated. "You have a lot to offer."

"But…"

"Remember how you mentioned Wendy, your favorite nurse? Why was she your favorite?"

"Because she understood that I wanted to watch videos other than *Barney* or *Blue's Clues.*"

"Right. She let you be a teenager."

"Yes," Amanda said. "Yes." She hadn't considered it in those terms but Lydia was exactly right. Wendy didn't treat Amanda like she was six years old, but she didn't expect her to behave like an adult, either.

"Other medical professionals need to know how to treat the teens on their wards. No one can explain how to do it better than someone who's been in that position."

Still Amanda hesitated. She'd never stood up before a group of adults, and the prospect was intimidating. She thought about Lydia who'd done so much for her. And she thought about Melissa.

"It's what Melissa would have wanted, isn't it?" Amanda asked.

"I think it is," Lydia said quietly.

Melissa Sengbusch had died five years earlier and although Amanda and Melissa had never met, the other girl had made a powerful impression on her and on so many other teenagers. Amanda would like to think that, had she lived, the two of them would've been good friends.

They had a lot in common. They'd both been teenagers with cancer. Both of them understood the struggles and the pain. Both were determined to live life to the fullest, no matter how long or short that life might be.

Amanda met Lydia's eyes. "Okay," she said, taking in a deep breath. "I'll do it." She wanted to honor Melissa and her Living Legacy Foundation. She could help others just the way Melissa would have wanted. It was what Amanda wanted, too.

SECOND WIND DREAMS
P.K. BEVILLE

One month shy of her 100th birthday, Flossie's dream came true. She got her very first motorcycle ride—in a pink leather jacket.

Flossie's dream ride was made possible through Second Wind Dreams, a nonprofit organization that fulfills the dreams of those living in elder-care communities—improving their lives and changing society's perceptions of aging. Flossie and hundreds like her have shown that our elders can still dream, and dream big, even when society is telling them they're too old.

Paula Kay (P.K.) Beville, Ph.D., began Second Wind Dreams with the goal of bringing seniors to the forefront of our society and making them feel what they are—special. Over the past eight years, Second Wind Dreams has made dreams come true in over 400 facilities in 41 states, Canada and India.

One woman's passion

P.K. is a trailblazer in her passion to bring something positive to nursing homes and develop ways to improve them. For the past twenty years P.K. has designed and implemented mental health services that are currently provided to more than 800 nursing homes throughout the United States. She co-authored *Second Wind,* an uplifting, heartwarming look at people in nursing homes, and she worked with seniors in nursing homes as a psychologist for over 20 years.

P.K. was continually struck by how much spirit and excitement residents had, even though they were frail and living in nursing homes. Yet, as a frontline caregiver, P.K. knew too well how these seniors were slipping into insignificance at the very time they should feel important and honored.

The idea for Second Wind Dreams came when P.K. asked some nursing home residents, "If you could have anything in the world, what would it be?" The answers were small and relatively simple requests, such as a new dress to attend a church group. P.K. realized that the hopes and dreams of residents were so simple that she was determined to make these dreams a reality. So P.K. gave up a six-figure salary to begin Second Wind Dreams, working single-handedly for one and a half years from the basement of her Marietta, Georgia, home. Even today as CEO of Second Wind Dreams, P.K. has never received a paycheck.

A forgotten population

Second Wind Dreams focuses on fulfilling the dreams of those living in nursing homes and elder-care communities. Nursing homes are where the frailest, weakest and, some say, the most burdensome among us spend their final days. These are the seniors who most need the program's assistance, yet nursing homes occupy the last rung on America's health-care ladder. Only 2% of nonprofit donations go to the elderly. Funding continues to be challenging, but P.K. believes that through programs like Second Wind Dreams, much can be done to improve the lives of those who live in nursing homes as well as those who work with them.

The lack of dreams and goals can have physical and mental consequences. The Dreams program stimulates residents both physically and mentally—fighting the triple threat of pain, boredom and loneliness found in so many of these residences, while giving seniors the special attention they deserve. As P.K. points out, you need only look at the faces of these seniors to see the results.

Dreams fulfilled

Second Wind Dreams makes possible about three dreams a day. Need-based dreams—something as simple as a cup holder for a wheelchair or a new pair of bedroom slippers—account for a humbling 22% of the dreams. Others are relationship-based dreams like the one of a resident who was flown across the country to reunite with a brother he hadn't seen in forty years. Many seniors dream of reliving past experiences such as driving a big rig again, or getting back out in the fresh sea air to catch the big one. And for residents like Kay, lifelong dreams are fulfilled. Ninety-two-year-old Kay, who never got the chance to graduate from university, was given full honors, with cap and gown and all the pomp and circumstance.

But as P.K. discovered right from the program's inception, an unbelievable 72% of the dreams are just for fun! The first dream P.K. fulfilled was that of ninety-two-year-old twins who wanted an Elvis impersonator to visit their nursing home. So many seniors are still kids at heart—like Mae, who was wheelchair bound, blind and on dialysis, yet dreamed of riding all seven roller coasters at a Georgia amusement park. In P.K.'s eyes the dreams are equal, big or small—even if the price tags for fulfilling the dreams differ. The dream itself is what it's all about.

Inspiring staff and the community

P.K. knows the only way to change society's perception of aging is through community involvement. Second Wind Dreams relies heavily on volunteers—individuals, families, church groups, student groups of all ages and corporations. Participating in a dream often leads to long-lasting partnerships with facilities and special relationships with residents. Those who have been a part of a dream-come-true are never sure who got the most out of it, the volunteer or the dreamer.

Those who work with the elderly are motivated by P.K.'s passion and vision. She pays positive attention to staff, knowing how hard they work and how they are underpaid and often feel unappreciated. P.K. recently completed a study to determine the impact of the Dreams program. The study showed that through Second Wind Dreams, depression among nursing home residents decreased by 56% and staff morale increased by 65%—proof that long after the dream has been fulfilled, the effects linger, giving all involved a sense of renewal and hope.

P.K. believes that the ability to dream is a life-affirming experience that can transform lives. She is so touched by each dream she witnesses that watching is like having her dream fulfilled, as well. P.K.'s dream has *always* been to enhance life in nursing homes and to honor the resilience and vitality of the human spirit in our elders. Because of P.K. Beville's vision and passion, Second Wind Dreams is changing the perception of aging…one dream at a time.

More Than Words

SHARON SALA

THE
YELLOW
RIBBON

SHARON SALA

This *New York Times* bestselling author sold her first book in 1991 and has since gone on to write over 50 novels—some under the pseudonym Dinah McCall. Her stories often explore controversial topics that affect women in everyday life. She believes that receiving letters from people her stories have helped heal is the most rewarding thing that can happen to any author. Sharon, who lives in Henryetta, Oklahoma, is the proud mother of two grown children and the doting grandma of three granddaughters and one grandson.

CHAPTER ONE

IT WAS ALMOST 9:00 a.m. and Frances Drummond was late. She was due to be at Just Like Home no later than nine. The residents of the assisted living center where she worked held her to a high standard and she tried never to disappoint them.

But disappoint them she would if she didn't get there in time to help with shampooing. Today was beauty day. Although she wasn't a licensed beautician, she was a perfectly willing shampooer, and was often called in to remove hair curlers so the beauticians could do comb-outs and styles more quickly.

Beauty day was the female residents' favorite day, and Frankie loved to see the women giggling and fussing over different hairstyles and nail polish colors.

A bread delivery truck was leaving the parking lot just as she drove in. The driver turned and stared as Frankie jumped out of her car. Self-consciously, she pulled up the neck of her pink cotton sweater, wishing she'd worn a turtleneck, and tried not to stumble as she hurried across the lot.

She entered the lobby of the home, breathless and limping more than normal from moving too fast. The girls, as she called them, waved at her from outside the little beauty shop, which was in a corner of the lobby. It was open only two days a week—one for the women, the second for the men—so no one wanted to miss out.

Haircuts and dye jobs were regular requests, both for men and women, along with the occasional permanent. The residents ranged in age from sixty-seven to ninety-eight. For Frankie, whose parents had died when she was twenty, these senior citizens had become the family she no longer had, and they took it upon themselves to give her advice, whether she asked for it or not.

Frankie had been in college when she and her parents were in the automobile accident that had killed her parents and left her with thick, puckered burn scars on her neck and arm and a painful limp. When she was tired, the limp was more noticeable. The scars and the handicap were usually enough to put most men off giving her a second look.

After years of disappointment, she'd given up hoping she'd ever find a decent man who could look past her imperfections to the woman beneath, and had created a satisfying life by helping others with much larger problems. This attitude was what had led her to the job she had now, working as the recreation director in a home for the aged. She loved her work and she loved the people. They had way more wrinkles than she had scars, and they all dragged their feet a bit when they walked.

The residents of Just Like Home were also funny, wise and to Frankie's unending surprise, often a little bawdy. She'd gotten more sexual advice from the girls than she'd ever be able to use.

Once she'd crossed the lobby, Frankie stepped into the site manager's office long enough to lock up her purse and hang up her coat.

"Good morning, Mrs. Tulia," Frankie said. "Sorry I'm late."

Mavis Tulia was on the phone, but she wiggled her fingers and mouthed a hello.

Frankie hurried back to the lobby, hugging girls on her way into the beauty shop, then waving at the three beauticians already at their chairs. One was in the midst of a cut, one was doing a dye job, and the third was putting curlers in Margie Potts's hair.

"Good morning, Margie," Frankie said.

"Hello to you, too," Margie replied. "I'm thinking of Ravenous Red for my nail color today. What do you think?"

"I think you would look ravenous," Frankie teased.

Margie laughed.

"Hey, Frankie," the beautician said. "Didn't think you were gonna make it."

"Traffic."

Margie rolled her eyes. She'd driven a cab for more than thirty years, and for the past five claimed to be working on a book about her life and her fares.

Frankie doubted the book was a work in progress, but it hardly mattered. It gave Margie an identity. Here in Just Like Home, she was known as the writer, just as she'd been the cabby before.

"What do you want me to do first?" Frankie asked the beautician working on Margie.

The woman pointed out to the lobby and the residents who were sitting there, waiting their turn.

"Louise is next. If you do the shampoo, Lori should be through with her cut and style by then."

"Will do," Frankie said, and stepped outside the little salon. "Louise, you're next, dear. Here's your cane. Let's go to the shampoo station."

And so the morning began. By noon, they were down to two beauticians, one having returned to her regular salon. When Frankie had Doris shampooed and ready for the stylist, she went back into the lobby to get the last resident.

Charlotte Grace was eighty-seven years young and never married. Some of the girls called her the Old Maid, but only in jest.

Charlotte never seemed to mind. She'd usually fire back a comment that being single didn't mean being a virgin, which always made the others laugh. Only Frankie saw the sadness in Charlotte that the other girls seemed to miss.

"Charlotte, you're next," Frankie said.

The older woman looked up from the magazine she'd been reading.

"About time," she said. "I was afraid I wouldn't get to show off my new do before they laid me out."

Frankie grinned. When she'd first begun working here, the death and funeral humor had taken her aback. But she'd long since gotten used to it. Only yesterday, Marvin Howard had flagged her down to look at some snapshots. When she realized they were of the new headstone set at his prepaid burial plot, she'd oohed and aahed the same way she might have done if she'd been looking at a picture of his great-grandchildren.

Charlotte's step was spry and her figure trim, her only frailty a slight tremble in her hands. She wore her hair short and fluffy, so the shampoo and styling wouldn't take long.

Frankie settled her into the shampoo chair and began to fasten a clean cape around her neck to protect her clothes. As she did, the Velcro fastener caught on the yellow ribbon that Charlotte always wore around her neck.

"Oh, wait…I've caught your ribbon," Frankie said.

"That's okay," Charlotte assured her. "I need to get a new one anyway. Can't let my locket go begging."

Frankie eyed the small oval locket hanging from the ribbon. She'd never seen Charlotte without it.

"That's really pretty," Frankie said. "Is it an heirloom?"

Charlotte's smile faded.

"I suppose it is now," she said, rubbing it between her thumb and forefinger. "Or at least it will be soon. That's what happens when you get as old as I am."

Frankie frowned. She'd said something wrong, but she wasn't sure what. She laid her hand on the back of Charlotte's neck.

"I'm sorry. I didn't mean to pry."

Charlotte shook her head and managed a teary smile.

"Oh, pooh, you're not prying. I'm just a sentimental old woman. I bought the locket for myself, you know. It wasn't handed down or anything."

"It's beautiful," Frankie said.

Charlotte opened it.

"So was he," she said softly, revealing the photo inside.

Frankie bent over for a closer look and saw a young man with a very sober countenance.

"Who was he...your husband?" Frankie asked.

Charlotte's chin trembled, but she didn't cry.

"I never married," she said at last, then looked up at Frankie. "But he asked. He did ask me to marry him."

Frankie pulled up a stool and sat down beside her.

"What happened?"

"I said no."

Frankie didn't know what to say. She could tell that Charlotte viewed this as a tragedy.

"Father didn't like him," Charlotte explained, then shrugged. "Back then, a father's opinion still held water. But he was wrong... my father...I should have married my sweetheart. His name was Daniel Louis Morrow."

"What happened to him?" Frankie asked.

A tear rolled down Charlotte's cheek. Frankie leaned over and blotted it with the tail of the cape.

"After I refused him, he didn't wait to be drafted," Charlotte told her. "He signed up for the army right after Pearl Harbor was bombed." Her voice shook a little as she added, "He never came home, you know. He was shot by a German sniper near a little town called Positano, in southern Italy. He's buried there."

She shut the locket with a snap, then pulled the cape down over the front of her dress and leaned back. It was obvious she was through talking.

Frankie got up and turned on the water, letting it flow until it ran warm, then began to work shampoo into Charlotte's hair, scrubbing gently until her scalp had a good massage and her hair was thoroughly clean.

She rinsed it twice, then wrapped a clean towel around Charlotte's hair and twisted it into a turban before helping her up and moving her to the stylist's chair.

Charlotte sat down, then took Frankie's hand.

"I always meant to go there...to his grave. All these years and I kept saying I would go. I even got myself a passport and took all my shots a couple of years back, then didn't do it. Now it's too late. Don't do that to yourself, you hear? If there's something you know you should do, don't put it off."

"I won't," Frankie said, and then leaned over and kissed Charlotte's cheek.

Charlotte smiled. "Thank you, dear. I don't know what I would do without you."

Frankie smiled back. "That works both ways," she said, then went to gather up the wet towels and clean up the shampoo area.

When it was time for lunch, Frankie played the piano for the residents as they ate. Quite often they would shout out a request. They rarely asked for any modern tunes, and Frankie was becoming quite competent at playing songs from the big band era of the thirties and forties.

She was in the middle of "Old Buttermilk Sky," a song Hoagie Carmichael had made famous, when she saw Charlotte come into the dining room. Her hair was freshly fluffed and styled, just as she liked it, and her expression pleasant. Frankie watched her nodding and waving at her friends as she took her seat at the table.

Since their earlier conversation, Frankie saw Charlotte in a different light. What she'd viewed as a calm, complacent demeanor was really a quiet sadness. And she knew now that Charlotte's shy personality was actually an expression of regret. The dress Charlotte had on was such a dark purple it looked almost black, and Frankie realized that the older woman never wore bright colors. It seemed to Frankie as if Charlotte were in permanent mourning.

Poor Charlotte Grace.

She'd lived an entire life without joy and it broke Frankie's heart.

Frankie thought about Charlotte all the way home, and even through her solitary dinner and a lingering bubble bath. As she was brushing her teeth, she caught a glimpse of her own reflection and froze. The scars were redder than usual from the heat of the bathwater. She glanced at them, then focused on her face. For a moment, everything looked blurred, and she could almost see her features aging and her hair turning gray.

She shivered, then shook her head to make the image go away. When she looked again, she was her normal self, but she'd gotten the message. If she didn't make some changes in her own life, she was going to wind up just like Charlotte—old and saddened by the things she'd missed.

Her mood was somber as she got into bed. She lay motionless, willing herself to relax, then wound up doing the opposite. She thrashed and turned until she'd messed up her sheets and was more awake than when she'd gotten into bed. Every time she closed her eyes, she imagined a lone tombstone in an empty field with Daniel Morrow's name on it.

Of course, she knew her imagination had exaggerated the facts, but she was certain the young soldier never dreamed his final resting place would be half a world away from his home.

Still wide awake at midnight, Frankie slapped the mattress with both hands, pushed herself up, and rolled out of bed. Within moments, she was heading for the library, where she kept her computer. She booted it up and got online, then typed in the words *Positano, Italy.*

To her surprise, a colorful Web site popped up. One of the more imposing facts about the little fishing village was that it had turned into quite a tourist spot, and the foremost hotel in the village was a former palace that had once been owned by Charles Murat, the brother-in-law of Napoleon Bonaparte. The palace had long since been turned into a hotel called the Hotel Murat, and boasted an aging elegance.

She sat there for a moment with her fingers resting on the keyboard, then impulsively clicked onto a form to e-mail the hotel and began to type.

Dear Sirs,
I am looking for the grave of an American GI who died during World War II. His name was Daniel Louis Morrow, and I was told that he'd been buried in a small cemetery in your area.
If there is anyone who can help me verify that, I would greatly appreciate it.
Time is of the essence, since the woman for whom I'm writing is very elderly. Please help me. It matters so much to her that we know for certain the location of his final resting place.
Sincerely,
Frances Drummond
Chicago, Illinois
USA

The moment she hit Send and the e-mail went out, she felt a weight roll off her shoulders. Her efforts might not amount to a thing, but whatever the outcome, she felt better for having made an attempt to verify this for Charlotte.

Frankie went to bed with a light heart, and as soon as she closed her eyes, fell fast asleep.

A HALF A WORLD AWAY, Giuseppe Longoria, the hotel manager at the Hotel Murat, was checking the hotel's e-mail. He was down to the last message, and when he opened it up, he realized it wasn't a request for reservations but a letter of inquiry instead. Being bilingual, he scanned it quickly, then frowned. This was beyond his expertise and had nothing to do with hotel management. He started to fire back a response that said as much, when one of the maids came into the office to empty the wastebaskets.

Her name was Maria Romano. She didn't read English, but he knew her nephew, Daniel Sciora, did. He also knew that there were several American GIs buried in the little cemetery on the outskirts of Positano where Maria lived. He explained the situation, asking if she would pass this message on to Daniel. When she agreed he printed it out and gave it to Maria.

It was after seven o'clock in the evening before Maria returned home. She had forgotten about the paper until she was changing out of her uniform. She took it from her pocket and laid it on the bed. Once she was dressed in her regular clothing, she headed across the road to her nephew's home.

THIRTY-SIX-YEAR-OLD Daniel Sciora was a lonely man, although his family was large, even by Italian standards. His aunt Maria and uncle Paolo lived across the road. Eight cousins and their spouses lived nearby in Positano, twelve cousins and their families lived a couple of hours north in Naples, while most of the others were in Sicily. Once a year, they made it a point to get together, renew family ties and catch up on family news. And every year, the aging grandmothers and aunts gave Daniel grief because he was still an unmarried man.

Daniel knew he was considered a good catch. He was tall and good-looking, and had inherited the vineyard and winery that his great-grandfather had begun. He could have had his pick of a dozen pretty women from the village, but he didn't want to settle for just any match. He wanted "love at first sight." A woman who took his breath away with nothing but a look, and he had yet to find her.

On this particular evening, he was about to serve himself dinner when there was a knock at the door. He dropped the spoon back into the pot and went to answer it. When he saw who it was, he smiled.

"*Zia* Maria! Come in! Come in! The pasta's ready. Have you come to eat dinner with me?"

Maria Romano rolled her eyes.

"Your *zio* Paolo would never get over it if I did," she said.

"Then bring him, too," Daniel offered. "I made plenty."

"You're a good boy," Maria said, and kissed him on both cheeks. "But food is not why I've come."

She handed him the e-mail that the hotel manager had printed out.

"This came to the hotel today, and Giuseppe asked me to bring it to you. He says it's a request for information from a woman in the United States. He thought since you understand English, you might be able to help."

Daniel frowned slightly as he took the paper.

"Sure, *Zia*, I'd be happy to help, but what is it?"

"I don't know. He didn't tell me. You read it. You're so smart, I know you'll understand what it's about. Now I must get back to the house and prepare our evening meal. *Ciao, bello*."

"*Ciao, Zia*."

He closed the door, and began reading the e-mail as he went back to the kitchen. But halfway there, he stopped. His throat tightened and he felt himself struggling for breath.

"*Dio mio!*"

There was little more to be said. A ghost from the past was staring up at him. Someone was asking about the grave of an American GI—a man by the name of Daniel Louis Morrow.

His aunt was right about one thing. He was definitely better equipped to answer this e-mail than the hotel manager. He knew for certain that there was a grave for Daniel Morrow. He knew because he was named for the man—the man who had been his grandfather.

What he had to decide was whether or not to answer the

e-mail. If this woman who was asking was family, she might get more than she'd bargained for. He knew she had no idea about his existence. Not even Daniel Morrow had known he had a daughter—Daniel's mother.

The infantry that Daniel Morrow belonged to had been bivouacked outside Positano for two days when he'd met Angelina Ricci. He'd been taken with the petite, dark-haired, dark-eyed beauty and a romance had ensued. But he'd died before he knew that Angelina was carrying his child—Daniel's mother. Daniel had grown up knowing about the GI who was his grandfather, and was proud of the fact. But it remained to be seen what these two American women would think of the truth.

He took the e-mail with him to the kitchen, reading it again and again as he ate his evening meal.

Even after he'd gone to bed, it was still on his mind. Whoever this Frances woman was, she seemed genuinely concerned about her elderly friend. Just as he was drifting off to sleep, he made a decision. He would tell her of Daniel Morrow's final resting place. The rest he would leave up to fate.

FRANKIE WENT THROUGH the next day on pins and needles, hoping for an answer to her e-mail. But there was an emergency at Just Like Home that evening. One of the elderly gentlemen who'd been living there for more than ten years sat down in his chair to read the paper and died. Of course, Frankie had stayed to help out, mourning his loss along with the others.

By the time she got home, it was almost midnight. The last thing she thought about was e-mail. She was aching all over and felt shaky and weak. She chalked it up to the trauma of the day, although death was something they dealt with at the home on a regular basis.

The next morning, she woke up with fever and chills. She sat up on the side of the bed for a few minutes, then got so dizzy she had to lie back down. There was nothing to do but call in sick.

Even if she'd felt well enough to drive, it was critically important not to expose the residents to any viruses. So she reached for the phone and dialed the home.

"Just Like Home. Mavis Tulia speaking."

"Mrs. Tulia, it's me, Frankie."

"My stars, dear…what's wrong with you? You sound terrible."

"I feel terrible," she said. "I felt weird last night when I got home, but blamed it on Mr. Ellard's death. But this morning I woke up feeling even worse. I have a fever, so I know I'm contagious."

"Well, you must stay home, of course. We can't have anything like this running through the residence if we can prevent it. Take care of yourself, dear, and call if you need me."

"Thank you," Frankie said. "I'm really sorry. I had planned some craft activities today, but since I won't be there to help start them, look in my locker for movies. It's Perry Monroe's turn to choose what the group gets to see. He's partial to World War II movies, which the women hate, but there are three that have love stories in them. Maybe you could offer him a choice between those three and everyone will be happy."

"Don't you worry," Mrs. Tulia said. "I'll make sure he chooses one that everybody can enjoy. I'm just sorry you're so sick. Get better soon. Love you."

"Love you, too," Frankie said, and hung up the phone.

After taking a warm shower and changing into a clean night-gown, Frankie made herself some hot tea and took it to bed. Once she'd finished the tea, she crawled beneath the covers.

Just as she was falling asleep, she remembered Charlotte and the e-mail she'd sent.

"When I wake up," she mumbled. "I'll check it when I wake up."

WHILE FRANKIE WAS fighting a flu bug, Daniel Sciora was fighting a battle of his own. He revisited the little cemetery where his grandfather was buried, and as he stood at the grave, it occurred to him that not once had he ever considered what Daniel Mor-row's life had been like before he'd come to Italy. All he'd known of Morrow was what his grandmother had told him, and that hadn't been much.

He shoved his hands in his pockets and read the name on the tombstone, as he'd done a thousand times before.

Pfc. Daniel Louis Morrow
Born October 10, 1919
Died May 8, 1943

"So, *Nonno,* you had your own set of secrets, didn't you?" Daniel's eyes narrowed. "I wish you were still here. I need someone to tell me what to do."

But there were no answers for Daniel, and to his growing dismay, no answer from the woman in America, either.

FRANKIE WOKE UP TWICE during the day, both times to go to the bathroom. She still had a fever, and her throat was dry and scratchy. When she went back to bed, she couldn't help but wish there was someone special in her life to tuck her in. Most of the time she didn't give much thought to her solitary state, but there were times, like now, when being alone felt like a failure.

The next morning was Saturday, and since she didn't work on the weekend, she was counting on the extra rest to help her feel better. She got up, weak and shaky, but minus the fever, to make some coffee. Once she'd poured herself a cup, she remembered the e-mail and took her coffee with her into the library.

When she checked her in-box, she was elated to see there was a response to the e-mail she'd sent to Italy.

She opened the message and began to read.

Dear Ms. Drummond,
I received the request you sent to the Hotel Murat regarding information on the grave of an American soldier named Daniel Louis Morrow.

There is, indeed, a soldier by that name who is buried in a small cemetery on the outskirts of Positano. If there is anything else I can do for you, please let me know.
Daniel Sciora

The news was all that Frankie hoped for and then some. Not only had Daniel Morrow's final resting place been verified, but the man had offered further help. She wasn't sure just what that might be, but she was definitely excited.

She hit Reply, her fingers pausing momentarily on the keys, and then she began to type.

CHAPTER TWO

THE AMERICAN WOMAN had responded. Daniel felt a kick of excitement as he opened her message.

Dear Mr. Sciora,
Thank you so much for answering so promptly. I would have replied sooner, but I've been a bit under the weather. This is the first day I've been out of bed in the last thirty-six hours. It feels good to be up and moving around.
My friend Charlotte is such a dear, but I'm going to have to think about how to tell her what I've learned. Her story is quite a sad one, you see, and I don't want to upset her needlessly. Daniel Morrow was her sweetheart. He asked her to marry him, but for some reason, her father didn't approve and refused his permission. Charlotte told me that she resented her father for his interference and regretted that she had followed his wishes. As a result, she never married.
Life is sometimes very sad, isn't it?

But then, I've never married, either, although not for the same reasons as Charlotte.

I am twenty-seven to Charlotte's eighty-seven and, as yet, unwilling to classify myself as an old maid.

I fear I'm rambling, but it's from joy. I do not yet know how I'm going to use the information you have given me, but I thank you again for taking the time to help me.

With much appreciation,

Frankie Drummond

Daniel was smiling. Her English was sprinkled with idioms he wasn't familiar with. *Under the weather* was a new one for him, but after further reading, he guessed it meant she'd been sick.

The reference to being an "old maid" must have to do with being unmarried, but it still made him laugh. He could almost hear her voice, full of life and laughter, talking about first one subject and then another, with hardly a breath in between.

His mother had been like that. Always laughing and teasing. His father, Antonio, had been a solemn man, but one who had loved his family dearly. It was a tragedy when he had died of a heart attack at forty-one. Daniel's mother had never recovered from the grief and had passed away within five years of his death. Sometimes it seemed to Daniel that he'd been alone most of his life.

This woman who called herself Frankie sounded like someone he would have liked to get to know better. However, distance prevailed. But he could answer her e-mail. It would be the proper thing to do.

FRANKIE HELD HER news close to her heart all weekend, wondering if telling Charlotte would be wise. What good would it do for Charlotte to know that Daniel's grave was, indeed, in the location where she'd been told? Frankie didn't imagine the older woman had enough money to get there now even if she wanted to.

Still, Charlotte's story was so sad. In the grand scheme of life, her wish to visit Daniel's grave seemed such a small thing.

By Sunday night, Frankie had pronounced herself well and was making plans to return to work the next day. She was out of the shower and preparing to dry her hair when she heard something from the television in the bedroom that caught her attention. She hurried into the room and sat down on the end of the bed to watch. A slender woman with delicate features and a confident, easygoing manner was being interviewed.

"So, the purpose of Second Wind Dreams is to grant dreams to the elderly?" the reporter asked.

"Yes, that's correct," the woman replied.

"Tell me, how does it work?"

"It's pretty straightforward. We all have regrets for something we didn't do. You know…that missed opportunity we turned down. Sometimes it's the reverse…there was something we wanted to do but were never given the chance. Well, it's my belief that age should never be the reason for giving up dreams. That's why I began Second Wind Dreams.

"Usually, the recipients of the dreams are discovered by someone else. Always, the recipients' doctors must pronounce them physically fit for whatever it is they dream of doing. Once that's accomplished, the rest is left up to us at Second Wind Dreams to make the magic happen."

"How can people contact you?"

Frankie's heart was thumping with excitement as she reached for a pen and paper. She took down the information, then ran to finish drying her hair. What if Charlotte qualified for something like this? What if these people could help Charlotte get to Italy to visit Daniel's grave? Frankie could hardly contain her excitement.

By the time she was ready for bed, she had a plan. Tomorrow she would have Second Wind Dreams fax her an information sheet. It might all come to nothing, but she wasn't going to give up on Charlotte's dream until someone told her it was impossible.

IT WAS JUST PAST NOON the next day when Frankie finished filling out the form that had been faxed to Just Like Home. She hurried into Mavis Tulia's office and sent it back to Second Wind Dreams, then breathed a sigh of relief. She had followed her heart and could only hope for the best. Whatever happened, it was out of her hands.

She worked late that night to get caught up after her time away, and when she got home she was so tired she forgot to check her e-mail. The next morning, to her delight, she discovered a message from Daniel Sciora.

Dear Frankie,
I must say that I like Frankie better than Frances. I like a very happy woman. I think you must also be a selfless woman. Not everyone cares for the older generation. You are to be commended for the life you have chosen to live.
I think your Charlotte is a very lucky woman to have you for a friend. As for being an "old maid," I take it that means an unmarried woman of a certain age. That makes me laugh. Twenty-seven is not old. At least I certainly hope not. I am thirty-six and to the disappointment of my large family, unmarried, as well. We could probably exchange amusing stories about what you Americans call "blind dates."
I wish you the best in giving your Charlotte the news of her sweetheart's final resting place. If it matters, please assure her that the grave site is well cared for and often bears fresh flowers.
If you have need to call me for any further details, my phone number is posted in the address of this message.
Ciao,
Daniel

Frankie sighed. Unlike Daniel, she didn't have amusing blind date stories. In fact, since she didn't date, there were no stories at all.

She reread the message, smiling to herself as she pictured him trying to figure out idioms of the English language.

He sounded nice.

She stared at the phone number.

She knew it didn't mean anything that he'd given her his number, but it *was* a generous offer of further contact. She wanted to tell someone about contacting Second Wind Dreams about Charlotte, but if it all came to nothing, then there would have to be explanations about why not. Still, she could call him without mentioning what she'd done.

Before she had time to change her mind, she grabbed the phone and punched in the numbers, hoping that it would already be morning in Italy.

DANIEL WAS ON HIS WAY out the door when the phone rang. He started to let it go, then changed his mind and ran back inside to answer.

"*Ciao?*"

"Hello, this is Frankie Drummond. Is this Daniel?"

Daniel's heartbeat stopped.

It was her!

The woman from America!

She sounded so young and happy. He shifted mental gears into English and took a deep breath.

"Yes, this is Daniel Sciora. It is a pleasure and a surprise to speak to you. Is everything all right?"

"Yes, yes, everything is fine. I just read your e-mail, and since you were kind enough to give me your phone number…well…I was just curious enough to call."

Daniel laughed. Her honesty was refreshing.

"Then I am happy you were curious. It is, indeed, good to hear your voice, as well. And how is your friend, Charlotte? Have you told her anything yet?"

Frankie sighed, and the sound made Daniel smile.

"No, I haven't. But I'm working on something that might prove to be exciting for her."

"Oh?"

"Yes, but I'm not going to say anything just yet for fear of jinxing it. If it happens, you'll be one of the first to know."

"Jinxing? What is this jinxing?"

Frankie laughed.

"Sorry. Your English is so good I forgot myself. A jinx is like having bad luck."

"Ah…that I understand," he said. "But your call is definitely not bad luck for me. It is good to hear your voice. Now all I need is a picture of you."

There was a moment's hesitation, and Daniel wondered if he'd pushed too far with such a request.

"That I can furnish," she said at last. "I'll scan one into an e-mail to you, but don't expect a glamour girl."

Daniel heard a change in the timbre of her voice, but thought nothing of it.

"I will send one to you, as well. As for glamour girls, that phrase I understand. Just so you know, Frankie Drummond, glamour girls are usually all glitter and no substance."

"I'll look forward to your picture."

"And I will look forward to yours," Daniel echoed.

"Yes, well, goodbye, then," Frankie said.

"Since I don't want to say goodbye, I will just say *ciao,*" Daniel told her. "And I hope there will be a next time."

EVEN AFTER the dial tone was buzzing in her ear, Frankie still listened, hoping for just one more word. Finally, she had no option but to hang up.

"Well," she said, and then grinned. She put her hand over her mouth to stifle a giggle.

She was acting silly and she knew it, but she didn't care. This was the most excitement she'd had in years. So much was happening. Even though she knew Daniel was nothing more than an e-mail pen pal, it made her very dull personal life suddenly interesting. She didn't know what the outcome of her request to Second Wind Dreams would be, but she would never regret the inquiry she'd sent to Positano.

Eight days later: Just Like Home

MAVIS TULIA STEPPED outside the office, searching the lobby for Frankie. She saw her in a corner, playing checkers with Al Janey. Al was their eldest resident and fancied himself quite a checker player, even though he often cheated by claiming he got the colors mixed up. As usual, Frankie was letting him win.

The manager glanced at the clock. It was almost time for lunch, so she didn't mind disturbing their game.

"Frankie! Frankie!" she called.

Frankie looked up, saw her boss waving at her from the office, and breathed a sigh of relief. Al had drifted off to sleep twice since they'd begun their game. Waiting for him to wake up each time was definitely an exercise in patience.

Frankie put her hand on Al's arm so that he would know she was talking. She suspected he'd turned his hearing aid off earlier and had forgotten to turn it back on.

"Al! Al! Mrs. Tulia is calling me. I have to go, okay?"

Al frowned. "I won, right?"

Frankie grinned.

"You sure did. Fair and square."

Al nodded.

"See you later," Frankie said.

Al was already setting up the checkerboard again just in case someone else came by and offered to play.

Frankie hurried over to the office.

"What's up?" she asked.

Mavis smiled. "I think this is yours."

Frankie took the paper and scanned it quickly. Then her heart skipped a beat. She looked up.

"Did you read this?" she asked.

Her boss nodded.

"So, what do you think?" Frankie asked.

"I think Charlotte Grace is lucky to have you for a friend."

Frankie clutched the paper to her chest. She couldn't believe it. Second Wind Dreams would make Charlotte's dream come true. If her doctor pronounced her fit to travel, Charlotte was going to Italy. Frankie wanted to scream—to shout the news from the rooftops—but she couldn't. Not until they knew for sure Charlotte's health was good enough for her to go. And Second Wind Dreams liked to make a big event out of the presentation, so that meant waiting.

During her afternoon break, Frankie called her bank and checked the amount in her savings account, then contacted a travel agent and asked what a first-class ticket to Positano, Italy would cost. The rate was staggering. Well over two thousand dollars. But she had the money, and if she could make it work, she wanted to accompany Charlotte on her trip.

Still, there was one person she could tell about her exciting news, and that was Daniel. She couldn't wait to get home and give him a call.

Yet that evening when she did get home, it occurred to her that he would most likely be asleep. Frustrated, she opted for e-mail, and scanned a snapshot of herself taken at Just Like Home to send along with her message. It wasn't a bad photo. You could see the scars on her neck and arm, but she had a nice smile on her face. It would have to do.

DANIEL WAS ON HIS WAY home after more than a week on the road, visiting his customers and taking orders for new shipments of wine. He'd been to Rome, then Milan, then back south to Naples. From there, he'd caught a flight to Sicily and made the rounds of his customers there.

As always, he'd been anxious to get home, but never as much as he was this trip. He'd thought of his new American friend several times while he was away and couldn't help but wonder if he'd have another message from her. He was also hopeful that she'd sent a picture. He wanted a face to go with that delightful voice.

He did, however, have reservations about the old woman's feelings. He couldn't help but worry about what might happen when she learned that the man she'd loved had fallen in love with another woman and left a part of himself behind when he died.

MARIA WAS OUTSIDE working in her garden when Daniel's car came down the road. She straightened up and waved as he passed. Only after he waved back did she return to her weeding.

Seeing his aunt in the garden gave Daniel a sense of homecoming. While many things in his life were in a constant state of flux, it was the things that never seemed to change that provided him with a sense of well-being.

Still, when he unlocked the door and carried his suitcase into the house, he felt a moment of letdown. If only there was someone in his life to come home to.

He glanced at the clock. It was just after noon. There were countless things he could do, from unpacking dirty clothes to checking mail and phone messages. Instead, he found himself heading for the computer.

It took a while for all the e-mail to download, but when he sorted through it, to his delight, he discovered a message from Frankie.

He opened it first and noticed there was an attachment. When he opened that and saw it was a photo, he leaned back and let himself absorb her image.

"So…hello, Frances Drummond," he said softly.

In the picture, she was standing behind an elderly woman, leaning down, arms around the woman's neck. There was a birthday cake in front of them, and they were both looking at the camera and smiling.

He caught himself smiling back.

Frankie had a pretty face and long, dark hair and he wondered what it would feel like to have her arms around his neck and her breath upon his cheek. He saw what appeared to be scarring on her neck and arm and winced, thinking of the pain she must have endured, then looked back at her face.

He knew what she sounded like. Now he knew what she looked like. For some odd reason, he wanted more.

He sat staring at her for the longest time before he remembered there was a letter that had come with the photo.

He opened the letter, then sat back and relaxed, as he would have if he'd been sitting face-to-face with her.

Dear Daniel,

I have the most marvelous news. There is an organization here in the States called Second Wind Dreams that makes dreams come true for the elderly. In this case, if Charlotte's health is good, they will pay for her trip to Positano so that she can visit her Daniel's grave.

I haven't told her yet, because I don't want to get her hopes up only to have them dashed, but I am so excited I can hardly contain myself. And I have another request of you that I hesitate to ask. However, since it's not for me, but for Charlotte, I will ask it of you, anyway.

If, indeed, she is able to travel that distance, I am going to pay my own way and come with her. So I was wondering, if it wouldn't be too much of an imposition, would you agree to be our guide and translator while we are there? Neither Charlotte nor I know any Italian.

I know it's a lot to ask, but I promise we wouldn't be any trouble. Charlotte is a very quiet, dignified woman and would not be demanding, and I promise not to cause you embarrassment.

However, if you feel this is asking too much, I will definitely understand, and hope that we will at least get to meet you while we are there.

Thank you in advance.

Frankie

Daniel's heart skipped a beat. Suddenly, every little fantasy he'd let himself weave about this Frances Drummond had the possibility of becoming true. He didn't know whether to be excited or alarmed. Then he glanced back at her picture and decided that it was definitely excitement he felt.

Before he did anything else, he got a snapshot of himself that had been taken in the vineyards near the winery and scanned it into the body of his message back to her.

IT HAD BEEN DAYS since Frankie had sent her photo to Daniel. Her first inclination was that he'd been disgusted by the scars and ended their long-distance chats. She'd been disappointed and had just gotten to the point of convincing herself it didn't matter, when she opened her e-mail and found a message from him.

"Fine, now you surface," she muttered as she clicked on the message to open it. But as soon as she started to read, her heart skipped a beat.

Dear Frankie, you are beautiful.

Frankie shivered. She could almost hear him saying those words, even though she knew he was just being kind.

I am sending a photo of myself. It was taken last year before harvest in front of my winery. As you see, I grow several varieties of grapes and make marvelous wines.

Frankie scrolled down to the bottom of the page, realized there was a photo attachment and quickly opened it.

"Oh, Lord," she muttered. "He's a bona fide hunk. The women in Positano must be absolutely stupid to have let you stay single. If I were there I'd—"

Then she sighed. So much for dreaming. She'd have no more luck with him than she did with the good-looking men here.

"Face it, Frances, you are what you are."

Having given herself a firm dressing-down, she printed out the photo and then returned to the body of the message.

I'm sorry I was so long in answering your message, but I have been traveling. It was business for the winery. Something I must do several times a year. I should hire a salesman, but I've always done it myself, and change is something that rarely agrees with me.

It is wonderful news about your friend Charlotte, and of course, if you are able to come, I will not only be your tour guide, but I would gladly offer myself to play host.

Please let me know how your plans evolve. I anxiously await your next message, and I also see that you have given me your phone number. Alas, it is night where you live now, so I will not give you a fright by calling at this time. However, do not doubt my intent to call you soon. I desire to hear your voice again.

Until later, bella signorina. And just in case you don't know what that means, I'm telling you that you are a beautiful young woman.

Daniel

If Frankie had been a puppy, she would have rolled onto her back and wiggled. As it was, she had to settle for a shriek, followed by a fit of hysterical giggles.

"Oh Lord, oh Lord, I'm too old to be acting like this," she said. Grabbing the photo from the printer, she managed a little two-step as she hurried down the hall.

CHAPTER
THREE

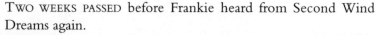

TWO WEEKS PASSED before Frankie heard from Second Wind Dreams again.

She was busy painting Margie's nails. The color Margie had chosen was Passionate Pink, to match her mood, she'd said. Frankie had finished her fingernails and was working on Margie's toenails when her cell phone rang. She glanced at the Caller ID and stifled a shout. It was Second Wind Dreams.

Frankie knew she couldn't let Margie know something was up. The woman couldn't keep a secret for beans.

"Excuse me a minute, Margie. I need to take this."

"I'm not going anywhere," Margie told her, waving her nails to let them dry as she leaned back in the lounge chair and closed her eyes.

"Thanks," Frankie said. As soon as she was out of earshot she answered the phone. "Hello, Frances Drummond speaking."

"Frances, this is Jean from Second Wind Dreams. I just thought you might like to know that Charlotte Grace's doctor cleared her for travel, so everything is a go. Does she have a passport?"

"Oh, my gosh!" Frankie squealed. "I am so excited, and Charlotte is going to be stunned. Yes, she told me a while ago that she has a passport. So what now?"

"Well, here's what we want to do. We always like to make a big surprise out of the news. Do you think she's up to it?"

"Oh, she'll cry," Frankie said. "We'll probably all be crying, but that's okay. She will be so happy."

"Then this is the way it will work. Continental Airlines has comped you both first-class, round-trip tickets. The Hotel Murat in Positano has comped your suite for a week. We have arranged for her to have a guide to—"

"Did you say *both* of us were getting complimentary tickets?" Frankie interrupted. "*And* a hotel suite?"

"Yes, I did. Second Wind Dreams always ensures the dream-weaver's costs are covered, too."

"Wow! This just keeps getting better and better. I assumed I'd have to pay my own fare."

"We couldn't do our work without people like you, Frances, so we're happy to arrange your plans, as well. Do you have a passport?"

"Yes." Even though she hadn't traveled since her parents' deaths, Frankie kept her passport up to date. "Oh, and one more thing. I have an e-mail acquaintance who lives just outside Positano. He has offered to be our guide. If you don't mind, I would really like to use him. I can give you his name and phone number. You can check him out. He owns a vineyard and winery in the area."

"I'm sure that won't be a problem, either. I didn't know you knew anyone there."

"Well, I didn't until I began trying to find Daniel Morrow's grave. I contacted the very hotel in which you've made Charlotte's reservations to ask if there was anyone in the area who could help me verify the grave location. They gave my request to this man, and he's been more than helpful in answering my questions and concerns. In fact, I've spoken to him on the phone now a couple of times, as well. He seemed excited to be able to help us."

"Fantastic," Jean said. "So…we'll go from there."

"Oh, I'm so excited for Charlotte," Frankie said.

"So are we," Jean echoed. "Until later."

She was standing in the middle of the office with a silly grin on her face when she remembered Margie's toes and dashed out.

Margie was right where Frankie had left her, feet up on the little plush pillow waiting to be finished.

"Sorry," Frankie said. "I didn't think it would take that long."

Margie smiled.

"No problem. I've been going through chapter eleven in my head and think it needs some punch. I believe I'll add the story about the time I got robbed."

Frankie's eyes widened. "You got robbed when you were driving a cab?"

Margie's eyes danced with delight. "Yeah, and guess what he took?"

"All your money?" Frankie said.

"No. My lunch. He stole my Big Mac and fries. And here's the funny part," Margie added. "He was wearing Armani. It just goes to show that thieves come from every corner of society."

Frankie laughed, then picked up the bottle of fingernail polish and finished what she'd started. When she was through with Margie, she went to look for Charlotte. She wasn't going to tell her anything. She just wanted to be with her—maybe judge her state of mind.

She couldn't help but worry just the tiniest bit that she might have breached Charlotte's privacy. What if Charlotte wouldn't go? What if she decided the trip would be too painful?

Frankie saw her sitting outside in a chaise lounge beneath a trio of ancient magnolias, working on her knitting. She took a deep breath and hurried out to join her.

"Hi, honey," she said, and pulled a chair up beside Charlotte's. "What are you working on?"

Charlotte smiled a hello as she held up a partially finished afghan.

"Charlie Coogan's birthday present. It's in a couple of months. Do you think he'll like it? The color is burgundy. That's sort of a manly color, don't you think?"

"I think it's great," Frankie said. "Charlie will love it."

Charlotte nodded. "Yes, Charlie gets chilled easily."

Frankie sat for a moment, watching Charlotte's fingers fly as she worked the knitting needles in and around the yarn. Then her gaze went to the bit of yellow ribbon at the neck of Charlotte's dress.

"Charlotte?"

"Yes, dear?" Charlotte said.

"Are you happy?"

Charlotte's fingers stilled. There was an odd little smile on her face as she looked up.

"Why…yes, I suppose I am," she said. "Why do you ask?"

Frankie shrugged.

"I don't know. After what you told me the other day about Daniel…"

Charlotte waved a hand in the air, as if to brush away the subject.

"Oh, my goodness, honey. I didn't mean for you to think I've been traumatized by my lack of spine. And that's what it was, you know. I never did know how to stand up to Father. Everything that happened was my own fault. I was grown. I could have defied him. But I didn't. I put Father's wishes above Daniel's. I have no one to blame but myself."

"I know, but it—"

Charlotte leaned forward and patted Frankie's hand.

"Do I wish my life had been different? Yes. But I have lived a good life, even if it wasn't as full as I might have liked." Then she shrugged. "Besides, you can't go through life wishing for things that will never be. That's why I told you not to live with regrets. If you see something…or someone…that you want, go after it with all you've got. You'll learn as you get older that it's not what you failed that haunts you, but what you never tried."

"I think I see what you mean," Frankie said.

Charlotte smiled.

"Of course you do," she said. "That's because I'm old and wise."

Frankie laughed out loud.

Charlotte smirked, then resumed her knitting.

They sat like that for a long while afterward. Charlotte with her knitting and Frankie with her dreams.

It was the perfect way to while away an afternoon.

SECOND WIND DREAMS WAS coming to the seniors residence in the morning to make the presentation to Charlotte. They would have the travel itinerary and tickets for the trip, which was scheduled to begin in eleven days. Frankie had also been told that they were bringing a film crew, and she was beside herself with anxiety. She needed to calm down, but there was so much riding on Charlotte's reaction, she couldn't relax.

It was almost 1:00 a.m. and she'd read the same page four times in the last fifteen minutes. She glanced at the clock again and then laid down her book. She wasn't certain, but she thought it would be early morning in Italy. Before she could talk herself out of it, she picked up the phone and punched in Daniel's number.

BECAUSE OF HIS marketing trip last week, Daniel had fallen behind on paperwork. He'd let it go until it was in chaos and was now forced to spend a perfectly beautiful morning stuck indoors. His mood was dour and his shoulders were slumped as he slogged through the stack of bills and invoices.

Just as he was about to enter another set of figures into the computer, his phone rang. Grateful for the interruption, he answered on the second ring.

"Ciao."

"Daniel? It's me, Frankie. Am I interrupting anything?"

A wide smile spread across his face.

"Frankie! Yes, you are definitely interrupting, and for that I am truly grateful."

She laughed, and the sound soothed the frustration Daniel had been feeling.

"I have news," she said.

"I hope it's good news."

"Oh, yes! The best! The surprise I told you I was working on for Charlotte is going to happen. Second Wind Dreams has agreed to grant Charlotte's dream to visit Daniel's grave. And we're both coming to Positano! Charlotte is going to get to say her goodbyes to Daniel the way she's wanted to for all these years. Isn't that wonderful!"

Daniel's heart was racing. Frankie was coming here?

"Is this true?" he said. "You are really coming to our village?"

"Yes! I hope you don't mind, but we want to take you up on your kind offer to be our guide and translator."

"Mind? Dear Frances…Frankie…I can think of nothing I would rather do." He bounded up from his chair and began to pace. "This is marvelous. Just marvelous. When are you coming? Are you flying into Milan? If so, you can take a smaller plane to Naples, but you will have to come by car from there. I can pick you up at—"

Frankie laughed as she interrupted him.

"Wait! Daniel! Take a breath!"

"Yes, yes, you are right. But it is such wonderful news. So tell me your plans."

"Second Wind Dreams has already organized everything all the way to Positano, including a reserved suite for Charlotte and me at the Hotel Murat. If we called you once we got there, maybe you could come and—"

"If you tell me when you are coming, I will be there waiting."

Then he realized that, for the first time in his life, he would have a chance to ask questions about the man who had been his grandfather. "This is the best news I've had in a long time. I am so happy for you, my dear."

"Anyway," Frankie said, "I just couldn't wait to tell you the news. I will send you an e-mail with our itinerary, and thank you again for being so generous with your time."

"Getting to know you and your Charlotte better is never a waste of time."

Daniel heard Frankie sigh, and imagined someone kissing her neck—or maybe the spot right behind her ear—and eliciting the same response.

"Frankie?"

"Yes?"

"I have never asked, but…do you have someone special in your life?"

"You mean a man?"

"Yes, I am speaking of a man…a boyfriend, as you Americans say."

"Hardly. You've seen my picture, so you must understand."

Daniel frowned.

"Yes, I saw that most beautiful picture, but I don't know what you mean."

Frankie laughed, but there was a bitterness in the sound.

"You're just being kind. You saw the scars. What you didn't see is that there's a limp to go with them. The only men in my life are all over the age of seventy, and one of them cheats at checkers."

Daniel's frown deepened. His voice was calm and quiet as he answered.

"I'm sorry, Francesca, but I think you do yourself an injustice."

"I'm just being honest," she said shortly. "It saves a world of hurt. But I must tell you that I do enjoy hearing the Italian version of my name."

Daniel realized that she wanted to shift gears. And, to be truthful, he didn't know that he'd called her Francesca, although he often thought of her by that name.

"Yes, it is a beautiful name," he said. "And I can't wait to meet you. I feel as if I already know you, but it will be wonderful to see you face-to-face."

"Yes, I know what you mean," she said, then added, "How about you? You must have girlfriends."

"I have many friends, but none of them special in that manner. I guess I've always wanted what my father and mother had."

"What was that?" Frankie asked.

"Love at first sight. That's what my mother told me. I never wanted to settle for less."

"That's good," Frankie said, and Daniel detected the note of longing in her voice.

"What is good?"

"Love at first sight. I don't know if I believe in it or not, but I'd sure like to experience it if it's for real."

"So would I," Daniel said softly. "So would I. Now rest well, little schemer. We shall meet soon."

"Yes, we will," Frankie said. "Until then."

"As you say…until then."

FOR THE PAST THIRTY MINUTES, a news van had been parked in the lot of Just Like Home. Every resident had been to the windows at least a half-dozen times, giving their opinion as to why it was there.

Frankie had had a smile on her face all morning, and there was nothing she could do to hide it. Even Charlotte had made a couple of trips to the windows with her knitting. When it was obvious that nothing was happening, she'd returned to her favorite chair in the lobby to finish Charlie's afghan.

Mavis Tulia bustled about like a warden, fussing with the potted plants and straightening pictures on the walls. The floors had been mopped a day early, and if the residents had taken the time to notice, the manager was wearing her best dress and her favorite perfume.

Another van drove up and two people got out. At that point, the news crew started unloading, as well.

"They're coming in!" someone shouted.

Everyone sitting in the lobby looked up. The residents standing at the window suddenly realized that if there was going to be a show, they wanted the best seats. They turned and made their way toward the empty chairs with surprising speed, and were seated when the visitors came in.

Frankie and Mavis greeted the group, and then the camera crew turned toward the residents. Everyone held their breath.

Charlotte's knitting was forgotten as she, too, was caught up in the excitement. Nothing like this had ever happened at Just Like Home.

Margie had announced to everyone that she had it figured out. She was positive someone had won the Publishers Clearing House Sweepstakes and had stuck to her story until she saw that the visitors weren't carrying balloons.

"They always have balloons," she'd said. "It's not them. It's not them."

Frankie's heart was pounding so fast that she was afraid she might pass out. One moment she wanted to laugh and kick up her heels, the next she felt as if she was going to cry.

"Oh, please God, let this be good," Frankie whispered, and then, as they'd planned, she went to stand beside Charlotte's chair.

To Charlotte's surprise, the cameras stopped where she was sitting. She looked up at Frankie.

"What's going on?" she asked.

Frankie knelt down beside her.

"Honey…we have a surprise for you," she said, and then nodded toward the Second Wind Dreams crew.

One of them stepped forward, then sat down beside Charlotte. "Charlotte Grace?"

"Yes, I'm Charlotte Grace."

The woman put her hand on Charlotte's arm.

"Charlotte, we're from Second Wind Dreams. If you've never heard of us, then all you need to know is that we make it our business to give senior citizens in this country a chance to realize lifelong dreams that they think have escaped them."

Charlotte took a slow breath.

"A little fairy told us that when you were young, you had a sweetheart named Daniel Morrow. She said that even though life carried the two of you in different directions, you still hold him close to your heart. Is that true?"

Charlotte nodded, then clutched at the locket around her neck, unable to speak.

"We also understand that he died during World War II and is buried in a cemetery outside a small village in southern Italy, and that your one big regret in life is that you never got to visit his final resting place. So we at Second Wind Dreams have made it our business to see that your wish comes true. In eleven days, you will be flying nonstop, first class to Milan, Italy. There you will take a smaller plane to Naples. A car will be waiting at the airport to take you to Positano. Upon your arrival, you will be the guest of the luxurious Hotel Murat, once the palace of the brother-in-law of Napoleon Bonaparte. You will have a translator at your disposal, and can spend as much time at Daniel's grave site as you wish."

Charlotte covered her face with her hands and started to cry. Frankie put her arms around her and cried, too. The camera scanned the lobby, capturing the shocked expressions of the residents, which quickly changed from surprise to delight and then tears.

"So, Charlotte Grace, are you ready to take a trip?"

Charlotte looked at Frankie, her face streaked with tears.

"Is this real?" she asked.

Frankie nodded.

"Yes, honey, it's real. And guess what else? You won't have to go all that way alone. I'm coming with you."

Charlotte threw up her hands and fresh tears flowed, but they were tears of joy.

"What am I going to wear?" she asked.

Everyone laughed. It was the perfect question for a woman to ask, no matter what age.

Eleven days later

THE FLIGHT WAS ALMOST as exciting to Charlotte as the news of the trip had been. Frankie took pictures constantly, so Charlotte would have a photographic record to show the girls back at the home. There were more perks on the first-class flight than either of them had ever experienced.

Champagne cocktails. Pasta salad with lobster. Chicken Cordon Bleu with steamed asparagus. Cheesecake and ice cream sundaes for dessert.

And all served on fine china and silver.

Frankie was just dozing off in the spacious reclining seat when she felt a tug on her arm. She quickly sat up.

"Charlotte, is anything wrong?"

"No. Were you sleeping?"

Frankie smiled.

"Not now. Can't you sleep?"

"No. I'm too excited, and at the same time a little nervous, you know?"

Frankie took Charlotte's hand.

"Yes, darling. I know…or at least, I can imagine." Then she lowered her voice and leaned closer to Charlotte's ear. "You're not mad at me, are you?"

Charlotte's eyes widened, then filled with tears.

"Oh, no, no. I could never be mad at you. You've given me the world. I thought you understood that."

Frankie relaxed.

"I didn't give you the world, Charlotte. Second Wind Dreams gave you the world. I'm just along for the ride."

CHAPTER
FOUR

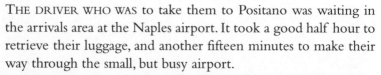

THE DRIVER WHO WAS to take them to Positano was waiting in the arrivals area at the Naples airport. It took a good half hour to retrieve their luggage, and another fifteen minutes to make their way through the small, but busy airport.

It wasn't until Frankie had Charlotte safely seated in the car and they were headed south out of Naples that she began to breathe easier. It was exciting to be in such a romantic country, but it was daunting not to know the language. Frankie kept thinking of Daniel waiting for them in Positano and finally allowed herself to relax.

DANIEL GLANCED AT HIS WATCH, then ordered another lemonade from the waitstaff at the Hotel Murat. He wasn't thirsty, but it was something to do to pass the time.

Two men he'd grown up with waved at him as they walked by on the street beyond the gates, but they didn't stop to visit. The outdoor patio of the Hotel Murat was for guests, although locals often gathered there in the evening for drinks or dinner. Daniel didn't regret their haste. He was too excited about Frankie and Charlotte's imminent arrival to spend time in idle talk.

Another five minutes passed and the ice in his lemonade began to melt. The scent of flowering vines filled the air, masking the faint, but ever-prevalent scent of fish and salt air coming from the Mediterranean and the beach below.

Finally, he abandoned the lemonade and walked around the patio to where he could better see the view. He knew this village as well as he knew his own face, but wondered how it would appear to the American women.

Tiny houses had been built all up the side of the mountain, linked by winding and narrow cobbled streets. Storefronts lined the spiral pathways in colorful array as owners spread their wares on tables or hung them along the high walls that bordered every pathway. Three-wheeled motorcycles had been modified for use as miniature trucks, complete with a cab and a small wooden bed in which to transport goods. They wheeled up and down the streets, weaving in and out among the locals and the tourists with surprising skill, while down on the beach, cafés and restaurants catered to the weary and hungry.

Small, privately owned fishing boats rocked upon the water, their anchors holding them close to the rocky shore. Farther out was an island that appeared to be floating on top of the sea. Gulls and other seabirds perched on mastheads and roofs, darting in and out among the swimmers braving the waters.

Would Frankie see his village for what it really was? Could she see beyond the tourist trappings to the good people who had endured for generations, living out their simple lives with no excuses or explanations? He hoped so. For reasons he didn't want to admit just yet, he wanted Frances Drummond to love his Italy as much as he did.

As he was gazing upon the pure blue of the sea, he became aware of a small car stopping outside the gates to the hotel.

He turned, and then his heart skipped a beat.

It was them.

Unaware he was holding his breath, he stood motionless, watching as two women stepped out of the tiny vehicle. One was young and slender, with wavy hair the color of dark chocolate. The other was small and fragile. Her silver hair was short and curly, and she leaned on the young woman as they walked. He saw the scars that Frankie was so self-conscious about, and he noticed her limp, as well. But they amounted to nothing to him. It was that near-perfect face that intrigued him, as well as the tenderness of her behavior toward the elderly woman.

He began to move, willing Frankie to look up.

Closer and closer he came until he could hear the younger woman's laughter. He felt himself go weak inside. He'd known it would sound like that.

Look at me, Francesca. Look at me.

She kept walking, her head bent to the older woman's ear as she helped her up the steps.

Francesca…Frankie. Turn around and look at me. I am here.

FRANKIE WAS RELIEVED to have reached their destination. As exhausted as she was by the traveling, her main concern was still for Charlotte's health. Charlotte had slept some on the plane, but not nearly enough to maintain her normal routine. Right now, Frankie's focus was on getting them to their rooms, then making sure Charlotte got some rest.

She was laughing at something that Charlotte said, a half eye on the man who was carrying their bags up to the hotel desk, when the skin suddenly crawled at the back of her neck.

She paused, almost stumbling, then caught herself and steadied Charlotte.

Again, the feeling came, only this time stronger.

"Wait," she said softly.

Charlotte stopped.

Frankie lifted her head, then slowly, slowly, began to turn, scanning the faces of the people around them.

And then she saw him, standing just outside the hotel beside a table with a wide, colorful umbrella. His eyes were dark, his expression fixed, as if he was waiting for a sign.

She took a deep breath, then exhaled on a sigh.

Daniel.

He was here, just as he'd promised.

She lifted a hand in a tentative wave and stifled the urge to run into his arms. Instead, she put a hand over the scar on her neck in a halfhearted gesture to hide it.

What's wrong with you, Frances? You don't know this man.

Even as she was dealing with that truth, there was another she still had to face. Something had happened just now that she couldn't explain.

When he started toward them, she didn't realize she was holding her breath.

Closer and closer he walked, until she could see the shadows his lashes cast upon his cheeks. He was wearing light-colored slacks and a white shirt, open at the collar, with the long sleeves rolled up almost to his elbows. His stride was long and graceful, and there was a steadiness in his expression that calmed her.

"Daniel?"

He clasped her hand, then lifted it to his lips and kissed it. She felt his breath, and then the firmness of his lips as they brushed the surface of her skin.

While her greeting had been a question, his was a confirmation.

"Francesca."

She smiled. "Yes, it's me." Then Frankie remembered herself and stepped aside to introduce Charlotte. "Charlotte, this is my friend Daniel. He's going to be our guide and translator. Daniel, this is my friend Charlotte Grace."

CHARLOTTE KNEW she had stopped breathing. It wasn't until a butterfly flitted past her line of vision that she took a quick breath and shuddered.

A ghost. She hadn't expected to see Daniel's ghost. Was he going to haunt her? Was he still angry after all these years for the way she'd let him down?

Oh, Lord, why did I come?

The man before her reached for her hand, as he had Frankie's, and brushed a soft kiss upon the thin, papery skin.

"May I call you Charlotte?" he asked.

Charlotte nodded, but her gaze never left Daniel's face.

"You must be exhausted," he said, and cupped her elbow with one hand, offering Frankie his arm. "Come, ladies, let me help you get settled in your room. You must have traveled all night. Did you get any sleep on the plane?"

Despite his lovely accent, it was the ordinary questions he was asking that settled Charlotte's nerves. She kept glancing at him off and on as they made their way to the suite that was to be their home for the next six days, until her notion of a ghost had passed.

Of course he wasn't Daniel's ghost. Just because they bore the same name didn't mean anything. Yes, he was tall as her Daniel had been, and he had a way of holding his shoulders as he walked that reminded her of Daniel, as well. But her Daniel's hair had been chestnut, his eyes a bright blue, and he'd had a cleft in his chin. This man's hair was dark and wavy, with eyes so dark they looked black, and a face that could have been carved by Michelangelo himself.

By the time they reached their rooms, she had regained her composure.

"Thank you for all of your help," Charlotte said, as the bellman unlocked their door.

Daniel looked at her and smiled. "You are most welcome…both of you," he said, and his gaze shifted to Frankie.

FRANKIE WAS SPEECHLESS. There was an invisible something in the air between her and Daniel that was almost frightening. She'd never felt so helpless. She was out of her element with this magnificent man.

"Are you hungry?" Daniel asked, as the bellman led them inside.

"Yes," Frankie said, and then gasped as she looked at their suite. "Lord have mercy. Would you look at this."

Charlotte was beaming, but far more practical in her acceptance.

"It used to be a palace, my dear. It's to be expected that some of the grandeur would have survived."

The blue-and-white floor tiles were Italian marble and the ceilings at least twenty or thirty feet high. The furnishings were old, but elegant, and spoke of a time long past. The bedroom was enormous, with floor-to-ceiling windows that opened out onto a small terrace, and there was a closet that ran the length of one wall. The bed was at least twice the size of an American king-size bed, and Frankie had a childish urge to jump on it, just to see how high she would bounce.

When the bellman showed them to the bath, even Charlotte had to gasp. Like everything else, it was massive, lined in amber-colored marble with gold streaks running through it. The sunken tub and shower were so wide and deep that it required six stair steps to get down into it. Had it been full, it would have been over Charlotte's head.

Charlotte actually clapped her hands in delight.

"Frankie, get the camera. Margie is never going to believe this unless she sees it for herself."

Daniel laughed, and the sound echoed within the room, filling Frankie with what could only be pure joy as she got the camera and took pictures for Charlotte.

"It is quite something, is it not?" Daniel said, then he took Frankie by the hand. "May I speak to you alone in the other room for a moment?"

Frankie managed a nod.

"Charlotte, will you excuse us?"

"Don't mind me," Charlotte said, as she dug in her purse for money to tip the bellman.

"Keep your money," Daniel said. "It's all been taken care of by the people who brought you to me."

"Oh! Well! This just gets better and better, doesn't it, dear?" Charlotte said, and then wandered back into the bedroom and sat down on the side of the bed.

Frankie followed her out and saw the exhaustion on her face.

"Daniel, will you give me a minute? I want to make sure Charlotte is…comfortable."

He understood.

"I'll be in the drawing room," he said, and walked out.

Frankie knelt at Charlotte's feet and began removing her shoes.

"Just lie back, dear. The room is nice and cool, and you can have a good nap. I'll have food for you to snack on when you wake, and we don't have to go anywhere tonight."

"I'm not going anywhere tonight," Charlotte said. "But if that gorgeous young man in there wants to take you somewhere, I'll be very disappointed with you if you don't go."

"Oh, but—"

"But nothing," Charlotte said. "You came as a companion, not a nurse. I'm not sick, just tired. I'm not dead, just old. So go have fun for both of us and tell me all about it when you get back. Right now, I just want to sleep and dream of Daniel, and then tomor-row…tomorrow…" Her voice trailed off and tears came to her eyes. She took a deep breath and made herself finish. "Tomorrow I shall go see him, again."

Frankie hugged her close, then helped her off with her dress, leaving Charlotte in her slip and undies.

"Here, let's pull the covers back," she said. "You might get too cool with the air-conditioning."

"That feels wonderful," Charlotte said, her head sinking into the pillows. "Oh, Lord," she added. "The pillows are filled with down. I haven't slept on a feather pillow since Mama died."

Frankie grinned. "Sweet dreams, dear," she said, and pulled a sheet and blanket up over the older woman's shoulders.

"Go away now," Charlotte ordered.

"Yes, ma'am," Frankie said, and tiptoed out of the room.

Daniel had opened the blinds and was standing at one of the windows overlooking the village below. At the sound of her footsteps, he turned and was again struck by the sight of her face. He could tell she was self-conscious about her limp, and to save her, he didn't wait for her to cross the room. Instead, he went to meet her, and when they were face-to-face, he opened his arms.

Frankie didn't give herself time to think about what she was doing. She just followed her heart and let his arms close around her.

"Welcome to Positano," Daniel said softly. "Welcome to my world."

Frankie shivered.

Daniel leaned back so that he could see her face.

"Are you ill? Do you need to rest, too? I can come back later tonight and—"

"I'm not ill," Frankie said. "As for sleep, I can do that when I go home. For now, I don't want to miss a moment of anything."

Daniel stilled. She'd done it again—said what he'd been feeling before he gathered his wits.

"So, you feel it, too, don't you, *bella?*"

Frankie looked away. She didn't want to get hurt, but she felt this was a chance of a lifetime. If the man was kind enough to pretend he didn't see her flaws, she wanted to make as many memories with him as she could—memories that would last the rest of her life.

She took a deep breath, and then made herself look at him.

"If you're talking about the rapid heartbeat, sweaty palms and loss of good sense, then yes."

Daniel laughed, then kissed her.

It was the litmus test that branded them goners.

The kiss sparked a hunger within Frankie that was so sharp she wanted to cry, especially when he finally tore himself away. The absence of his lips was actually painful.

"Starvation," she muttered.

Daniel cupped her face. "I am sorry. Of course, you are hungry. You already said so once. Come, come. We will go down to the beach. There are some wonderful little cafés. You can eat and I will watch you smile. Then we will both be fed."

Oh, Lord, it isn't enough that he's unbelievably gorgeous. He has to talk pretty, too.

"I didn't mean I was starving for food," she said. "But you can feed me just the same."

After she freshened up, Daniel took her by the hand and escorted her from the room, taking care to lock the door behind them, leaving Charlotte to her rest.

Careful not to go too fast, Daniel held tight to her arm as they walked all the way down to the beach. They strolled past a church and bell tower, as white as the clouds above the horizon.

"Oh, my gosh!" Frankie exclaimed with delight. "It looks like something out of *The Godfather.*"

"What is this godfather?" Daniel asked.

Frankie grinned.

"Sorry. It's an old, but very famous American movie made about Italian immigrants who came to America and who were part of the Mafia. I was speaking of the church. There is one just like it in the movie."

Daniel nodded. "Yes, I believe I do know of this film. I had just forgotten the name." He glanced at her and smiled. "Americans are very fascinated with the Mafioso, are they not?"

"Yes, I suppose we are," Frankie said, looking all around her. "This village is marvelous. So many different styles of architecture."

Daniel nodded.

"Just about every country in ancient Europe with an army and ships raided these shores. The faces of our people and the architecture of our homes and buildings are evidence of these invaders."

Frankie couldn't quit talking and pointing, and Daniel couldn't quit looking at her. Even as they were seated at a table underneath a colorful awning and sipping cool drinks, he was trying to come to terms with the truth of what had happened to him today.

He'd known the first moment he saw her, head bent to the needs of another, laughter only a whisper away, that he'd found the woman he'd been looking for. His mother had been right. There was such a thing as love at first sight. Daniel knew he'd been smitten, and he had only six days to do something about it.

They ate and they laughed and watched the sun go down behind the mountains. Then Daniel took her by the hand and walked her back up the winding paths. The streetlights cast shadows on her delicate features. He wished he didn't have to say good-night.

All too soon, they were at the hotel. He escorted her through the lobby, then up the staircase until they were standing outside the suite.

Frankie turned to Daniel and put both hands on his chest, feeling his heart beating steadily beneath her palms.

"I don't know how to thank you," she said softly.

"I do," he said, and cupped her face with his hands.

The kiss was tender, yet the depth of emotion behind it was anything but. This bond between them made no sense, and yet there it was.

Frankie's hands slipped up around his neck and suddenly she was kissing him back, but when Daniel slid his hands to the back of her neck, she flinched.

The scars. He'd felt the scars. Surely he would be disgusted. She pulled away from him first, unable to bear the hurt and embarrassment of his rejection.

Daniel knew what had happened, but he wouldn't let her go. He continued to hold her, his fingers locked at the back of her neck and his thumbs rubbing against the curve of her cheeks until she was breathing easy. Only then did he bend down until their foreheads were touching.

"I will dream of you tonight," he said softly, brushing a second kiss upon her brow. "Sleep well. Tomorrow I will take you and Charlotte to see Daniel's grave."

Frankie waited as he opened the door, then handed her the key. "Lock it after I leave you," he said.

"Yes, I will."

"Until tomorrow."

Frankie sighed. "Until tomorrow."

Inside the room, Frankie listened to the fading sound of his footsteps. She was setting herself up for a great big hurt, but God help her, she didn't care. She wanted whatever he would give her, even if it didn't mean anything to him.

Blissfully tired, Frankie quickly showered and got ready for bed. She checked on Charlotte, who hadn't seemed to have wakened since she'd left, then gratefully crawled into her own bed in the next room and closed her eyes.

BREAKFAST WAS a hasty affair. Charlotte had been so distracted that morning she'd put on two different shoes, and it was all Frankie could do to get her to settle down and eat.

"You have to eat something," she argued. "You skipped dinner last night, so you don't have a say in the matter."

"Oh, pooh," Charlotte said as she slathered a soft cheese on some warm bread and took a bite. "Umm, good." She took a piece of melon that Frankie had put on her plate.

Frankie ate without tasting. Her thoughts were filled with Daniel, and she was afraid. She'd let herself become infatuated with a man she hardly knew. She could only imagine what he must be thinking of her. She was a novice when it came to worldly men, but as she'd told herself last night, she wouldn't regret the sadness she might feel later. Even if she did wind up getting hurt, she wasn't going to deny herself the luxury of Daniel's company.

Just as they were finishing up, there was a knock on the door and a bellman was on the stoop, telling them that Daniel was waiting for them below.

They gathered up camera and film and hats for the bright Italian sun, then as soon as Charlotte took her daily meds, they were off.

"BUON GIORNO," Daniel greeted them in the lobby. "Forgive me for not coming up myself, but I've been on the phone all morning with an unhappy customer."

Frankie frowned. "If there's a problem with you taking time away from your work, I'm sure we can—"

Daniel put a finger on her lips, then shook his head.

"There is no problem. Only the wishes of two beautiful women to grant."

Charlotte smiled and clapped her hands lightly.

"Well said, young man, and you must know how anxious I am to get started."

"Then we are off," he said grandly. "We must walk about the length of one block up this street to a small courtyard where my car is parked. Unfortunately, it is too wide for our narrow streets. Is that all right?"

"Perfect," Charlotte said. "I like to walk. It's good for my constitution."

Daniel slipped his arm through Charlotte's and Frankie did the same on the opposite side, almost carrying the older woman to the car. Daniel helped Charlotte into the backseat and buckled her in, then settled Frankie in the seat beside him. Soon, they were scooting through the streets and out onto the highway.

"It's not far," Daniel said. "Enjoy the sights, and if you have questions, please feel free to ask."

"I have one," Charlotte said. "What are all these trees?"

"Olive trees," Daniel said. "But it's not yet time for harvest."

"I like green olives," Charlotte said.

"Not these, you wouldn't. They are very bitter. It is the process they go through as they are bottled that gives them a milder taste."

"Is your home in this direction, too?" Frankie asked.

Daniel ventured a glance at the woman beside him.

"Yes, it's less than a half kilometer from the cemetery."

He hoped Frankie would come to his home before her visit was over.

Finally they arrived at the cemetery. It was quite large and scattered up and down a hillside, its boundaries marked by a three-foot wall built from the rocky earth on which it stood. There were all manner of gravestones and tombs, some grand, some little more than a cross. Flowers in different degrees of decay decorated the graves, making it obvious which ones had been recently visited.

Daniel parked, and they got out. "I'm sorry, but it is a bit of a walk to where we must go."

All the joy was gone from Charlotte's face, and had been from the moment they'd stopped.

"That's all right," she said. "I've come this far. A few more steps can't matter."

"Then take my hand," Daniel offered.

"And mine," Frankie added.

"I want my camera," Charlotte said.

"I have your camera," Frankie told her. "And a blanket, as well. I thought you might like to stay there awhile."

Charlotte nodded, her soft curls bouncing lightly around her face. But her eyes were already on the tombstones.

Daniel took a bundle from the trunk of the car and led the way. Countless times he had come with his grandmother and mother to place flowers on the grave.

No one spoke as they walked, and when Daniel suddenly stopped, Charlotte stumbled. If he hadn't been holding her, she would have fallen.

"This is it," Daniel said, and pointed down.

The tombstone had been hand-carved out of local stone, the words cut roughly into the surface, and then worn smooth by the passage of time.

Without thinking, Charlotte reached for her locket as she read the words on the stone. Her hands were shaking, her chin trembling as she struggled with her emotions.

Frankie spread out the blanket, then took Charlotte by the hand.

"Sit here, dear," she said. "Stay as long as you like. We'll be on that bench just over there, okay?"

Charlotte nodded without looking, unaware that Frankie had just taken her picture at the grave.

Frankie glanced at Daniel and started to speak, then caught a strange expression on his face. He wasn't looking at Charlotte at all, as she might have expected. Instead, he was staring intently at the tombstone marking Daniel Morrow's final resting place.

To her surprise, he walked over and removed the dead flowers from the vase beside the marker, unwrapped his bundle, and put a fresh bouquet of flowers in their place.

He took Frankie's hand, and as they turned to go, they heard Charlotte say, "Hello, Danny, it's me, Charlotte. I've come to say I'm sorry."

Frankie bit her lip to keep from crying. Her toe caught on the uneven ground, and she stumbled. If it hadn't been for Daniel's quick reflexes, she would have fallen headfirst onto the rough ground. Her face turned bright pink as she righted herself and looked away.

"Sorry," she said. "I'm always so clumsy."

"Sssh," Daniel silenced her. "No explanation is necessary. I am just glad you're not hurt."

Frankie nodded, but was still unable to look at him. When they reached the bench, she was thankful to sit down.

Daniel dumped the paper he'd had around the flowers into a trash bin beneath the tree, then sat down beside her. For a few minutes, he just held her hand without talking.

Finally, it was the chirping of a bird that started their conversation.

"He sounds happy," Frankie said, pointing to the creature perched high in the tree.

"He should be," Daniel said. "Here he has nothing to complain about."

Frankie sighed.

"Thank you for this."

He nodded while still eyeing the old woman on the blanket a short distance away.

"Is she strong...your Charlotte?"

"You mean healthwise?"

"Yes."

"She seems to be," Frankie said.

"Her heart is strong?"

"To my knowledge." Frankie frowned. "Why do you ask? Is something wrong?"

Daniel didn't answer. He wanted to, but he didn't know what to say. Then he turned to her, staring long and hard into the sweetness of her face.

"This trip for Charlotte...it is filled with sadness and regret, is it not?"

Frankie nodded.

"Life is so short." Daniel lifted his hand to smooth away a stray strand of hair that had blown near her eyes. "Do you remember what I said about love at first sight?"

Frankie felt the blood draining from her face and wondered if she looked as faint as she felt.

"Yes. I remember."

He took her hand, absently threading his fingers through hers.

"I'm going to say this now, because I don't want to be like Charlotte someday. Old and filled with regret for what I should have said or done. I felt it, Frances. Yesterday, when you turned around and looked into my eyes. The breath left my body and then came back like a blow to my belly. I didn't know whether to grab you and run and never look back, or trust fate to promise you would return my feelings in kind."

Frankie panicked. She'd dreamed of hearing something like this from a man one day, but this man was a stranger.

"Oh, Daniel, if—"

He put a finger on her lips.

"Say nothing now. It's enough that you know how I feel."

Frankie was trembling. She didn't know whether to laugh or cry. Like Daniel, she was troubled by what she was feeling. It was too much too soon. Then she reminded herself that it wasn't so soon at all. In fact, she'd been waiting twenty-seven years for this moment to happen. That it was happening in a cemetery in a country foreign to her own seemed immaterial. The miracle was that it had finally come.

She leaned against Daniel's shoulder. He put an arm around her and pulled her close.

The bird continued to sing as Charlotte Grace said her goodbyes.

CHAPTER FIVE

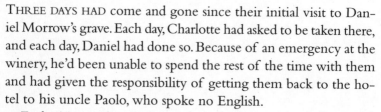

THREE DAYS HAD come and gone since their initial visit to Daniel Morrow's grave. Each day, Charlotte had asked to be taken there, and each day, Daniel had done so. Because of an emergency at the winery, he'd been unable to spend the rest of the time with them and had given the responsibility of getting them back to the hotel to his uncle Paolo, who spoke no English.

Each visit was shorter than the previous one, until on the fourth day, Charlotte came only to place fresh flowers on the grave. After that, she was ready to go. Neither Daniel nor Frankie knew what had transpired for Charlotte during these visits, but whatever it was, she'd come to terms with her loss.

CHARLOTTE STEPPED BACK from the flowers she'd laid on the grave and glanced up at Daniel. Again, as she had done so many times before, she felt as if she was staring at a ghost. This time, she decided to mention it.

"You know something, Daniel?"

He smiled at her.

"Yes, but probably not your something."

She shook her head in pretend disgust, although her eyes were dancing with delight.

"Such a tease. That's good, though. A man should have a sense of humor."

His grin widened, and a chill ran through Charlotte.

"I don't understand it…maybe it's because we're here in this place and it's the closest I've been to my Daniel in more than sixty-seven years…but there are times when you look like him."

Daniel reeled as if he'd been slapped. He tried to recover his smile, but it just wouldn't come.

"Really," he said.

She nodded, then tugged at the yellow ribbon around her neck until she had pulled the locket out.

"Yes, really. Look. This is a picture of him when he was about twenty."

She opened the locket.

Daniel leaned down.

Charlotte watched his eyes narrow and his nostrils flare. Again, she was struck by the notion that this man had secrets he wasn't willing to share.

"Do you see it?" she asked.

He straightened, then momentarily looked away. When he turned back to Charlotte, she was still there, waiting for his answer.

He put a hand on her shoulder.

"Yes…I do see it, Charlotte. It's a strange thing to see oneself in another's face."

She wanted him to say more, but it was obvious he would not. There was a moment when she wondered if he knew something about her Daniel that he couldn't tell. She shook off the thought as nothing but an old woman's foolishness. How could he know anything? He was far too young.

Charlotte tucked the locket back into the neckline of her collar and smoothed her hands down the front of her dress as they walked back to the car.

"Thank you so much for being so generous with your time," she said. "I won't be needing to come back again. I've said my goodbyes, you know."

"Have you now?" Daniel asked.

She nodded.

"I hope they were fond goodbyes?"

"They were as they should be," she said, and then changed the subject as they reached the car. "Where's Frankie?"

Daniel frowned slightly as he looked around, but his frown disappeared as he spied her.

"She's over there." He pointed to an outcropping of rock beneath some trees.

"What's she doing?" Charlotte asked.

"I don't know," Daniel said. "But I'll go get her."

Charlotte got into the car as he went to get Frankie. Just as he was walking up, he saw her drop something into her pocket.

"Hey…I thought we'd lost you. What are you doing?" he asked.

"Leaving a piece of myself behind," she said, and pointed at the dead tree trunk.

Daniel's gaze immediately caught on the heart she'd cut into the bark, and the initials she'd carved inside.

F.D. loves D.S.

Daniel smiled as he traced the shape and words, then took her in his arms.

"Ah, Francesca…again, you…how do you say…beat me to the drink."

Frankie laughed. "The phrase is, beat me to the punch."

He frowned. "I thought a punch *was* a drink."

She jabbed him lightly on the shoulder with a clenched fist.

"That's the punch referred to in the expression," she said.

"The English language is a puzzle," he mused. "Still, you say what is in your heart, while I seem to fall short of doing the same.

So, you carve your feelings in this bark, as you have carved your-self into my soul. I cannot think of life without you. The fact that I've had to be away from you so much these past three days has been a big disappointment. I had planned so much for us to do, and yet life kept interrupting."

"I know it couldn't be helped," Frankie said.

She couldn't think of life without him, either, but wasn't will-ing to get her heart broken by saying any more. The way she looked at it, what happened to them next was up to Daniel.

"Will you and Charlotte come to my house for dinner tonight?"

The question both surprised and delighted Frankie. "Yes. We'd love to."

"If I ask, would you both stay the night, as well?"

"Yes, so please ask."

Daniel started to smile. "So, Frances Drummond, then I am ask-ing you to stay with me tonight."

"Yes."

He shook his head, then kissed her gently.

"Tonight I have things to say to Charlotte that she might not want to hear, and I need you with me."

Frankie frowned.

"I can't imagine what they could be. She likes you, you know."

"And I like her, as well. Now come. I need to get you back so you can both pack an overnight bag for the visit."

CHARLOTTE FUSSED over her clothes like a girl going on a first date, then fussed again about what to take to spend the night at Daniel's house.

Frankie packed her bag almost as an afterthought. She knew what she wanted to happen tonight, and if it did, a nightgown was going to be the last thing on her mind. Still, she prepared for a dis-appointment by packing it anyway.

Daniel picked them up just as the sun was going down. He spoke to the hotel clerk, letting him know that the two American women would be spending the night at his home, and that, when they were ready to come back, he would return them to the hotel personally. With that, they walked the short distance up through the narrow streets to his car.

Daniel alternated between bouts of nervousness and bouts of elation. He knew what he wanted to happen tonight, but after he revealed the truth about his family, he had no idea if either woman would speak to him again.

The drive was brief. They arrived at his home just as the sun disappeared over the mountains, although the vineyards could still be seen, clinging to the mountainside. The winery was a distance from the house, maybe a quarter of a mile, but still visible in the fading light.

Daniel helped both women out of the car.

"Welcome to my home," he said. "Come inside. *Zia* Maria has fixed some special dishes for us tonight and there is much for me to show you."

Frankie could see how anxious Daniel was, and knew that he was working up his nerve to tell them whatever it was he had to say.

"Does your aunt live close by?" Charlotte asked.

Daniel smiled and pointed to the small house just across the road.

"Yes, she and *Zio* Paolo live right over there. Actually, she is the reason we met. She works at the hotel where you are staying. The manager gave her your first e-mail to bring to me."

"Really?" Frankie said. "I wonder why?"

"Because I speak English, and because he knew we both lived near the cemetery where the American GIs were buried."

"Oh." Frankie glanced at the house across the road again. "Will we be eating with them?"

"Not this time," Daniel said. "But maybe another."

"We leave in two days."

Daniel's eyes darkened.

"Don't remind me," he said, and then shook off the dark feelings. "Come, come, we'll go inside now. We'll eat…laugh…make memories."

Charlotte took the arm that he offered.

"I like that phrase…making memories. It's a good thing to do."

When they finished the main meal, Charlotte wandered about the living area while Daniel and Frankie carried dishes into the kitchen, then prepared coffee and dessert on a tray.

Charlotte walked over to a massive fireplace at the end of the room and glanced absently at the framed photos sitting on the mantel.

Reaching up, she took one down and turned it toward the lights to see it better. She was still staring at the photo as Daniel came into the room with a carafe of coffee and three cups on an ornate silver tray.

He set it down and started to speak, then realized what Charlotte was doing. He glanced at Frankie and took a deep breath. It was time.

"Charlotte."

She looked up. Her eyes were bright with unshed tears, and even though he was at the other end of the room, he could tell her chin was trembling.

"Who is this woman and this child?" she asked.

"Daniel, what's wrong?" Frankie sounded concerned.

He squeezed her hand, then let it go and crossed the room to Charlotte.

"That's my mother, and that's me when I was eight months old."

Charlotte took a deep breath and shivered slightly.

Daniel took her by the hand and led her to a nearby chair. Frankie followed, aware something momentous was happening.

"Charlotte, I have come to care for you a great deal, and because I do, this is very difficult for me to say. I don't want to hurt you…ever. But if the truth is to be told, I have to risk that. Will you hear me out without judging me?"

She nodded.

"My grandmother was seventeen years old when the war came to Europe. She was barely eighteen when the American GIs liberated Italy."

Charlotte gasped and reached for her locket, clutching it tightly in her hand.

Daniel saw her fingers wrap around it and groaned inwardly.

"She met and fell instantly in love with one of the soldiers."

"Danny," Charlotte said softly.

Daniel nodded. Frankie gasped.

"All my life I've known that Private first class, Daniel Louis Morrow was my grandfather. I have lived with that knowledge with a sense of pride. But you also have to realize that he knew my grandmother less than six weeks. He was killed by a sniper before he learned that she carried his child."

Charlotte moaned and leaned back in her chair, closing her eyes. The picture she'd been holding fell into her lap.

Frankie leaped forward and knelt at Charlotte's side.

"Charlotte…sweetheart…are you all right?"

At first there was only silence, and then they heard Charlotte sigh. To their relief, when she opened her eyes, they were clear and dry.

"I think I've suspected this from the moment I saw you, then when I saw this picture, I could no longer deny the truth. Your mother is the image of Danny." Charlotte looked up at Daniel. "You know what my first impression of you was?"

"What?" he asked.

"I thought I was seeing a ghost."

"Oh, Charlotte, I'm so sorry," Frankie said. "I would never have done all of this had I known."

Charlotte grabbed at Frankie's hand.

"Oh dear…oh, no…you both misunderstand. This was somewhat of a shock, but not in a bad way. You see, I don't view this as any kind of betrayal on Daniel's part. I'm the one who turned him down. I'm the one who sent him away." Then she did start to cry. "This is actually the best news I could have been given."

Daniel was so stunned, he sat down with a thump.

"How so?" Frankie asked.

"All these years, I've pictured Danny brokenhearted, then dying and being buried alone in a foreign land. Knowing that he'd found some happiness again, however brief, lifts a burden of guilt that I've carried for most of my life." She looked at Daniel again. "You have just given me the best gift. Seeing you is like seeing Danny again. He's still alive to me now, because of you."

Daniel couldn't speak. He took both of Charlotte's hands and lifted them to his face, then kissed the palm of each.

Charlotte removed her hands from his and cupped his face, smiling through tears.

"You poor dear. All this time you were afraid you were going to hurt my feelings. Thank God you found the courage to tell me. I wish I could make you understand what a miracle this is for me."

Suddenly she clapped her hands.

"Oh! I just realized! You have family in the States. A lot of family, and most of them still live in the state of Illinois, where we're from. This news is going to send them over the moon."

"Then you're not angry with me," Daniel said.

"Haven't I just been saying that?" Charlotte wiped her eyes and sat up. "I can't wait to get home and give the Morrow family a call."

Daniel hugged her, then turned and hugged Frankie, too.

Smiling, Charlotte pointed to the coffee.

"Weren't we about to have dessert?"

Daniel glanced at the melted gelato. "I'm afraid it's ruined."

"It's just as well," Charlotte said. "I have to watch my girlish figure. And on that note, if you don't mind, I think I'd like to go to bed. This has been a long day and I have a lot to sleep on."

"I'll go with you," Frankie said, then touched Daniel briefly. "Be right back?"

"Of course," he said.

A few minutes later, Frankie returned. Daniel was standing in the open doorway, looking out into the dark. She walked up behind him and touched his shoulder.

As she did, he turned. There was an expression in his eyes that she didn't want to decipher.

"She's smiling," Frankie said. "I haven't seen Charlotte smile like this...well...ever. It's as if she's a young, carefree girl all over again."

Daniel turned and hugged her, then whispered in her ear.

"I want to make love to you."

Frankie's heart almost stopped. She was afraid—so afraid. But not of letting him see her scars. She was afraid that if they did make love, she would die when they had to say goodbye. Still, she wanted him and these memories more than she'd ever wanted anything in her entire life.

"Then do it," she whispered.

A light glittered in Daniel's eyes, and then he swept her off her feet and into his arms.

His bedroom was at the other end of the house, and Frankie had brief glimpses of wide hallways, low ceilings and arched doorways as he carried her there.

The massive four-poster bed was turned back, revealing gold satin sheets beneath a red-and-gold tapestry spread.

"Daniel! This is beautiful," she said.

He laid her on the bed. "No more than you are, Frances Drummond. I have been dreaming of you and this moment all my life," he said softly. "I don't want you to ever forget our first time."

Frankie's heart skipped a beat. First time? Did that mean there would be others?

"Love me, Daniel. Let me love you back."

AND SO THE NIGHT PASSED in passion, until finally they fell asleep in each other's arms. The next morning Daniel was the first to wake. He had been watching her for some time when he saw her eyelids beginning to flutter. She was waking.

Daniel raised himself up on one elbow and looked down at her face.

"Good morning, Francesca."

Frankie smiled lazily, then stretched like a cat that had been sleeping in the sun.

"It's not a good morning, it's a great one," she said.

Daniel smiled and nuzzled the side of her neck, raking his lips across the puckered flesh. Almost immediately, he paused. There was a moment of silence, then she heard him sigh. When he looked up at her, the smile was gone.

Her heart skipped a beat. *This is it. This is the part where he finally admits that those scars he just kissed repulse him.* She braced herself for the pain.

"I can't bear for you to leave me," Daniel said. "I've waited so long for you to come. Please love me back, Frances Drummond. Please say you will marry me and share my world and my life."

Frankie's shattered senses suddenly focused. This was the last thing she'd expected him to say.

"Oh, Daniel, you don't know how long I've dreamed of someone saying those very words to me, and yet we've known each other such a short time. I'm afraid you'll come to regret your offer, and I just couldn't bear to face your rejection."

Frowning, Daniel shook his head and gathered her up in his arms.

"My only regret will be if I lose you," he whispered. "Please, don't make me beg."

Frankie rose up on her elbows and cupped her face with both hands.

"I have things to deal with back home," she said. "I have property and—"

"I'll come with you," Daniel told her. "Please say I can come with you. We'll make it happen faster if we do it together, and… and I can meet my grandfather's family at the same time. After that, I will ask you the same question again, and if you say yes, which

I pray you will, then we can get married in your town and have a reception in mine. What do you say?"

Frankie started to cry, but they were wild, happy tears.

"I say yes."

CHARLOTTE SMIRKED when she was told the news.

"I suspected it all along," she said, grinning at both Daniel and Frankie.

"Then, if things work out, will you be my matron of honor?" Frankie asked.

Charlotte's features crumpled.

"Oh, darling, you always seem to know the very best thing to say and do. Being a part of your wedding will be the closest I'll ever come to the ceremony I should have had with my own Daniel. I would be honored."

Daniel put his arms around her and hugged her gently.

"The honor will be ours," he said.

"I want to have it at Just Like Home," Frankie told Charlotte. "That's where my very best friends are, you know. Daniel and I have talked about it." She looked at him. "Once we get to the States, if he still thinks he can't live without me, we'll have the wedding there and then the reception here when we return."

Charlotte's smile slipped.

"Oh. Yes. Of course you'll be coming back here." She forced a smile. "And that's as it should be."

Daniel glanced at Frankie and she nodded. Now it was time to break the rest of their news.

Daniel sat down on the sofa beside Charlotte and took her by the hand.

"I haven't known you nearly as long as Frankie has, but I've known you long enough to realize that it would be a great loss to leave you behind. So, when we marry…"

Frankie interrupted. "No…*if* we marry. I'm serious when I say you have to ask me again in a few weeks. Your feelings may change, and if they do, I will understand."

Charlotte just shook her head. How different young people were today. Still, she'd made a mess of her own life. It seemed that Frankie and Daniel were trying to do the right thing.

Daniel frowned at Frankie and put a finger against her lips to silence her, then turned to Charlotte again.

"As I was saying…before my dear Francesca interrupted to tell me what my true feelings are… We want to ask you to come back to Positano with us. My mother and grandmother have been gone for years, as have Frankie's. You are all she has. Will you come and live here in my home and share her with me?"

Charlotte's mouth dropped open and she unconsciously fingered the locket around her neck. There was a hope in her eyes that nearly broke Frankie's heart.

"Oh…you two won't want an old woman interfering with your new life."

Daniel shook his head.

"On the contrary, dear lady. You forget, this is Italy. We love to have our *nonnas* around. My house is huge. You will bring love to this place. Besides, if you don't come, who's going to teach our little girls how to knit?"

Charlotte beamed as she looked from Daniel to Frankie and back again.

"Are you sure?"

"Positive," they both said at once.

A quiet joy came over her face as she leaned back in her chair. Her gaze moved to the window, and she realized how close she would be to Danny for the rest of her days.

"I accept," she said softly.

Daniel grinned. "I will be the envy of every man in Positano. I will have not one, but two beautiful women in my life."

"Then if you don't change your mind later, it's a deal," Frankie said.

Daniel looked at her and laughed.

"Yes, my love. It is, as you say…a deal."

WHEN THE THREE OF THEM arrived back in the States, they were met at the airport by a contingent from Second Wind Dreams. It seemed that after receiving Frankie's call about a possible wedding at Just Like Home, Mavis Tulia had phoned the director of Second Wind Dreams. The sadness in Charlotte Grace's life had been transformed into joy. The story generated so much news across the country that the charity was the recipient of unusually large and much-needed cash donations to further their good works.

True to his word, Daniel met his grandfather's family, and in doing so, felt as if a part of him had come home. He knew that was how the Morrow family felt. They had part of their Danny back, even if it was in an unexpected way.

And also as he'd vowed, Daniel Sciora had once more proposed to Frankie, but this time with a stern expression on his face. He told her that he was unaccustomed to having his word doubted, and hoped that he wouldn't have to propose to her every year or so, just to reassure her that he couldn't live without her.

Frankie had cried and accepted his offer, and then they married in the small chapel on the grounds of Just Like Home. She walked herself down the aisle, but when it came to the point where the preacher asked who gave this woman to this man, everybody in the congregation shouted out a loud, "We do."

That brought tears to Frankie's eyes and put a big smile on Daniel's face. He would say later that he'd thought his family was large, but he believed hers was larger.

Charlotte had become the center of attention, which was, for her, a bit disconcerting. She'd lived so many years in the background of life that she wasn't sure how to take all this fuss. But she still managed to find time to knit, and on the day she was to fly back to Italy with Frankie and Daniel, she presented Charlie with the finished afghan.

"It's a little bit early," she said. "On your birthday, eat a piece of cake for me."

Charlie blushed and kissed her on the cheek, then beamed with delight as he and the other residents of the home waved goodbye to two of their own.

Charlotte and Frankie walked out of the door, paused on the step and looked at each other. Then they smiled and walked arm in arm to Daniel, who was waiting with their cab.

Daniel knew it was difficult for them to leave their old friends behind. But he also knew that these two women belonged together, and with his help, he would make sure that they soon had a new family to fuss over them.

"So, my two beautiful women…are you ready to go home?"

"Yes," they said in unison.

Daniel opened the door of the cab, then stepped aside.

"Your chariot awaits."

Four years later

CHARLOTTE HAD been gone a whole year now, and still, from time to time, either Daniel or Frankie would start to ask if she was coming down to dinner, then they would remember and smile through their tears.

Today would have been her ninety-first birthday. They were going to stop by the cemetery on their way to Positano, and Frankie was trying to get dressed and still keep their baby girl out of mischief at the same time.

Frankie was doing up the last button on her blouse when she heard a crash behind her. She flinched and turned just as Daniel came running into the room.

Their eighteen-month-old daughter, Charlotte, had pulled a potted plant down from a stand. The pot had shattered, spilling dirt and broken stems all over the floor.

"Oh, Charlotte…no, no," Frankie cried as she leaned down and picked her up.

The baby howled.

"Is she hurt?" Daniel asked, running practiced hands over her black curly hair, feeling for bumps.

"No. Just scared, I think." Frankie frowned. "I'll have to clean this up before we go."

"The housekeeper is here," Daniel said. "I'll tell her while you dry little Miss Nosey's tears." He placed several tiny kisses along Charlotte's arm, all the way to her cheek, and the baby giggled.

With a wink at Frankie, Daniel hurried out of the room.

Charlotte automatically grabbed at the yellow ribbon at her mother's throat.

"You can't have that, either," Frankie said, gently taking the locket out of Charlotte's hands before it could go in her mouth. "But you will someday, when you're older. I promised. Now, let's go find the flowers we're going to put on Grandmother's grave."

Charlotte Grace had lived long enough to see her namesake born, and had rocked her to sleep many times. Then one night she had gone to bed and simply hadn't woken up.

When they arrived at the cemetery a short time later, Frankie took the flowers from the trunk of the car while Daniel got his daughter out of the backseat.

"Come with Papa, little girl. We will visit your great-grandfather and Grandmother Charlotte while Mama brings the flowers."

It sounded like a fine idea to Charlotte, except for the flowers. She pointed to the bouquet that Frankie was carrying and let out a screech.

"Me do," she said.

Daniel grinned as Frankie chose two of the more sturdy flowers from the bunch and handed them to her baby.

"Here you go," she said gently. "One for Great-grandfather, and one for Grandmother Charlotte."

Clutching the stems tightly, the little girl squirmed to get down. She held her father's hand as they made their way to the graves.

When they got to Daniel Morrow's grave, Charlotte put one of the flowers down on the ground, then patted it goodbye and pointed up the hill.

"Yes, Grandmother Charlotte is up there, isn't she?" Daniel said, and took her hand once more.

Together, the trio started up the hill to the spot where Charlotte Grace was buried. In death, as in life, there was still a distance between Charlotte and the love of her life. But Frankie was comforted by the thought that all their sadness had been left behind.

When they reached Charlotte's grave, Frankie stepped forward and replaced the old flowers in the vase with the new ones she'd brought.

"Look, Charlotte, it's wisteria, your favorite."

The little girl moved closer to her mother. Before either one of them could stop her, she'd placed her flower on the grass and then lay facedown on top of it, arms outstretched.

Frankie picked her up and began brushing her off.

Charlotte pointed to her flower.

"Hug," she said.

Frankie smiled. "Yes, you gave Grandmother Charlotte a big hug. She would have loved that."

"Here, give her to me," Daniel said as he kissed Frankie's cheek. "She's getting too heavy for you to carry this far."

As they were walking away, baby Charlotte turned and looked at where they'd been, then began smiling and waving.

Frankie felt the skin crawl on the back of her neck, just like the first day she'd seen Daniel.

"Wait!" she said softly, and stopped.

Daniel took her arm.

"Are you hurt? Did you turn your ankle?"

She shook her head. Her heart was pounding so fast that she thought she would faint, but she had to look. She had to know.

Slowly, slowly, she began to turn around.

They were barely visible, like the shadow of a cloud on the rock-strewn hill. But they were there, just the same.

A young man and a young woman, standing hand-in-hand on the horizon. When Frankie blinked, they were gone.

Daniel frowned.

"What is it? Are you okay? Did you forget something?"

Frankie shook her head, furiously fighting back tears.

"No, darling. Everything is okay. In fact, it's more than okay. It's perfect."

Daniel smiled.

DRESS FOR SUCCESS LOS ANGELES
JANET LAVENDER

We've all spent time in front of our closet or at the mall selecting just the right suit to give us that edge at an important client lunch or business meeting. But for many low-income women the professional attire we take for granted is a major barrier to entering the workforce. Without a suit, how can she get a job? But without the job, how can she afford the suit?

Janet Lavender, founder and executive director of Dress for Success Los Angeles, knows firsthand the difficulties presented by something so basic as lacking a suitable outfit for job interviews. Janet herself was once homeless and on welfare after losing her job in the banking industry, where she'd worked for twenty years. But Janet got back on her feet thanks to a one-year stay in a women's shelter, a business degree and a passionate desire to help other disadvantaged women. In 1996, Janet's dedication led to the founding of Dress for Success Los Angeles, which to date has provided over 10,000 women with professional wardrobes, job training, career coaching and job advancement opportunities.

Dress for Success Los Angeles is an affiliate of Dress for Success, the not-for-profit organization that each year provides business suits and career development to more than 45,000 women in more than seventy-three cities, including nine locations outside the United States.

More than a suit

Clients are referred to Dress for Success Los Angeles from a diverse network of not-for-profit member organizations that include homeless shelters, domestic violence shelters, job training programs and other agencies that focus on welfare-to-work. Each Dress for Success client receives two suits: one for the initial job interview and an additional suit when she gets the job. A volunteer "Personal Shopper" assists clients with the utmost dignity and respect. Services are always provided to the client at no cost, and every suit that is donated is given directly to a woman interviewing for a job. For a client who is struggling with self-worth, the suit that she is helped to choose symbolizes the faith Dress for Success Los Angeles has in every woman's ability to succeed.

Motivated by compassion and growing need

The majority of clients helped by Dress for Success Los Angeles are Latina and African-American women. Many are single mothers. As an African-American and single mother herself, Janet is motivated to make a difference in the lives of other women whose struggle she knows all too well and for whom she has deep compassion. Most of the women have little or no work skills and are unprepared for job interviews. In addition, many lack basic skills in their personal lives and so cannot transfer life experience to their workplace challenges.

Over the past ten years Janet has been greatly concerned with the serious rise in the number of families living on and below the poverty line. The hardest hit by this trend are women. Los Angeles County statistics show that the percentage of single-mother households living below the poverty line in 2000 was 30%. These alarming figures, the critical need for her services, as well as her own personal experience, are what motivate Janet to continue her efforts to develop much-needed programs through Dress for Success Los Angeles.

From survival to success

The interview suit itself is just one step in empowering a woman to make that difficult transition from welfare to employment and true self-sufficiency. Janet has spearheaded programs that are specifically designed to facilitate the transition from the hardships and insecurity of day-to-day survival toward self-sufficiency and success. These programs address issues that face clients well before the actual job hunt begins, and provide the support and education needed to secure the job.

In 2001, Janet established the Professional Women's Group— the first and only job-retention model that moves low-income women toward self-sufficiency by addressing their social and economic needs in relation to work, home and the community. The Professional Women's Group offers the support and information needed by women unfamiliar with the workplace to continue to develop skills and advance in their careers. The program provides a comfortable atmosphere for women to share, grow and network with other women who have recently made the same transition into the workforce. Monthly meetings cover a variety of topics, including communication skills, the "unwritten rules" of the workplace, child-care issues, financial planning, stress management and juggling responsibilities.

Volunteers…and a community that cares

Janet's tireless energy and innovative ideas are an inspiration to all who become involved in Dress for Success Los Angeles. Operating on a minimal budget, Janet could not have managed to develop this effective series of client programs, including a recently added one-on-one mentoring program, without the dedication of a small paid staff, the generosity of many community volunteers and the support of local businesses—all of whom recognize the valuable benefits not only to the clients in need, but also to the community at large.

Janet has developed close relationships with over 100 services and referral agencies throughout Los Angeles County. She has also formed partnerships with the Los Angeles Unified School District and with leading companies in order to establish job training, placement programs and innovative career development initiatives.

Approximately 70% of the clothing Dress for Success receives is gently used items women donate—most notably business suits. The remaining thirty percent of inventory is donated directly from manufacturers. Shoes are sometimes in short supply, even with the generous participation of footwear companies. Volunteers have been known to take the shoes off their feet to save a client from having to purchase shoes she can't afford.

This level of passion and commitment from individual volunteers, corporate sponsors and community groups reflects the belief that every client who walks through the doors of Dress for Success Los Angeles is a true success story. And that success began with the compassion and vision of Janet Lavender, a woman who transformed her personal hardships into a way to help thousands of other women…by turning a suit into a career.

More Than Words

JASMINE CRESSWELL

THE
WAY
HOME

JASMINE CRESSWELL

With well over 60 titles in series romance fiction to her credit, *USA TODAY* bestselling author Jasmine Cresswell is a pillar of the romance community and has the great admiration of her peers. She has been nominated for numerous RITA® and *Romantic Times* Awards. Indeed, she has been nominated for the *Romantic Times* Career Achievement Award for Romantic Suspense on four occasions and was twice selected as Rocky Mountain Fiction Writer of the Year. Jasmine and her husband make their home in Sarasota, Florida.

CHAPTER ONE

THE DOORBELL RANG and Amy Duran stopped to cast one final glance into the full-length hall mirror as she hurried to the door. She knew that her need to be perfectly groomed bordered on the obsessive, but she'd grown up wearing shabby hand-me-downs, and memories of the dingy, never-quite-clean look of her high school years still had the power to sting. It was a great confidence-booster to know that these days she could afford a new outfit for any and every special occasion.

Her mirror provided the reassurance she sought. Her unruly auburn hair was styled and sprayed into submission. Her mascara hadn't smudged. The cocktail dress she'd bought last week still seemed just right for the occasion, and no threads hung from the hem. She wore no jewelry except earrings, but the fake diamond falls made a dramatic statement. Were they over the top? She wrinkled her nose, considering. Probably not, she decided, hurrying across her little entrance hall. This was a gala affair, after all. And if she'd judged Brian's mood correctly over the past couple of weeks, it might even end up being a gala occasion in her personal life, too.

Smoothing a nonexistent crease out of her satin skirt, Amy quickly opened the door. Brian did a double take in mock amazement when he saw her. "Wow and double wow! You look fabulous."

He handed her a bouquet of tiny red rosebuds, then leaned forward and kissed her lightly on the lips. Drawing back, he gestured for her to twirl around so that he could admire her sparkly black cocktail dress from all angles.

"You have the cutest tush in L.A.," he said, grinning. "You look perfect." He kissed her again, but gently, so as not to smudge her lipstick. "As always, you do Maitland Homes proud."

"Thanks. I try my best." Amy felt herself blushing. "Your dad has been a great boss and I'm very appreciative." Having spent her teenage years listening to her foster parents yell that she was stupid, ugly and ungrateful, Amy still had trouble accepting praise gracefully. More than a decade had passed since her eighteenth birthday freed her from the tyranny of the Smith household, but some wounds were so deep and jagged that they never quite healed. To conceal her embarrassment, she buried her nose in the bouquet of flowers. The roses looked pretty, she discovered, but had no smell.

"I should put these in water before we leave." She walked into her spotless kitchen, selecting a vase from the shelf that held neatly ranged rows of containers, candles and assorted decorative items.

Brian watched in silence as she quickly arranged the roses and carried the pewter vase over to her tiny breakfast nook. She put it in the exact center of her table, which was already set with a place mat and napkin for tomorrow morning's breakfast.

He shook his head as she wiped up an errant droplet of water. "Jeez, Amy, you're something else. I've never met anyone as compulsively neat and organized as you."

"I can't think straight if I'm surrounded by mess." Amy smiled brightly, as if being organized were an unimportant quirk of her personality instead of the rock around which her entire life was centered. Organization meant control, and Amy was determined to be in control of her life. Too many people blamed their problems on bad luck instead of their own poor judgment. Her parents had been prime examples of that, and she had no intention of following in their irresponsible footsteps.

Brian leaned against the wall, the picture of relaxation. "For all you know, you might discover a whole new creative side to your personality if you were surrounded by mess."

She shook her head. "Absolutely not—"

"How would you know? I bet you've never tried it." Brian was laughing as he spoke.

"I did once—"

"Are you sure? When you were in kindergarten, maybe. Never since then—"

"Wrong." She returned his teasing smile as she picked up her evening purse and pashmina wrap. "I was in fourth grade at least. And that was enough to prove that mess doesn't work for me."

Brian held open the door. "Hey, one of these days you should stage a rebellion against your inner self and not empty the trash for two days. And if you want to do something really wild, you might even leave a soda can on the coffee table."

Amy could think of few forms of rebellion that held less appeal for her, but she didn't argue. She rarely argued, having seen all too often the mess that ensued when disagreements spiraled out of control. "Speaking of being organized, we need to get going. I ought to arrive at the hotel a few minutes early in case there are any last-minute crises."

"A crisis in an event you're responsible for organizing? You're joking, right?" Brian held out his arm, tucking her hand into the crook of his elbow. The gesture was so friendly that Amy decided she must have imagined the thread of sarcasm in his last remark.

Brian had parked his BMW at the curb outside her town house, indifferent to the huge No Parking sign posted right overhead. Miraculously, he'd avoided a ticket, or even being sideswiped by a vehicle trying to pass on the narrow street. Anybody else's car would, of course, have been both ticketed and dinged. It often seemed to Amy that Brian was surrounded by a protective cloak that had descended over him at the moment of his privileged birth to Glen and Gloria Maitland. That cloak had never blown away or ripped in the thirty-five years of Brian's existence; instead it had snuggled him safely throughout his blissfully spoiled childhood and continued to envelop him today.

Amy envied Brian his carefree life and sublime self-confidence, but she wasn't jealous of his many privileges. On the contrary, she simply wanted to share his good fortune—to be draped under the comforting mantle of his protection by assuming the role of Mrs. Brian Maitland. His wife.

She was hopeful that tonight their relationship might take another step toward greater commitment. Recently, Brian's father had begun to drop broad hints that it was time for his son to give up the bachelor life and settle down. Brian had apparently taken the lecture to heart. A couple of weeks ago they'd stopped in a jewelry store and looked at engagement rings, "just for fun." He hadn't bought one, but she couldn't help hoping that he might have gone back to the store and picked one out as a surprise. She might not like surprises as a general rule, Amy thought with silent self-mockery, but a surprise proposal from Brian she could handle.

She refused to dream too many dreams about her relationship with the boss's son, but the temptation was always there. As his wife, every fantasy she'd indulged during her neglected childhood would come true. Having a real family, and children of her own, remained her deepest and most passionate wish. But bringing children into the world was a huge responsibility, which meant that she needed to choose their father with care. Not for her the sort of husband who walked out the moment he got restless, or the first time the bills started to pile up and threaten his supply of beer money. Her children, she swore, were going to enjoy all the security and love she herself had lacked.

Traffic was no worse than usual, and since Brian seemed to know every short cut in greater Los Angeles, they arrived in good time at the hotel where the fund-raiser was being held. Once there, Brian cheerfully waved her off so that she could confer with the executive director from L.A.'s Dress for Success, the organization that would benefit from tonight's gala event.

That was another great facet of her relationship with Brian, Amy mused as she tracked down her quarry. He wasn't possessive. As the only son and designated heir to Glen Maitland, CEO of Maitland Homes, he understood how important her job responsibilities were, and he never gave her a hard time about the long hours she worked, or the weekends when an emergency cropped up and she needed to cancel their plans at the last moment.

Amy's official job title at Maitland Homes was Project Coordinator, but in reality she simply did whatever Glen Maitland asked of her. Her boss was a big supporter of community charities, particularly when his support was likely to garner positive press coverage for his company. Five months ago Glen had handed her the assignment of putting on a glamorous, media-worthy fund-raiser on behalf of Dress for Success, and she'd squeezed the assignment into her already crowded schedule, determined to fulfill his command to glittering effect.

Amy would have worked hard for any gala being organized by Maitland Homes, but she'd thrown an extra splurge of energy and enthusiasm into this particular one. She'd called in every favor she could scrounge up, and even elicited a promise of a feature segment on tonight's late local news. There was nothing like TV coverage to generate extra contributions and positive buzz, and she was thrilled when she saw that a camera crew from Channel 13 had turned up as promised.

She knew from firsthand experience how vital a service L.A.'s Dress for Success provided for women attempting to enter the mainstream job market after major setbacks or years on welfare. By the time she finished college, Amy had been carrying a debt load of thirty thousand dollars, and it had taken every last cent she could scrape together to buy herself an outfit suitable for job interviews—and even then she'd been shopping in consignment stores and praying for bargains. If she'd known about Dress for Success, she'd have leaped at the chance to use their services.

In the course of planning tonight's event, Amy had spoken many times to the staff and volunteers at the organization's headquarters downtown in the heart of the garment district, and she'd been impressed not only by their dedication but also by their efficiency and the great ideas they'd developed on how to expand their services. As the executive director had explained, it was no use offering a woman a smart business suit for a job interview if there was no backup support to show that same woman how to conduct herself not only at the interview, but at the job.

Some of the clients at Dress for Success had never held a job in their lives. Others came from single-parent homes where two or three generations had failed to graduate from high school. Not surprisingly, they hadn't a clue how the business world operated. One of the most common problems for women entering the workforce for the first time was the fact that they didn't own an alarm clock and had no idea how to guarantee that they would wake up each morning in time to get to work. A ten-dollar clock could make the difference between success and failure for the new employee. Amy's own background had been skimpy in the love and caring department, but she had to acknowledge that the Smiths had placed a lot of emphasis on the importance of education and self-discipline, so from that perspective she'd been well-prepared to enter the work world.

Amy finally hooked up with the Dress for Success director and managed to get her alone long enough to check off the last few items on their joint To Do lists. The director fielded at least three interruptions in the five minutes she and Amy spent chatting, but her smile remained friendly and relaxed as if she were well accustomed to juggling half a dozen conversations simultaneously.

"Okay, I think that does it," she said, snapping her Palm Pilot shut and allowing herself the luxury of a small sigh of relief.

"Yep, we're definitely done." Amy slipped her own Palm Pilot into her evening purse. "Now all we have left to do is enjoy the evening."

The director took Amy's hand and folded it inside both of hers. "Thank you for everything you've done to make tonight a success. We're all *real* grateful for the support from Maitland Homes. This is an amazing turnout, and the money we raise tonight is going to provide help to a lot of women, and that means a lot of kids will benefit, too. It's always the kids I worry about the most."

"It's been my pleasure working with you and your staff." Amy's smile turned into a grin. "And you're wasting valuable schmoozing time. Instead of talking to me, you'd better get out there and buttonhole some of those big donors I noticed gathered around the bar."

The director laughed. "I sure will if you're certain there's nothing else you need me to do here?"

"Nope. I checked in with the hotel banquet manager this afternoon and finalized all the dinner arrangements, so I have almost nothing left to do."

"Great, then I'm outta here." With a tip of her hand, the director left to start her schmoozing.

The final task on Amy's checklist was to thank Tracey, the florist who had donated the table centerpieces, charming confections of candles, mirrors, rosebuds and trailing ivy. Tracey had started her own business four years ago and was just breaking into the big time. She and Amy expected the publicity from this event to pay off in future sales, but it was a gamble for a relatively new operation, and Amy was grateful that Tracey had been willing to take the risk.

Brian waved to her from across the reception area, beckoning to her to come and speak to the TV reporter, but Amy had no desire to be interviewed and knew Brian would do a fabulous job of promoting both Dress for Success and Maitland Homes. He was so good-looking and articulate that she'd often thought he would make a great on-air reporter himself.

Leaving Brian to charm the news crew, Amy decided she could take another couple of minutes for herself. She'd persuaded the manager of Della Robia, one of L.A.'s most upscale clothing boutiques, to put on a fashion show, and the manager planned to present the store's exclusive line of fall business clothes after dinner. Fashion shows were a standard feature at charity benefits, of course, but the theme was particularly appropriate as a support for Dress for Success, and Amy was eager to get a behind-the-scenes glimpse at the models and their finery.

She had anticipated finding a hive of activity, but the scene inside the makeshift changing room was one of anarchy verging on chaos. Panty hose hung off the edge of mirrors, and the buzz of hair dryers competed with the cries of models who couldn't find their lipstick or who needed surgical tape to stick foam cups over their miniscule boobs. Despite the racket, the PR manager from Della Robia assured Amy everything was not only under control but even ahead of schedule.

Winding her way expertly around scurrying, half-naked bodies, the PR manager led Amy to a relatively quiet corner of the room and introduced her to a trio of nervous volunteers who were already garbed in their first outfits of the night. The three women, one petite, one average and one plus-size, were recent graduates of the Dress for Success program and would be mingling with the professional models to show off the boutique's extensive inventory. The outfits the volunteers were wearing had been donated by the store and would be auctioned off at the end of the show. Amy was optimistic that the presence of the three former clients, once welfare recipients and now successful career women, would persuade guests to write some generous checks.

Brian caught up with her as she came out of the changing room. He handed her a glass of champagne. "Here, take a break. You're making me tired just watching you zoom around."

"Thanks." She sipped appreciatively, relishing the festive bubbles and the sense of celebration that champagne always inspired. "How did your interview with the TV people go?"

He shrugged. "Okay, I guess. You should have joined us. You know far more about what's going on tonight than I do."

"But you look so good on camera." She smiled and gave his arm a quick squeeze. "Sexy and trustworthy both at the same time. That's a killer combination."

He rolled his eyes, but she could tell that he liked the compliment. "You've had a chance to talk to a lot of people already," she said. "From your perspective, does it look as if everything's going okay?"

"More than okay. You've done a great job, Amy." He grinned. "The hors d'oeuvres even taste good, and that's a major miracle. Not a piece of rubber cheese in sight. How the hell did you achieve that?"

She laughed. "I gave the banquet manager a hot tip on a town house for sale in Laguna Hills. She ended up buying it for a bargain price. I guess the hors d'oeuvres are her way of saying thank you."

"I guess. Anyway, I officially pronounce you a miracle worker." He put his arm around her waist, guiding her toward the center of the room. "Come on. Time to take off your organizer hat and start enjoying the evening. I want you to meet the Secretary of State. He's here with his daughter. Jayne and I have known each other since high school and I'm sure you'll like her."

Brian was going to introduce her to the Secretary of State for California? Amy swallowed a giggle. Sometimes she found it surreal to contrast her life nowadays with her life growing up. Back then, a good day meant that her foster father hadn't beaten her and there'd been enough food on the table at dinnertime for everyone to go to bed without feeling hungry. A *really* good day meant all of the above, plus her foster brother, Dan, hadn't been locked in the basement for mouthing off at the Smiths. In the five years she'd spent in the Smith household, there hadn't been more than a few dozen really good days.

Amy drew in a quick breath, dispelling the hurtful memories. She reminded herself that the Secretary of State pulled on his pants one leg at a time the same as anyone else and that there was no reason for her to feel out of her depth just because she was a kid who'd been dragged up by the Department of Children and Family Services instead of being raised by a real family.

The Secretary of State turned out to be a jovial, middle-aged man with a politician's knack for interesting small talk. His daughter, however, was nowhere near as pleasant. Jayne gave Amy a swift once-over, which was apparently all she needed to slot Amy into the category of Too Unimportant to Bother About. Barely acknowledging their introduction, she commandeered Brian's attention with a series of anecdotes about various friends from their school days, pointedly excluding Amy from the conversation.

The Secretary of State stepped into the breach left by his daughter's rudeness, but was soon called away, leaving Amy plenty of time to notice that Jayne was wearing a dress that shrieked Designer Original. Her makeup, of course, was exquisite, and her dead-straight blond hair fell to her shoulders in the sort of sleek curtain usually seen only in ads for expensive shampoo. Watching her, Amy could almost feel her hair frizzing, her mascara clumping and her sequins glittering with vulgar excess.

She waited for Brian to remember that she didn't actually know the Miffy, Buffy and Todd he and Jayne were gossiping about, but he seemed lost in the world of prep school memories. Quelling a spurt of annoyance that Brian was such a willing captive of Jayne's bad manners, Amy murmured an excuse. The other two barely acknowledged that she was leaving.

Fortunately, Amy's feelings weren't hurt. She'd learned to ignore insults from the Jaynes of the world years ago, and as for Brian, she knew he was never intentionally cruel or cutting. He was simply self-absorbed and tended to forget that other people didn't necessarily share his interests.

Amy took another glass of champagne from a passing waiter and made her way into the ballroom. The space had been set up exactly as she'd requested, with a podium for speeches, and a velvet-draped catwalk for the fashion show, as well as a dance floor flanked by four dozen tables.

She exchanged greetings with several colleagues, mentally noting that people were starting to congregate at the tables. She glanced at her watch. 7:55. Time to make an announcement asking all attendees to find their seats so that the hotel staff could begin serving dinner.

Her boss had evidently reached the same conclusion. Glen Maitland was waiting at their reserved table right in front of the speaker's podium. As soon as he saw her, he expertly rid himself of a group of colleagues congratulating him on his generosity in sponsoring the fund-raiser.

He greeted her with his usual friendly smile. "Hi, Amy, you look great. Where's Brian? I thought he was escorting you tonight."

"He is, but he's met up with an old friend from prep school so I left them to reminisce."

Glen gave an admiring shake of his head. "That boy manages to keep up with more of his old friends than anyone I've ever met. Anytime I need a contact, whatever it's for, Brian always seems to know just the right person for me to call."

"That's certainly a useful skill." She supposed knowing all the right people could be called a skill.

Glen beamed. "It sure is. Everyone likes my son, and that's a valuable talent in the construction business. In any business, for that matter."

"I'm sure it is." Although it wouldn't hurt if Brian spent a lit-

tle less time socializing and more time taking care of the less en-
joyable aspects of his job as Director of Sales. Amy spent quite a
few hours a week covering for Brian's neglect.

"Anyway, we need to get this banquet started," Glen said. "I was
just talking with the catering director. Her staff is ready to go, so
I'll make the announcement that it's time for people to sit down
for dinner."

Amy nodded her agreement. "The hotel staff seems to be keeping right on schedule, thank goodness. That's a relief."

"Choosing this hotel was a good call on your part. You've done
a terrific job, Amy. Thanks." Glen was much too politically correct to make the mistake of hugging her, but he stepped aside so
that his wife could kiss the air on either side of Amy's cheeks while
he walked up to the mike to make the announcement.

"You look lovely, my dear," Gloria said. "Such a pretty little
dress. Only a slim young woman like you could get away with all
those sequins."

"I'm glad you like it." Amy returned Gloria's bright, insincere
smile with one equally bright and equally insincere. She was well
aware that she'd been insulted, but if Gloria had hoped to discon-
cert her, she had failed, just as Jayne had a few minutes earlier.
Amy's childhood had armored her against cruelty and insults; it
was kindness and compliments that left her floundering. In a way
it was flattering that Gloria often seemed so hostile. She doted on
Brian, her only child, and clearly saw Amy as a threat to her role
as the number-one woman in her son's life. Amy considered that
good news.

Fortunately, Glen Maitland more than compensated for his
wife's hostility. He and Brian returned to the table at the same time,
and Glen made a big fuss of seating Amy between the two of them
and introducing her to the other guests. The VIPs at Glen's head
table were all business acquaintances of the Maitlands, including
a county commissioner, the mayor of Laguna Niguel, and several
important subcontractors who worked for Maitland Homes.

These were people who dealt with Amy on a regular basis in the course of her work, and conversation flowed easily. In fact, Amy realized, it was Brian who sometimes appeared marginalized in the rapid-fire exchanges about current projects and the perennial issue of development versus conservation in Southern California. Glen brought up the thorny topic of the role overdevelopment might have played in the devastating combination of floods and fires that had besieged the region over the preceding six months, and Amy found the diverse, well-informed views of the participants fascinating.

Dessert was being served when a middle-aged man whom Amy didn't recognize came up and, apologizing for the intrusion, leaned down so that he could speak directly into Glen's ear, his words inaudible to the other guests.

Glen listened in silence. Then he pushed back his chair, his expression suddenly grim. "Sorry, folks, but I have to leave you for a few minutes. I'll be right back. Please enjoy dessert while I'm gone. Amy told me we're going to have a bittersweet chocolate torte with fresh raspberries. My absolute favorite."

"No prize for guessing that's why you chose it," Brian muttered when his father was out of earshot.

"Well, yes." Amy was puzzled by the note of resentment she detected in Brian's voice. "But most people like chocolate and raspberries, so there didn't seem any harm in picking something popular that your dad would also really enjoy. Don't you approve?"

He gazed at her, eyes wide with astonishment. "Honey, you misunderstood. I wasn't criticizing. I'm thrilled that you take such good care of my dad. Nobody else has ever paid that much attention to all his likes and dislikes. Hell, you're probably the only reason he wasn't hospitalized months ago for stress and working too hard. You've removed so much of the administrative burden from his shoulders that he finally has time to spend on the strategic decisions he needs to make. Everyone in my family is just delighted that you're on board."

Brian's praise sounded genuine, almost gushing in fact. Most people would have taken his words at face value, but for some reason Amy doubted his sincerity. However, this wasn't the place or the time to pursue the subject, especially since she wasn't sure exactly what subject she needed to pursue. She would surely seem paranoid if she suggested to Brian that he sounded jealous of her relationship with his father.

With a slight mental shrug, she changed the topic of conversation and asked if he had seen the report that next week the vice president and his wife were going to spend two nights in the town of San Clemente, which was where the Maitlands lived. Brian hadn't heard. He turned to pass on the snippet of news to his mother, and talk flowed back into safe, noncontroversial channels.

Almost fifteen minutes passed before Glen Maitland returned. He came alone. He was a big man, with bushy gray eyebrows. At the moment, those eyebrows were pulled into a ferocious frown. His lips, tightly compressed, mimicked the snarling line of his eyebrows and emphasized the anger he was fighting to control.

Gloria Maitland stared at her husband in dismay. "Oh, my! What's happened, Glen? You look as if you've heard some really bad news."

Her boss wasn't good at pretending and Amy could see how much effort it cost him to adjust his expression into the semblance of a carefree smile. "Don't worry, honey, it's nothing important. Just an annoying piece of business that needs to be taken care of."

"Not right now, I hope?"

"'Fraid so, honey. I'm going to need Amy to come with me, but I'll be back lickety-split. Y'all behave yourselves while we're gone. Brian, make sure my guests all have after-dinner drinks to go with their coffee. The bartender was telling me earlier on that they have some real fine vintage cognac if anyone's interested." He turned to Amy, although he didn't quite meet her gaze. "Amy, please come now."

Glen Maitland had been born in Alabama, but he'd moved with

his family to California when he was seven. Most of the time he spoke exactly like any other Californian. The only time his speech patterns ever betrayed his Southern heritage was when he was stressed—and he'd just said *y'all* and *lickety-split,* surefire indications that he was deeply bothered about something.

Amy almost needed to run to keep up with him as he strode through the nearly deserted lobby. Even his back looked angry, she reflected. She mentally reviewed the projects most likely to cause Glen such stress on a Saturday evening. There had been no looming problems when she left work yesterday at six, but that was no guarantee of a peaceful weekend. Unfortunately, when you made your living in the construction industry in California, problems were never more than a few feet around the corner. If lightning or sliding subsoil didn't get you, a government agency was always looming on the horizon, waiting to inform you that you'd disobeyed some vital environmental regulation or violated some fine-print section of the building code. Who was the man who'd come and whispered in Glen's ear? Not one of the construction site managers, she was sure. She knew all of them, at least by sight. Still, if the problem was big enough, the manager might be holding down the fort, and the man who came to report the news might be one of his assistants. She didn't know all of the junior construction personnel.

Glen pushed open the door to a small, deserted room that seemed to be used chiefly for stacking chairs. He gestured for her to precede him, then swung around to face her, his expression even more ferocious than before.

"What is it?" she asked, fishing out her Palm Pilot, ready to take notes. "Don't tell me we have another problem with the Mission Valley project?"

He cut her off with a brusque, chopping movement of his big, calloused hand. "Don't," he said. "It's over, Amy. You've been found out."

"I've been found out?" She blinked, puzzled. "What do you mean, *found out?*"

"Goddammit, Amy, don't make this situation worse than it already is. You're fired. I want you to leave the hotel right now. It's embarrassing to have you around. I'll make your excuses to the other guests—tell 'em you're sick, I guess. I'll also arrange to have your desk cleaned out and any personal items sent to you. I don't want you in the Maitland Homes offices ever again."

Amy opened her mouth, but like the goldfish swimming endless circuits in the bowl on her kitchen counter, no sound came out.

Glen slammed his fist onto the table. "I trusted you like my own flesh and blood. How could you do it? Goddammit, Amy, how could you?"

CHAPTER
TWO

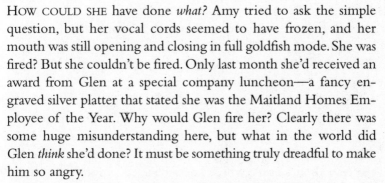

HOW COULD SHE have done *what?* Amy tried to ask the simple question, but her vocal cords seemed to have frozen, and her mouth was still opening and closing in full goldfish mode. She was fired? But she couldn't be fired. Only last month she'd received an award from Glen at a special company luncheon—a fancy engraved silver platter that stated she was the Maitland Homes Employee of the Year. Why would Glen fire her? Clearly there was some huge misunderstanding here, but what in the world did Glen *think* she'd done? It must be something truly dreadful to make him so angry.

"I see that you're smart enough not to protest that you're innocent." Glen's mouth twisted as if he'd swallowed something bitter. "Don't you have anything at all to say? Other than a cliché like it's all a terrible mistake."

She cleared her throat, still searching for her voice, but Glen spoke before she found it. "Perhaps you're worried about incriminating yourself. You shouldn't be. In fact, I'd be a whole heap happier if you had the guts to confess to what you've done. Bottom line, if you make full restitution of the missing funds, I'll cut you a break. I won't prosecute, although I damn well should."

He wouldn't prosecute? That final threat jolted her out of her paralysis. "Prosecute?" she said. "Prosecute *me?* Glen, I have no idea what you're talking about. Why would you prosecute me? What's going on, for God's sake?"

"Don't lie anymore," he said wearily, pinching the bridge of his nose as if to relieve intense pain. "I can't stand it. Like I said, the game's up. As soon as I realized the fifty thousand was missing from the subcontractor account, I hired Tony Kresge to find out who'd stolen the money. Kresge is an investigator with Corporate Safety and, in case you don't know, they're the best forensic accountants in L.A. Hell, they may be the best in the country. It cost me fifteen thousand dollars in fees, but it was worth every cent, because it took Tony less than three days to discover that you were the person who'd stolen the money."

"Me? *Me?*"

Glen made a chopping motion with his hand. "He's accumulated enough evidence to demonstrate that you weren't nearly as clever as you thought you were. Trust me, Kresge has left you no wriggle room for denial."

"You think I stole fifty thousand dollars from the subcontractor account. You're accusing me of being a thief." Amy repeated the crazy words, hoping that hearing them spoken out loud would give Glen's accusations some vague connection to reality. She had often read about people whose knees buckled and she'd wondered what, exactly, that meant. Now she knew. Her legs felt as if the bones had turned to mush and her knees suddenly bent, unable to support her weight. She had to grab on to the back of a nearby chair to prevent herself from falling.

"Glen, I swear I don't know what you're talking about. Until you brought me in here, I had absolutely no clue that any money was missing."

"Cut it out, Amy. I'm not impressed by your protestations of innocence. You'd do better with me—a whole lot better—if you owned up to what you've done." Glen's eyes contained no shred of warmth or sympathy. "Hell, if you needed cash, why didn't you just ask me for a loan—"

"I didn't need cash. I don't need cash—"

"What was the problem? Do you have sick relatives? Too much credit card debt? A drug habit—"

"No," she exploded. "I don't have sick relatives. I'm not in debt. I didn't steal any money. And I sure as hell don't do drugs!" The suggestion that she might be hiding an addiction sent her over the top. She'd suffered way too much from her mother's cocaine habit to be able to respond rationally. A wave of anger restored steel to her spine and powerful volume to her vocal cords. She stepped away from the support of the chair, feeling her cheeks grow hot and her eyes flash fire.

"You ought to know me by now, Glen, since I've worked with you for more than three years. I'm loyal, I'm honest and I'm hard-working. How dare you accuse me of hiding a drug addiction and stealing company money!"

"The evidence is cut and dried." Glen spoke curtly. "You took the money in three installments over the past eight weeks. You stole the first ten thousand on July 6, almost two months ago. You covered your tracks very cleverly, but at crucial moments in each transaction you had to provide a password or enter an access code. To penetrate the account, you used your password, and codes only you and I knew. You disguised your withdrawal as a business transaction, and you did a good enough job to fool our accounting department until they conducted an in-house mini-audit last week. Just your bad luck that the new accountant is so darn good at her job, isn't it, Amy? She came straight to me, and I went straight to Corporate Safety. I have to say, you're just about the last person I expected to get fingered as the culprit."

Her mind whirred at lightning speed, trying to make sense of what Glen was saying. The thefts, apparently, had all been made electronically, which meant the evidence couldn't be anywhere near as cut and dried as Glen was claiming. "Just because my passwords were used doesn't mean that I made the transaction. Anybody could pretend to be me in cyberspace."

"I suggested that possibility to Tony Kresge," Glen said. "Although God knows how anybody would have discovered your passwords—"

"If somebody wanted to set me up, it wouldn't be impossible."

"Maybe not. But Tony just finished double-checking every detail of his investigation, and there's no doubt about his conclusions. The use of your passwords might not be considered definitive, but what about the access codes? For this particular account, there isn't another soul in the company who knows those except you and me. Besides, the transactions were all made from your computer—"

"Maybe when I was at lunch, or in a meeting—"

Glen shook his head. "On one occasion, the transfer was made on a Sunday, when everyone has to sign in to gain access to our offices. It was the last Sunday in July and you were the only person signed in that day, Amy. And here's the clincher: Kresge has uncovered the numbered account in the Cayman Islands where you sent the money."

The so-called proof of her guilt certainly sounded damning, but the idea of her owning a numbered bank account in an island notorious as a tax haven for criminals and billionaires struck Amy as somewhere between insane and hilariously funny. She gave a wild gasp of laughter, stopping abruptly when she saw Glen's appalled expression.

"I don't have a numbered account in the Caymans or anywhere else," she said, her voice shaking from a combination of stress and outrage. "Where in the world would I get enough money to need a secret bank account?"

"Good question," Glen said harshly. "I wondered that myself.

Have you stolen anything more, Amy? I've sent Kresge back to the office to run checks on all the other accounts to see what other funds might be missing. Clearly, I was very mistaken about you, Amy. I sure as hell hope there isn't going to be more bad news waiting for me on Monday."

"I've never stolen a penny from Maitland Homes, much less fifty thousand dollars. If there's more money missing, it's nothing to do with me. I've worked hard for you and your company for the past three years—"

"I agree." For the first time, Glen looked sad rather than angry. "That's the only reason I'm cutting you some slack. I can't stand dishonesty, and in the normal way of things, trust me, you wouldn't be standing here, arguing the fine print of the accusations. You'd be on your way down to the police station, facing charges of grand theft. But, as you say, you've worked damned hard ever since you joined our company, and I can only assume you got in over your head somehow and didn't have the guts to come to me and ask straight-out for a loan. Stupid of you, because I'd have been happy to give you one. Anyway, too late now for regrets. In view of your good work in the past, I'm going to give you much more of a break than you deserve. Bring me the fifty thousand dollars by the end of next week and I won't lay charges. After that, I recommend you move somewhere far enough away that when you look for a new job, nobody is going to be calling me to ask for a reference."

"How far away would that need to be?" Amy demanded. "The planet Mars?" Her stomach lurched sickly at the prospect of searching for a new job when her previous employers wouldn't give her a reference. In the small world of the building industry, it wouldn't be long before somebody whispered in somebody else's ear that Amy Duran had been fired for theft, and her chances of ever finding employment would plummet to right around zero.

"You should have thought about the consequences back in July when you took ten thousand dollars that didn't belong to you, and followed up with another twenty and another twenty on top of that. It wasn't just one theft, Amy, that's what really burns my ass. Your criminal behavior was ongoing. You had all the time in the world to think about what you were doing and you kept right on doing it. I can't excuse that. I want my money back, and if you want to stay out of prison, you'd damn well better give it to me. For our sake, I hope you haven't spent it all—"

"I never had it to spend—"

"That's it. End of discussion." Glen strode out of the room, slamming the door behind him.

Amy had no idea how long she stood, clutching the back of the chair, before her brain actually formed a coherent thought as opposed to spiraling in freefall panic. She had to get home, she realized. There was too much noise here at the hotel, and way too many people. In the sanctuary of her neat, quiet town house she'd be able to think the situation through and find a logical way to explain to Glen why he was so badly mistaken.

It was a relief to have a plan of action, even if the plan was nothing more profound than going home. Legs still wobbly, she walked back into the lobby. Festive music spilled out from the ballroom and the voice of the announcer mingled with a scattering of applause as the fashion show swung into action.

Darting behind a column to avoid one of the staffers from Dress for Success, she contemplated the problem of how she could actually get home. Would Brian be willing to drive her? Would he understand, as his father apparently did not, that she was incapable of stealing from his family's company, or from anyone else for that matter?

Brian would believe her, Amy decided. Of course he would. They had been dating for months, and were close in a way that she and Glen couldn't possibly be. There was even a measure of comfort to be derived from the thought of Brian's laid-back company. Glen wasn't willing to listen to her, but he'd listen to his son, and Brian would surely be eager to convince his father that the hotshot forensic accountant had made a mistake and that Amy was innocent. The roiling in her stomach eased a little as she scribbled a note asking Brian to meet her in the lobby since she wasn't feeling well and needed a ride home.

She handed the note to one of the waitstaff, folded inside a five-dollar bill, and gave the man directions on how to deliver it to Brian. While she waited, she paced the lobby, her rambling thoughts punctuated by music, applause and occasional bursts of laughter. Everyone seemed to be having a really grand time, she thought cynically. Her final effort on behalf of Maitland Homes was proving a huge success.

The server returned, but Brian wasn't with him. Instead, he handed Amy a note. "Your friend asked me to give you this," he said.

"Thank you." When all else failed, pride came to Amy's rescue and she managed to take the note with a casual smile, as if she'd never expected any other form of reply. She turned away and read what Brian had written. His note was brief and to the point.

My father has explained what you've done and I never want to see or speak to you again, much less drive you home. Use some of the money you stole from us to pay for a cab. Brian

She knew that Brian's callous reaction ought to make her furious. Despite months of intimacy, he apparently had paid her so little genuine attention—knew her so superficially—that he was willing to accept his father's insulting accusations without a murmur of protest. She should be steaming with rage that he couldn't summon the compassion to at least drive her home, even if he doubted her innocence.

But in fact Amy didn't feel angry; she felt sick to her stomach, as if instead of sending an offensive note, Brian had delivered a hard punch straight to her gut. How could this be happening to her, the queen of control? The person who believed that there was no bad luck, only bad management? Why was she teetering right on the absolute edge of disaster? Where had she gone wrong in her plan to surround herself with pleasant, successful people so that she could lead a perfect, organized life?

The nausea was so intense that she had no energy for worrying about anything other than controlling the urge to upchuck in the lobby. She hurried into the ladies' room and sank down onto a banquette, resting her back against a cool granite column until the worst of the nausea passed.

When she was sure she could stand without making an exhibition of herself, she hauled herself upright and made her way to the revolving doors of the main entrance. Her feet dragged across the marbled floor of the lobby as if she were an old, sick woman.

She had only fifteen dollars left in her purse, she realized. She'd tucked in a few five-dollar bills to have some money for tips, but fifteen dollars was nowhere near enough to get her home to Laguna Niguel. Fortunately, she'd brought a credit card in case she wanted to bid on something during the auction, and she could only hope the cabdriver would be willing to take that. Bottom line, if he wanted to get paid, he'd have no choice.

The parking valet came up as soon as she left the lobby. "Good evening, miss. Can I get your car?" He held out his hand for the expected claim check.

"I don't have a car." Amy swallowed. "Could you call me a cab, please?"

"My pleasure." He hesitated for a moment, his kindly brown eyes gleaming with sympathy. "You sure you're okay, miss? You don't look all that good."

"I'm fine, thank you." She sounded curt, she knew it, but she was afraid she'd start sobbing her heart out if he offered any more overt kindness.

He turned away, barely concealing a shrug, and whistled up a cab. Amy avoided his eyes as he held open the door for her to get in, tipping him with another of her five-dollar bills. She couldn't afford that big a tip, of course, but when you had a fifty-thousand-dollar debt looming over your head, and no cash to pay for your ride home, five dollars didn't seem all that significant one way or the other.

Amy gave her address to the cabbie and sank inside, relieved to discover that her driver was fully occupied in conducting a conversation on his cell phone in some language she didn't recognize. As they sped along the freeways, relatively clear at this hour on a Saturday night, the sickness in her stomach gave way first to apathy, then to astonishment at the huge mistake Glen was making. Finally, her astonishment coalesced into a rage so all-consuming that she was literally sweating from the heat of her anger. Glen was jumping to conclusions and giving her no chance to defend herself. How dare he? Her whole life was on the line and she wouldn't—couldn't—allow him to get away with such rotten behavior.

She tapped on the glass to attract the cabdriver's attention. "I've changed my mind," she said. "I don't want to go to Laguna Niguel anymore. Take me to San Clemente, please."

She gave him the Maitlands' address, indifferent to the fact that it might still be a couple of hours before Glen and his wife arrived home. It was a fine night, not at all cold, and she sat on the waist-high wall that hid the swimming pool motors and heaters until she finally heard the sounds of their car arriving.

The Mercedes sports coupe swept into the driveway, expensive engine purring, and she ran to position herself in front of the garage doors. She heard Gloria scream as Glen slammed on the brakes, squealing to a halt not more than a foot or two from where she was standing.

Glen shot out of the car. "What the hell are you doing? I could've run you down—killed you! Are you crazy?"

"I didn't steal the money," she said, hands clenched at her sides. "You've made a terrible mistake and you owe me an apology. A big apology."

Gloria clambered out of the passenger side and teetered around the car on her high-heeled evening sandals until she was clutching her husband's arm. "Come inside," she begged her husband, tugging at his sleeve. "She looks demented...out of her mind. She...she might hurt us."

"Of course I'm not going to hurt you." Amy felt the wild laughter return, bubbling up into her throat. She gulped in air, reasserting control. "Don't be ridiculous, Gloria. This is me, Amy—"

"And you're trespassing," Glen said, his voice icy with contempt. He draped his arm protectively around his wife's shoulders as if he really expected Amy to resort to physical violence. "Get off my property, or I'll call the police and explain to them exactly why I don't want you anywhere near me or my wife."

"No, I won't leave." She clenched her jaw. "I'm not leaving until you show me the so-called evidence that Tony Kresge dredged up against me. I'm entitled to see what he found—"

"Like hell you're entitled," Glen said. "You must think I'm real stupid. I'm not handing over the details of the case against you just so that you can pick it to pieces and invent some cockamamy defense."

"That's not my plan. Don't you care about discovering the truth? Don't you want to find out who's really stealing from you?"

"I sure do. That's why I hired the best forensic accountant in the business, and he fingered you." Glen's voice rose. "Now get out of my way. My wife is tired, and so am I. It's been a lousy night and I want to drive my own car into my own garage without interference from a thief."

"I'm not moving until you *listen* to me—"

"I've listened long enough. This is your final warning, Amy, and you'd better take it seriously: don't come back here, or you'll find yourself chewing over the wisdom of your past actions from the comfort of your very own jail cell."

She felt tears well up, but she wouldn't let them fall. She never cried. Maybe Gloria was right to be worried about her physical safety, Amy thought wryly. Her frustration level was so high she wanted to pound on Glen's chest to make him listen. He was responding to her words, but he wasn't even trying to hear what she was really saying.

"I didn't steal the money! If you'd only let me see the so-called proof, I'd be able to convince you." She heard despair in her own voice. "You have to believe me, Glen!"

Gloria opened her cell phone and handed it to her husband. "Call the police," she said in a low voice. "Let them deal with her."

Glen took the phone and started to dial, then stopped. "Last chance, Amy. Is this what you want?" he asked quietly. "It's your choice. I can lay the evidence in front of the police right now since you're so gosh-darn anxious to review it."

Should she take the risk? No, she thought, anger and heat slipping away, replaced by an icy chill of fear. No, she didn't want him to call the police. She'd watched her mother, Jinny, get arrested and taken to the police station too many times when she was a kid, and she had sworn she would never, ever, ever put herself through that humiliation. The image of Jinny, hands cuffed behind her back, the cop's hand heavy on her head, forcing her to bend down in order to climb into the squad car, was burned into Amy's soul. She wasn't going to let those indignities happen to her. She couldn't let them happen and retain her sanity.

"No, don't call the police," she said dully, moving away from the garage entrance. "I'll leave."

"About time," Gloria muttered, teetering back to take her seat inside the car.

"How are you getting home?" Glen asked. He sounded angry again, as if he was annoyed with himself for caring about Amy's transportation problems.

"I have my cell phone. I'll call a cab."

"That could take hours—"

"Don't worry, I'll wait on the sidewalk, so I won't be trespassing."

Glen hesitated for a moment, then shook his head without saying anything more. He got into the car and drove into the garage, closing the door behind him. The lights went out, leaving Amy in darkness.

The night suddenly felt cold after all. Amy wrapped her arms around her waist, huddling inside the scanty protection of her pashmina evening wrap. It was a long time before she found the energy and focus to retrieve the business card given her by the cabbie and call for a ride home.

Until tonight, she'd almost forgotten how much it hurt to feel totally alone in a hostile world.

CHAPTER
THREE

AMY GOT UP from the table and went into the kitchen to pour herself another cup of coffee, but the pot was empty. Six cups of coffee before 9:00 a.m., she thought with bitter amusement. This was clearly not going to be one of her more relaxed Sundays.

She set a fresh pot of coffee to brew and went back to her spreadsheets and bankbooks. Unfortunately, however many times she did the math, the balance in her checking account remained stubbornly at $597. Her savings account yielded another $1,210, not counting this month's interest, which hadn't yet been reported. She had eight thousand dollars in a 401K savings plan at Maitland Homes, but she knew she wouldn't be allowed to take all of that out, since half of it had been contributed by the company. In addition, she owned approximately five thousand dollars' worth of stocks and shares—her own small stake in the American dream.

On the plus side, her student loans had been paid off six months ago after years of scrimping, and she had only a few hundred dollars in credit card debt. Bottom line: even the sum of all her investments came nowhere near fifty thousand dollars. That meant she couldn't solve her problems by paying Glen the money he was demanding.

Amy refused to accept her own calculations. There must be some way she could raise the extra cash. She could sell her car, an eighteen-month-old Mazda Miata. She could hope to get sixteen thousand bucks, maybe even seventeen. But she still owed ten thousand and change on the loan, so she'd net less than six thousand, plus she'd have no way to get to work. This was L.A., after all, where there were probably more private helicopters than public bus routes. Of course, she might never manage to get another job, she reflected grimly, in which case transportation to the office wouldn't be an issue.

Amy felt tears sting the back of her eyes, something that had happened more in the past twelve hours than at any time since her engagement to Daniel Redmond ended. But crying never helped solve a problem, she reminded herself. It sure as hell hadn't done anything to mend her relationship with Dan. She ought to know by now that there was no point wallowing in useless emotion.

Think, she ordered herself, pacing the length of her living room. You're smart and you have a good education. That's everything you need to solve any problem.

The pep talk didn't work. For the first time in years, she felt helpless. Her emotions ricocheted between terror that she didn't have the funds to buy her way out of an arrest warrant and a stubborn relief that she couldn't make restitution. Paying Glen fifty thousand would be a tacit admission of guilt, and she would almost prefer to face jail rather than confess to a crime she hadn't committed. Almost.

Another pot of coffee and four hours later, she was still staring at the same sheets of paper and making the same hopeless calculations when a ring at the doorbell jerked her out of her escalating dejection. She ran to the door, trying to convince herself that Glen would be on the other side, ready to make an apology for his dreadful mistake. Or, at the very least, it would be Brian, offering to go to bat on her behalf with his father.

Yes, that must be it, she decided. Brian had come to apologize for his miserable behavior. He sure as hell owed her an apology after abandoning her last night without a single word or gesture of support.

She peered through the spy hole and saw a young man she didn't recognize. He wore a biker's helmet emblazoned with the logo of a delivery company often used by Maitland Homes. One hand rested on the handles of his bike; in the other he carried a flat envelope.

Amy felt a momentary letdown that her visitor wasn't Brian. Then she allowed hope to surge again. Okay, so neither Glen nor Brian had come to apologize in person, but who could be sending her a package by special messenger if not her boss? Probably Glen had reconsidered his decision to withhold the details of Corporate Safety's investigation into the missing money. The package most likely contained the so-called proof that Tony Kresge had uncovered. Once she examined the details of Kresge's investigation, surely she'd be able to poke holes in the false case that had been built against her.

She opened the door, leaving the chain in place.

"Hi, miss." The messenger held out the brown envelope and an electronic pad. He gestured to the pad. "Could you sign here, please?" He tipped his helmet back to get some air. "Nice day, isn't it?"

"Lovely." Until the messenger commented on the weather, Amy wouldn't have been able to say if it was sunny and warm or cold and rainy. She unlatched the door chain long enough to sign her name and take the package. Her hands were shaking, she noted almost abstractly.

"Thanks," she said.

"My pleasure." The delivery man hopped onto his bike and pedaled off as she relocked the door.

As she'd hoped, the return address displayed the personal logo of the CEO of Maitland Homes, indicating that the package had indeed come directly from Glen Maitland. Thank goodness! The fact that her boss had paid the huge premium required for a Sunday delivery surely suggested that he was having second thoughts about his precipitous actions of the previous night. Her task for the rest of the day would be to read through the documents with great attention so that she could demonstrate to her boss precisely where and how Tony Kresge had made false assumptions about her guilt.

She ripped open the envelope as she made her way back to the living area. There seemed much less material than she would have anticipated, only a short covering letter and two attached pages. She read the letter so fast that she didn't understand it, and had to go back and read it again.

Dear Ms. Duran:

Attached please find a copy of the lease agreement concerning the town house you occupy, located at 5636 Siesta Drive. This town house is owned by Maitland Homes and rented to you at 75% of assessed market value as a benefit of your employment with our company.

The enclosed contract, signed between you and Maitland Homes on January 5, 2002, states that you may occupy the said premises only for such time as you remain an employee of Maitland Homes, Inc. Your employment with our company terminated yesterday, September 10, 2005. Therefore, in accordance with clause 4, section (ii) of the aforementioned lease, you are hereby notified that you are required to vacate said premises within thirty days, i.e. before October 10, 2005.

Very truly yours, Glen R. Maitland, President

Amy read the letter a third time. She wished she could summon a fortifying dose of anger at the mean-spiritedness of Glen's action. The haste with which he'd invoked his legal right to evict her was almost vicious, and she sensed the jealous hand of Gloria Maitland behind the move. Unfortunately, she couldn't feel anger. All she could feel was stark, overwhelming fear.

She was willing to work her tail off to get her life back on track, but where would she live? It wasn't as if she had dozens of kindly relatives all eager to stretch out a helping hand. Last she'd heard, her mother was in yet another compulsory drug rehab program in a locked facility, trying to avoid a lifetime conviction under the three strikes law. She had no clue whether her father was alive or dead. He might as well have dropped off the edge of the earth when he walked out on her and Jinny twenty-three years ago. Her paternal grandparents had been dead for more than a decade, and her maternal grandparents, along with a couple of uncles, all lived in Iowa. They hadn't cared enough about her to take her in when she was a homeless child of nine and Jinny was hauled off on her first trip to jail. It seemed unlikely they would be willing to offer her a home or cough up a loan of fifty thousand bucks now that she was supposedly a self-sufficient adult.

What was she going to do? Maybe she could take out a bank loan so that she could repay the fifty thousand dollars that she hadn't stolen. For a moment Amy clung to the idea as a lifeline. Then she realized that she'd already lost her job and was about to lose her home. In those circumstances, a bank officer was about as likely to offer her a loan as he was to stand on the sidewalk and toss dollar bills into the air. And even if, by some miracle, her bank was willing to cough up the fifty thousand based on her previous good credit, how in the world was she going to find a job that would enable her to pay back the loan?

The harder Amy thought, the less chance she saw of coming up with enough money to buy her way out of an arrest warrant.

That meant by the end of next week Glen would be notifying the police of her supposed crime and handing over his file of incriminating evidence. The fact that the evidence was wrong wouldn't matter. She had a terrifying suspicion that once the police got their hands on her, they would never let go. Why would they believe her protestations of innocence once they discovered that she'd spent most of her childhood in foster care because her mother was in prison?

She had no faith in the fairness of the justice system. The quaint notion that you were innocent until proven guilty applied only in theory, not in practice. She knew damn well that where the real world of law enforcement was concerned, the opposite applied to people like her. She'd seen what had happened when Dan tried to protest about their foster father's brutality: she and Dan had been ridiculed by the authorities and the Smiths had punished them for tattling. Absolutely nothing had happened to the Smiths. Before that, she'd seen the system at work with her mother. Much as she despised Jinny's addiction, Amy also knew that several of her mother's trips to the police station weren't justified—the cops had simply come looking for an addicted ex-con whenever they needed a scapegoat in a drug case they couldn't solve.

As for children not being tarred with their parents' sins, that was a real joke. People with a background like hers were automatic suspects whenever a crime was committed in their vicinity.

You have to call Dan. He's a lawyer, after all. Right now, he's the only person who can help you.

Amy shoved the insidious thought aside, her breath coming hard and fast. The temptation to seek Dan's help was so strong that her hands actually made a little pushing movement to thrust it away.

It would be a professional call. You don't have to rehash the past or get into a load of personal stuff.

"No!" She realized she'd spoken out loud. Not just spoken; she'd yelled. Good grief, she was really losing it. But where she and Dan were concerned, nothing had ever been tepid or impersonal. From the moment she'd walked into the Smiths' horrible home and been introduced to their other foster child—surly, angry Daniel Redmond—Dan had been the most important person in her life. They'd been so close for so many years that there were no boundaries to mark off the different areas of their lives and no dividing line between the personal and the professional.

Having watched Jinny go to pieces in the wake of her father's disappearance, Amy had sworn she would never allow herself to be made vulnerable by love. Dan had made her forget that vow. She'd sworn she would keep her relationships with men low-key and polite. Dan only needed to smile at her in his special way and she had forgotten all about polite and easygoing. She had sworn she would never mistake sex for love. With Dan, every gesture and every touch had been an act of love, so how could she make a distinction?

At least Dan was always a hundred percent on your side.

Unlike Brian, who had tossed her aside at the first hint of trouble, Dan had always been there for her. He'd been a hundred percent on her side when they endured the careless cruelty of other kids at school who mocked their poverty. He'd taken the blame when she sneaked into the kitchen late at night to steal milk or a slice of bread to staunch the hunger pangs of Patty, their newly arrived foster sister. He'd been there when five-year-old Patty died from pneumonia too long neglected by the indifferent Smiths. Amy had been overcome with guilt and grief, as if she were somehow responsible, and only Dan had been able to assuage her grief. He'd been there when they struggled to make it through college with no financial help beyond the scholarships they could win by sheer hard work and outstanding grades. And he'd been there— magnificent and fascinating—when she fell so deeply and passionately in love with him that it seemed the whole world was painted in brighter colors every moment they were together.

Swallow your pride. Call him. You need him.

Yes, she did. Except that Dan wasn't on her side anymore. She'd broken their engagement and sent him away. She'd told him never to come back. And he hadn't.

She'd last seen Dan Redmond six years ago, and their parting had been the stuff of many subsequent nightmares. The emotional wounds they inflicted on each other toward the end of their engagement had been so deep that their final meeting had degenerated into a hideous example of everything Amy most despised about human relationships. She had ended up screaming insults and sobbing hysterically, incoherent with rage and grief. Her feelings had been so raw that she could only bear the pain by making sure she wounded Dan as badly as he had wounded her. And she discovered to her chagrin that she was unexpectedly good at inflicting emotional pain.

Dan, two years older by the calendar but usually a hundred years wiser, hadn't behaved much better than her on this occasion. Amy's barbs and taunts had been much too successful in finding their mark, and for the first time in all the years she'd known him, he lost control.

She recognized now, although she hadn't at the time, that her barbs had been almost lethally effective. He'd been hurting, but he'd also been so furiously angry at her decision to end their relationship that he'd actually punched his fist into the wall of the room she rented from a professor in the English department at USC. He'd smashed a giant hole that went right through the plasterboard to the stud behind. When he finally left, all she'd wanted to do was curl up into a ball and sob the night away. Instead, she'd had to run out to the hardware store to get the materials to patch up the hole before the professor noticed the damage.

Just thinking about that hideous parting left Amy dry-mouthed and trembling. She hated the intensity of the emotion that Dan had provoked in her. Loathed the fact that six years after their final encounter she could still summon up a vivid memory of the way he'd kissed her right before he stormed out of the door. His tongue had thrust deep into her mouth, and his hands had twisted in her hair, pulling her head back so that he could see her face.

She couldn't hide her feelings from Dan. He knew her much too well and he'd recognized that, despite everything, she still wanted him. He'd jammed his body up against hers, her back against the damaged wall, forcing her to acknowledge not only that he was aroused, but that she was, too. She'd trembled in his grip, a hair's breadth away from surrendering to desire and pulling him down onto her bed so that they could heal the hurt of their argument in hours of making love. It had taken every last ounce of her willpower not to surrender to the force of their mutual passion. She had bitten her tongue until she tasted blood to prevent herself from telling him that his career choices didn't matter, that she loved him no matter what.

Amy shuddered, closing her eyes to shut out the images of a scene that retained far too much power to hurt. She'd thrown aside a lifetime of caution when she fell in love with Dan, and she'd paid a heavy price. Her love for him had brought her to the very edge of a precipice. If she had tumbled over, she would never again have been in control of her life.

It was her experience with Dan that had made Brian feel like such a safe choice for a potential husband. She found Brian an agreeable companion and he seemed to have lucked out in the gene lottery; he was handsome, athletic and reasonably smart—a decent choice of father for her children. Even the events of the past twenty-four hours didn't change her opinion that choosing Brian as a life partner had been a sound decision, despite the fact that she had never loved him. Love always ended up hurting. If she'd been in love with Brian, his refusal to help her right now would have been devastating. As it was, his betrayal was no more than a pinprick, a reinforcement of the lesson that you should never place trust in anyone other than yourself.

Amy realized that while her brain had been occupied with justification of her loveless relationship with Brian, her feet had taken charge and walked her over to the shelf in the kitchen where she kept her phone book. She already had it open to the letter *R*.

She fanned the air in front of her face, her hand not quite steady. Okay, she'd come this far. There was probably no harm in thumbing through the pages in search of a Daniel Redmond. Of course, she didn't really expect to find a listing for him. Dan might have moved to Montana by now. Or to Monrovia or Mongolia for that matter, a volunteer for some international corps of do-gooders. She could just picture Dan in a community so poor that the pigs and the kids played in the same mud hole, while he—idealistic to the depths of his stubborn soul—sat on a stoop exploiting his near-magic powers of persuasion to convince the village elders that they needed to establish a legal system with property rights for women, and education for all the children, and judges in the courts who didn't take bribes.

Her fingers skittered to a halt at an entry for Daniel and Elizabeth Redmond, living at an address in Long Beach. Daniel and Elizabeth.

Amy drew in a shaky breath. Funny, but somehow it had never occurred to her that Dan would be married. But he was thirty-two years old, magnetic in the extreme, and it was six years since they'd ended their engagement. Why on earth wouldn't he be married?

Amy swallowed hard. From her point of view, it was good news that Dan now had a wife. If there had ever been any possibility of his misunderstanding her reasons for getting in touch with him, the existence of a wife would stop speculation before it even began. In fact, since he was married, there was no reason in the world for her not to call him.

Quickly, before she could succumb to cowardly second thoughts, Amy dialed the number. An unfamiliar male voice answered on the second ring. "Hello?"

"Yes, hello. My name is Amy Duran, and I'm looking for Daniel Redmond."

"You've got him. I'm Dan."

But he wasn't her Dan. Amy made no attempt to analyze why her heart gave a leap of irrational joy. She wished Dan well, but surely she couldn't be stupid enough to care one way or the other if he was married?

"I'm sorry to bother you—"

"You haven't bothered me…yet. What do you want?"

"Probably nothing. I believe I've called the wrong number. I'm looking for the Dan Redmond who's a lawyer. He attended USC in the early nineteen-nineties and then went on to law school at Pepperdine."

"Young lady, I wish that had been me, but I'm eighty-eight years old and I didn't even make it through high school. Back when I was a teenager, high school was a luxury, let alone college. We had to go out to work or the family didn't get to eat. And in the nineteen-nineties, I was already retired, sitting on the porch and driving my wife crazy, or so she tells me."

Amy apologized again for disturbing him and hung up. There were no more listings for Daniel Redmond in the residential phone book, but when she searched the Yellow Pages she found a listing for Redmond and Kolachik, defense attorneys. The full names of the two partners were listed as Daniel M. Redmond and Robert F. Kolachik, and their office was located in Torrance. A tagline announced that the firm specialized in criminal law and handled no civil lawsuits.

Dan's middle initial had been *M*, for Matthew. It would surely be a real coincidence if there were two Daniel M. Redmonds practicing law in this area; the name wasn't that common. She dialed the phone number, taking comfort in the near certainty that on a Sunday she wasn't likely to reach anyone. With luck, however, there might be a recorded message that would provide office hours and possibly even driving directions. Between now and Monday morning she had plenty of time to decide whether or not she was going to humble herself and contact Dan in person.

Sure enough, a recorded message clicked in after a couple of rings, a pleasant female voice informing Amy that she'd reached the offices of Redmond and Kolachik, attorneys at law. Office hours were Monday through Friday, nine to five. Daniel Redmond was out of town until Monday, but in an emergency—presumably that meant if you were about to be hauled off to jail—Robert Kolachik could be reached by cell phone. The pleasant voice gave a number to call.

Amy was about to hang up the phone when somebody picked up. "This is Bob Kolachik."

She hesitated for a moment, almost deciding not to answer. At the last moment, she found the courage to speak. "I'm looking for the Daniel Redmond who was a student at USC in the early nineties. He went to law school at Pepperdine. Is this his office?"

"Yes, it seems like you've called the right place. Dan and I both went to Pepperdine. Can I pass on a message? Tell him who's calling?"

Her brain went blank. "No. No, thank you." She slammed the phone back into its cradle, hoping that Bob Kolachik didn't have caller ID, or if he did that he would be much too busy to call her back. Speaking to an actual person brought home the realization of what a bad idea it had been to contemplate retracing her steps into the murky depths of her past. She was lucky that the phone had been picked up by Bob Kolachik and not by Dan himself.

In this small thing, Fate had smiled on her. She'd caught a break by not reaching Dan and she needed to use the next twelve hours to get her head on straight again. No more weak thoughts of calling Dan. She was sure that sometime soon she'd come up with a much better plan for keeping herself out of jail than contacting the man who had broken her heart and not even bothered to hand her back the pieces.

CHAPTER FOUR

AMY STILL WASN'T SURE how in the world she'd ended up at the offices of Redmond and Kolachik, attorneys at law. She'd been telling herself that she wouldn't approach Dan right up to the moment when she parked her car in the crowded lot outside his office. And yet, here she was.

"How may I help you?" The receptionist was in her late fifties, well-groomed and attractive. She had the competent appearance of a woman who had been keeping hotshot young lawyers in line for at least a couple of decades. Like the offices themselves, her image was more upscale than Amy would have anticipated, given that Dan had always disdained the idea of using his law degree to make a profit.

Amy had pointed out that people without money had no power, and that he would be able to help the underdogs of the world much more effectively if he succeeded in climbing to the upper reaches of the legal hierarchy. Dan had countered that she always confused lack of material goods with poverty, and that it was possible to be rich in moral authority even if you didn't have money.

Their conversations had started out as abstract discussions but rapidly degenerated into highly personal arguments about their future together, until one night they found themselves in the midst of the hideous screaming match that ended their engagement.

"Miss? Can I help you?" The receptionist repeated her question. "Who have you come to see?"

Amy responded with an apologetic smile. "Sorry, I was distracted for a moment. My name's Amy Duran and I'm here to see Dan…Mr. Redmond."

The receptionist ran a neatly manicured pink nail over the entries in a calendar on her desk. "Do you have an appointment? I don't see any notation here."

"No, there wasn't time to make an appointment. Actually, my situation is…it's…kind of an emergency. Something cropped up over the weekend and I need legal advice right away."

The receptionist looked at her consideringly. "You do know that our firm only deals in criminal cases?"

"Yes." Amy made no attempt to explain why she needed the help of a criminal defense lawyer. She'd been in the business world long enough to know that sometimes silence was the very best answer.

The receptionist shook her head, sympathetic but firm. "I'm sorry, but Mr. Redmond can't possibly see you today. His schedule is jam-packed this morning and he has court this afternoon and tomorrow, as well. It might be possible for him to fit you in on Wednesday—"

"Unfortunately, I need to see him today. Right now, in fact." Amy swallowed her pride, an action that was as hard for her as swallowing a lump of rancid food. At this point, she was desperate, and if she needed to beg, so be it.

"I'm in really urgent need of legal advice," she said, allowing a trace of the panic she felt to creep into her voice. "If you tell Dan

I'm here, I think he'll agree to see me. We're…old friends. I've known him since I was thirteen."

The receptionist gave Amy yet another considering look, then pressed a speed-dial button on her phone. "There's a Ms. Amy Duran waiting in the reception area," she said. Impressively, she remembered the name without asking Amy to repeat it. "She wants to see you this morning, as soon as possible."

The receptionist paused for a moment, listening. "She says she has a legal emergency. I have told her that you handle only criminal cases."

The receptionist listened again, then hung up the phone. This time, the look she directed at Amy was openly curious. "Mr. Redmond says he would be happy to see you. He'll be with you in ten minutes. If you'd like to take a seat over there by the window, we have plenty of magazines to help pass the time. Could I get you a cup of coffee while you're waiting?"

"No, no, thank you." Amy was still wired from the quantity of caffeine she'd ingested yesterday. Or maybe it wasn't only excess caffeine creating the sensation that at any moment she might explode out of her skin. She'd been an emotional basket case for at least two years after she broke up with Dan, and this meeting was forcing old wounds to open wide. Still, perhaps it was a good thing she was obsessing about the humiliation of being forced to plead with Dan for his help. At least that prevented her from obsessing about Glen Maitland and the possibility that this time next week she'd be viewing the world through the bars of a jail cell window.

Aware that the receptionist's gaze was still fixed firmly on her back, Amy attempted to walk casually over to the chairs grouped by the window. Of course, the harder she tried to appear nonchalant, the more she felt like a malfunctioning robot. She plopped into the first seat she came to and grabbed a magazine from the top of the pile. The print danced in front of her eyes, and she stared at the page with blind incomprehension. Nevertheless, she kept her gaze glued to the magazine as if she found the articles fascinating. At least pretending to read provided an excuse not to look at the receptionist.

How was she going to cope with meeting Dan again? That was the burning question. She would be polite but cool, Amy decided, just as if she hadn't made the same decision a dozen times in the past few hours. She would present the image of a sophisticated career woman who had left behind all the uncertainties and gaucheness of the naïve young girl he'd known. She would be friendly, but slightly distant, so that Dan would realize at once how far she'd traveled since their parting. He would be impressed by her elegance and…

"Hello, Amy."

Oh, my God, Dan.

She jumped to her feet at the sound of his voice, heart thudding in double time. The magazine fell to the tiled floor with a noisy splat. She hurriedly bent to pick it up and saw that she'd been reading *Curve,* which claimed in a banner headline to be the nation's bestselling journal for lesbians. Good grief, she didn't want Dan to think she'd traveled that far!

She dropped the magazine back onto the table and straightened to find that Dan was now positioned a mere few inches away from her. He wore a dark suit, crisp white shirt and a gray silk tie. She could never remember seeing him in an actual suit before. Khakis and a blazer had been as formal as he got. He looked achingly familiar and utterly alien, the man who was her soul mate and a man she didn't know. She shivered, her skin sparking as if she'd been jolted by an electric charge.

Her skin might be twitching, but her facial muscles felt frozen. Amy did her best to twist her mouth into something that might, with luck, resemble a carefree smile. She didn't offer to shake his hand, which reminded her that he hadn't offered, either. No time to analyze what that might mean.

"Well, hello yourself. How are you, Dan?" For somebody aiming at casual and sophisticated, she wasn't doing too well. Her voice cracked in midgreeting and she could feel the heat rushing into her cheeks, no doubt leaving them bright red. In other words, she must be presenting an image about as sophisticated as SpongeBob SquarePants.

Dan had always been good-looking, with an eye-catching Black Irish combination of bright blue eyes and dark hair, but the past six years had changed him from merely handsome into devastatingly charismatic. A rush of erotic memories washed over her, followed by a totally unexpected wave of new desire. It was so long since she'd experienced honest-to-God sexual need that for a moment she couldn't quite place what the strange sensation in the pit of her stomach actually was.

"I'm well, thanks. It's good to see you, Amy." Dan's voice was polite, but so devoid of enthusiasm that he might just as well have said *the temperature this afternoon is forecast to reach a high of eighty degrees.*

"It's good to see you, too." Amy's cheeks were in danger of cracking, her smile was so forced. "It's been a long time."

She almost groaned out loud at the banality of her remarks. She'd had eighteen hours to plan this meeting and she couldn't come up with a more interesting line than that?

"Yes, it has been a while." Dan's response contained no hint of regret for their separation, let alone any indication that he was interested in revisiting the past. On the contrary, he immediately switched the subject to the business at hand. "It must be something important to bring you here?"

"I'm in pressing need of some legal advice." Before Amy could say anything more, a young and attractive woman came rushing into the reception area, the businesslike impact of her tailored shirt countered by the fact that her tight black skirt ended about ten inches above her knees.

"Excuse me," she said with a perfunctory nod in Amy's direction. "Dan, any chance you could come right now and make a phone call? I've spoken with Professor Fineman at UCLA, and he's agreed to testify in the Andromeda case. But he wants you to call him back immediately."

"I'm glad he's agreed to testify. You must have been very persuasive." Dan rewarded the newcomer with a slight smile. "Could you let him know that I'll call him back before lunch?"

"Fineman was really hoping to speak to you now—"

Dan shook his head. "Not possible, I'm afraid."

The woman grimaced. "You know how full of his own importance the professor is. He might renege…."

Dan shook his head. "Not likely. I saved his ass on the Bullen case, and he owes me. By the way, Chris, this is an old friend of mine, Amy Duran. Amy, this is Christine Diaz, my paralegal assistant and general lifesaver."

"It's nice to meet you, Amy." Christine's greeting was polite, but mechanical. Clearly, when her boss was around, she had eyes for nobody else. "Dan, remember you have that ten-thirty conference call scheduled and you simply can't miss it—"

"I've remembered. I'll rely on you to keep everyone out of my office for the next half hour so that Amy and I can finish up before the ten-thirty deadline." This time Dan sent his assistant one of his full-blown, killer smiles.

Amy's breath caught in her throat. She'd thought she remembered the potency of Dan's smiles when he chose to turn up the heat. She'd underestimated by a factor of at least ten.

Chris almost visibly melted. "I'll see what I can do. You know what Mondays are like, though."

"Yeah." Dan grinned. "Almost as bad as Fridays." He glanced toward the receptionist, raising his voice slightly. "Linda, can you direct any incoming calls to Chris, please? And if they insist on speaking to me personally, let them know it will be late this evening before I'm available to return any phone calls."

"Yes, I'll make sure you're not interrupted." The receptionist wrote herself a brief note and Chris dashed away, presumably to placate Professor Fineman.

If Dan had set out to provide an objective lesson in how valuable his time was and how fortunate she was to be getting half an hour of his undivided attention, he couldn't have done a better job, Amy reflected ruefully.

"Let's go to my office, shall we?" Dan gestured to indicate that she should follow him through a heavy paneled door that led from the reception area into a carpeted corridor lined with shelves of law books.

His office was at the end of the short hallway. The windows, screened by expensive metallic mesh blinds, looked out over nothing more exciting than the parking lot, but the carpet was thick plush, the giclée prints on the walls were signed, and the desk was glossy dark cherry. The décor was definitely fancy enough to re-assure nervous clients that they were in the presence of a lawyer who won most of his cases. Amy tried not to feel intimidated by the trappings of such evident success.

Dan sat down and gestured to the chair facing his desk. "How can I help you, Amy? Linda told you that I only handle criminal cases, I believe. If you have any other sort of legal problem, I'll be happy to recommend someone who works in the area you need."

"I definitely need a criminal lawyer." Amy's words ground to a halt. She was silenced by the shameful need to admit that she was on the verge of being arrested for stealing fifty thousand dollars from her employer. She hadn't realized how disorienting it would be to sit face-to-face with the man she had once known more intimately than anyone else on the planet and now knew hardly at all. She wished she understood how the idealistic Dan of six years ago had been transformed into this hard-driving, commercially successful criminal lawyer.

"I was surprised to discover that you're working in private practice," she said, the need to know overcoming her reluctance to refer to the subject that had ended their relationship. "I assumed you would still be working in the public defender's office."

"I left the public defender's office almost five years ago." The hesitation before Dan replied was so slight that anybody else might not have noticed it. "Bob Kolachik was a couple of years ahead of me in law school, but we knew each other quite well. He'd already established a successful criminal defense practice and he asked me to join him. I leaped at the chance."

On the surface, Dan seemed to have answered her question, but he was too smart not to realize his response actually did nothing to explain why he had abandoned his original goal. Amy wanted to inquire what had happened to his crusade for the disadvantaged and the oppressed, but she no longer had the right to question him about something so personal if he chose to be evasive. It also occurred to her, a bit on the late side, that he was now a sufficiently successful lawyer that she might not be able to afford his fees. That would certainly add a touch of irony, she reflected wryly.

"I don't want you to think that I've come looking for personal favors," she said quickly. "Naturally, I expect to pay your usual fees, whatever they are."

"Naturally." Dan's expression didn't change by the flicker of an eyelash. "If I take you on as a client, my time is billed at two hundred and fifty dollars an hour. We use our paralegal staff for as much of the research and routine work as possible. Paralegal time is charged at ninety dollars an hour. We request an up-front retainer from new clients. The amount of the retainer depends on the nature of the case."

If he could be all business, so could she. "I understand and I accept. If we decide to go forward, that is." Amy knew from bills for legal fees that had come across her desk at Maitland Homes that two hundred and fifty bucks an hour wasn't an outrageously high charge. And since she couldn't possibly pay back the fifty thousand, she might as well use what savings she had in an attempt to keep herself out of prison.

Dan leaned across the desk, his gaze meeting hers with an intimacy that had been lacking in their encounter so far. "You're still as lousy as ever at hiding what you're thinking," he said softly.

She refused to succumb to the warmth in his voice. "Most people complain that my expression is hard to read."

"Then most people must be blind. You want to know why I'm not working for the public defender's office anymore."

Despite her curiosity, Amy was almost tempted to lie, since that would keep a safe emotional distance between them, preventing the exchange of personal information on a topic that was at the heart of their past problems. Unfortunately, she couldn't bring herself to lie to Dan, even if she could have gotten away with it, which was highly doubtful.

"I did wonder," she admitted. "You were so determined to use your skills to help people who were disadvantaged by the system."

"You're right, I was determined." He shook his head, dismissing his former self with visible impatience. "I was also arrogant and hopelessly naïve, two characteristics that I've decided often go together. It didn't take me more than a few weeks to realize that working in the public defender's office was a complete waste of my time and professional training."

Amy couldn't help the bitter smile she gave him. "What, Dan? Don't tell me you discovered that if you're poor, you get shafted by the system—even if you have a noble public defender on your side?"

"That's exactly what I discovered," he said quietly. "You were right and I was wrong about what I could achieve. You told me that I couldn't help people unless I operated from a position of strength, and you were right. At the public defender's office, I had no power at all. I was carrying an annual workload in excess of five hundred cases—"

"Five hundred?" Amy was startled into interrupting. "You must mean the whole office, not you personally?"

"Unfortunately, I mean me. Alone. Every other lawyer working there carried similar loads. Do the math. I was representing two clients per day, five days a week, fifty-two weeks a year. I tried to even the odds by working ten-hour days, seven days a week. That barely bought me enough time to meet each of my clients once before negotiating a plea bargain with the prosecutor's office."

"What about the trials? Who took care of that?"

"Me, if they were my clients. Who else?" He laughed without mirth. "And that was the worst travesty of all. Most of the cases never got as far as a courtroom, of course, because if everybody who was accused of a crime demanded their right to a trial, the system would grind to a halt within a week. But if for some unexpected reason the case did go to trial, I quite likely found myself reading the discovery documents as I was walking along the corridor on the way into court."

"At least you tried. You gave each case your best shot. You did read the documents."

He grimaced. "More or less. It didn't take me long to realize that I wasn't making a difference for my clients, much less helping the cause of universal justice. On the contrary, I was participating in a charade that pretends poor people accused of crimes in this country actually get a fair shake from the legal system. They don't, and after two years, I wasn't willing to keep up the pretense anymore."

Dan sounded deeply angry, and she knew it was anger directed at himself, because of his failure to defeat the injustice of a system creaking along on the brink of implosion from the sheer weight of cases. "I expect you helped more people than you realized at the time," she said.

He shrugged. "I wish I could believe that, but you're giving me way too much credit. The best I can claim is that I managed to get a not-guilty verdict for a couple of men unjustly accused of murder. Two victories in two years isn't much cause for celebration."

"It is for the innocent men you helped free. For them, it was huge."

He smiled. "Yeah, I guess it was. Thanks for reminding me of that. Anyway, I haven't completely abandoned my old dreams. Bob and I have plenty of clients who can afford to pay for our services and we utilize half of our net profits to take on pro bono cases. It's not a perfect solution, but I guess part of growing up is learning to modify your dreams."

She had forgotten how brutally honest Dan was with himself. Unlike her, he never made excuses or tried to paint his actions in a better light than they deserved. She felt a surge of painful regret that they had ended their relationship over a dream that he had abandoned within months of their parting, but she could only admire him for admitting that he'd failed—to the very person who'd told him all along that his dream was impractical.

She smiled at him, her first genuine smile in two days. "It sounds to me as if you and your partner have worked out a great compromise. You've built a successful career, and several people each year get legal advice they otherwise couldn't afford. Surely that's much better than sticking to your original plan and ending up achieving nothing?"

AMY'S SMILE WAS AS magic as ever, Dan thought. Somehow—God knows how—he'd managed to forget in the past six years just how incredibly beautiful she was. The sight of her when he walked out into the reception area had literally taken his breath away, and having her seated three feet away wasn't helping to return his brain to anything approaching functional mode. When they were in college, he'd thought she must have the softest, most kissable lips in the entire world. Seeing her now, he was sure of it. He was having one hell of a time thinking about anything other than how much he wanted to kiss her.

Still, he had just enough active brain cells to know he wasn't about to do anything as flat-out stupid as getting involved with her again. He had no intention of exposing himself to another dose of the potent Amy Duran virus. His last bout had been damn near fatal, leaving him sick, wounded and barely functional for months. He could only hope that one potent attack of the disease had been enough to make him immune for life. But in case it hadn't, he would make damn sure that he didn't do anything from here on out that might lead him into temptation.

"I'm sorry to be abrupt," he said. "But I have a killer schedule for the next few days and we need to stay focused. How can I help you, Amy?"

He picked up his pen and pulled a clean legal pad in front of him—props to help him avoid looking at her. Too much time spent gazing into her smoky green eyes was a surefire way to end up with a fresh dose of Amy fever. It was astonishing how quickly his body was succumbing to all the old familiar yearnings. He'd read a scientific article only last week proclaiming that there were few things harder to rekindle than the passions of a once-hot love affair. Clearly, the authors of the article hadn't been studying the right sample of people.

Dan heard the shaky breath Amy drew in, but he still didn't permit himself to look up.

"I've been accused of stealing fifty thousand dollars from the company I work for." Her admission came out in a headlong rush.

His head jerked up, the reaction involuntary. "*You? Stealing?* Are they crazy?"

She stared at him in total silence. Suddenly her eyes weren't smoky anymore; they were emerald-bright. She quickly turned away, reaching into her purse for a tissue, but not before he saw tears spill out and trickle down her cheeks. In all the years they'd spent together, Dan could count the number of times he'd seen her cry on the fingers of one hand, and the impulse to comfort her was so strong that he had to grip the sides of his chair to prevent himself from walking around the desk and taking her into his arms. He ached to hold her close and stroke her hair until the tears ended. Instead, he gripped the studded arms of his fancy leather chair and willed himself not to move.

"Damn!" She found a tissue and scrubbed fiercely, leaving her cheeks flushed and the tip of her nose red. Perversely, he found her more beautiful than ever when her appearance wasn't quite so flawless.

"I'm not sure what I said to make you cry." He spoke lightly, giving her time to recover.

"It wasn't your fault. Not at all. I overreacted. I'm sorry, Dan. It's just that you're the first person who hasn't automatically assumed I'm guilty. Until I saw how astonished you were by the accusation, I hadn't realized how much it bothers me that people who are supposed to know me well apparently know nothing about me."

He scratched something meaningless onto his pad, just to distract himself from his continuing urge to comfort her. He reminded himself that this meeting needed to be kept as impersonal and professional as possible, for both their sakes.

"I'm sorry you've been disappointed in your friends," he said. Jeez, he sounded like a pompous ass, Dan thought ruefully. Hell, he *felt* like a pompous ass. He saw that he'd written Amy's name on the pad in front of him and was in the process of doodling a heart around it. Good God, he hoped she hadn't seen that piece of insanity! He quickly crumpled the page and threw it into the wastebasket.

"Okay, if we're going to get these accusations put to rest, I need information," he said crisply. "Lots of it."

Yeah, that sounded better. Brisk and efficient. Dan leaned back in his chair, genuinely focused on the problem for the first time since the moment when Linda told him Amy was waiting in reception. He'd almost run out of his office to see her. Then he'd forced himself to sit down and wait ten minutes in the pathetic hope that he might actually be able to present the appearance of a man whose heart wasn't thumping with the force of a jungle drum and whose tongue wasn't almost hanging out with eagerness. Fat chance.

"Tell me where you work, what your position is, and why you're the person who's been accused of stealing the money," he said. "Give me details. Lots of them."

Amy had a neat, orderly mind, and even though it was clearly painful for her to discuss what had happened, she was able to give him a clear account of Saturday night's events and her boss's accusations. Glen Maitland, Dan decided, was not only an asshole, he was an outsize idiot. If the man had worked with Amy for three years and still didn't recognize that she was incapable of stealing, then the guy didn't have the judgment to be the CEO of a lemonade stand, let alone a company that built three hundred million dollars' worth of homes each year. As for Brian, the boss's nitwitted son and apparently Amy's sometime lover…Dan would derive significant pleasure from giving the guy a swift kick in the balls at the first available opportunity.

"I have one comment and one question," he said. "First, the comment. It's obviously important for us to get the details of Tony Kresge's investigation from Glen Maitland. I'll work on some legal stratagem that might work for that. And second, the question. Who do you think really stole the money?"

Amy looked at him blankly for a moment, and then she laughed. A brief laugh, but genuine nevertheless. "A very good question, and I haven't a clue about the answer. Now you see why I need your help. I've spent every waking minute for the past thirty-six hours agonizing about what I should do, and how this could possibly have happened to me. In all that time it never once occurred to me to concentrate on identifying the thief who really stole the money."

The intercom on Dan's desk buzzed. He snatched up the phone. "Yes?"

"It's ten-thirty," Chris told him. "And you know Judge Collins hates to be kept waiting."

"Place the call, and get everyone on the line. I'll pick up in two minutes—"

"He'll be furious if you keep him hanging."

"I won't, I promise." Dan put the phone back in its cradle. "Amy, I'm sorry, but I can't put off this conference call any longer, and the rest of my day is jam-packed—"

"No, I understand. I'm grateful for the time you've already given me—"

"Meet me for dinner tonight, will you? We both have to eat, and that will give us time to decide on the best strategy for compelling Glen Maitland to turn over the documents we need. He paid for the investigation, so legally they're his property and getting our hands on them is by no means a slam dunk. Also, give some serious thought as to who the real culprit is and why they chose to use your password and your computer. Was it happenstance? Or is somebody angry enough with you that they deliberately tried to set you up?"

"It must be sheer chance—"

"Perhaps. But think about it some more before you come to that conclusion. Anyway, there's a pretty decent restaurant a couple of blocks from here on Magnolia Street, The Manor House. Can you be there at eight?"

Dan was cursed with far too much insight into his own motives, and he knew damn well that he was giving Amy special treatment. With any other client, he might have suggested meeting at eight if that was his earliest free moment—but he'd have located the meeting in the office, and he'd have eaten a sandwich first.

Amy hesitated, probably because she was smart enough to realize that having dinner with him was a seriously bad idea. He didn't want to give her the chance to refuse—what was that about not getting involved with Amy again in this lifetime?—so he got up and escorted her to the door, his manner implying that their dinner date was a done deal.

She paused in the doorway, catching him off guard when she turned to look up at him. "Thank you," she said. "For the first time since Glen Maitland sprang all this on me, I actually feel there's a chance I might not end up on the wrong side of the jailhouse door."

"Don't worry," he said. "I'll take care of everything."

By some great stroke of good fortune, she didn't tell him to stop sounding like a conceited dick. "Thank you," she said again, her smile a little wobbly around the edges. "You've no idea what a relief it is to have your help."

Dan, who normally prided himself on his ruthless self-awareness, decided he had too many other things going on right now to dwell on just how happy he felt. The phone buzzed, Chris's signal for urgent. At least the need to confer with Judge Collins provided justification for his claim to be too busy to waste time wondering why his pulse raced simply because tonight he would be seeing Amy.

Just the two of them; just like old times. Except there was no way in hell that they would end up in bed together as they always had in the past. He would make sure of it. He was way too smart to deliberately self-destruct.

Snatching up the phone, Dan forced his attention back to Judge Collins and the Garcia case, grateful for the lifeline to sanity.

CHAPTER
FIVE

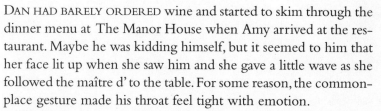

Dan had barely ordered wine and started to skim through the dinner menu at The Manor House when Amy arrived at the restaurant. Maybe he was kidding himself, but it seemed to him that her face lit up when she saw him and she gave a little wave as she followed the maître d' to the table. For some reason, the commonplace gesture made his throat feel tight with emotion.

She looked even more stunning than earlier in the day. She was wearing silk slacks and a cropped jacket in a muted shade of green that, to his untutored male eye, seemed to impart a creamy glow to her complexion. Instead of pulling her hair back into a tight knot as she had this morning, she'd styled it in a loose twist, reminding him of the days when they'd been lovers and how erotic he'd found it to pull the combs out of her hair so that her curls tumbled in a heavy auburn cascade over the pillows.

He knew that she had no clue how sexy men found the wispy fronds that tended to escape and cluster around her face whatever hairstyle she chose, but he wasn't surprised to observe that every pair of male eyes in the room turned toward her as she walked by. He experienced a juvenile burst of pride until he reminded himself that he had no right to any such feelings. This was a business meeting, and Amy was his client. At most, this reconnection was a chance to establish a downsized version of a relationship once vitally important to both of them.

He rose politely to his feet when she reached the table. The more he could keep up the pretence of professional formality between the two of them, the safer he would be from making a total horse's ass of himself.

Amy murmured her thanks to the maître d' as the man slid out her chair and handed her a leather-bound menu. "I'm sorry if I kept you waiting," she said as soon as the maître d' left. "There was an accident on the freeway."

Her voice mirrored his own carefully polite attitude to an uncanny degree, which suggested that perhaps she didn't feel any more at ease than he did, despite her superficially composed appearance. That insight cheered him.

"You're not late," Dan said, closing his menu. "I was a couple of minutes early."

It took a while before he realized he was gazing deep into her eyes and that his last coherent thought had occurred several silent seconds ago. So much for keeping up the façade of professionalism, he reflected ruefully. He gave a slight shake of his head, hopefully restoring brain function, and opened the menu again. Maybe he should stop working so hard at maintaining his cool. Maybe he should just relax and act normally.

Relax around Amy Duran. Now there was a radical concept.

"The linguine with clam sauce is very good here," he said. "And also the broiled New Zealand lamb chops with purple Peruvian potatoes." He had an embarrassing suspicion he sounded like a particularly annoying waiter touting the day's specials.

"I'm not sure I'm up for purple potatoes," she said, setting the menu aside with a slight smile. "I'll have the linguine. It's always one of my favorites."

In the old days, she would have spent twenty minutes discussing the pros and cons of every entrée with him. But then, in the old days, they wouldn't have eaten at a fancy restaurant more than once a year, so their selections would have been worth lingering over.

Better to get straight to business, Dan decided, not happy with the way his thoughts kept backtracking relentlessly down memory lane. It was one thing to aim for relaxed, another to tap-dance on the edge of quicksand.

"Did you have any success in identifying the real thief?" he asked briskly, offering her the basket of bread. He helped himself to a crusty roll dusted with sesame seeds when she refused. He'd forgotten to eat lunch again, he realized.

"Not much." She wrinkled her nose, a once-familiar gesture indicative of frustration. "In some ways, it would be easy for any of the managers to put the blame on me, but in other ways it would be very difficult. My password and the bank access codes are the major sticking points. I've racked my brains all afternoon, and I still don't understand how anybody could have discovered those."

"Do you change your password often?"

She gave a guilty shake of her head. "Not as often as I should. The last time was right around my birthday."

"June 14," he said automatically. "All the thefts have occurred since then, haven't they?"

"The first was on July 6, according to Glen."

He nodded. "So the thief only needed to ferret out your password once and he or she was good to go."

"True. But how did the thief discover it even that one time? I don't have it written down anywhere."

He pulled a face. "Nowhere at all?"

"Nowhere," she confirmed. "I pick something I'm not going to forget so that I don't need a written reminder. This last time I happened to be reading a biography of Ronald Reagan, so I picked Ronald40, because he was the fortieth president. How could anyone possibly guess that? And my password isn't even the most difficult thing for the thief to acquire. He or she would need the bank account access codes, too, and Glen changes those on the first of every month."

"Do you record those anywhere?"

"Not on paper. It's a ten-digit code, so I keep a record in my Palm Pilot, disguised as a phone number."

"A ten-digit code isn't something you can guess at," Dan commented, silently agreeing with Amy that it was damn difficult to imagine how anyone had acquired the information they needed to fake her identity. "There are millions of possible combinations."

Amy looked miserable. "Even if the thief had some whiz-bang piece of technology to attach to my computer, surely it would take hours to crunch through all the combinations and hit on the correct number."

"I'm no expert, but I would think so," Dan acknowledged. "What about Glen? Where does he keep his record?"

"Same as me, in his Palm Pilot. But nobody has access to Glen's office, let alone to his Palm Pilot. Glen and I are both pretty obsessive about keeping our PDAs right next to us." Amy swirled ice in her glass, the gesture disconsolate. "The truth is, Glen has some justification for suspecting me. It isn't as if he leaped to a totally unreasonable conclusion."

"Except for the minor fact that he ought to have known you're incapable of stealing."

She flashed him a glance replete with gratitude, but the wine waiter arrived at that moment with the bottle of Russian River chardonnay Dan had ordered earlier and she had no chance to say anything. Dan went through the ritual of tasting and approving and gestured for the waiter to pour a glass for Amy. She accepted with a smile, but made no reference to the fact that this was the wine they'd drunk the night he asked her to marry him. Maybe that was because she'd forgotten, Dan thought wryly. Or maybe she was just a whole heap better than he was at walking away from the past.

He smothered a frustrated sigh. What the hell did he want from her, anyway? He ought to be grateful that at least one of them seemed aware of the dangers of walking on the edge of a precipice. They gave their dinner orders to the waiter and Dan turned back to the issue that was supposed to be uppermost in his mind.

"Okay, if you can't guess how anybody discovered your password and the bank access codes, let's switch away from that problem for a moment. Have you thought of anyone at the office who has a grudge against you?"

"Yes, there is someone," she said. "Marilyn Milanov, who's in charge of payroll. She was passed over for a promotion last year and I was given the job. She had almost three years' seniority over me and she was angry enough to threaten to resign."

Dan mentally filed the name. "Since she works in accounting, she's a good candidate. She would know the subcontractor bank account exists, and would have a general idea how to access it and make a transfer."

"Yes, that was my reasoning, too. Except that I'd stake my life on the fact that Marilyn is totally honest. She's also happily married to one of the regional managers for Safeway, and I can't think of a single reason why she'd be so desperate for cash that she'd resort to stealing. Plus, she doesn't have enough imagination to invent a scheme that pinned the blame on me. Lack of creativity is precisely the reason she's finding it so hard to take the next step up the career ladder."

Kids with bad-tempered foster parents like the Smiths couldn't afford the luxury of misunderstanding other people's moods, so learning to predict likely behavior had been a necessary survival skill for both of them. Dan figured that if Amy didn't suspect Marilyn, then he wouldn't waste too much time suspecting her, either.

"Anyone else who dislikes you? Maybe somebody smart enough to keep their dislike hidden?"

"Nobody I can identify, although I guess that's the problem. I'm not supposed to suspect this person, am I?" Amy made a frustrated gesture. "One of the reasons I enjoyed working at Maitland Homes was because it's such a friendly environment. People there tend to enjoy each other's company. I'm not aware of any tense undercurrents, not even with Marilyn. She expressed her disappointment over the promotion and that was that. We weren't about to get together for lunch or a movie after work, but if she'd been really mad, surely she'd have left?"

"You'd be surprised. What seems rational to you and me doesn't always seem that way to a criminal."

The word *criminal* caused her to look momentarily stricken. "That's what Glen and Brian think about me, isn't it? That I'm a criminal."

"Yes." No point in sugarcoating the truth, but he wasn't about to let her wallow in self-pity. "And it's our job to prove them wrong. If we can't pin down the thief's motive for setting you up, let's move on to means and opportunity. Who could have accessed your computer?"

"Almost anyone, unfortunately." She shook away her momentary blues. "All the managers are in and out of each other's offices several times a day, and we usually leave our computers up and running. Plus I routinely meet subcontractors and clients in one of the conference rooms. That would open up plenty of occasions for somebody to use my computer."

"But the thief would be running a risk, because he or she could never be sure when you might return," Dan suggested.

"Not much of a risk. It would be fairly easy to dream up an excuse for being in my office. The person could bring me a site plan, or blueprints, or any one of a dozen different administrative forms. In a construction company, there's always something that has to be signed or approved, and everyone knows that I sign off on a lot of routine stuff for Glen Maitland."

"So the bottom line is that any of the managers could have found occasions to sit in front of your computer and pretend to be you."

Amy gave a frustrated grimace. "That about sums it up. It's the reverse of the problem with my password and bank codes. This time there are too many suspects instead of too few."

He needn't have worried about this meeting becoming too personal or too nostalgic, Dan reflected wryly. So far, they hadn't exchanged a single word that couldn't have been overheard by any and every member of his office staff.

"Okay, enough negativity." He leaned across the table, forcing Amy to meet his gaze. "You need to stop listing all the reasons why nobody could have acquired your password or the bank account access code. Here's the fact: somebody acquired both of them. Start from there. Somebody did this to you. How did they do it? *Who* did it?"

"I already told you: I haven't a clue—"

"Wrong answer!" He glared at her. "Tell me how somebody could have acquired your password."

"They couldn't." Amy glared right back. "I don't have my password written down anywhere, so the only way the thief could have acquired it is by reading my mind." She gave a mock start of surprise. "Oh, of course! Why didn't I think of that before? The thief is telepathic! Gee, he should be real easy to find. Maybe there's a little antenna growing out of his or her forehead—"

Her sarcasm snapped Dan's brain into action. "We're making this too complicated. How about if the thief stood behind you on at least one occasion while you keyed in your password? All the person has to do is watch you type and—voilà. He's found out your password, which you were then obliging enough not to change for almost two months."

Amy opened her mouth to retort and abruptly closed it again.

She drew in a short, quick breath. "I don't remember anyone peering over my shoulder." But for the first time, he heard doubt in her voice.

"You weren't supposed to remember. I'm guessing the thief asked you to pull up some information, something that he or she knew was confidential. Sales figures, perhaps, or the bids from subcontractors. That would require you to key in your password to access the necessary data. It's such a routine request that there's no reason for you to remember the occasion or the person. Is that a possible scenario?"

She nodded, visibly reining in a burst of excitement. "Yes, it's possible. It could have happened that way. I was responsible for keeping most of the confidential records." Relief flooded her expression, then quickly shut off. "But that still doesn't explain how the thief discovered the bank access codes."

They finally seemed to be getting somewhere, thank God. "Remember Sherlock Holmes?" Dan said. "He told Watson that once you rule out every impossible solution to a problem, what you're left with—however unlikely—must be the answer. That's the case here for us. The only place you and Glen had records of the bank codes is in your Palm Pilots. Therefore the only possible explanation of how the thief acquired the codes is that he or she found a way to access either your Palm Pilot or Glen's."

As he was speaking, the waiter arrived with their meals, and by silent agreement they broke off their discussion of the case and took a few minutes to enjoy the excellent food. Dan had ordered sea bass, and it arrived arranged on a bed of saffron rice, topped with curls of shaved vegetables. Amy commented with a laugh that his meal looked too pretty to eat.

The sound of her laughter warmed Dan's heart. This time he didn't try to analyze his reaction, or to deny it. As he watched her wind linguine around her fork, his happiness faded into an overwhelming sensation of regret for the years they'd been apart.

"I'm glad you came to see me this morning," he said quietly, needing for once to speak the truth.

She looked up and met his gaze, her cheeks turning faintly pink. "I'm glad I came, too. Thank you for helping me, Dan. Most of all, thank you for believing in me. For knowing without a quiver of doubt that I'm not a thief."

"How did we screw up so badly?" The question jumped out from the dark recesses of his subconscious. "We were so much in love. What the hell happened to us, Amy? I've never understood."

"I'm...not sure. Could it have been as simple as the fact that we were too young? We could manage the sex, the passion and even the falling in love part, but not all the more difficult stuff that makes up a day-to-day adult relationship."

"Is that all?" Dan shook his head. "It seems to me it was something more."

"We were too young...and we'd been too badly hurt by our parents," she said after a brief hesitation. "We'd been betrayed by the people who should have been our first line of defense against the world. Then we were betrayed all over again by the system that was supposed to take care of us. In the end, I guess I needed to protect myself even more than I wanted to love you. I already had too many scars, and I was too frightened to take a chance." She put down her fork, abandoning the pretense that she was eating. "You were braver than I was, Dan. You always have been."

"No." He finally admitted the truth, to himself as well as to Amy. "I wasn't brave at all."

She gave a slight smile. "In that case, you had a brilliantly effective façade."

"I sure worked hard at it. I was able to fake bravery pretty well, especially around you, but only if I didn't look too deeply into myself. I wasn't willing to face the fact that I'd been almost mortally wounded, first by my parents and then by the Smiths. I figured that if I had you to lean on, I could make it through life, blazing a trail of justice, and that would somehow compensate for everything that we'd both missed out on when we were little kids."

"We had more to deal with than a lot of other kids while we were growing up," Amy said, "but in a way, we owe the Smiths. They didn't love us, they had terrible tempers, and they should never have been approved as foster parents. But despite everything they did wrong, they did impress on us that the one way we could get ahead was through education. Remember how Mrs. Smith would drive us to the library each Saturday morning? It was the only activity she did with us. And Mr. Smith always asked us if we'd done our homework first thing when he arrived home from work—"

"Yeah, and beat the crap out of us if we hadn't done it to his satisfaction." Dan grimaced. "I'm not quite ready to forgive the Smiths, even if my original motivation for going to law school was revenge. I had some crazy idea of suing the pants off them for abuse and neglect when I finally graduated."

"You never told me that."

"I assumed you'd tell me it was a waste of time and mental energy. That the Smiths weren't worth my attention. By the time I passed the bar exam, I realized you'd have been right."

Her smile contained a hint of pain. "You're giving me too much credit. I'd have been standing right beside you, urging you to throw the statute book at them. I hated the Smiths for years. I guess I finally realized that hating them gave them too much power."

He was thoughtful a moment, then took a sip of wine. "Maybe you're right. Perhaps our relationship exploded simply because we were too young and too inexperienced to cope. Not inexperienced in the usual sense of the word, but we'd had too many of the wrong experiences and not enough of the right ones."

"But we had each other," Amy said. "We gave each other hope."

"The truth is, you rescued me," Dan said. "I was about to give up when you came to live with the Smiths. Without you, I'd never have made it through high school. I'd have rebelled and ended up in jail, just to prove that I didn't give a damn. I knew that even as a kid. I recognize it even more strongly now."

"We rescued each other," she said. "I wouldn't have survived the Smiths without you."

"Then how the hell did we lose each other?"

Amy looked at him, her gaze tainted with regret. "I think that's how we started this whole conversation. Maybe the only true answer is to admit that we were both idiots and leave it at that."

"Works for me." He reached across the table, laying his hand over hers. Her skin felt smooth and warm beneath his fingertips. "We can take this as slow as you want, and maybe we'll still end up apart. But we don't have to be idiots the second time around, do we?"

Amy turned her hand palm upward, her fingers closing around his. "No, we absolutely don't."

Dan felt a rush of desire so intense his skin burned with the heat of it. He lifted Amy's hand and kissed her palm, his gaze locked with hers. The hazy desire in her eyes reflected his own, and he wasn't sure whether to feel frustrated as hell that they were nowhere near a room with a bed and a door, or relieved that he was going to have to exercise some self-control and give them both some breathing room.

For good or ill, their waiter chose that moment to return. "I hope your dinners are to your satisfaction?" His voice rose in a question as he surveyed their still-brimming plates.

"Everything's delicious," Amy said. "Thank you."

"We're just catching up on old times," Dan told him. "Too busy talking to eat."

"Sorry to have disturbed you." The waiter tactfully backed off.

The intimacy of the previous few minutes was broken, but Dan sensed a change of mood in Amy as well as in himself. They'd let down their defenses, and he suspected they'd both been surprised by how much they still cared for each other.

"Tell me what you've been doing for the past six years," he said.

"And what are your plans now that Glen Maitland has been dumb enough to lose you?"

"I was doing temp work after we split up, and got sent to a small company that was trying to build affordable housing—apartments that were designed to be rented out and stand up to hard usage from kids and busy families."

"It's hard for companies to make a profit on low-cost housing in this real estate market," Dan commented.

Amy nodded. "Very hard. The company I worked for actually needed subsidies from local government to make ends meet. They hired me on as a permanent employee when they got a grant from the county, and I had a great time until their federal funding was pulled and they went belly-up. That's when I took a job at Maitland Homes."

"That must have been a contrast! Glen Maitland caters to a different segment of the real estate market."

"It seemed a smart move at the time and I learned a lot about the building trade." She shrugged. "Now I realize how much I missed the pleasure of seeing an immigrant family take possession of the tiny house they'd always dreamed of owning. I guess I'd like to get back to that. I was really impressed with the Dress for Success organization and the people working for it when I organized the fundraiser. In between obsessing about my own problems, I've found myself wondering if there might be some way to take the skills I've learned working for Glen Maitland and utilize them in a company dedicated to building low-cost housing. Wouldn't it be great if the women using the services of Dress for Success also had access to an organization set up to help them find safe, affordable housing?"

"If you could pull that off, you'd be filling an almost desperate need for a lot of people," Dan said. "And you're right about the skills you've learned with Maitland Homes being useful. Bottom line, if you could help some company to design and build decent, cheap housing that also made a slight profit for the builder, you'd be the toast of L.A."

"And a lot of other cities, too. It's a challenge all over the country." Amy finally took another bite of her linguine. "Anyway, it's a goal I'd like to aim for even if I can't make it happen right away."

"I'd much prefer to talk about your plans, but I suppose we've got to get back to discussing this crazy accusation your boss threw at you," Dan said, not bothering to conceal a sigh. "It's annoying that we have to waste so much time on something so bogus."

Right now, what he really wanted to do was find out if Amy liked the latest Nelson DeMille thriller, and what she'd thought about *Ocean's Twelve,* since Brad Pitt had once been her favorite movie star. He needed to know if her favorite late-night snack was still a peanut butter and strawberry jam sandwich. He wanted to tell her that he'd found his father, and that after he'd gotten through yelling at him for taking off and never looking back, he'd even kind of liked the guy.

Amy echoed his sigh. "Yes, I guess we do. We'd actually made some headway before our food arrived."

"Then let's work fast. My goal is to wrap this up before dessert."

"Right." She rolled her eyes. "I vote in favor of that."

"Then let's get started. According to Glen Maitland, one theft occurred on the last Sunday in July, when you were the only person signed into the office. Does that narrow the field of suspects at all?" he asked.

"You'd think it would, but Maitland Homes builds houses, not nuclear submarines, so our security is pretty minimal. I don't think it would be too difficult to bypass security."

"Even on a weekend when you're required to sign in?"

"Even on a weekend. If I were a thief, and I'd set my mind to stealing money and incriminating one of my colleagues, I'd plan in advance and might duplicate a master key to the office. Or I'd find some way to get in through a fire door or the back service entrance. Or I'd come in with a cleaning crew, if the timing was right. It would take some ingenuity, but it would be nowhere near as difficult as getting hold of my password and the bank access codes."

Instead of being depressed by Amy's comments, Dan had a sudden inspiration. His desire to get out of here and be alone with Amy seemed to be pushing his analytic power to a higher level. "How many people knew you would be working that particular Sunday? It's an important question, because if you were the designated fall guy, the thief needed to know for sure you would be there. He or she couldn't risk you coming up with an unbreakable alibi. How could the thief know that you wouldn't be spending the entire weekend out of town, for example? Or singing in the church choir at the precise time the transaction was made? In fact, when you really analyze it, impersonating you on a Sunday was a very risky proposition unless the thief could be a hundred percent sure you'd be signed in at the office."

He sensed a sudden stillness in Amy, a withdrawal into her own thoughts, and he had to prompt her before she replied. "I only knew I would be going into the office at the last moment," she said finally. "We were way behind on two important projects. I tried working on them at home, but there were site plans I needed to refer to and they were in the office. So I came in and worked for a couple of hours…" Her voice trailed away.

"What is it?" Dan asked. "What aren't you telling me, Amy?"

"Nothing—"

"No, don't lie. Anything but that."

She let out a tight breath. "Okay. The truth is I had a date with Brian for that Sunday night. I called to let him know I'd be going into the office for a couple of hours." Her voice was painfully flat. "He was the only person who knew."

The son of a bitch had set her up. "Brian?" Dan queried, as if he didn't recollect perfectly well who Brian was. "Remind me who Brian is?"

"Brian is Glen Maitland's son. Remember, I told you he's the director of sales."

Dan pulled a face, wanting to do something—anything—to chase away the misery of betrayal he could read in Amy's expression. "Oh, yes! Now I remember. He's the prince of a guy who escorted you to the fund-raiser on Saturday night and then dumped you miles from home, with no transportation."

Amy winced, as if she were the person who'd behaved badly. "His father told him not to—"

"And he obeyed? I guess that makes him a wimp as well as a jerk. So explain to me how Brian got through security without signing in?"

"Brian is very outgoing," she said. "He's one of the few people in the building who probably knows all the security guards by name. And, of course, they all recognize him as the boss's son. I imagine he just waved at the guard on duty, exchanged some chit-chat and walked through."

"Did he have a chance to use your computer once he was inside?"

She didn't have to think about her answer. "No, absolutely not. Brian isn't the sort to hang around while other people finish up their work. He arrived at the office around six-thirty. I shut down my computer, and we left five minutes later. There's no way he had time or opportunity to transfer twenty thousand dollars to an offshore bank account before we left for dinner." She gave Dan a look that was almost pleading. "It's impossible for him to be the thief."

"I don't agree. Remember this was the second theft. He'd already worked out any kinks in his system, so he could presumably have been quite speedy making the transaction. Are you sure you didn't go to the restroom before you left?"

"No. I didn't even stop by the water cooler. I remember we were going to a movie before dinner, and we needed to hurry."

"Then Brian must have managed to get to the office before you arrived. In other words, the money had already been stolen by the time you signed in. How much time elapsed between the moment you called him and the time you arrived at the office?"

"About an hour."

"Where does Brian live? Would he have had enough time to get in and out of the office before you?"

Dan could tell from Amy's expression that the answer was yes. The son of a bitch had learned she would be in the office and immediately decided to take the opportunity to steal a few more thousand bucks. A kick in the balls didn't seem anywhere near adequate punishment.

"Brian lives about ten minutes away from the office," Amy said. "He would have had time to make the transaction. But he wouldn't do it, Dan. He couldn't deliberately choose to set me up—"

"Why not?"

"We were dating—"

"Yeah. I can see from the way he behaved Saturday night that he took his relationship with you real seriously." Dan didn't bother to hide his sarcasm. "And here's another reason to suspect Brian. Which employee of Maitland Homes would have the easiest time getting his hands on either Glen's Palm Pilot or yours?" He answered his own question. "Brian is the obvious candidate. You and Glen may keep your PDAs right by your side when you're in the office, but at home, I expect you leave them by the phone, or on the desk where you pay bills. Brian has access to both your houses. It would be a snap for him to get the information he needed."

Amy had turned pale as he spoke, but she still wasn't ready to acknowledge that the man she'd been dating—presumably the man who'd been her lover—could have betrayed her so viciously. "Brian can't be the thief," she protested. "For God's sake, Dan, why would Brian Maitland steal fifty thousand bucks from his own father's company? He sure as hell doesn't need the money—"

"How do you know?"

"Because he's Glen and Gloria Maitland's only son! The Maitlands are multimillionaires, and Brian is their sole heir. If he wants something—anything—he only has to ask."

"Are you sure? Suppose he wants something his parents disapprove of?"

She looked puzzled. "Such as what?"

He shrugged. "Drugs would be an obvious example."

"No," she said flatly. "Brian doesn't have a drug problem and he drinks in moderation. You know I wouldn't have gone out with him if he'd shown the slightest sign of having a problem with addiction."

With an alcoholic father and drug-addicted mother, Amy had seen chemical dependency up painfully close, and she wasn't likely to be mistaken about the telltale signs. Dan decided it was a safe bet that Brian wasn't shoving his inheritance up his nose or injecting it into his veins. That didn't mean they needed to abandon Brian as a suspect. Dan would really like to stick it to the guy.

"There are plenty of reasons aside from a drug habit that Brian might need money and not feel able to ask his parents for a loan. What if Brian is being blackmailed?"

This time Amy stopped and thought for a moment before rejecting his suggestion. "Brian strikes me as a very unlikely candidate for blackmail," she said eventually. "His life's an open book. He counts half the movers and shakers in greater Los Angeles as his friends, and has a nodding acquaintance with the other half. It's not as if he has dark secrets in his past. The Maitlands are pillars of the community—"

"How about dark secrets in his present?" Dan hesitated for only a second before asking his next question. "What if he has some offbeat sexual fetish, for example?"

"Then he managed to keep it well hidden from me," Amy said. "His sexual tastes struck me as boringly chaste and normal." Her pallor vanished in a vivid blush when she realized what stress had prompted her to reveal.

Dan made light of the revelation. "Boring? Chaste?" He quirked an eyebrow. "Poor guy. What an epitaph."

For a moment he saw the gleam of laughter in her eyes, but after a second or two, she managed to produce a frown. "Glen is going to be devastated," she said. "He's not going to accept the idea of his son's guilt just because we point out that Brian had the means and the opportunity. Glen is going to need a rock-solid motive before he'll even contemplate the possibility that Brian not only stole from him, but also set me up to take the fall."

"It's enough if we can demonstrate to Glen that his son is seriously in debt," Dan said. "We don't have to explain why and how he got that way. And if it turns out Brian isn't in debt…well, I guess we would have to rethink our conclusions in that case."

Amy perked up again. "It shouldn't be too difficult to order a comprehensive credit report. If I were still working at Maitland Homes, I could get it in a heartbeat."

"I can get it," Dan said. "Bob and I have a subscription to one of the most comprehensive background-checking services. We need it for our work."

"Could you check tonight?"

"Of course." He looked at her. "I live less than five minutes' drive from here. We can go back to my place and do it right now, if you want."

Amy met his eyes, her gaze steady. She clearly recognized that he could easily have suggested going to his office but had chosen not to. "I'd like that," she said.

Dan pulled out a credit card and managed to catch the eye of a waiter. He turned to Amy with a grin. "Hey, what do you know? We wrapped this up before dessert after all."

CHAPTER
SIX

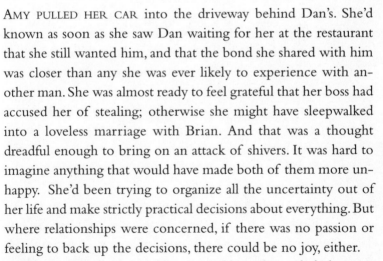

AMY PULLED HER CAR into the driveway behind Dan's. She'd known as soon as she saw Dan waiting for her at the restaurant that she still wanted him, and that the bond she shared with him was closer than any she was ever likely to experience with another man. She was almost ready to feel grateful that her boss had accused her of stealing; otherwise she might have sleepwalked into a loveless marriage with Brian. And that was a thought dreadful enough to bring on an attack of shivers. It was hard to imagine anything that would have made both of them more unhappy. She'd been trying to organize all the uncertainty out of her life and make strictly practical decisions about everything. But where relationships were concerned, if there was no passion or feeling to back up the decisions, there could be no joy, either.

Dan opened the door of her car and leaned in to help her out. She was barely standing before he dragged her into his arms. "I've been waiting six years to do this," he said, slanting his mouth across hers in an urgent, demanding kiss.

He kissed her with a passion that mirrored her own, and with a tenderness that brought back a hundred bittersweet memories. Amy reached up and linked her hands behind his neck, holding him tight. A hot wave of pleasure swept over her when his tongue found hers, reminding her of how long it had been since she'd experienced the joy of acute sexual need. The knot of desire in the pit of her stomach grew tighter, and she moved closer to Dan. Her body, she discovered, remembered perfectly how to mesh with his. She wanted their kiss to last forever, and she gave a soft groan of disapproval when Dan lifted his mouth from hers.

"We should probably go inside," he said, and there was a hint of laughter in his voice. "I'm sure the condo association has rules about owners making love in their driveways."

She blinked, returning to reality with a jolt. Good grief, they were still outside, standing in a pool of light cast by the streetlamp. How had that happened? She'd spent the years since their separation telling herself that Dan's kisses were the same as any other man's. She'd lied. Worse, at some level she'd always known that she lied.

She followed him into his town house, blind to its style and layout despite the fact that her professional interest usually kicked in the moment she stepped into a home she hadn't visited before. Dan took her hand again, holding her close as he led her upstairs, using his shoulder to push open the door to his bedroom so that he didn't need to stop kissing her.

His clothes might have changed, but his body was lean, his skin was hot and his muscles still as hard as when he'd been in college. Her desire spiraled several notches higher, overcoming inhibitions. This time, she took the lead as she grabbed his hand and stumbled through the darkness in the direction of the bed.

Dan stopped her. "Wait!" He reached up to pull out the combs she'd used to hold her hair off her face. The combs dropped to the floor and he gave a sigh of sheer pleasure as her hopelessly unruly hair tumbled around her shoulders.

"God, I've dreamed so many times of seeing you like this again. You have to be the most beautiful woman in the world, Amy Duran."

His husky voice was the most erotic thing she'd heard since the last time they had made love. She was having a terrible time remembering how to breathe and could have sworn her bones were melting. Heat scorched and sizzled through her veins, intense enough to be painful, but when Dan pulled her down beside him on the bed, everything suddenly felt right, at once beautifully familiar and dazzlingly new.

"How in the world did we survive without this?" she murmured.

"I have no clue. Maybe we didn't. Maybe we've died and gone to heaven."

How could she have forgotten, even for a moment, how wonderful it was to make love to Dan? What stupid stratagems had she used to convince herself that she could survive for the rest of her life without ever again being held in his arms? She must have been suffering from a six-year attack of insanity. Dan was her soul mate, Amy realized. He was her best friend as well as her lover, her source of light and hope in the darkness.

God, how she'd missed him.

IT WAS CLOSE TO MIDNIGHT before they could bear to leave the magical oasis they'd created in the bedroom, but eventually the need to check on Brian's financial situation spurred them into moving. Exhilarated and exhausted from hours of lovemaking, Amy sat in the living room, wrapped in one of Dan's robes and eating a bowl of ice cream to compensate for the dinner she'd barely touched, and the dessert they'd never gotten around to ordering.

She yawned. "Are you getting anything useful on Brian?" she asked, giving the spoon a regretful last lick.

"Lots of good stuff." Dan remained focused on the monitor in front of him. "I can tell you already that our friend Brian is in a deep financial hole. He has a second mortgage on his town house, his credit cards are maxed out, and he has delinquent debts out the wazoo. I'm trying to find something that would indicate why the hell he's in such trouble when he's making over a hundred thousand a year. His two biggest debts are to Evander Corporation and Milheiser Associates. Thirty-one thousand to Evander and twenty-three to Milheiser. Ever heard of either of those companies? There's nothing here to indicate what products they sell."

Amy shook her head. "I've never heard of either of them. Can you run a search on the companies?"

"I'm getting something on them now. Yep, here it comes." Dan gave a triumphant exclamation and swiveled around on his chair to face her. "Well, wadda ya know? Our boy is addicted after all."

"Addicted?" Amy couldn't believe what she was hearing. "Brian has a drug problem? I can't believe it, Dan. Honestly, he's never shown the slightest sign—"

"Not drugs. He's a gambling addict. Evander and Milheiser are parent corporations for Las Vegas casinos. Brian is in hock up to his overprivileged eyeballs."

A dozen images flashed in front of Amy's inner eye, then rearranged themselves like a kaleidoscope into a coherent, vivid pattern. "Of course," she said as everything became clear. "I picked up on all the clues but never put them together. I wondered why Brian's favorite weekend date so often seemed to be an early Saturday brunch. He'd take me to some fabulous resort or restaurant right on the coast, and then by noon, we'd be done. He'd disappear for the rest of the weekend, claiming he had to play in a golf tournament with his father, or some such thing."

"And what do you bet Brian told his dad he was spending the weekend with you? Meanwhile, he'd actually hopped a commuter plane to Las Vegas."

"Using his relationship with me for cover." Amy pulled a face. "He really played me for a sucker, didn't he?"

"What would you expect?" Dan shrugged. "He's an addict, and just because his fixation is gambling, not drugs or alcohol, that doesn't change the reality of his addiction. He used you and betrayed you because that's what addicts do. You know too much about addiction to need reminding that you played no part in Brian's problems. They're all his, every one of them."

Dan was right, Amy acknowledged silently. For once, the years of experience with her mother were useful; they reinforced the truth of Dan's statement with poignant efficiency.

"We still have a problem," she said. "Glen not only loves his son, he's blind to Brian's faults—"

"Perhaps deliberately blind," Dan suggested. "It's easy to acknowledge your kids have a problem if the problem isn't very big. I guess most parents work pretty damned hard to avoid seeing that their kids are wading into really deep trouble."

"Like us with our parents," Amy said softly. "Remember how the other kids in school would bitch and moan all the time about what morons their parents were? Or how totally unreasonable their parents' rules were?"

"But we just kept quiet, and if we ever said anything about our birth parents, it was always to defend them." Dan frowned. "My guess is that Glen Maitland will try hard *not* to believe us, because otherwise he has to accept his son is an addict and a thief. Am I right?"

"I'm sure you are." Amy put her empty ice-cream bowl in the sink. "Right now we might even have a problem getting Glen to listen to me. There's a good chance he'll refuse to speak to me."

"I'll request the meeting with Glen," Dan said. "He's not likely to refuse me, especially if I hint there's a lawsuit pending. But I have court tomorrow morning at nine, and the case will last at least the whole day." His frown deepened, then vanished. "You know, we're approaching this the wrong way. Maybe we shouldn't tell Glen what we've discovered. We need to confront Brian first and persuade him to confess to his father."

Amy's immediate thought was that Brian would never voluntarily confess. It took strength of character to make such a confession and Brian lacked the necessary strength. She recognized his weakness now—at some level, she'd always recognized it. The amazing thing was that she'd wasted three months dating such a loser. She hoped—she really hoped—that if he had ever gotten around to proposing, she would have taken a long, hard look at him and realized that she had to refuse.

"Brian is armor-plated by his years of privilege," she said. "Piercing that armor is going to take a lot more than simply informing him we know he's in debt."

"No problem." Dan made a show of flexing his biceps. "It will give me significant pleasure to beat the crap out of him until he's willing to confess."

"Despite your muscular advantage, I think we might need to move to Plan B. Brian has enough friends in high places that you're likely to end up arrested for assault and battery."

"Okay. Plan B. How about I beat the crap out of him and contact my friends in high places before he can get to his?"

She hid a smile. "We need a Plan C."

"Personally, I find Plan B mighty appealing. But an alternative would be for you to worm a confession out of him when he thinks the two of you are alone. Actually, though, you'll be wearing a wire and I'll be outside in my car, recording every sordid detail."

"Isn't that illegal? To record somebody without their knowledge?"

"Yes, it's completely illegal. But we don't intend to take the tape to law enforcement or the courts. We only plan to send it to Glen, along with Brian's damning credit report."

Since Dan would be unavailable tomorrow, it would be Wednesday at the earliest before they could put their plan into action. Amy sighed at the delay. "I hate having to wait, but I guess I can use my free time while you're in court to buy the audio surveillance equipment."

"No need. I already have everything we'll need, left over from another case." Dan stood up, reaching for the cotton sweater hanging over the back of his chair. "So why don't we pay Brian a visit right now?"

"Because it's one-thirty in the morning!"

He smiled and kissed her on the tip of her nose. "I know that, Ms. Prim and Proper. But we're not paying a social call, we're trying to nail a criminal. It'll be all the better for us if Brian starts spouting off at the mouth when he's only half-awake."

"Shouldn't we at least call first?"

"Why? So he has time to notify the cops, think up a good alibi, or leave the premises? Stop picturing him as your boss's son and start picturing him as the criminal asshole who stole a lot of money and pinned the blame on you."

"I can do that. In fact, I'm getting a Technicolor image."

"Good. Then let's get moving."

"But what about your trial tomorrow? I don't want your client to end up in prison because I kept you up all night."

He smiled and put his arm around her, hugging gently. "Thank you for being so thoughtful, but you don't need to worry. I'm already prepared for the trial, and I've pulled all-nighters plenty of times before. As long as I can crash tomorrow night, I'll be okay."

Amy realized she felt something close to excitement. "You make sure the audio equipment is working, and I'll get dressed. Give me fifteen minutes."

"You can have ten. We'll plan tactics while we drive."

AMY PUT HER FINGER on the doorbell of Brian's town house and kept it there. When that produced no results, she banged the heavy wrought-iron knocker. It would be anticlimactic, to say the least, if it turned out that Brian was spending the night away from home.

A light went on and she saw Brian's blurred outline through the mottled glass panel set into the door. He must have recognized her, because he stopped abruptly. Fortunately, he seemed too disconcerted by the sight of her to just turn around and go back to bed.

"What do you want?" He opened the door a crack, leaving the chain in place.

"To talk to you. Let me in, Brian."

"Do you know what time it is?" He rubbed his eyes, chasing away sleep. "Get off my doorstep, Amy, or I'll call the cops."

"Go ahead, call the cops. That would be fine by me. You, however, might need to worry about what I have to say to them."

"I have nothing to worry about from the cops. What the hell do you mean?" But he didn't shut the door, and he didn't sound at all sure of his claim.

"You have a lot to worry about," she corrected him. "Not least the hundred and twenty thousand bucks you still owe to the casinos in Las Vegas, despite the fact that you've borrowed every penny you can lay your hands on. There's a second mortgage on this house. Your credit cards are maxed out. You have an overdraft at your bank—"

"Who the hell gave you the right to poke around in my private affairs?"

"You did when you stole fifty thousand dollars from your father's company and pinned the blame on me. Too bad you screwed up with your alibi, isn't it, Brian?"

"How did I screw up?" He was finally wide enough awake to make an instant correction to his tacit admission of guilt. "I haven't the faintest idea what you're talking about."

"Then let me come in and I can explain."

She expected him to refuse. Instead, he unlatched the chain and stood aside to let her into the hallway. The living room was located just to the right of the front door, and she quickly walked in, flicking on the light. She set the printout of his credit report on the coffee table and gestured to it.

"Brian, look at that spreadsheet."

He gave the figures a cursory glance, then stood up and walked over to the bar. He poured himself a shot of brandy and drank it down in a single gulp.

"What's this got to do with the money you stole from Maitland Homes?"

"I didn't steal any money, as you very well know. You did."

"The transactions were made at your computer, with your password, using access codes only you knew—"

"No, you knew them, too."

"How could I?"

"Easily. Glen and I both kept a record of the access codes in our Palm Pilots, and you had free run of my house as well as your father's. It must have been astonishingly easy for you to set me up. The only thing that might have stopped you was a conscience. And you're an addict, so you don't have one of those right now."

"I'm not an addict! You're saying that because you're just like my dad, a workaholic. Well, I'm not. I'm just a regular guy and I don't want to spend my whole damn life on a building site. No wonder I need to get away on the weekends and have a few hours of relaxation. Have you any idea what it's like being the only son and heir of Glen Maitland? It's a pain in the ass, that's what."

"You don't have fun on the weekends, Brian. You gamble money you don't have. You need professional help and you need it now. My lawyer and I made a rough calculation, and we estimate that over the past year, you've run up gambling debts that total close to a quarter of a million dollars."

"It can't be that much. I just play blackjack occasionally. Not even every weekend…" His voice petered out and he sank down onto the couch. "A quarter of a million dollars? My God, surely it can't be that much?"

The fact that Brian didn't know the exact amount he owed was precisely what Amy would have expected from somebody whose addiction had spiraled out of control.

She spoke more gently than she and Dan had planned. "Face it, Brian. You're not going to be able to lie, cheat and steal your way out of the hole you've dug for yourself. It's too big and it's too deep. Your father is going to be auditing the company books on a regular basis, and I'm gone, so you can't blame me anymore. Next time the situation gets desperate and your creditors are threatening all sorts of dire consequences, what are you going to do?"

"I don't know." He buried his face in his hands. "I have no idea what I'm going to do."

"You can tell your father the truth. You can tell him you have a gambling problem, that you're in debt, and that you stole the fifty thousand dollars, not me. You have excellent company health insurance. Check yourself into a residential program. Get counseling. It's your only hope."

"I can't tell him—"

"If you don't tell him, my lawyer and I will."

"He won't believe you. That's how I get away with everything. Dad isn't willing to believe that *his* son is anything but perfect."

Amy's moment of sympathy vanished. She marveled anew at

the similarities between Brian's addiction and her mother's. Everything was always somebody else's problem, never theirs, and any excuse or stratagem was acceptable as long as they didn't end up having to take responsibility for their own lives.

"Let me make this real easy for you, Brian. We have proof that you're thousands of dollars in debt. We have proof that you were in the office when all three thefts occurred. We can demonstrate exactly how you acquired my password and the access codes for the bank. We also have proof that I'm not in debt and that I have absolutely no reason to need stolen money. Glen Maitland is a smart man. He isn't going to like hearing that his son is a thief, but he'll accept it. Eventually."

"You're underestimating me, Amy." Brian had recovered himself enough to gloat. "It would be easier to make my dad believe the sun rises in the west than that his beloved son and heir is a thief."

"But you *are* a thief."

He shrugged. "Okay, so I stole the money. So what? My father is convinced you're the culprit and I'm going to make sure he keeps believing that."

"It might be a little difficult for you to maintain your protestations of innocence when he hears the tape I've made of this conversation."

"Tape? You made a tape of what I just said?" Brian swore viciously. "Why, you bitch! Give it to me." He lunged for her, reaching for her shirt and trying to rip it open.

She dodged behind the couch, but Brian kept grappling with her, searching for the wire. "Brian, stop! You don't think I was crazy enough to come here alone? My lawyer is waiting outside—"

"No, he's not." Dan erupted into the room. "Your lawyer is right here." He hauled Brian off her and punched him hard on the chin.

Brian staggered for a moment, then came at Dan swinging wildly. But Dan was a veteran of more street fights than Brian had seen in the movies, let alone lived through in real life. The guy never saw the uppercut coming that laid him out cold on his own floor.

Dan dusted off his hands. "Plan B," he said, laughing. "I told you it would work."

CHAPTER SEVEN

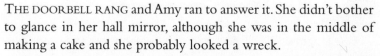

THE DOORBELL RANG and Amy ran to answer it. She didn't bother to glance in her hall mirror, although she was in the middle of making a cake and she probably looked a wreck.

She opened the door and her heart gave its inevitable lurch of happiness when she saw Dan. He stepped inside and kissed her hungrily, pulling her hard against him. When they finally had to come up for air, he put his arm around her waist and propelled her into the kitchen. He stuck his finger into the batter and licked appreciatively. "Yum, cinnamon. It's good."

He reached for another scoop and she pushed it away. "Raw batter will give you cooties."

"No, that's girls. And only when you're in fifth grade. Besides, you owe me one today."

"I always owe you one."

"No, you don't." He kissed her again, then grinned. "Except maybe today you do. Look what I have for you." He reached into his jacket pocket and pulled out a heavy cream envelope. "Open it."

She rubbed her slightly sticky hands on the seat of her jeans and opened the envelope. Inside was a check. Puzzled, she pulled it out. The check was drawn on Glen Maitland's personal account, and it was for fifty thousand dollars.

"I don't understand. What's this for?" she asked.

"Compensation for slander, false accusations and wrongful dismissal. I suggested to him that you would be generous enough not to sue for wrongful dismissal in exchange for this extremely token payment from him that, not coincidentally, is exactly the amount he accused you of stealing."

Amy stared at the check, not at all sure how she felt. "I appreciate your efforts, Dan, but I'm not sure I want his money."

"Of course you do. If you prefer to donate it all to your favorite charity, then feel free. But it was the very least Glen owed you."

"Maybe you can use it for your legal defense fund. For some kid who's facing charges that might ruin his life."

He kissed her. "You're a kind woman, Amy Duran, and I'm madly, insanely in love with you. Will you marry me?"

She laughed. "I will. As I told you the last three times you proposed."

"Ah, but this time, I'm making it official." He reached into his pocket again and this time he pulled out a dark blue velvet box, holding it open to display the diamond solitaire nestled inside. His expression suddenly serious, he reached for her left hand and slowly slid the ring onto her finger. "Marry me soon, Amy."

Her fingers were still sticky with cake batter. They were in the kitchen instead of at an expensive restaurant overlooking the ocean. For all she knew, she probably had cake mix on the end of her nose. Trust Dan to have chosen the perfect place to give her his ring.

"I love you," she said. "Would next week be soon enough for us to get married?"

"It would be perfect," he said, and kissed her.

STREET HAVEN AT THE CROSSROADS
PEGGY ANN WALPOLE

Peggy Ann Walpole was advised to abandon her dream of nursing even before she began. The physical demands would be too much for a woman whose lifelong struggle with illness had begun in childhood. But Peggy Ann was determined, and at the age of eighteen, she entered nursing school at St. Michael's Hospital in Toronto.

It was the 1950s and St. Michael's was near the city's skid row. In the emergency room Peggy Ann witnessed the debilitating effects of street life on women—drug overdoses, alcohol withdrawal, mental illness and beatings from prostitution. Peggy Ann wondered where these women went after they left the hospital. There were hostels for destitute men. But what about these desperate women?

Peggy Ann continued her nursing, but believed she could do something more to help. For years she dedicated herself to the care of women ravaged by life on the streets, and dreamed of opening a drop-in center to provide shelter and support. By 1965 Peggy Ann was able to rent the beverage room of an old skid-row hotel…and Street Haven at the Crossroads was born.

Since that time, Street Haven at the Crossroads has helped tens of thousands of women, and become a multifaceted agency offering an integrated continuum of services—from immediate support for women off the streets, to long-term programs addressing issues such as mental health, addictions, violence, poverty and homelessness. Street Haven has an open-door philosophy, and all of the programs are based on a nonjudgmental, total acceptance of the person. Street Haven believes that all women are worthwhile and that they deserve to be treated with dignity.

Women from all walks of life find themselves facing high housing costs, limited job opportunities and family problems that too often result in their living on the street. These women's lives are made more difficult by personal problems ranging from a history of abuse to a life of seemingly insurmountable challenges. Each month Street Haven helps hundreds of these women develop and maintain healthy, productive and independent lifestyles.

The Heart of Street Haven

Peggy Ann began Street Haven as a drop-in center for women, and 40 years later, The Haven and The Drop-In remain at the heart of the agency. Women who live daily with poverty, mental illness and other critical issues are often trying to manage alone. They may be isolated from friends and support within the community. The Haven is a 24-hour emergency, short-term shelter where each day 40 to 60 women are given shelter, food, clothing, medical attention, counseling and support. The Drop-In provides art therapy, crafts, spiritual groups and recreation activities, while the Learning Center helps women develop basic skills in reading, writing, math, computers and job-search techniques.

Each day Street Haven prepares 200 meals. For the many women literally living on the street, a nutritious meal can mean the difference between life and death. As women become healthier they start to take control over their lives again. Even the act of getting the women to share a warm meal provides them with a much-needed sense of community.

Helping toward lasting change

Street Haven at the Crossroads also offers long-term programs. Joubert House is a home where women with a history of psychiatric illness and homelessness are helped to achieve their personal goals toward greater independence. The Addiction Case Management program and Grant House, a residential treatment center, help women with alcohol and chemical dependency make positive choices toward significant and lasting changes in their lives, and develop the skills they need to live free of alcohol and drugs. Street Haven also owns and manages two apartment buildings to provide safe, affordable, permanent housing for single women. In addition, a significant amount of work is done assisting women in the community to find suitable housing.

Street Haven is a challenging place to work, but the staff is dedicated to their clients—and to Peggy Ann, who treats clients and staff like family. For many people who work at Street Haven, Peggy Ann *is* their family. Women who came to Street Haven after life on the streets were taken under Peggy Ann's wing, and now they are helping others in situations they were once in themselves. Street Haven has brought out the same passion and devotion in thousands of volunteers, corporations and foundations who have dedicated time, money and support over the years—and continue to care.

Women helping women

Peggy Ann believes that the key to Street Haven's success is its client-centered approach—and that it is run by women, for women. Clients, with the assistance of the staff, shape their own recoveries and help in deciding on the programs and activities at Street Haven. Their voices have significance—and it's the women themselves who've helped shape Street Haven into the agency it has become since opening its doors in 1965.

Peggy Ann and the staff see so many women come to Street Haven seeking help. Some come for a day or two, some stay months at a time. Sadly, many return after unsuccessful attempts to rebuild their lives. But one thing that is always constant at Street Haven is the care the clients receive. Every woman is helped no matter how many times she comes back. For women who are not ready for change, Peggy Ann and the staff are there to listen to them, to cry with them, counsel or just let them be. When a woman senses that love, and knows she's believed in, she is often able to face overwhelming obstacles to a better life. These women, who so desperately need someone to care, are the only motivation Peggy Ann and the staff need.

Street Haven at the Crossroads continues to provide help and comfort to women from the streets, and to provide programs for them to turn their lives around. But it is the women themselves, their strength and courage, that make the changes happen; it is *they* who beat the odds. And for 40 years, Peggy Ann Walpole has been their guiding light....

The operating details and conventions of the fictional women's shelter in *Shelter from the Storm* are of the author's creation and are not those of Street Haven at the Crossroads.

BEVERLY BARTON
SHELTER
FROM THE
STORM

BEVERLY BARTON

USA TODAY bestselling author Beverly Barton wrote her first book in 1989 and to date has written over 50 books. This sixth-generation Alabamian's books have consistently hit the Barnes & Noble bestseller list, Waldenbooks series romance bestseller list and have appeared on the *New York Times* paperback extended list. Beverly currently writes series romance for Silhouette, mainstream romance for Harlequin's HQN imprint and mainstream romantic suspense for another publisher. The author currently lives in Tuscumbia, Alabama.

CHAPTER ONE

CATHY BLAMED her restlessness and discontent on the sweltering July heat. Ninety-five degrees in the shade and a heat index of one hundred was enough to wreak havoc on anyone's nerves, wasn't it? Just walking from her car into the air-conditioned building a few hours earlier, she'd broken out into a sweat. It was the darn humidity. If only it would rain, things might cool off a bit. But glancing out the window of her office at Shelter from the Storm, the women's shelter she had founded here in Chattanooga, Tennessee, seven years ago, she saw a cloudless, clear blue sky and bright sunshine.

She turned back to the stack of mail that she'd been doing her best to wade through since eight this morning. Lifting the black-and-gold paper cup from her desk, she took a sip of lukewarm coffee and grimaced. She liked her coffee either black and hot or iced with loads of whipped cream. This morning she'd picked up an iced coffee with extra whipped cream and chocolate sprinkles from her favorite coffee shop, but that had been—she glanced at her wristwatch—three and a half hours ago. She had no more sat down at her desk than her phone rang, and it hadn't stopped since. The first calls came from two local businesses on the brink of making sizable donations to the shelter. Another had been from a former resident who wanted to return as a volunteer, one from a minister seeking a place for a battered wife whose husband had been abusing her for thirty years, and the last from Eric Vinson, a police officer and friend who was looking for a shelter for a homeless woman and her six-year-old daughter.

Cathy walked across her office, entered the small adjacent bathroom and dumped the distasteful residue from her cup into the sink. As she tossed the cup into the trash, her stomach growled, reminding her that she hadn't eaten breakfast and it was nearly lunchtime. She usually prepared breakfast every morning for Michael and her, but her son had spent last night with his best friend.

That's probably what's wrong with you, she told herself. *You're worried about Michael.* Of course, she had no need to worry. After all, he was with Justin Russell and his father, Tate, who was Michael's Little League coach. The boys had been best friends for over a year and were practically inseparable now that it was summer. For the last few months she had joined the boys and Coach Russell on various outings, getting to know and like both father and son. Besides, she needed to get used to the idea that Michael was no longer a little boy, that he was fast approaching his teen years and would want and need more independence. But how did a single mother of an only child learn to let go?

By slow degrees. Cathy could almost hear the warm Southern drawl of Earline Muhlendorf, her friend and volunteer co-worker here at the shelter. Earline had raised four boys, now all adults, all married and two with children of their own. Although she was old enough to be Cathy's mother, Earline had become her dearest friend and cherished confidante. She was the only person in Chattanooga who knew all the details about Michael's father deserting her long before he was born.

Do not dredge up old memories, Cathy warned herself. Most of the time, she kept the past in its place and seldom thought about Sean

Williams, the boy she'd loved with all her heart and trusted with her very life. She would have followed Sean anywhere...and did. All the way from South Carolina to Canada, to a job that didn't pan out for him, a one-room flat and only enough money to eat once a day, if that. But at nineteen, she had foolishly believed that you could live on love.

She had learned better. Learned the hard way.

And how many times since she founded Shelter from the Storm had she seen young girls like herself come in, brokenhearted, penniless, abandoned and pregnant? And each time, she would remember her own past and the women of Street Haven in Toronto who had saved her and her unborn child. Without their help, she wouldn't have been able to build a new and better life for herself and Michael.

"We have two new residents and one returnee." Earline opened the door to Cathy's office—always without knocking—and breezed in. "Pearl Isom is back from rehab and she looks great. She asked to speak to you later today, if you have time."

"I'll make time," Cathy said. There was something special about Pearl, an inner beauty and kindness that masked the horrors of her young life. At twenty, she had been through more than most people in a lifetime, yet her experience mirrored that of numerous girls and women who sought solace at the shelter. "How did she seem to you?"

"Clean and sober. Smiling that sweet smile of hers." Earline shook her head sadly. "She has no idea how truly lovely she is. And I'm afraid she may still equate physical attractiveness to sexuality. I can't imagine what it must have been like for her, molested by her own stepfather at thirteen, and then on the streets as a prostitute at sixteen." Earline glanced at the stack of correspondence piled high on Cathy's desk. "I can take care of some of that when I return from lunch, if you like. Daniel is taking me to The Southern Star today. Want to go with us?"

"No, thanks. Tate Russell is supposed to bring Michael by soon. And I've invited Justin and him to join us in the cafeteria today. But as far as the mail goes, yes, please take half of it...or more." Cathy indicated the wooden armchair to the right of her desk. "Please, sit."

Like all the other furniture at Shelter from the Storm, the chair had been a donation. Often she and Earline and the other volunteers would jokingly refer to the center's decor as "Secondhand Rose." But as time went by, more and more merchants donated new items, like the two side-by-side refrigerators and freezer in the cafeteria-style kitchen, which now had to accommodate nearly fifty women when at full capacity.

Earline plopped her plump behind down in the chair and studied Cathy curiously. "What's wrong? I can't put my finger on it, but you're not quite yourself."

Cathy forced a smile. "It's nothing. Just this horrible heat. And Michael is growing up and I'm getting older and—"

Earline laughed. "I'm sorry, honey, but when you're my age, you'll need to worry about growing old. You're only thirty-two. You are definitely in your prime. My thirties were some of the best years of my life."

"Age, like everything else, is relative I suppose."

"What's really bothering you? It's not that gorgeous hunk, is it?"

"What gorgeous hunk?"

Earline laughed again.

"I was referring to Tate Russell, of course. How many gorgeous hunks do you have in your life? If there's more than one, you'll have to share."

"I don't *have* Tate Russell. I mean, we're friends, of course, but that's all."

Earline tsk-tsked. "For the life of me, I can't figure out why you haven't made a play for that man. He's handsome, rich and single. And he loves kids. I've seen him with the boys. He'd make a great dad for Michael."

Heat flushed Cathy's cheeks. "I told you, Tate and I are just friends. He dates and so do I. Just not each other."

"Humph! When is the last time you had a date?"

Cathy had to think before she answered. For a couple of months, she had dated Glenn Digby, a fellow teacher at Soddy-Daisy High School, where she taught English. He had been interested in more than casual dating, and when she'd made it perfectly clear that she wasn't, he had ended things. Six months later, he'd married someone else. That had been… No, it couldn't have been that long ago. But there had been no one since then. Not that she hadn't been asked, but she had been busy with her son, her students and her volunteer work at Shelter from the Storm. There simply wasn't time in her life for romance.

"Two years," Cathy reluctantly admitted.

Earline shook her head disapprovingly. "You need a man, sweetie. You should ask Tate out."

"We've been going out for several months now."

Earline groaned. "Family outings with the boys, right? I'm talking about a date. Just you and Tate."

"Tate has girlfriends," Cathy protested. "He's not interested in me in that way. And he's not my type." That last statement came rushing out of her mouth without thought.

"Honey, Tate Russell is every woman's type."

"You're wrong. Besides, it's a moot point. He and I are friends. Period."

"If I were twenty-five years younger and unmarried, I'd—"

"Well, you are married," a male voice said from the doorway. "And you'd better not forget it."

Daniel Muhlendorf was six-three and barrel-chested, but Cathy knew the man was a gentle giant. He walked into the room and went directly to his wife, then leaned over and kissed her on the cheek. When he glanced at Cathy, his mouth curved upward in a warmhearted smile, lifting his thick white mustache.

"You don't need to worry," Earline told her husband. "There's only one man in the world for me." She reached out and grasped his big hand. "I was just trying to play matchmaker for Cathy."

"Too bad all our boys are married," Daniel said. "I'd love to have

Cathy for a daughter-in-law." He helped his wife to her feet, then turned to Cathy. "Want to join us?"

"I've already asked," Earline told him. "She's expecting Tate Russell to come by with Michael and his son Justin. They're going to eat in the cafeteria."

"Tate Russell," Daniel repeated. "The building contractor?"

Cathy nodded.

"Hmm… He'd make a fine catch, and he's on the shelter's board. Earline didn't tell me you two were dating."

"We're not."

"They're just friends," Earline said.

"Humph," Daniel said. "No man would want to be just friends with a lovely girl like you."

Earline gave Cathy an I-told-you-so glance before slipping her arm around her husband. "I'm starving. Let's go."

After they left, Cathy walked over to the windows and gazed down into the garden. A generous but anonymous donor had recently given Shelter from the Storm the old house next door, allowing the organization to offer temporary housing to more women in need. These two buildings in the St. Elmo area of Chattanooga were utilized to the maximum, including the basements and the attics. This last addition, an old three-story Victorian, had a carriage house that Cathy and her colleagues hoped to eventually convert to office space so they could free up more rooms in the main house. The shelter also rented two other houses, both in undisclosed locations within Hamilton County. These were used mostly for women whose lives were threatened by abusive spouses.

The garden below was a work in progress, spearheaded by some of the residents themselves. At present, it was little more than a cleared grassy area with two old oak trees and a couple of wrought-iron benches in great need of sanding and painting. Cathy noticed that, despite the oppressive heat, two people were sitting in the garden. On closer inspection, she realized that it was Andrew Hudson and a young woman. Andrew was one of the shelter's few male volunteers. A youth minister at Cathy's church, he had devoted a great deal of his free time to working tirelessly with street kids even before Cathy asked him to volunteer at the shelter.

When she recognized the young blond woman with Andrew, Cathy sighed. She should have known the moment Pearl Isom returned from rehab, Andrew would be here to greet her. It had been Andrew who had brought Pearl to Shelter from the Storm two months ago. The rules here were simple. Any guest who was an addict was allowed to stay for three days, then she had to agree to go through a rehabilitation program or leave the shelter. This program was for women who not only needed assistance but were willing to work hard to help themselves.

When Andrew placed his arm around Pearl's shoulders, Cathy glanced away, feeling somewhat like a voyeur. The two people in the garden had no idea anyone was watching them. And there was no reason to assume anything improper was going on between them just because Andrew had his arm around Pearl. But curiosity and a niggling sense of concern forced Cathy to look again. Sitting together on one of the rusty old benches, the two were talking. Just talking. Cathy released a deep, pent-up breath.

The last thing Pearl needed was to think there was even the slightest chance she and Andrew had a future together. After all, Pearl was a high-school dropout, a reformed drug addict and former prostitute. She was four months pregnant and had no idea which of her many clients had fathered her child. On the other hand, Andrew was a college-educated, straight-arrow Christian, a young man who had dedicated his life to good works.

Cathy understood about impossible dreams. Her own hopes had been harshly torn apart when she was Pearl's age. She simply did not want the young woman to go through any more heartache than she'd already endured. If only she could infuse Pearl with the wisdom gained from her own experience, Cathy thought. If only she could make Pearl understand that there were just certain dreams that could never come true for women like them. Women who didn't dare trust life to treat them fairly.

Cathy turned away from the windows and sat down at her desk to tackle the stack of correspondence. Maybe she could get through some of it before Tate arrived with Michael and Justin.

TATE RUSSELL PULLED into the parking lot at the back of Shelter from the Storm. The instant the car came to a stop, his son Justin and Justin's best friend, Michael, opened their doors, jumped out and raced toward the back door. At thirty-seven, Tate was in his prime, but there were times when he envied the energy those twelve-year-olds possessed. After they'd gotten home from last night's Lookouts game at Bellsouth Park, he had let them stay up until one, and then they had slept until well past ten this morning. Despite the fact that both boys were growing up in one-parent homes, they were great kids. Typically rambunctious and not certain their parents knew much, if anything, Justin and Michael nevertheless were well-behaved and, when the occasion called for it, mannerly. Up until two years ago, Justin had gone to private school, but when he'd become friends with a group of public school kids at Little League games, he had asked Tate to allow him to attend Loftis Middle School in Soddy-Daisy. Reluctantly, Tate had agreed that they'd try it for one year. As it turned out, the change had been good for him as well as his son. Heck, this year, he had even coached Justin's Little League team.

It wasn't so long ago that Tate had spent most of his waking hours at work, trying to modernize his father's old construction firm. Then his wife Hannah died suddenly from a brain aneurysm when Justin was seven. Too late, Tate had realized what was really important in life. The ironic thing was that in the past five years, he had learned how to balance work with life, and his business had not suffered in the least.

Tate finally caught up with the boys just as they flung open the door to Cathy's office. He stood outside in the hallway and watched as she rose from her desk and came rushing toward her son, a welcoming smile on her face, her arms held open. Michael halted and glanced at Justin. As if sensing her son's reluctance, Cathy lowered her arms and laughed.

"So, how was the game last night?" she asked. "And just how late did Tate let you guys stay up?"

Cathy was such a good mom, Tate realized. She knew it wasn't cool for twelve-year-old boys on the verge of adolescence to kiss their mom. Tate could remember shying away from his own mom at that age. She'd died three years ago, and now he'd give anything for one last chance to feel her arms around him.

He studied Cathy as she talked with the boys. She had a way about her that made people instantly feel at ease, and he suspected it was because she genuinely liked people and cared deeply about their welfare. Over the past year, he'd seen her at various school functions and whenever Justin and Michael got together. But it wasn't until Little League season began this year that he'd invited her to join him and the boys for pizza after one of their games. He'd hoped she would see it as an invitation to date. After all, who better for a single father than an attractive single mom? But it quickly became apparent that Cathy had no interest in dating— him or anyone else. So he had accepted what she was offering, and their casual acquaintance had grown into genuine friendship.

Not that Tate didn't want more. Just looking at her put all kinds of lascivious thoughts into his head. Dark-haired and dark-eyed, with a willowy figure most runway models would envy, Cathy seemed to have no idea how gorgeous she was. Or how sexy. And whenever he tried to steer their conversation around to just the two of them, she effectively sidestepped the issue.

Tate figured he had two courses of action—either persuade Cathy to date him or start going out with someone else. Oh, he still had the odd date now and then, and though there was a lot to be said for being a sought-after bachelor, he wasn't getting any younger. He wanted to get married again, maybe have another child or two. If Cathy wasn't interested, then…

The problem was, Cathy was the woman he wanted. She was perfect for him. He liked everything about her, including her son. He suspected that Justin and Michael would like nothing better than to become brothers, and he was certainly willing to do his part to make that possible. But how did he get Cathy to see what she was missing?

"Mom doesn't want to get married," Michael had blurted out recently. "I think my dad broke her heart real bad."

Not wanting to cross-examine Michael, but curious to know more, Tate had asked, "Your father doesn't seem to be a part of your life. Is he—"

"Nah, he's not dead," Michael had replied. "At least not as far as we know. He walked out on Mom before she got a chance to tell him she was pregnant. When I turn eighteen, if I want to find him, she'll help me. But I figure he had to be pretty stupid to let my mom go. I don't know if I want to meet the guy."

Tate had silently agreed. He would never have let Cathy go.

"Well, are you going to stand out there all day?" Cathy asked, effectively jerking Tate from his thoughts.

Grinning, he stepped over the threshold into the small, cluttered office.

When Cathy smiled at him, his gut tightened. Did she have any idea how badly he wanted to kiss her? Probably not. If she did, she'd run in the opposite direction.

"Are you three guys sure you're ready to work here all afternoon?" Cathy asked, glancing from one to the other. "Painting is no easy job." She focused on Tate. "And don't you have a construction firm to run?"

"I took the day off. Besides, I need to be here for the board meeting at four. By the way, I've promised the boys that if they stick it out the entire afternoon, we'll take them to that new sci-fi movie tonight."

"And we can get anything we want from the concession stand," Michael reminded him.

"Yeah, and we get to pick where we eat supper afterwards," Justin added.

She ruffled Michael's dark hair, then Justin's blond curls. "Not a bad deal." Glancing at Tate, she asked, "Is it a bribe or a reward?"

"Whatever works, right?"

"Right. We have a whole house that needs painting, so all volunteers are appreciated." She motioned to the door. "They're already serving lunch in the cafeteria downstairs. I believe we're having chicken casserole today."

Both boys grimaced, and Justin groaned.

Tate gave his son a you'll-eat-it-and-like-it glare.

"It's okay," Cathy told them. "We always have either peanut butter sandwiches or grilled cheese sandwiches and sometimes hot dogs for the kids who stay here with their moms."

The boys grinned, obviously relieved.

"May we get colas out of your little fridge to take with us?" Michael asked.

Cathy sighed. "I'd rather you didn't, honey. None of the other kids will have colas and it wouldn't be fair—"

Michael shrugged. "No problem. Milk or juice will be okay."

"Why don't you two go on down," Tate suggested. "And choose a table for us. We'll be there in a few minutes."

"Grown-up talk," Justin said, then both boys laughed and shot out of the room. Tate heard their rowdy footsteps as they ran down the back stairs.

"You didn't feed them sugar for breakfast, did you?" Cathy asked. "They're both super energized today."

"Actually, they didn't have breakfast. They slept until ten, then showered and dressed and we headed down here."

Smiling, she eyed him speculatively. "Is there something you want to discuss with me?"

"Huh?"

"You sent the boys ahead and Justin implied we were going to talk about grown-up stuff, so—"

"It's nothing earth-shattering," he said. *Unless you count the fact that I think I'm falling in love with you.*

"So what is it?"

"I was just thinking about the kids here at the shelter not having colas, not even as treats," Tate said. "What if Russell Construction donates several cases to start with, and then as a member of the board, I'll contact a few of the local distributors and see what we can work out."

"Tate Russell, have I ever told you what a wonderful man you are?"

"No, Cathy, you haven't." He grinned at her.

"Then let me tell you—Tate, you are a wonderful man. And I'm so very glad that I…that Michael has you in his life. You're a true role model for my son."

"That works both ways. You're the kind of woman I want Justin to know, the type of female role model a boy needs. You're warm and caring and generous and—" He looked at her questioningly. "What's wrong?"

Cathy was suddenly solemn. "Please, don't put me on a pedestal. There are things about me that you don't know. When I was younger—"

"I don't expect you to be perfect," he told her. "God knows I'm not. And if we're going to compete as to who had the wildest youth, you just might lose. I was the bane of my parents' existence for several years back when I was in high school."

When he walked over to her and reached out, intending to caress her cheek, she drew back, as if she couldn't bear the thought of him touching her. "We'd better go," she said. "The boys will wonder what happened to us."

"Sure. Let's go."

He had to be patient and understanding, give Cathy all the time she needed to accept the fact that sooner or later, they were going to be lovers. And more. Much more.

CHAPTER TWO

"THE BOARD MEETING WENT WELL, didn't it?" Cathy cornered Tate directly after the meeting ended.

"It was a great idea having two volunteers from the shelter and a representative from the residents on the board," Tate said. "But then you always have great ideas."

"And you, Tate Russell, have a silver tongue. You always know the right thing to say. But I can't take credit for the idea. There's an organization in Toronto called Street Haven that has a board of directors made up of members from the community, such as lawyers and business people, as well as staff and Street Haven clients. All I did was borrow their model."

"My mother always said that knowing where to find the answer was the next best thing to already knowing the answer."

"Your mother was a wise woman." In her peripheral vision, Cathy caught a glimpse of Andrew Hudson as he approached the exit. She called out, "Andrew, I'd like to speak to you."

Andrew paused, then acknowledged her request with a smile and a nod.

"Want me to wait around?" Tate asked.

"No, thanks. You go on."

"Don't forget about this evening."

"Oh, I haven't forgotten, and if I did, Michael would remind me at least half a dozen times."

"I think the movie starts at seven-fifteen. Why don't we pick y'all up around six-thirty?"

"Sounds fine."

Tate spoke to Andrew as the two men passed each other. Andrew was twenty-six, five-seven and skinny, with wavy black hair and golden-brown eyes hidden behind a pair of glasses that weren't all that flattering. He usually wore jeans and a cotton pullover shirt and today was no exception. Although he wasn't handsome, he was cute in a boyish, slightly nerdy way. But what he lacked in looks, he more than made up for in personality and heart.

She should never compare the two men, Cathy thought. It was like comparing apples to oranges. Tate was older by eleven years and possessed the rugged good looks other men envied and women drooled over. At six-one, broad-shouldered and lean-hipped, Tate had the swagger of a confident man who knew his place in the world. He wore his light brown hair short and neat, and his gray-blue eyes always had a sparkle in them. Smiling eyes. He was the kind of man who made others feel comfortable, perhaps because he was so comfortable in his own skin. A trait Cathy envied.

"What's up?" Andrew asked.

Cathy glanced casually around the meeting room, noting that it was now almost empty. Only a couple of stragglers remained, but they were deep in conversation near the door and weren't likely to overhear Andrew and her.

"How is Pearl? I haven't seen her today, but I plan to find her before I leave here and welcome her back to the shelter."

"Pearl is doing well," Andrew said. "She looks rested and prettier than I've ever seen her. She returned from rehab with a positive attitude."

"That's wonderful. She's quite special, isn't she?" This conversation would be so much easier if she could just come right out and ask Andrew if there was anything going on between Pearl and him. But considering the fact that it was really none of her business, she had to choose her words wisely.

"Yes, Pearl is very special," he replied.

"She's fortunate that you took an interest in her and have done so much to help her."

"I wish I could do more for her and other girls like her."

"Yes, of course. We all wish that."

"Was that what you wanted to talk to me about?" Andrew asked.

"Oh…well…not exactly."

"Is something wrong? You're acting sort of strange."

When Cathy realized that the final two stragglers had gone out into the hall, she took a deep breath and said, "Tell me if I'm stepping over the bounds here, but…do you think perhaps Pearl has…is…well, it's possible Pearl might misconstrue your kindness for something more."

Andrew wrinkled his brow, and frown lines formed around his mouth. "Are you accusing me of something?"

"Mercy, no. All I'm saying—and doing it badly, I'm afraid—is that Pearl is vulnerable and I wouldn't want to see her get hurt. If she mistakes your attention for love, then—"

"Look, Cathy, I know you mean well, but you are sort of stepping over the bounds a little. Both Pearl and I are adults, and if we—"

"Oh…oh, mercy."

"You're acting as if we…as if Pearl and I are doing something wrong. We aren't. I swear to you that I haven't even kissed her. But I do care about her."

"I see."

"And she cares about me, too."

"I'm sure she does, but you have to realize how impossible a personal relationship between the two of you is. Right now, you feel sorry for Pearl. We all do. And she is a very pretty girl. Any man would find her attractive. But she's so vulnerable right now, so needy. If you allow her to think of you as her salvation, as a way out, you'll be doing her a disservice. She has to learn to stand on her own two feet and not think that Prince Charming is going to come along and take care of her and make all her problems vanish."

Andrew looked her square in the eyes. "What happened to you, Cathy? Who hurt you so badly that you don't believe in happily ever after for yourself or anyone else?"

Cathy drew in a deep breath and exhaled slowly in an effort to calm herself. "I'm sorry. I apologize. You and Pearl *are* adults. I hope you know that I spoke to you only because I care for both of you and I don't want to see either of you get hurt."

Andrew laid his hand gently on Cathy's shoulder. "I know you meant well. I'm not questioning your motives. Will it ease your mind any if I promise you that I'll never hurt Pearl in any way?"

Cathy forced a smile. "I know you wouldn't. Not intentionally. You're a good man."

"Don't you think Pearl needs a good man?"

"Of course she does. But consider what you'd have to deal with if you became personally involved with Pearl. She's an unwed mother whose baby could possibly be born with physical and mental handicaps because of her drug abuse. She earned her living as a prostitute from the age of sixteen. What would the people at church think? How would it affect your career?"

Andrew removed his hand from her shoulder and stared at Cathy as if she had two heads. "I never realized you could be so judgmental, so unforgiving. I thought you of all people believed everyone was entitled to a second chance."

"Oh, Andrew, that's not what I meant." Cathy reached out to him pleadingly. "I do believe everyone is entitled to a second chance, and sometimes a third or even a fourth. I'm not judging Pearl, at least not the way you mean. But whether we like it or not, others can and do judge us on our past actions. You may truly believe that you can accept Pearl for who she is now, that her past doesn't matter. But what if you discovered later on that it did matter, that you couldn't deal with it as easily as you thought. You could wind up breaking Pearl's heart and…"

"You don't need to say any more." Andrew held up a restraining hand, signaling Cathy to stop. He stood there staring at her for a full minute, tears glistening in his eyes, then turned and rushed out of the room.

Cathy heaved a deep sigh. Had she simply made matters worse by speaking to Andrew? Initially she had intended to forewarn him that Pearl might have a crush on him and misconstrue his kindness and attention for something more. But then she'd realized Andrew had deeper feelings for Pearl, romantic feelings, and she'd butted in when she shouldn't have. But why? Had she projected her own fears of being rejected onto Pearl's situation?

She often wondered what people would think if they knew about her past. She had once been a teenage runaway living with her boyfriend, who had deserted her only days after learning she was pregnant. A high-school dropout, she'd had no skills, and without family or close friends to turn to, she had considered both abortion and suicide. She had even thought about prostitution as a temporary solution. Thank God, she had found out about Street Haven before she'd made another huge mistake. As long as she lived, she would be grateful to the wonderful people at Street Haven in Toronto who had taken her in. With their support and her own determination, she had made the most of the chance they'd offered her.

It wasn't that she had lied to anyone about her past. She just hadn't talked about it. She was ashamed of having been such a foolish young girl, yet she could deal with the truth if it ever came out. But what about Michael? It was her duty as his mother to protect him, wasn't it? When she had come to Chattanooga seven years ago, most people assumed she was divorced, and she hadn't bothered to correct them. Earline knew the truth, of course, and probably Daniel because he and Earline had no secrets from each other.

The only person she had lied to was Michael. To protect her son, she had told him that his dad hadn't known she was pregnant.

Cathy knew only too well the overwhelming sense of worthlessness that came with being unloved and unwanted. She had lived with that emotional burden all her life. Sean Williams had made her believe he would love her forever, and she had suffered even more when he had deserted her. His rejection had left deep emotional scars that made it difficult for her to trust anyone.

For women like Pearl and her, taking a chance on love was like asking to be kicked in the gut—again.

WITH DRIED PAINT SPRINKLED in his hair, smeared on his clothes and face, Michael looked like a ragamuffin. Cathy had placed an old towel in the passenger seat of her SUV to protect the upholstery before letting him in.

As she drove up Broad Street, heading for the Interstate ramp that would take her onto Highway 27, she tossed her son an antibacterial wipe. "See if you can clean your hands."

He scrubbed his hands with the wipe, then tossed it into the small trash container attached to the passenger door. "Could we stop on the way home and get a cola? I'm really thirsty."

"Maybe." She glanced briefly at her son. Michael was hers and hers alone. She seldom thought about the man who had fathered him. Her son had inherited her dark hair and eyes and her facial features, but he had a much better personality than she did. He was far more gregarious.

"Did you have fun painting?" she asked. "Or was it just work?"

Michael shrugged. "Both, I guess. I did have fun at first, but after the first hour, it was work. No way am I going to be a painter. I want to do something a little easier."

"Such as?"

"Gee, Mom, I don't know."

"At least you don't have to decide right now. You're only twelve, but in a few years, you'll need to do some serious thinking about your future. Right now just make good grades and stay out of trouble."

"I guess that's what all parents want for their kids, huh? Justin says his dad rewards him for his good grades. He actually gets ten bucks for every A he brings home on his report card and he can spend that money any way he wants to."

Cathy laughed. "I hope you aren't expecting me to pay you for your grades. For one thing, I'd go broke, considering you're a straight-A student. And don't forget that Coach Russell is wealthy and your mom is *not*."

"I know. I was just telling you what Justin told me."

As she drove onto Highway 27, she asked Michael, "So, where do you want to stop for colas? I'm not rich, but I think I can spring for a couple of cold drinks."

"Anywhere is fine with me," he replied. "Mom?"

"Yes?"

"You like Tate, don't you?"

"Tate? When did you start calling Coach Russell by his given name?"

"Since last night. He told me I should just call him Tate."

"Oh, I see."

"Well, Mom, you *do* like him, don't you?"

"Yes, of course. He's a very nice man."

"I like him," Michael said. "He's a really great guy and a wonderful dad."

"Yes, he is."

"Aw, Mom, you're not getting it, are you?"

She took her eyes off the road just long enough to glance at Michael and see the frown marring his precious face. "Apparently not. What are you talking about, honey?"

"I'm talking about the fact that I like Tate and you like Tate, and Tate and Justin like us. You and me."

Cathy laughed. "Okay, I agree that we all like one another. So?"

"So, Justin and I have been talking, and we think it would be great if you and his dad got together."

Now she got it. "You mean you and Justin would like Tate and me to date?"

"Yeah. Dating first, then get engaged and married. Justin thinks you'd make a great mom and I think Tate would make a great dad. So, what do you say? Don't you think it's—"

"Oh, Michael, Tate and I are just friends."

"Lots of people are friends first, before they get married."

"Just when did you and Justin hatch this marvelous plan?"

Michael grinned sheepishly. "Last night."

"Whose idea was it?"

"Mine and his. We've both been thinking about it for weeks now, but he never said anything to me and I never said anything to him."

"Look, honey, I know you miss not having a dad, but—"

"Just go out on one date with him, okay? That's all."

How did she respond to that? What could she say to him? She could hardly admit to her twelve-year-old son that she would never, as long as she lived, completely trust another man. Not even a great guy like Tate Russell.

"One date, huh?"

Turning in his seat, Michael said, "You'll do it? You'll ask Tate for a date?"

"I…uh…I'll think about it."

"Yea, Mom!"

Cathy's heart sank. Even if she did wind up going out on one date with Tate to appease Michael, she knew nothing would come of it. She wouldn't let it. She didn't dare.

CATHY HAD BEEN UNUSUALLY QUIET all evening. Not that she was ever a big talker, Tate thought, but she'd spoken only when spoken to ever since Justin and he had picked Michael and her up at six-thirty. At the movies, they had intended to place the boys between them as they had done on two previous outings, but both kids had insisted that they be allowed to sit alone, a couple of rows down from their parents. Tate knew what they were up to, but he wasn't sure Cathy did.

On the ride home from the St. Elmo shelter this afternoon, Justin had confided in him about his and Michael's lengthy discussion concerning their parents.

"I need a mom and Michael needs a dad," Justin had said. "I really like Ms. Brennan and Michael thinks you're great."

"Are you saying what I think you are?"

"If you two got married, Michael and I would be brothers and—"

"Whoa, son. Marriage? Cathy and I haven't even been out on a real date."

"So ask her already. Ask her tonight."

Tate had given Justin's suggestion a great deal of thought and admitted to himself that he'd like nothing better than to get to know Cathy on a more personal level, but she had shown no indication that she felt the same. And a guy really hated to get shot down. But who was to say that would happen? After all, he and Cathy had been around each other often enough to realize they were compatible. They had more in common than a lot of married people. They both loved baseball, sci-fi books and movies. They attended the same church and were both interested in outreach work. She was the volunteer director of Shelter from the Storm and he served on its newly formed board of directors.

Tate pulled his Navigator SUV into Cathy's driveway.

"Is it okay for Justin to come in for a while so we can play video games?" Michael asked his mother. "Just thirty minutes. Please."

"Just thirty minutes, huh?" Cathy smiled at Tate and his stomach knotted painfully. Did she have any idea just how lovely she was or what effect her innocent smiles had on his libido?

"It's fine with me, if it is with Tate." She tossed the ball into his court.

"Sure," Tate said.

The boys shot out of the SUV and raced to the front door. Tate got out, rounded the hood and helped Cathy down onto the driveway. He allowed his hand to linger on her arm, and much to his surprise, she didn't brush it aside when he guided her up the sidewalk to her front door.

She retrieved her keys from her purse, unlocked the door and flipped on the light. Her house was a modest three-bedroom, two-bath in Hunter Trace, one of many neat, vinyl-sided homes in the nice neighborhood. He suspected that making payments on this house, albeit modest by his standards, stretched Cathy's budget to the limits. After all, she was a single mother, without child support, surviving on her pay as a high-school teacher.

By the time he and Cathy entered the small foyer, the boys were already halfway down the hall to Michael's room.

"Would you like something to drink?" Cathy asked. "I'm afraid I don't keep anything alcoholic in the house, but I have iced tea, apple juice and orange juice."

"Nothing for me, thanks."

Cathy's living room was furnished with sturdy, inexpensive pieces that managed to create a warm, comfortable feel. If she were his wife, Tate thought, she could decorate their home without such tight budget considerations. He'd lay the world at her feet. The house of her dreams, fine furniture, expensive clothes…pretty much anything she desired.

She's not your wife, he told himself. But if he were honest, he had to admit he was on the verge of falling in love with Cathy Brennan.

"Come on in and sit down." She welcomed him with a wave of her hand.

Instead of sitting, he came up behind her, clasped her shoulder and leaned down. She gasped.

"Cathy, I need to ask you something."

She whirled around, freeing herself from his hand. "You sound so serious."

"Dating is a serious matter. Or at least it should be."

"Dating?"

"Are you aware that our sons would like us to go out on a real date?"

Cathy laughed. "Oh, I see Justin has spoken to you. Michael filled me in on the way home this afternoon."

Tate breathed a sigh of relief. "Those two have become best bud-dies, and since you and I are single, they think we should be dating."

"I know. I hope you don't mind, but I promised Michael that you and I would go out on a date."

"You did?"

"Just one date," she told him. "It seems to mean so much to him that I couldn't say no. I hope you don't mind."

"I understand. It means a great deal to Justin, too."

And to me, he wanted to tell her, but didn't. Just one date? She might intend for their first date to be their last, but if he had his way, it would be the first of many.

CHAPTER THREE

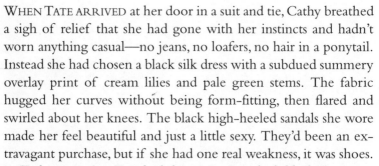

WHEN TATE ARRIVED at her door in a suit and tie, Cathy breathed a sigh of relief that she had gone with her instincts and hadn't worn anything casual—no jeans, no loafers, no hair in a ponytail. Instead she had chosen a black silk dress with a subdued summery overlay print of cream lilies and pale green stems. The fabric hugged her curves without being form-fitting, then flared and swirled about her knees. The black high-heeled sandals she wore made her feel beautiful and just a little sexy. They'd been an extravagant purchase, but if she had one real weakness, it was shoes.

To her surprise, Tate had driven up in a sleek black Corvette. Cathy was accustomed to seeing him in the Navigator, an upscale family ride. A Corvette was a bachelor's vehicle, a playboy's toy. But tonight, it seemed to fit Tate perfectly. And that unnerved her. In all the time they'd spent together with the boys, she had tried not to notice how devastatingly attractive he was.

Their conversation was stilted at first. They had both agreed to this date to pacify their sons and Tate probably felt as awkward as she did.

After he turned off Hixon Pike onto Amnicola Highway, Cathy hazarded a glance his way and immediately wished she hadn't. Her stomach did a wicked flip-flop, and although she tried to tell herself it was only nerves, she knew better. Everything feminine within her responded to Tate's overwhelming masculinity.

"You're awfully quiet," he said. "You're not already regretting this date, are you?"

"No, of course not. We both know why we're doing this. After tonight, nothing will be different. We'll still be friends."

"Mind if I ask you a personal question?"

"It depends on just how personal." Despite laughing softly to indicate she was joking, in her heart of hearts, Cathy was dead serious. There were some things far too personal to share, especially with Tate Russell.

"Why haven't you gotten married?"

Cathy's heart sank. She could lie by omission as she usually did when asked a question about her marital status. On any legal forms she had to fill out, she always marked *SINGLE,* rather than *DIVORCED.* All her records plainly showed that her maiden name was Brennan, the same as Michael's. But the general public didn't know she'd never been married to his father, and it wasn't something she proclaimed to the world. Despite more tolerant moral standards, Cathy preferred not to be thought of as an unwed mother.

"I've never been married," she said. "Michael's father and I went our separate ways before he was born."

"Yes, I know. Michael told us that his dad never knew about him, that he took off before he found out you were pregnant."

Cathy sensed the question in his statement. "Yes, that's what I told Michael."

"But it's not what happened, is it? Michael's father left you after he found out you were pregnant, didn't he?"

"Oh, yeah. He couldn't leave fast enough." After all these years, the memory of Sean Williams's desertion still had the power to hurt her.

"If my opinion matters, I think you did the right thing in not telling Michael the whole truth." Keeping one hand on the wheel, Tate reached across the console and grasped her hand, entwining their fingers. "He told me that he doesn't intend to ever try to find his father, because any man who'd walk out on his mom is an idiot." Tate squeezed her hand. "I agree with him completely."

A warm rush of pleasure swept over Cathy. Tate's opinion shouldn't matter so much to her, but it did. "It hasn't been easy for Michael growing up without a dad."

"You could have given him a father if you'd gotten married."

She sighed. "I could lie to you and tell you that I haven't married because I never met the right man or because I've been too busy, first going to college and then teaching and helping found Shelter from the Storm. But the truth is I haven't been looking for a husband."

He squeezed her hand again. "Michael's father must have hurt you terribly."

"Something like that." She forced the words out through partially clenched teeth.

"When Hannah died, I thought I'd die, too." Tate untwined his fingers from Cathy's and placed his hand back on the steering wheel. "I hated myself for having spent too much time at work instead of with her and Justin. Actually, I hated the whole world, and I even hated God there for a while. But in the end, knowing Justin needed me is what saw me through the really rough times. I imagine Michael has been your salvation, hasn't he?"

"He's my reason for living."

"I understand."

They both stopped talking, as if they needed to regroup after sharing such deeply personal feelings. For several miles, they drove along in silence.

Finally, when Cathy noticed they were on Chestnut Street, she said, "We're downtown, heading toward the Aquarium. Just where are you taking me for dinner?"

"Can't you guess?"

"No, not really—" That's when she saw the riverboat ahead, docked at Pier 2 on Riverfront Parkway. "We're dining on the *Southern Belle?* Oh, Tate, what a lovely idea."

"I aim to please," he told her as he whipped the Corvette into the parking lot. "I wanted our first date to be special."

"Oh." What could she say? Surely he understood that this was a one-time thing.

Tate rounded the hood of the sports car, opened the passenger door and helped her out. The minute the humid evening air hit her skin, she felt hot. But she wasn't sure if the heat was weather-related, or a reaction to having Tate's arm around her.

THE CAESAR SALAD WAS perfect and so were the prime rib, baby red potatoes, green beans and scrumptious rolls. But there was no way Cathy could eat all this food. Even through her twenties, she'd been able to eat as much as she wanted. But after turning thirty, her metabolism had seemed to slow just enough that she'd been forced to start watching the amount she consumed. Only one roll, she told herself. And no dessert.

Since arriving on the *Southern Belle,* she and Tate had avoided talking about anything deeply personal and chitchatted about the hot July weather, her work at the shelter and his position on the board, the Lookouts' season so far this year, and their sons. Always their sons.

The riverboat was one of Chattanooga's many tourist attractions, but the restaurant also appealed to local residents, and Cathy could see why. The mood was one of luxury and comfort, as well as romance.

"Why don't you and Michael come to the house Sunday afternoon?" Tate suggested. "We can grill steaks and burgers and swim in the pool and take the boat out for an afternoon excursion."

"That sounds really nice." He wasn't asking her for a second date, Cathy told herself. They'd be a foursome, with Michael and Justin. "I'll bring the salad fixings and dessert."

His smile ignited something entirely unexpected inside Cathy.

A giddiness she could only vaguely recall from her teen years. She was being silly. What on earth was the matter with her?

"We seem to be chalking up several firsts," Tate said.

She looked at him inquiringly.

His smile broadened. "Well, this is our first date tonight, and Sunday you'll come to my house for the first time."

"Oh, yes, you're right." Her sudden nervousness eased a little. "I've heard so much about your place from Michael that I almost feel as if I've been there. And you know, I just now realized that I've never picked Michael up. You've always brought him home."

"That's okay. We're both busy single parents with full-time jobs, but I have a great deal more help than you do. I have a housekeeper and a gardener at home. Besides that, I'm my own boss and can take time off without having to get anyone's permission."

Cathy smiled, then sliced one of the small new potatoes in half and speared it with her fork. Before she could take a bite, her cell phone rang. Hurriedly, she laid the fork on her plate, lifted her clutch purse from the table and retrieved her phone.

As she flipped it open, she looked apologetically at Tate. "Cathy Brennan."

"Cathy, this is Earline." Her friend sounded agitated. "I hate to interrupt your dinner but we have a situation at the safe house in East Ridge."

Cathy's heart leapt to her throat. "What kind of situation?"

"Tonya Allen is certain she's seen her husband's car drive by three times in the past couple of hours. She's terrified that he's found her and the children."

"Did you call the police?"

"Yes, of course I did. They've promised to have a patrol car pass by every hour, but until Derin Allen does something illegal, there's nothing the police can do."

Cathy cursed under her breath. "We have to move Tonya and the kids as soon as possible. Actually, we need to vacate the house, take all four women and the six children and relocate them tonight."

"I agree, but we're pretty much at full capacity at the shelter in St. Elmo, and the other safe house is full, too," Earline reminded her. "Any suggestions? I'd be willing to bring one of the women and her children home with me."

"Okay, let's see…" Cathy tried to figure out who she could call for help. "You can take one woman and I'll take one. That leaves two. We'll have to make some more phone calls and see what we can come up with." Many of the shelter's volunteers simply didn't have enough room in their homes to accommodate several other people, but perhaps for one night… "Can you and Daniel meet me at the East Ridge safe house in—" She glanced across the table at Tate. "I have to move four women and six children ASAP. I hate to ask—"

"Tell Earline and Daniel we'll line up help and meet them there," Tate said. "I'll phone Jeff Clark, one of my employees. He owns a van and an SUV. He and his wife will help us transport these people. They live in the area and can get there a lot quicker than if we drive back to pick up my Navigator."

Cathy relayed Tate's plan to Earline, then added, "If we have to, we'll put cots in the halls at the shelter."

"And I'll have Daniel guard the door with his shotgun," Earline said, only halfway joking.

"We'll be there as soon as we can," Cathy promised.

"Take a deep breath," Earline told her. "Thank goodness Tonya noticed and called us before her husband did more than drive by. What I can't figure out is how he found them."

"Who knows? Somebody told somebody who told somebody else. These things happen, no matter how careful we are."

"Let's pray we get there before Derin Allen actually stops at the house."

Cathy closed her cell phone and shoved it back into her purse. "I'm so sorry about this."

Tate called the waiter over and asked for a check. "Immediately," he said. "We have an emergency and have to leave." Then he used his cell phone to contact Jeff Clark.

The bill was taken care of in a snap, and Tate escorted Cathy off the riverboat and onto the pier. Once they were safely belted into the car, Tate headed over to Market Street.

"From what you were saying to Earline, I take it that an abusive husband has discovered the location of the East Ridge safe house, and now you need to vacate that house, but you don't have room anywhere for ten people. Is that right?"

"Yes, that's right."

"I believe I can solve your problem, at least temporarily."

"You can? How?"

"I have a showcase house on Signal Mountain in a new neighborhood," he told her. "It's fully furnished and the utilities are on. There are four bedrooms and four baths."

"Oh, Tate, do you mean it? You'd actually…" Emotion tightened her throat.

"Of course I mean it. You have a problem. I have a solution."

"The terrible thing is that we probably won't be able to use the East Ridge house again. If Derin Allen discovered it this easily, other men could, too."

"Then we need to come up with another house as soon as possible. The place in East Ridge is a rental, isn't it?"

"Yes, we rent both of the safe houses for this very reason."

"Then why don't you let me, as a member of the board, find a new residence where we can relocate those four women and their children."

Tears gathered in Cathy's eyes. "Tate Russell, you're too good to be true."

As she looked at him in the semidarkness of the car, Cathy had an almost irresistible urge to slide across the console and kiss him.

ANDREW CARRIED the packages to his car, put them in the trunk and then helped Pearl into her seat. He had taken her to an early movie followed by shopping at Northgate Mall. He'd bought her a new pair of sensible shoes and some slacks and tops. Now that she was nearly five months pregnant, very few of her old clothes still fit her. And in all honesty, she didn't own many things that weren't part of her "working girl" attire.

"Want to stop by Panera Bread and grab a bite?" Andrew asked.

"Oh, can we?"

"Sure."

"You've already spent so much money on me, I hate for you to—"

"You've thanked me at least a half-dozen times, and I'll tell you again that I'm only too happy to help you."

When Andrew smiled at her, Pearl felt warm and fuzzy inside, something she never felt except when she was with him. Andrew was kindness personified, and he represented safety and security; his friendship was as much a safe haven as Shelter from the Storm. But there was more to her feelings for Andrew and that worried her. While going through the rehab program to kick her drug habit, Pearl had thought of Andrew every day and occasionally dreamed about him at night. He had been the one constant in her life for nearly a year now, but only after he rescued her—literally— from an abusive john, had she thought of him as more than a do-good youth minister trying to "save" her and all the other sinners in her profession.

Once at Panera Bread, Pearl found a booth for them while Andrew placed their order. She glanced around at all the people in the bakery/café and wondered what they would think if they knew she was a former prostitute who had no idea who the father of her unborn child was. Tonight, on her excursion with Andrew, people had smiled and spoken with her, treating her as if she were like any other pregnant young woman. She suspected they thought Andrew was her husband and the father of her child.

She sighed. If only that were true. If only… What would it be like? she wondered. It would be heaven. Absolute heaven.

For me. Not for Andrew.

When he married, he would choose a good girl, a respectable girl, one whose past would never embarrass him.

"Here we go." Andrew removed their food from the serving tray, set the tray at the back of the table and slid into the booth on the opposite side. "Eat up. Remember, you're eating for two."

Pearl eyed the glass of milk and thick sandwich. After three months of not being able to eat much of anything, she now had the appetite of a horse.

She laid her hand tenderly over her slightly protruding belly. "I hate myself every time I think that I might have hurt my baby."

"Don't look back," Andrew told her. "Unfortunately, none of us can change the past. We just have to do the best we can do today…and tomorrow."

"What if she's seriously damaged?" At Pearl's last doctor's appointment, the sonogram showed she was having a girl and there were no obvious signs of any physical deformity. "How will I ever be able to forgive myself? How will she ever be able to forgive me?"

Andrew reached across the table and grasped her hands in his. "If she has any mental or physical problems, we'll make sure she gets the best treatment possible. And we'll love her and take care of her and give her a good life."

Pearl stared at Andrew, wondering if he realized he had said "we" repeatedly, as if he intended to be a part of her child's life, not only now, but in the future. "If only I had gotten help sooner. If I had listened to you…" Tears choked her.

He squeezed her hand. "Don't do this to yourself. Remember, think ahead, not back. If the Good Lord forgives us for our mistakes, why is it that we often have so much trouble forgiving ourselves?"

Pearl dried her tears with a paper napkin. "I promise that I'll try to be a good mother."

"I know you will. You have a kind heart, Pearl."

"You've always seen the best in me, even when I was… But you're not always going to be around."

"I could be," he told her. "I'd like to be."

She looked him directly in the eyes. "What are you saying?"

"I'm saying that I have feelings for you, Pearl. Feelings that go a lot deeper than a minister or a shelter volunteer wanting to help others."

She snatched her hand away and shook her head. "No, no, Andrew, you can't do this."

His face turned pale. "Forgive me if I've stepped over the line here, but I thought…I had hoped you had feelings for me, too."

How could she saddle a man like Andrew with her problems? Pearl thought.

"I—I care about you, Andrew," she told him. "But I'm just not ready for…please understand."

He offered her a weak smile. "I understand."

"This won't change our friendship, will it?"

"No, of course not." He glanced at her untouched glass of milk and sandwich. "Let's eat, then I'll drive you back to St. Elmo."

She lifted the sandwich and took a large bite, but she barely tasted the food. The thought that Andrew cared deeply for her, that he wanted to be there for her and her baby, consumed her. Those thoughts filled her heart with hope and her mind with dreams. Dreams of a future that could never be.

WHEN TATE AND CATHY ARRIVED at the safe house in East Ridge, Jeff Clark waited in his van in the driveway, his wife Ashley parked behind him in her SUV. Tate pulled over to the side of the road, then got out and walked over to speak to his friend.

Cathy raced up to the house and knocked on the door, making sure her face was visible to the security camera. Tonya Allen opened it immediately and all but threw herself at her. Cathy hugged the woman reassuringly.

"He's parked across the street," Tonya said. "He knows that if he comes into the yard, he'll be violating the restraining order I have against him, but…" She gulped down terrified sobs. "I don't think that will stop him."

Cathy led the petite blond woman back inside the house. The

other three women waited in the living room, obviously anxious about their own fate as well as Tonya's.

"Everything is going to be all right," Cathy told them. "We're going to relocate all of you tonight. We have vehicles waiting outside. Pack as quickly as you can."

"Where are we going?" A doe-eyed young Latino woman named Paloma held her six-month-old son on her hip.

"Y'all will be staying in an unoccupied house that belongs to a friend of mine. It's fully furnished and the utilities are on. As soon as we can rent another house, we'll move you there."

"How did Tonya's old man find out where she was?" Holly Jean Klyce asked.

Holly Jean was a twenty-eight-year-old who looked forty. She had married at sixteen, had her first baby at seventeen, divorced at twenty, remarried at twenty-one and had another child. Both husbands had been brutes. But with two children, no skills and nowhere to turn for help, she had stayed with her second husband—until he started beating her son from her first marriage. Holly drank, smoked, had a potty mouth and an attitude that grated on Cathy's nerves, but to her credit, she wanted to keep her kids safe. Cathy could relate to her as a woman-in-need who wanted what was best for her children.

"We don't know how he found out," Cathy admitted truthfully. "We may never know."

"How are we going to leave here without Tonya's husband following us?" Christelle Fulmer asked, her seven-year-old twin daughters clinging to her.

"Don't worry about that," Cathy said. "I'll make sure Mr. Allen doesn't follow."

"How you going to do that?" Holly Jean asked sarcastically.

"Officer Meadows is going to stay with Mr. Allen," Tate said as he walked into the living room.

All eyes turned to him.

Cathy crossed the room and laced her arm through his. "Who is Officer Meadows?" she asked softly.

"He's the policeman who's been driving by here every hour," Tate said. "I stopped him on this round and explained the situation. He's across the street talking to Mr. Allen right now, and he plans to see to it that the guy stays put until I phone him and let him know we're far enough away that Allen won't be able to find us."

Once again Cathy had the overwhelming urge to throw her arms around Tate and kiss him. But as before, she managed to restrain herself.

"Thank you. You're wonderful, you know."

Tate just grinned.

Cathy turned to the group of women. "Hurry up. We need to leave as soon as we can."

CHAPTER FOUR

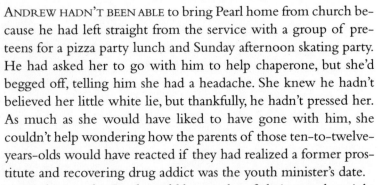

ANDREW HADN'T BEEN ABLE to bring Pearl home from church because he had left straight from the service with a group of preteens for a pizza party lunch and Sunday afternoon skating party. He had asked her to go with him to help chaperone, but she'd begged off, telling him she had a headache. She knew he hadn't believed her little white lie, but thankfully, he hadn't pressed her. As much as she would have liked to have gone with him, she couldn't help wondering how the parents of those ten-to-twelve-years-olds would have reacted if they had realized a former prostitute and recovering drug addict was the youth minister's date.

Maybe one day Pearl would be worthy of their trust, but right now she wasn't even sure just how much she trusted herself. Oh, she'd never go back to working the streets, not as long as she had any other option, and Shelter from the Storm provided those options. But drugs were another matter. Over the years, she had tried a little bit of everything, starting with marijuana. She had smoked pot at fourteen, then moved on to crack by sixteen and had even sampled heroin and LSD. But crack was her first choice.

Pearl walked up the stairs to the second floor, where her room was located. The bedroom was one of the smaller ones, with only two beds, two dressers and a long window that overlooked the south side of the house. When she arrived at the end of the hallway, she noticed that her door stood wide open and Brenda Collins, the resident house mother, was in the room with another woman. When Pearl reached the doorway, she cleared her throat. Both women turned to face her. Short, plump and fifty-something, Brenda smiled warmly. The other woman was young, probably no older than Pearl herself, and redheaded.

"Pearl, dear, come on in and meet your new roommate." When Brenda placed her hand on the redhead's shoulder, she flinched. "This is Whitney Nesbitt. Whitney, this is Pearl Isom."

"Hello." Pearl offered the new resident a tentative smile as she entered the room. She was never overly friendly with anyone on first acquaintance. She had learned the hard way that it was better to be cautious than sorry later.

"Hi," Whitney replied.

"I'll leave you girls to get to know each other." Brenda paused outside in the hallway. "Whitney, if you need anything, my room is downstairs. I'm available twenty-four hours a day."

Whitney nodded, then as soon as Brenda was out of earshot, she looked Pearl over from head to toe.

"Your baby got a daddy?" Whitney asked.

"No."

"Figures. Girls like us are the ones who get knocked up by worthless pieces of trash." She plopped down on the bed by the window, obviously claiming it as her own even though it was the one Pearl had chosen for herself upon arriving yesterday. "So why didn't you get rid of it?"

Pearl wanted to tell her it was none of her business, that she shouldn't be butting into other people's affairs. But instead she just shrugged and said, "I want my baby."

"You must be nuts. How are you going to take care of a baby when you can't even take care of yourself?"

"That's why I'm here at Shelter from the Storm," Pearl said. "They'll help me. They help women all the time to get a GED and even go on to college or find a job."

"And who's going to take care of that—" she pointed at Pearl's belly "—while you're going to school or working?"

"Cathy is planning to open a day-care center by this fall, if she can get some grant money and find some generous donors."

"Cathy, huh? Is she the head honcho around here?"

"She founded Shelter from the Storm and is the volunteer director. You'll like Cathy. Everyone does. She's a single mother herself."

Whitney stretched out on the bed and looked up at the ceiling. "Would you believe that old bat Brenda went through my suitcase and my purse? She confiscated my cigarettes and switchblade." Whitney rolled over on her side, unbuttoned her blouse just enough so she could slip two fingers into her bra, and pulled out a small plastic bag. "She should have done a body search." Laughing, she held the bag of crack over her head.

"You can't have that stuff here," Pearl said. Oh, God, why had this happened, and on her second day after being released from rehab?

She hadn't realized she was staring at the plastic bag until Whitney asked, "Want some?"

Pearl sat on the edge of the other twin bed and clasped her hands tightly together. She shook her head.

"Hey, you're breaking out in a sweat," Whitney told her. "You want some real bad, don't you? How long's it been?"

"I just got out of rehab yesterday. And yes, I want some. But I'm not going to…. Please, get rid of it. If you don't, I'll have to tell Brenda."

Whitney shot straight up in bed and glared at Pearl. "Aren't I the lucky one, getting a snitch for my roommate."

"There are rules you have to follow in order to stay here. I need this place. I need all the help I can get, so don't think I won't turn you in. I've got more than myself to think about now." Pearl laid her hand over her belly.

"Don't get your panties in a wad." Whitney tossed the bag of crack cocaine to Pearl. It landed in her lap. "I'm heading off to rehab day after tomorrow and I wanted to make sure I had some stuff before I go. You know, up to the very last minute. If you don't want any, that's fine by me. I was just trying to be neighborly."

Pearl stared at the plastic bag. Her pulse quickened. Her heartbeat hammered in her ears. She picked up the bag and held it for a couple of minutes, tempted beyond all reason. Then she threw it back to Whitney, got up and walked out of the room.

"Are you going to tell on me?" Whitney called after her.

Pearl didn't answer. The last thing on her mind was telling Brenda that her new roommate had hidden drugs inside her bra. No, Pearl had more immediate problems. She had to get away from Whitney's friendly little offer before it was too late. For her...and for her baby.

CATHY FELL IN LOVE with Tate's house the minute she saw it. The large, two-story brick featured a traditional front facade with a sprawling porch and navy blue shutters. At the back, walls of windows, a screened porch and three layers of decking faced out to the lake, which was actually the backwaters from the nearby Tennessee River. Stone steps led to the pier where Tate's thirty-five-foot cruiser was docked. At the side of the house, a pool and patio were surrounded by decorative fencing.

Michael had worn his swim trunks under his shorts and was in the pool within minutes after they arrived. While she and Tate labored in the kitchen and over the barbeque grill, the boys frolicked in the water. Michael was an adept swimmer. She'd made sure of that, starting his lessons the first summer they moved from Toronto to Chattanooga.

"You look mighty pretty today," Tate said casually. "Like sunshine."

She smiled. "Thanks."

Had she consciously dressed to attract Tate? Maybe. She had to admit that she had lain out the yellow sundress before she and Michael left for church this morning. She had chosen it for several reasons. First, she looked good in the fifties-style dress. It hugged her waist and crisscrossed her breasts, then tied with straps at the back of her neck. Second, she had a pair of snazzy yellow sandals that matched the dress and a yellow two-piece bathing suit. She liked things—clothes, furnishings—to be color coordinated.

It wasn't like Cathy to think about how a man would react to what she was wearing. She loved clothes and liked to look her best, but she dressed for herself and for no one else.

And even if she *had* dressed to impress Tate, was it wrong to want him to think she looked nice?

"Want to take a swim while the burgers and steaks are cooking?" Tate asked. "We've got everything under control and I can finish things up on my own."

She sighed. "I think I'll wait until after lunch."

"I thought that after we ate, I'd take you and the boys out on the boat."

"Oh, I'd like that and I'm sure Michael would, too."

Tate had opened a bottle of wine before they began meal preparations and had offered her a glass, but she had declined. Now, as he sipped on his wine, he asked, "Are you sure you don't want some?"

She shook her head. "No, thanks. I'll stick with my diet cola." She patted the can sitting on the kitchen counter.

"Well, if you don't want to join the boys in the pool, would you like a grand tour of the house?"

"I'd love it."

Setting his wine down, he led her from room to room on the main floor. She had seen the living and dining rooms when she first entered the house because they flanked the two-story foyer, but she enjoyed getting a closer look. And she'd already inspected the huge kitchen, breakfast room and family area.

"This place is breathtaking," she told him. "But I should have expected nothing less, considering you're a builder."

"I designed the house," he told her. "It's really too big for Justin and me, but someday I'd like to marry again and maybe have more children."

Cathy's breath caught in her throat.

"I can't take credit for the decorating," he said when it became apparent she wasn't going to comment on his last statement. "I hired an interior designer."

He led her down the hall and into the master suite. A massive king-size bed dominated the bedroom and a marble fireplace was the centerpiece of the sitting room.

"How long have you lived here?" Cathy asked. Had he built this house for his wife? Was it filled with memories of the woman he had loved and lost?

"Justin and I moved in here four years ago." Tate led her back to the foyer and the spiral staircase. "Six months after Hannah died, I sold our house and Justin and I moved in with my mother for a while. Then I invested in a condo downtown."

After touring the four bedrooms, four baths and rec room up-stairs, Cathy laughed, "With all this room, you really must be plan-ning on having more children."

"I'd like at least two more." He placed his hand in the small of her back.

Feeling his warm touch through her sundress, she tensed momentarily.

"Wouldn't you like to have more children?" he asked.

She should just jerk away to let him know he shouldn't be touching her, but the truth was, she enjoyed the feel of his big hand on her back, loved the feel of him so near.

"I—I haven't really thought about it," she said.

"If the right man came along…?"

She hurriedly changed the subject. "We'd better get out to the patio and check on those burgers before they burn."

He chuckled. "Yes, I guess we'd better."

As they walked down the stairs, side by side, Tate took her hand in his. They held hands all the way out to the patio. The gesture seemed so natural, Cathy thought. So pleasantly, enjoyably natural.

"Look at them," Justin said. "They're holding hands."

Michael glanced at his mother and Tate as they walked out onto the patio. "Yeah, man, you're right. And they're smiling. Heck, they're laughing."

Justin swam over to the wide steps at the shallow end of the pool and sat down on the top one. "Think they'll kiss?"

"I dunno," Michael said, swimming over to join his friend.

"I really like your mom. If my dad married her, I wouldn't mind having her for a mother."

Michael nodded. "Same. It would be great having your dad for a father."

"So how do we get them to fall in love?" Justin asked. "You know more about it than I do."

Michael looked aghast. "What do you mean? I've never been in love."

"What about Tiffany Raines?" Justin teased. "I thought you were in love with her. Ooh…kiss, kiss."

"No way, man. You're the one who likes her." Michael splattered water playfully in Justin's face, then pushed off the step and swam away. Justin followed, and within minutes, they were racing to see who could swim across the pool the fastest.

Cathy rested in the rocker on the deck, watching the fading rays of sunlight shimmer across the lake from a sky rich with shades of pink and lavender. Tate sat beside her in an identical rocker, and when she glanced at him, she realized that instead of enjoying the glorious scene before them, he was staring at her.

"I suppose you're used to this incredible view, aren't you?"

"Yes, I'm used to it, but it never ceases to impress me."

"So why were you looking at me instead of—"

"Because you, Ms. Brennan, are a pretty impressive sight yourself."

"Tate…I—I don't know how to respond to that."

"Just say, thank you, Tate."

"Thank you, Tate."

He nodded toward the closed French doors that led inside to the family room. "Did you notice how the boys insisted we stay outside and enjoy ourselves while they went in to watch TV?"

"They weren't very subtle, were they?"

If Justin hadn't been equally guilty, Cathy would have been embarrassed by Michael's blatant comments at how great the four of them were together.

"My son wants a mother and your son wants a father. And it would seem you and I are their top picks for those jobs."

"I'm sorry that Michael was so—"

"Justin was just as bad."

"Maybe it's our fault," Cathy said. "After all, we have been spending a great deal of time together these past few months, and then last night we agreed to go out on a date. I hope we haven't given them the wrong impression."

"And what would that impression be?"

She looked at him quizzically. "That we're a couple. That there's more to our relationship than just friendship."

"And there's not?" he asked.

"No, I... You don't want more than friendship, do you?"

Tate rose from his chair, came over to her and held out his hands. Instinctively, she lifted her hands and placed them in his. He tugged her up and onto her feet, then pulled her into his arms. Startled, she gasped.

"Yes, I do want more," he admitted.

"But...I...we..." She couldn't think straight when Tate was so close, when her body was pressed so intimately against his, when she could feel—oh, mercy! She could feel his arousal.

Without saying another word, he lowered his head and took her mouth. Gently. Giving her time to withdraw. But she responded, kissing him back, opening her mouth in invitation. His arms held her firmly, but as he deepened the kiss, he eased his hands down her back to cup her buttocks and press her closer. She melted against him, loving the taste of him, the scent of him, the feel of him.

When they were both breathless, Tate ended the kiss. Burying his face against her neck, he whispered, "I want you, Cathy. I want you so much."

Her body tingled, the sensation beginning between her thighs and radiating out to every nerve in her body. It had been forever since she'd felt this kind of desire, this sweet uncontrollable rush of longing.

Keeping one hand on her hip, Tate eased the other between them to cup her breast as he dotted kisses along her neck. Feeling hot and cold at the same time, she shivered and whimpered his name. "Tate…Tate…"

"Tell me you want me, too."

I want you. I want you desperately.

The thought jolted Cathy back to reality.

"I can't—I'm sorry…" She jerked out of Tate's arms and turned away from him.

"Cathy, what's wrong?"

She walked across the deck and grasped the banister railing, as she stared out at the colorful twilight. What was wrong? Everything was wrong. She had come so close to succumbing to desire, to giving in to her baser instincts. But she couldn't. She didn't dare. What if she fell in love with Tate? What if he used her and cast her aside? What if he thought of her as damaged goods? No, Tate wouldn't…. Just because she thought of herself that way didn't mean Tate would. He was a good man. He'd never intentionally hurt her.

But having sex didn't equal commitment. And a man like Tate wouldn't want a woman with Cathy's past as his wife.

What if she became involved with Tate and got Michael's hopes up, only to have them dashed to smithereens? She couldn't take that chance. She couldn't risk having her heart broken and definitely not her son's.

Tate came up behind her, but didn't touch her. "Did I push too hard too fast? Is that it?"

"Yes. No. Oh, Tate, I'm sorry if I sent out the wrong signals. But I just can't do this. Not now. Maybe not ever."

"Are you that afraid of caring for someone?" He grasped her shoulders and turned her to face him. "I'm not Michael's biological father. I'm not the man who got you pregnant and deserted you. I'm not the man who broke your heart."

"I know that. It's just…"

"You're punishing me for what another man did. That's not fair. Not to me or you."

"I know, but I can't help it."

"We can slow things down," he told her. "I can wait."

"No. You shouldn't wait for me. You should find someone else." Someone worthy of you.

CHAPTER FIVE

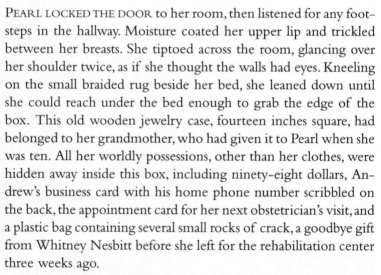

PEARL LOCKED THE DOOR to her room, then listened for any footsteps in the hallway. Moisture coated her upper lip and trickled between her breasts. She tiptoed across the room, glancing over her shoulder twice, as if she thought the walls had eyes. Kneeling on the small braided rug beside her bed, she leaned down until she could reach under the bed enough to grab the edge of the box. This old wooden jewelry case, fourteen inches square, had belonged to her grandmother, who had given it to Pearl when she was ten. All her worldly possessions, other than her clothes, were hidden away inside this box, including ninety-eight dollars, Andrew's business card with his home phone number scribbled on the back, the appointment card for her next obstetrician's visit, and a plastic bag containing several small rocks of crack, a goodbye gift from Whitney Nesbitt before she left for the rehabilitation center three weeks ago.

When she had pulled the box out, Pearl rose to sit on the edge of the bed. She glided her fingertips over the jewelry case on her lap, the hunger inside her urging her to give in, to stop fighting and ease the pain eating away at her. With both nervousness and guilt bearing down on her, she flipped up the lid and opened one of the three inner compartments. For several minutes she sat staring at the folded plastic bag, her mind and heart at odds with her addiction.

Why hadn't she simply thrown the stuff away, flushed it down the toilet after Whitney had given it to her? Or why hadn't she turned it in to Brenda Collins or even to Cathy? If she'd done either, she could have spared herself three weeks of torment, twenty-one days of struggling with her inner demon.

Brenda and Earline and Cathy suspected something was bothering her, but she swore to them that it was nothing, just normal worry about her unborn child and her own uncertain future. But Andrew knew it was more and had asked her point-blank what it was. She had tried lying to him, but when he didn't believe her, she had screamed at him to leave her alone. That had been two weeks ago, and although he had tried his best to talk to her again, she had done everything possible to keep her distance.

Andrew was far too good for her. He deserved a much better woman than she could ever be. How could he even trust her when she didn't trust herself?

But you've had the stuff for three weeks and you haven't used it, she reminded herself. *That has to count for something.*

But she wanted it. Wanted it desperately.

Pearl removed the plastic bag from the jewelry case and laid it on her pillow, then closed the box, leaned over and shoved it under the bed. She knew what she had to do, the only thing she could do if she wanted a chance for a decent future for herself and her baby.

CATHY AND EARLINE SHARED lunch in Cathy's office. Earline had brought club sandwiches and some of her delicious homemade pickles. Cathy both loved and hated it when Earline prepared their lunch. Loved it because it was so good, but hated it because it was always scrumptiously fattening, from the thick-sliced homemade bread and potato salad to the oversize slab of made-with-real-butter pound cake.

As they sat across from each other on either side of Cathy's desk, she frowned at Earline. "If your goal is to destroy my willpower, you've achieved it."

"Once a week won't hurt you." Earline patted her round tummy. "My problem is that I eat like this all the time. I love my own cooking."

"I used to never have to worry about my weight." Cathy sighed.

"If you think it's difficult at thirty-two, just wait until you hit forty and then fifty. I hate to tell you this, but it gets harder and harder to keep the weight off."

Cathy eyed the pound cake as if it were her enemy. "Would you be upset with me if I don't eat the pound cake?"

"Not at all. Save it for later or take it home for Michael. But I intend to eat mine. Every last bite."

Cathy smiled at her dear friend. "While you're enjoying dessert, I'll clear away this mess." She stood and picked up sandwich bags, napkins and paper plates.

As she dumped the debris into the wastebasket, she glanced out the side window of her office and across the yard to the carriage house behind the second of the shelter's houses. If only they had enough money to renovate the carriage house, she could move her office in there and free up another room and bath for clients.

Carrying her cake on a paper plate, Earline got up and walked over to the window beside Cathy. "By Christmas, you should be moved over there."

"Hmm…"

"You're thinking about Tate, aren't you?"

No, she wasn't, and maybe she wouldn't have thought about him for the rest of the day if Earline hadn't mentioned his name. For the past three weeks, she had tried to convince herself that she had done the right thing telling Tate that she wasn't interested in more than friendship.

But if she had made the right decision, why was she so miserable?

She still saw Tate whenever he picked up Michael or brought him home. But their outings had come to an abrupt halt. Not once in three weeks had Tate done more than say hi and bye. Oh, he was always cordial, and nothing seemed to have changed between their sons, something for which she was very grateful.

"Don't be silly, I wasn't thinking about Tate," Cathy said. "Why would you assume I was?"

"Maybe because you're in love with the man and you blew your chance to nab him before someone else does."

"I am not in love with Tate Russell," Cathy proclaimed vehemently.

"Yeah, sure. And people mistake me for Pamela Anderson almost every day." Laughing, Earline glanced at her breasts. "It's the big boobs—people can't tell us apart."

Cathy laughed, too—genuinely laughed—and it felt good. It had been a while since she'd even smiled. "Okay, so maybe I do have feelings for Tate, but…"

Earline laid her crumb-dotted plate atop a file cabinet. "But what?"

"But I did what was best for both of us when I, as you say, blew my big chance."

"If Tate loves you, then—"

Cathy glowered at Earline.

"Okay, okay." Earline held up a restraining hand, letting Cathy know it was unnecessary to correct her. "If he cares about you and you care about him, how was it best for both of you to nip romance in the bud?"

Cathy could be honest with Earline in a way she could never be honest with anyone else. "This way, Tate can never fail me, never let me down. I don't have to trust him and worry that he will betray that trust. And…and Tate never has to know everything there is to know about my past, and the day will never come when he might be embarrassed to introduce me to his friends as his girl-friend or perhaps his wife."

Earline groaned loudly. "Oh, Lord, that's what I was afraid of—you've overanalyzed things and looked into a future that won't happen. Tate is not Sean Williams or anything like him. You've known the man for a year. You've seen him with his son, with his friends, with his co-workers. He's an honorable man and you know it."

"Honorable men sometimes—"

Earline cut her off. "Yes, they do, but not often. Cathy, sweetie, nothing in life is one hundred percent guaranteed. But the odds are in your favor that Tate is the kind of man who would never let you down."

"What about me? Don't you think Tate would be terribly dis-appointed in me if I told him about my past? And I'd never go into a permanent relationship with him or any man without be-ing completely honest."

"So be honest," Earline said. "My goodness, do you actually be-lieve Tate would think less of you if you told him you were a teen-age runaway who experimented with drugs when you hooked up with Sean Williams and followed your heart—all the way from South Carolina to Toronto? He already knows you weren't mar-ried to Michael's father and that the jerk dumped you when he found out you were pregnant, which, by the way, wasn't your fault."

"Tate doesn't know that I considered aborting my pregnancy, and even went as far as making an appointment at a clinic. And he has no idea that I considered prostitution as a solution to my problems, as well as suicide. Don't you see? My building a fu-ture with Tate is as absurd an idea as Pearl having a future with Andrew."

Earline put her arm around Cathy's shoulders. "Oh, sweetie, I think you're wrong on both counts. And I simply do not under-stand your reasoning. You're the person who believes that everyone deserves a second chance, and yet you won't allow yourself a second chance. And Pearl—"

"Reminds me of myself at her age, only my drug experimentation was over by the time I got pregnant, thank God. And I found Street Haven before I actually became a prostitute." Emotion welled up inside Cathy. Old wounds, never quite healed, seeped painfully with regret and hopelessness.

Earline hugged Cathy comfortingly. "Andrew is a remarkable young man, and if he truly loves Pearl and wants to make a life with her, then it would be wrong of anyone—even you—to stand in their way."

Cathy eased away from her friend's embrace. "Is that what you think I've been doing—keeping Pearl and Andrew apart?"

"Haven't you advised Andrew not to let their relationship develop into something serious?"

"Guilty as charged." Was Earline right? Cathy had thought she was doing what was best for both Andrew and Pearl. And for her and Tate. "I believed that I was helping Andrew and Pearl, but maybe I was interfering in something that's really none of my business. It's just that since I first met Pearl, I've seen so much of myself in her…the girl I was at her age."

A sharp knock sounded at the door and the very person they had been discussing rushed into the office.

Pearl's eyes were red and swollen from crying, her face splotchy. Sweat dotted her forehead and upper lip. As she came to a sudden stop several feet into the room, Pearl held out her trembling hands, pressed together in front of her, almost as if she held a tiny treasure cupped between her closed fingers.

"I have to talk to you right now." Pearl's words were a whimpering cry for help.

"Pearl, what's wrong?" Cathy asked. "Are you all right? Is the baby—"

"My baby and I will both be fine just as soon as you take this…." She opened her clasped hands and revealed a plastic bag.

Cathy and Earline immediately recognized what was inside the small bag.

"Where did you get this?" Earline asked.

Cathy walked over and lifted the bag out of Pearl's hand. "You haven't used any of this, have you?"

Pearl shook her head. "No. I swear I haven't." She looked pleadingly at Cathy.

"I believe you," Cathy said.

Pearl turned to Earline, tears trickling down her cheeks. "I've had it for three weeks, ever since Whitney Nesbitt gave it to me before she left for rehab."

"You've had crack cocaine hidden in your room for three weeks and you haven't used any of it," Earline said, her words a statement, not a question. "That must have taken tremendous willpower on your part. You must want to stay clean very badly."

"I do." Pearl choked back tears. "I don't want to do anything else that will hurt my baby. I want to be a good mother. I want…" She burst into tears.

Earline hurried to Pearl and wrapped the girl in her arms. "Everything will be all right now." Earline patted Pearl on the back, the way a mother would comfort a child. "I'm so…we are so proud of you. And you should be proud of yourself." Earline glanced over her shoulder at Cathy. "Shouldn't she be proud of herself, Cathy?"

"Yes. Yes, she should." Cathy tried to keep her emotions under control, something she'd been doing for the past twelve years. Only with Michael did she allow herself to feel freely, to love with all her heart. And only with Earline could she be herself and not a phony who hid a past she was terribly ashamed of and would give anything to change.

"Why don't I go with you back to your room and we can talk," Earline suggested.

"Wait," Cathy said. "I'd like to speak to Pearl alone for just a few minutes."

Earline smiled. "Why don't I go to the cafeteria and get some iced tea for Pearl and me." She glanced at Pearl. "I'll be waiting for you upstairs."

As soon as Earline left, Cathy indicated a chair in front of her desk. "Please, won't you sit down?"

Pearl sat, entwined her fingers together and rested her hands across the lower part of her slightly protruding tummy.

"Earline is right," Cathy said. "It took a great deal of courage for you to keep this—" she dropped the plastic bag on her desk "—for three weeks and not use it. And it took just as much courage for you to bring it to me, to get rid of it."

"I wanted it, you know. I wanted it really bad."

Nodding, Cathy offered Pearl a sympathetic half smile. "You should tell Andrew. He will be very proud of you."

"Andrew and I…well, we aren't…I mean, I decided it wasn't fair to him to let him think we have a future when I know we don't. How could we, considering the kind of person I am."

"The kind of person you *were*," Cathy corrected. "You're not a drug addict or a prostitute. You're a mother-to-be who is being helped by friends to get back on her feet. And you've just proven to me and hopefully to yourself that you're strong and brave and deserve to be trusted. And you deserve a second chance. Why shouldn't that second chance include Andrew?"

"But I thought…I mean, how can he forget about all those men…I don't even know who fathered my baby."

"Andrew has a big heart and an unwavering ability to understand why people do the things they do. That's why he went into the ministry. He's in the business of forgiveness."

"Are you saying that it's all right for Andrew and me…for us to be together?"

"That isn't for me to decide," Cathy said. "That's up to you and Andrew." *You've said enough,* she told herself. *Let it go at that.* But she couldn't help adding, "Why don't you call Andrew and ask him to come to see you this evening."

Pearl's quivering smile and tear-streaked face touched a deep emotional chord inside Cathy. The hope in the young woman's bright blue eyes reinforced Cathy's opinion that, this time, she had indeed done the right thing.

When Cathy rose from her chair and picked up the plastic bag, Pearl stood and watched while she went into the adjacent bathroom, dumped the crack into the commode and flushed it down the drain. Pearl let out an audible sigh of relief.

When Cathy stepped back into her office, she went over and gave Pearl a hug. "Let me know how things work out for you and Andrew."

"I will." Pearl hugged Cathy. "I'm going to call him right now."

Cathy indicated the telephone on her desk. "Why don't you use my phone? I need to go over to the carriage house and check on a few things."

"Thank you." Pearl picked up the phone and punched in the number she had obviously memorized.

Cathy paused in the doorway until she heard Pearl say, "Andrew, it's me, Pearl. I—I've missed you so much. Could you come to see me this evening?"

PEARL HAD NEVER BEEN so nervous in her entire life. But then, nothing had ever been this important. What if she said or did the wrong thing? What if Andrew had changed his mind? What if he didn't really love her?

She looked at herself in the mirror and wished she had more makeup, more than just blush and lipstick. Earline had told her that she was so pretty she didn't need any artificial help. Her complexion had cleared up and her color was good now that she wasn't taking drugs and had a decent place to live.

Pearl ran her hands over her long blond hair and tried to not think about how many men had touched her hair, wound their fingers in it and told her how beautiful it was. None of that mattered now. All those men were in the past. Andrew was the only man in her life, and if he wanted her, he would be the only man for as long as she lived.

She wished she had on a pretty new dress and maybe some pearls, something demure and ladylike, but the only dress she owned was this pale pink rayon one. She'd salvaged it from her "working girl" clothes—the only outfit that didn't scream "whore"—and tossed the rest into a Dumpster.

After taking a deep, calming breath, Pearl headed down the stairs. When she entered the common room, Andrew jumped up from the sofa and took a tentative step toward her. He looked so handsome tonight in his dress slacks and sports coat. She glanced around the room nervously and noticed that they were not alone.

"You look awfully pretty," Andrew said.

"Thank you."

The two women who were watching television glanced at each other, then at Andrew and Pearl. They giggled, turned off the TV and, none-too-subtly, left the room.

"I guess they could tell we wanted to be alone," Andrew said.

Trying her best to relax, Pearl walked toward Andrew. There was no point wasting time on idle chitchat, so she got right to the point. "Do you still care about me? I mean, in a special way?"

He reached out and took both of her hands into his, looking her right in the eyes. "Yes, Pearl, I care about you in a very special way. I love you. There, I've said it." He sucked in a deep breath, then let it out in a relieved whoosh.

"Oh, Andrew." *Tell him. Be honest with him.* "I—I have to tell you something."

"Whatever it is, I'll understand."

She began with the day Whitney Nesbitt had come to the shelter three weeks ago and ended by saying, "I've changed. I swear I have. I will never take drugs again or turn tricks or—"

Andrew clasped her face between his hands and kissed her on the lips. Softly, gently. She sighed with pleasure.

"I believe in you, Pearl. I trust you. And I want the two of us to build a life together."

"Are you sure? I mean, can you ever forget about my past, all those men…"

"I'm not interested in your past, only your future. Our future together." He slid his hand into the inside pocket of his sports coat and pulled out a small velvet box. "I've been carrying this around for weeks." Before she realized his intentions, he knelt down on one knee, held her left hand in his and asked, "Pearl Isom, will you marry me?" He popped the lid on the jeweler's box to reveal a small half-carat diamond.

"Oh!" Pearl gasped, completely shocked by his proposal. "Oh, Andrew."

He looked up at her, his eyes filled with uncertainty. "If you don't love me—"

She placed two fingers over his lips to silence him. "I do love you, but I'm not sure it would be fair to you. You deserve so much better."

He rose to his feet and pulled her into his arms. "I love you. I want you. Don't I deserve the woman I love?"

She gazed longingly at the engagement ring. "I'm not saying no. And you must know I want to say yes. But I need a little time. Can you give me that? Just a day or two?"

He kissed her forehead, and her cheeks, then took her mouth in a hungry kiss that told her just how much he wanted her. When she was breathless and quivering from head to toe, he ended the kiss and released her. Then he handed her the open ring box.

"You keep this," he told her. "Maybe it will help you decide. It's not a big diamond because I can't afford luxuries, not on a youth minister's salary. And I probably won't ever be rich because I'll always use part of my salary to help others. But if you marry me, I swear I'll take care of you and the baby and do everything I can to make you happy."

She caressed his cheek. "I don't doubt that for a minute, but the question is—can I make you happy, not just now, but for the rest of our lives?"

CHAPTER SIX

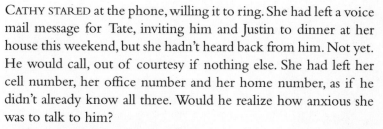

CATHY STARED at the phone, willing it to ring. She had left a voice mail message for Tate, inviting him and Justin to dinner at her house this weekend, but she hadn't heard back from him. Not yet. He would call, out of courtesy if nothing else. She had left her cell number, her office number and her home number, as if he didn't already know all three. Would he realize how anxious she was to talk to him?

She missed Tate, missed the four of them doing things together. Tate had been a good friend both to her and to Michael. She wanted that easy camaraderie they had shared. She wanted her friend back.

Don't lie to yourself. You know why you're in a panic.

Yesterday evening during supper, Michael had said, "Tate's dating a really pretty lady with all this frizzy blond hair. Her name is Lori and she's got a toy poodle named Pinkie."

Cathy had almost choked on a piece of chicken. After swallowing and clearing her throat, she'd asked, "Have you met her?"

"No, not yet, but Justin told me all about her. He said she's okay."

After that bit of news, Cathy hadn't been able to get the thought of Tate with another woman out of her mind. She had slept fitfully, tossing and turning half the night, dreaming about Tate and some leggy blonde, who in her dream looked a great deal like Nicole Kidman.

On her drive that morning to Shelter from the Storm, two things had occupied her mind to the exclusion of all else. First, today was her last full day at the shelter. School would be starting soon and she had to report to work next Monday. She hadn't accomplished half as much as she'd hoped during the summer, but then she always set her goals too high. For herself and others. Her second concern was the situation with Tate. He had every right to date another woman. Hadn't she told him to find someone else? Yes, damn it, she had. And she'd been a fool. Even if she wasn't quite ready to jump into an intimate relationship with Tate, she wanted him back—their friendship, their closeness, their wonderful times together.

He had said he wouldn't rush her. Why hadn't she taken him up on his offer instead of turning him down flat? What had she expected—that he'd wait around for her to change her mind? He was a man in his prime who wanted and needed a sexual relationship with a woman. But the prospect of sex hadn't been what had scared her off. It had been the fact that Tate wanted more—he wanted a wife.

Most women would jump through hoops to land a man who possessed half of Tate's wonderful attributes. But not Cathy Brennan. And why? Because she was an idiot.

As usual, Earline opened the office door without knocking and breezed in, but this morning, she had someone with her—Pearl. And they were both smiling like the proverbial cat who ate the canary.

"Good morning, ladies." Cathy glanced from one to the other. They actually giggled. "What's going on? Something's up? Come on, spill the beans."

Earline urged Pearl forward. "Show her."

Hesitantly, a glow of sheer ecstasy on her face, Pearl walked up to Cathy and held out her left hand. A diamond ring sparkled on her third finger. Cathy's heart skipped a beat. Did this mean—? Of course it did.

"Andrew asked me to marry him last night," Pearl said. "I told him I needed time to think about it. He insisted I take the ring with me while I was thinking. Then when I got back here and went to bed, all I could do was lie there and wonder what was wrong with me. An incredible man like Andrew loves me, wants to marry me and be a father to my baby, and I told him I had to think about it. I must have been out of my mind. So at midnight, I called him and said yes. A thousand times yes."

"Oh, Pearl…"

Pearl's smile vanished. "You aren't going to try to talk me out of it, are you?"

Cathy grasped Pearl's hands. "No. No, of course not. I'm very happy for you. And for Andrew."

"I know it won't be easy for us. I can't change my past, but Andrew knows everything there is to know about me and he still loves me. He still wants me."

Earline came over and put her arm around Pearl's shoulders. "They want to get married soon. I thought a mid-September wedding at Andrew's church. Something small and personal. I think we should be able to pull that off, don't you, Cathy?"

"Yes, of course we can." Her mind swirled with ideas. "You'll need a wedding dress."

"No problem," Earline said. "My daughter-in-law Jennifer was about five months along when she and that youngest son of mine got married. I think her dress should fit Pearl just fine. It's a cream silk with a white lace overlay."

"We'll need flowers, music and a reception," Cathy said. "If we can't come up with anything else, we can have the reception here at Shelter from the Storm."

"I have a cousin who's a florist," Earline said. "And the pianist at the church will provide the music, and we're having the reception at my house. It's only a few miles from the church."

"Well, it seems you two have everything planned," Cathy said.

"Not quite everything." Pearl looked hopefully at Cathy. "I'd like you to be my maid of honor."

"Oh, Pearl…I don't know what to say."

"Say yes," Earline told her.

Cathy laughed. "Yes, I'd be happy to be your maid of honor."

Pearl hugged Cathy, her action totally spontaneous. Then she turned and headed for the door, pausing to glance back at them. "Andrew will be here soon. We're going out to lunch to celebrate our engagement and then we're going to the jewelry store to pick out wedding bands."

"Do you have the money to buy him a ring?" Cathy asked.

"She does," Earline said.

"I have ninety-eight dollars and Earline gave me a little more, so I'm set. But thanks for asking. Y'all have been so wonderful to me."

When Pearl sailed off down the hall, her feet barely touching the ground, Earline zeroed in on Cathy. "How does it feel knowing a twenty-year-old is smarter than you are?"

The question startled Cathy. "What?"

"You heard me."

"Yes, I did, but I don't know what you mean."

"If anyone should be afraid to trust in love and happiness, it's that poor child. But she's too smart to let the mistakes of her past keep her from reaching out and grabbing everything she's ever wanted—someone to love and someone to love her. And here you are, with a dozen years between you and your past, and you rejected the love that was offered you practically on a silver platter."

"Well, please, don't hold back. Tell me what you really think." Cathy spoke lightly, doing her best not to cry. And she wanted to cry her heart out because she knew Earline was right.

"What I think is that you should pick up that phone and call Tate Russell."

"I've already called him and left a message. I did that first thing this morning."

"And he hasn't called back?"

"No. Not yet."

"Exactly what did you say in your message?" Earline asked.

"I invited him and Justin to my house to have dinner with Michael and me tomorrow night."

Earline groaned. "No wonder he hasn't returned your call. You should have asked him for a date."

"He's already dating someone else."

"Who says?"

"Justin told Michael that Tate is dating some frizzy-haired blonde named Lori. And she has a toy poodle named Pinkie."

Earline shrugged. "So you have a little competition. I seriously doubt that Tate is interested in a future with Ms. Frizzy."

"But what if I ask him out and he says he *is* serious about this Lori person."

"Take a chance." Earline picked up the phone and held it out to Cathy. "Call the man and find out."

Cathy had punched in the first three digits on the phone when her cell phone, which was in her purse in her desk drawer, chimed with a distinct tune, "Chattanooga Choo Choo." In her effort to replace the receiver, she almost dropped the phone. Earline grasped it and returned it to the base. Then Cathy yanked open the drawer and removed her purse, but when she rummaged inside for her cell phone, her hands were trembling so badly that Earline had to snatch the purse from her and retrieve the phone.

"Answer it," she ordered, thrusting the phone at Cathy.

"Hello, Cathy Brennan here."

"Cathy, it's Tate Russell."

Widening her eyes, Cathy looked right at Earline. "Hello, Tate. How are you?"

"I'm okay. You?"

"I'm okay, too."

Earline grinned, then waved and headed for the door. Cathy rushed after her, nabbing her by the arm. Realizing that Cathy did not want her to leave, Earline sat down, crossed her arms over her ample chest and waited.

"I got your message," Tate told Cathy.

"Oh, good. I thought it might be nice if we could—"

"Justin would love to come for dinner with you and Michael tomorrow night," Tate said. "But I'm afraid I can't. I...uh...have a date."

"Oh."

Earline mouthed the word *what?*

Cathy took a deep breath. "I understand. Maybe some other time."

"Yeah, maybe. What time do you want me to drop Justin off?"

"Um...around six-thirty, or earlier if you'd like. And if Justin wants to spend the night, he's welcome. Just send along his church clothes."

"Thanks, Cathy, I'll do that. I'm sure he'd love to stay over."

"Good. Then it's all set."

"Yeah, it's all set."

"See you tomorrow evening."

"Yeah."

"Bye," Cathy said reluctantly.

"Goodbye."

The minute she flipped her cell phone closed, Earline bounded out of the chair and practically pounced on Cathy. "You didn't ask him out!"

Cathy shook her head. "No, I didn't."

"Why not?"

"He already has a date for tomorrow night."

"Does he really?"

"Yes."

"Now, don't let this setback stop you from doing what you want to do." Earline studied Cathy's expression. "Oh, sweetie, you're on the verge of tears and here I am, ready to give you a lecture."

Cathy forced a smile. "Hey, it's not as if I'm in love with the guy or anything." Several stray tears trickled down her cheeks.

"What would you do if Tate changed his mind, cancelled his date and was standing in front of you right this minute? Would you tell him you aren't in love with him, or would you be honest with him and with yourself?"

"Earline, I don't know—"

"Sure you do. Just listen to your heart and not your fears. What's your heart telling you?"

"That I'm an idiot, that I should have given Tate and me a chance, that yes, damn it, I am in love with him."

Earline smiled triumphantly, then urged Cathy to stand. When Cathy did, Earline clutched her shoulders from behind and marched her to the bathroom. "Go in there and take yourself a good cry, then wash your face. I've got an errand to run, but I'll check on you later."

Like a windup doll, Cathy followed her friend's instructions. The minute she entered the bathroom, she closed the commode lid, sat down and cried.

IN HER MIND'S EYE, Cathy could still see Pearl's and Andrew's happy faces when they stopped by a couple of hours ago to show her the wedding bands they had chosen. Two wide gold bands. Simple circles representing the never-ending cycle of love.

The longer she thought about her own situation, the more Cathy realized that she needed to borrow some of Pearl's courage and not give up on Tate. So what if he had a date tomorrow night? He wasn't married or even engaged. He was still single, still free. And she had as good a chance of winning his heart as anyone else, even a frizzy-haired blonde named Lori. When she took Justin home Sunday afternoon, she'd invite herself and Michael in and stay long enough to ask Tate out on a real date, just the two of them.

Instead of worrying about her personal life for the past few hours, she should have been concentrating on shelter business. Lord knows she had tried. But all she could think about was Tate and how she was going to make things right with him.

Cathy checked her watch. Four-fifteen. She had promised Michael they would leave here today no later than five, so that gave her forty-five minutes to actually get some work done—unless Michael got bored watching TV or shooting hoops with the kids living at the shelter.

A soft rap sounded on her closed office door. "Come in, please."

When the door opened, the largest bouquet of roses she'd ever seen filled the doorway. Dozens and dozens of roses—red, pink, yellow and white—in a basket almost as wide as the door.

"Delivery for Ms. Cathy Brennan," said a muffled male voice.

That's when she noticed a pair of legs beneath the massive bouquet.

"Uh…I'm Cathy Brennan. But are you sure these are for me?"

The man placed the basket on the floor and replied in a familiar voice, "I'm very sure they're for you."

Cathy gasped when she saw Tate standing there, an ear-to-ear grin on his face. "Tate? What are you…? Why did you…?"

"I'm trying to make an impression," he told her. "I thought ten dozen roses might do the trick. Was I right?"

Slightly rattled and completely puzzled, she simply nodded.

"Roses are your favorite flower, aren't they? I just didn't know which color you prefer. In the future, I'll make sure I always send you your favorite. So what is it?"

"What?" Something didn't make sense to her. Had she fallen asleep at her desk and was now dreaming?

"What's your favorite color rose?" he asked.

"Oh. I love all colors, but if I had to pick a favorite, it would be yellow."

"Okay. Yellow it is. For birthdays, Mother's Day, Valentine's Day and anniversaries."

"I'm confused," she admitted. "What are you doing here? Why did you bring me flowers?"

He took a step toward her. She held her breath.

"When we spoke earlier today, why didn't you tell me that you'd changed your mind about us?" he asked.

Cathy suddenly felt as if all the air had been knocked out of her. "How did you— Earline! She called you, didn't she? What did she tell you?"

"Oh, nothing much, just that you were upset that I was dating someone named Lori who had frizzy blond hair and a toy poodle named Pinkie." Grinning, Tate took another step closer. "And for your information, Earline didn't just call me, she tracked me down to talk to me in person."

When he took another step, bringing them almost face-to-face, Cathy sucked in a deep breath.

"She shouldn't have called you. She should have minded her own business."

Tate leaned down, so close that she felt the warmth of his breath on her lips. "She also told me that you're in love with me. Was she right?"

"Oh, Tate…"

He cupped her face with his big hands. "Are you in love with me, Cathy?"

Take a chance, an inner voice advised her. *Trust your heart. Trust Tate.*

"Yes, I'm in love with you," she told him.

He kissed her. Tenderly, as if she were made of spun glass. Then he lifted his head. "And you already know I'm in love with you. So, do you want a long courtship?"

"You love me, too?" She swatted at his chest as he wrapped his arms around her. "If you love me, then why are you dating—"

"I'm not dating anyone," he confessed. "You'll have to forgive me for using my son to lie to you."

"What did you do?"

"I told Justin to tell Michael that I was dating a blonde named Lori." Tate chuckled. "The frizzy hair and the toy poodle named Pinkie was Justin's invention."

"Then you don't have a date tomorrow night?"

"Yes, I do have a date—with the woman I plan to marry."

He was moving too fast, taking her breath away, making plans before she had a chance to adjust to their new relationship. "Wait a minute. You're talking marriage and we've had only one date."

"So, we'll date some more. For a month, two months, six months. And then we'll get married." He nuzzled her neck.

"Tate, are you asking me to marry you or—"

"I'm asking." He shoved his hand into his pants pocket and pulled out a ring box.

Cathy gasped. He snapped open the lid on the box. When she saw the beautiful yellow diamond nestled on a bed of midnight-blue velvet, she gasped again, even louder.

"If you don't like it, we can exchange it for whatever you want."

"Tate, when did you buy this ring?"

"Today."

"Today?"

"Why do you think it took me so long to get here after I talked to Earline? I was buying out the florist and picking out an engagement ring." He removed the ring from the box and clasped her left hand. "Here, try it on and see if it fits. Earline told me what size to buy."

"Earline certainly has been a busy lady, hasn't she?"

"I consider her our fairy godmother and think we should name our first daughter after her."

"Our *first* daughter?" Cathy laughed and wriggled her ring finger. "So put it on and let's see if it fits."

He slid the ring onto her third finger.

"It's a perfect fit," she told him.

"Just like you and me." He looked directly into her eyes. "Will you marry me, Cathy?"

"My past is not something I'm proud of," she told him. "And I have all kinds of issues with trust, and I'm dragging around a great deal of emotional baggage. Are you sure you want—"

"I want you, honey. You and your past and your trust issues and your emotional baggage."

"You can't say I didn't warn you." She wrapped her arms around him and hugged him, then held her hand up and looked at her ring. "I want a five-month engagement, then a New Year's Day wedding."

"Five months?" Tate groaned. "Are you going to make me wait that long?"

"Five months isn't all that long." She leaned into him, feeling his body react. "That gives us time to get to know each other better." She gave him a deep, passion-filled kiss, then pulled back. "Just think. We can get in five whole months of practice."

"Practice for what?" he asked, a smirking grin on his face.

"For the honeymoon, of course. And you know what they say—practice makes perfect."

Tate lifted her off her feet, whirled her around and around, then eased her down his lean, hard body. When her toes touched the floor, she wrapped her arms around his neck.

Suddenly they heard footsteps and laughter. Keeping her securely in his arms, Tate pivoted so they could see who had just come into the office. There stood a beaming Earline, with Michael and Justin in tow.

"When Tate dropped Justin off downstairs with Michael, the boys couldn't wait to come up here and find out what was going on," Earline said.

"I just asked Cathy to marry me and she said yes," Tate told them.

Michael and Justin came rushing toward them. Tate and Cathy reached out and drew their sons into a shared embrace.

"Hey, man, we're going to be brothers for real," Justin said.

"Too cool!" Michael yelled. "So Tate's going to be my dad?"

"You bet," Tate said.

"And it means I'm going to be your mom," Cathy told Justin.

"That's great. It's just what Michael and I want."

"It's what we all want," Tate said. "The four of us are going to be a family."

Cathy savored the moment, thankful that at long last she had found her own personal shelter from life's many storms in the arms of the man she loved.

GROOVE WITH ME
ABIGAIL ROSIN

In the fall of 1996, Abigail Rosin, a twenty-three-year-old Brown University graduate, carried a bag of tap shoes and a radio to New York City's Lower East Side to offer free dance classes to under-privileged girls. Two students showed up that day. But Abigail per-severed, believing, from her own involvement in dance and theater, that dance could be a source of joy and community—and break the cycle of underachievement faced by so many inner-city girls. And she was right. Today, Abby's Groove With Me dance program provides 21 classes a week to 220 students.

Groove With Me is an award-winning Manhattan-based non-profit organization providing free dance classes for underprivileged girls. Most participants are Latinas and African-Americans ages four to eighteen, and most live in single-mother households in New York City's most deprived neighborhoods. Groove With Me provides role models, group belonging and a venue for lead-ership. Classes in hip-hop, tap, ballet, jazz, funk, choreography and African dance instill pride in the girls' heritage while teaching dis-cipline, focus and teamwork.

A chance for at-risk girls

After-school programs for New York City girls have long received less financial support than those for boys, with only one
quarter of youth programming directed toward girls. And at a time
when funding for programs has been slashed drastically, Groove
With Me plays a critical role in the lives of inner-city girls. Through
the medium of dance, Groove With Me teaches self-respect and self-
worth, helping deter at-risk girls from prostitution, gang involvement, substance abuse, teen pregnancy and domestic violence. Dance
builds self-esteem in the girls as they learn how to achieve their goals.

Abigail is passionately devoted to giving girls the self-confidence
to make healthy choices. Even if the classes only provided an hour
of joy each week, that would be a gift for the girls—and Abigail.
But Abby continually sees the greater benefits of Groove With
Me. The students are more disciplined, affectionate and confident,
and quiet girls are helped to overcome their shyness. As one
mother of a Groove With Me student expressed, "Abby has been
able to capture the confidence of some of the most needy dance
students, to calm agitated youngsters and to motivate discouraged
children to keep trying their best."

The need for permanence fulfilled

January 2001 was a milestone for Abigail. After five years scattered around the city in borrowed spaces such as high school caf-
eterias, Groove With Me opened its own studio in Spanish
Harlem—thanks to the passionate commitment of staff and volunteers, and the generous donations of enthusiastic supporters.
Permanent space is crucial to the students' sense of security and
continuity. The Groove With Me studio and the classes themselves
provide stability for the girls in an unpredictable world. For many,
the studio is a second home. The Groove With Me environment
provides a safe place for girls, an alternative to unsupervised homes
or negative influences on the street.

But nothing boosts self-esteem like being on stage and having people tell you how great you are! So every six weeks Abby gives students an added incentive to master their dance steps and team routines by arranging for public performances throughout New York. The students have appeared at venues such as the Museum for the City of New York, the Central Park Bandshell and even *The Today Show.* Performance broadens the girls' horizons, exposing them to colleges and community groups—opening them to possibilities for their own lives. Abby and the Groove With Me teachers also take the girls to watch professional dancers audition for parts. Abigail loves to hear the girls dream aloud about being on Broadway or dancing in music videos.

Groove With Me provides the connections for students who are serious about developing as dancers, but the program's main goal is to instill a confidence in students that will allow them to pursue options beyond dance. Abigail's vision is not to have the girls master dance techniques, but to build a strong sense of self. Abby's vision carries through in the dance classes themselves. The warmth and mutual respect between students and teachers is evident.

Volunteering from the heart

The teachers at Groove With Me are all volunteers. Some are women who were given a break when they were growing up and want the opportunity to give back to the community. Other teachers are dancers sidelined by injury, aspiring choreographers, dancers who work nine-to-five jobs and people who want to help disadvantaged children. The Groove With Me teachers are completely devoted to their students, giving their time, their expertise *and* their hearts. One teacher even makes new costumes for every show.

The students love and idolize their teachers, and miss them when they're away. And the teachers are as positively affected as the girls—sometimes in extraordinary and moving ways. In one instance a teacher was facing the death of her mother, and it was her students who cheered her up.

It's moments like this that refuel Abigail's motivation every day. Her father says her eyes light up and her voice rises ten octaves when her students are mentioned. Very often Abigail's inspiration comes from things she does that no one ever sees, like walking a girl to her home in the projects at night in the cold, or accompanying a girl to an audition. The walls of Abby's apartment are covered in drawings the girls have made for her with messages like "Thank you for teaching me hip-hop," "You are the best dance teacher" and "You are like a second mother to me."

Backstage at shows the students put up a mural and everyone writes on it what they've learned or why they love Groove With Me. The girls write how they've learned to express themselves, to not be shy, to never say, "I can't." And how, at Groove With Me, "you don't have to be in the front and be perfect"…to be a star.

More Than Words

JULIE ELIZABETH LETO
INTO
THE
GROOVE

JULIE ELIZABETH LETO

A romance reader from age 16, *USA TODAY* bestselling author Julie Elizabeth Leto knew these were the stories she was destined to write. The native Floridian discovered her niche with Harlequin Temptation's sensuous, sexy tone and character-driven stories. Her constant desire to "push the envelope" made her a natural choice to be one of the launch authors when Harlequin Blaze made its debut. A former dance student with a Latina heritage (Italian and Cuban), Julie lives in Tampa, Florida.

CHAPTER ONE

"HE'S STILL OUT THERE."

Despite the singsong lightness of Marcy's announcement, Georgia Rae Evans bristled. Nothing annoyed her more than a man who didn't know the very basics of acceptable behavior. She stomped over to the window beside her protégé, pleased to be accompanied by the sharp, staccato beat of her tap shoes, and with one decisive yank, cleared away the blinds that Marcy had been using as cover to spy on their mystery man.

Marcy scrambled away. "Georgia, what are you doing?" she whispered desperately.

"I'm trying to open this window," she said. Her voice strained as she struggled with the latch. "What does it look like I'm doing?"

"You're going to yell at him, aren't you? Georgia, he could be dangerous! This isn't Cobb County, sweetheart. This is Spanish Harlem. He could be a Latin King from the looks of him."

With her thumb wedged beneath the latch, Georgia Rae gave it one last tug. She accomplished nothing except putting a wicked indentation in her skin. Dangerous gang member, she doubted. She'd already sent the neighborhood cop to check him out. Georgia had watched from the window while the guy showed ID and, she later found out, assured Officer Bill that he was simply waiting for someone. Still, his presence had disturbed her afternoon. He was too…darn, but she couldn't quite find the right word. *Disruptive* was the closest she could come up with. He captured her attention, even when common sense told her to ignore him.

But he wasn't an easy man to overlook. He wore his hair long, but in a shaggy way that made her think he'd just forgotten to show up for his regular haircut. And while he'd mostly kept his hands in his pockets and his eyes hidden behind reflective shades, he didn't exude that dangerous vibe she'd learned to detect, the one that had kept her safe during her past four years in New York City.

Recently and painfully, Georgia had learned not to ignore her instincts, especially when it came to men. Consequently, she wasn't backing down today just because of a sticky window. Bottom line was—he'd been watching the dance studio all day. And good or bad, his intentions would make the difference between her calling the police again or just running him off herself.

With a grunt, she gave up on the window and glanced over at the clock hanging above the floor-to-ceiling mirrors in the dance studio. Most of the area middle schools had let out just minutes ago. The students for her first class would start trickling in very soon, and in order to get to the studio, they'd have to pass the loitering Hispanic man who'd parked his butt in front of the furniture store across the street. And while he seemed to be paying attention to the entire neighborhood around him, his gaze kept wandering back to the second-story dance studio where Marcy and Georgia had been working all day, picking out music and designing low-cost costumes for the girls' performance at a fundraiser three weeks from Saturday.

Waiting for someone, huh? The man possessed more patience than any New Yorker she'd ever met.

She'd noticed him on her way into the studio because, well, he was hard not to notice. His dark skin, dark eyes and swaggering smile at the women who dared walk by him reminded her of Antonio Banderas in *The Mask of Zorro*. Intense, menacing, and with a sense of self that warranted immediate notice. Georgia contained her sigh, not allowing her fantasies of being Catherine Zeta-Jones to interrupt her ire. Spanish Harlem could be a rough place, a scary place, even for the young girls who lived in the neighborhood and traveled to the studio several times a week for their dance lessons. The last thing her charges needed to deal with was some sicko who'd been watching the building since rush hour.

The decision to act was made for her when two of her girls, dressed in T-shirts and sweats with their tap shoes laced together and dangling over their shoulders, emerged from the deli across the street. The mystery man slid off his perch and approached them. The girls, fourteen and street smart, didn't so much as flinch, but Georgia felt her blood pressure rise to explosive levels.

"I don't give a rat's ass if he's recently been released from Attica, Marcy, I won't have him messing with my girls," Georgia insisted.

She grabbed her wrap sweater and dug her arms into it, twisting the tie around her waist.

Marcy's café-latte skin paled. "Girl, you've lived in this city long enough to know you don't go out looking for trouble!"

Georgia jammed her legs into her black warm-up pants, but left her tap shoes on. She'd need the height of the two-inch heels, and the machine-gun-fire sound wouldn't hurt, either. When she marched over to tell that man to get the hell away from her students, a soundtrack would come in handy.

"I'm going to look for Officer Bill first," Georgia conceded. "But if he's not anywhere to be found, then I'm going to stroll on over and see what Zorro's apprentice is doing on this fine, autumn New York day."

Her Southern accent thickened ever-so-slightly as she turned on the charm—not that the accent could congeal much further. Georgia Rae had been born and bred just outside of Atlanta, where cultivating a sugary Southern twang increased a girl's chance of bagging a wealthy husband. Not that Georgia Rae had gone on that particular spouse safari—much to her mother's chagrin— but even though she'd been surrounded by Yankees for quite some time and had completed her college studies in the heart of the

Midwest, she could turn on her bred-from-birth charm when it suited her purpose.

Marcy shook her head and returned to her task, which was cueing the music for the first of Georgia's three afternoon classes. Georgia turned on her heel, determined to find out who the man was and why he thought it was perfectly all right for him to talk to her girls.

The street was crowded with people, many of whom she knew by name. The day was a little brisk, being October in New York City, but the weather was clear and breezy. This part of Harlem—heck, any part of Harlem—had a reputation for being chancy, but Georgia Rae had learned firsthand that despite the bad press, most of the people who lived in East Harlem did care about what happened here. Just like she cared what happened to her students.

The minute she walked out the door, she saw the mystery man's face snap up. His gaze traveled across the street and slammed her with keen intensity. The girls he'd been chatting with dashed away, hurrying to the street corner before they crossed. Georgia stood there, her stare locked with Mr. Leather Jacket's, until her students approached.

"Who's that man you were talking to?" she asked.

Lupe, popping on her ever-present bubble gum, shrugged her shoulders. "Some *papi chulo* who asked us if we danced."

"Yeah," Lisette replied with a snort. "Like we carry tap shoes around for our health."

Georgia waved the girls inside. She should have known these two could handle themselves, but not all her students had sharp tongues and attitudes like Lupe and Lisette.

After double-checking the crisscross tie on her sweater to make sure her tight leotard was covered, Georgia gave the man, who was still watching her, a quick grin, then looked both up and down the block for any sign of Officer Bill.

Nothing.

He'd come around soon. He tried to make a pass down 124th and 3rd Avenue around the time the girls were heading toward the studio, but Georgia had called him earlier, thus disrupting his beat. But she was in no mood to wait around or play games. She had classes to teach and needed to ensure her students arrived at the studio safe, sound and without being accosted.

Continuing to grin, she stepped out quickly between a Buick and a pickup parked out front, looked both ways and, still brimming with righteous indignation, crossed the street.

By the time she reached him, his eyebrows were high on his forehead.

"Hi," she said saucily.

He slid off his sunglasses, revealing inky dark irises surrounded by thick lashes that were almost too pretty to belong to a man. Almost.

"Hola," he answered, and his voice, a combination of pure male baritone and Hispanic timbre, struck her with its reluctance.

She thrust out her hand. "I'm Georgia Rae Evans."

He glanced at her hand, and then looked around as if he needed witnesses to this odd behavior before he could respond.

His hands were out of his pockets, but he made no move to accept her friendly gesture, even after several seconds ticked by.

Despite the tingle up her spine, Georgia pushed her hand a little closer to him, just in case her intentions were somehow lost in the translation.

"And you are?"

"Not interested in whatever you're selling, *chiquita.*"

Her smile didn't waver, despite a new impulse to fist her outstretched hand and smash it into his smug face.

"Well, that's not the most polite response you could come up with, now is it? You'd think, after sitting out here all day doing nothing but staring at my building, you'd have had time to come up with a cleverer retort to a friendly hello."

"*Your* building?"

She leaned on her left hip, offsetting the unsteady balance caused by her shaking. She didn't know if she was more angry than scared or more scared than angry—but it really didn't matter. The result would be the same.

He'd pushed the wrong button.

She smiled sweetly. "No, not technically my building, of course, but for the time being, I'm one of the people responsible for the children who will be arriving for our dance classes in just a few minutes. See," she said, turning to point to the sign in the bay window above the door. "We're a dance studio. What you might not realize is that our clientele is young girls. Or maybe you do realize it and that's why you've been loitering all day and talking to my girls in the street. Please understand that I've been watching you for hours and can give an incredibly detailed description to the police, should the information be needed."

"Do you always talk so fast?"

"I talk fast?"

"And a lot."

She grinned. "Yes, well, it's a stereotype for people to believe that all Southerners talk slowly. I grew up in a household of six children. If you didn't talk quick, you didn't get a word in. Now, can I assume I've made my point about the inappropriateness of a grown man hanging out just outside a dance studio that caters to young girls? I'm not accusing you of anything, mind you, I'm just pointing out that so far as comfort zones are concerned, your continued and unexplained presence isn't appreciated, so I'd be very happy if you moved along."

"It's not a stereotype."

"Excuse me?"

Georgia Rae attempted to rewind her diatribe and find which sentence he was referring to.

Luckily, he filled in the blank.

"That Southerners talk slow. I'm from the South."

"Whereabouts?"

"Miami."

She laughed. "That's not the South! That's the tropics." She leaned forward and whispered sweetly, "It doesn't count."

"Tell that to all the good old boys in my neighborhood."

She arched a brow. "Oh, really. And what were their names? Billy Bob? Rufus, maybe?"

"More like Juan Pablo and Miguelito, but trust me, they knew their grits from their *arroz con pollo*."

He made his claim with such emotional emphasis that Georgia immediately caught on.

"You're teasing me."

"I'm trying to lighten you up a little, *sí*."

"Why?"

"Because I'm not hanging around here to check out your students, okay? That's why I'm across the street instead of on your doorstep. I didn't think anyone would mind if I hung out while I waited for someone."

She frowned, realizing that she might have overreacted.

"Well, it's not like I personally mind," she said, feeling a little guilty for making the implication that he was some sort of predator—but not too guilty. First and foremost, her concern was for her students, and a stalker could as easily wait across the street, where he wouldn't be as obvious as he would be right beside the door. "But I can't be too careful."

He pressed his lips together and nodded. Georgia Rae caught a look in his eye that briefly seemed impressed. But only briefly.

"This is good," he said. "I mean, I never thought about how the teachers would have to look out for the kids outside the dance class."

She crossed her arms. "We care about them all the time. You know, if you don't mind me being bold again, who are you and why are you here?"

"You're good at bold."

"It's a gift."

"Or it's an excuse to be nosy."

"Now, that's just rude. I'm not the one hanging out in a neighborhood filled with children and no verifiable reason for being here."

He stepped forward, breaking through the personal space barrier that most New Yorkers radiated like laser-triggered alarms. He was tall. Not that a man had to be much more than five-seven to put a crick in Georgia's neck, but this guy was close to six feet.

And even through his clothes—snug-in-the-right-places blue jeans, a faded gray T-shirt and a black leather jacket—she could tell that every inch of him was lean and muscled.

"You're right," he said, his voice husky. "I've been rude. Manners aren't my thing, okay?"

"What is your thing, Mister—" She stuck out her hand again, and this time, with a reluctant grin, he accepted her palm in his.

"Diego Paz."

"Well, Mr. Paz…"

"Please," he said. "Call me Diego."

"I hardly think I should. I don't want to give you the impression that we're in any way headed toward a first-name-basis relationship."

He shook her hand with one quick pump, followed by an echoed shake that brimmed with more gentleness than she expected.

"I can't see how that could possibly happen, either, but the way you pronounce my last name sounds more like those little toy candy dispensers than it should."

She paused and realized he'd just insulted her Spanish pronunciation. Wasn't anything she hadn't heard before. The girls at the studio had a great deal of fun teasing her about the way she mispronounced their Spanish names and surnames, not to mention the way she destroyed their slang.

"Diego, then. And since we're on a first-name basis, even under duress, then maybe you'll tell me exactly why you've been watching the studio all day. Just who have you been waiting for?"

He glanced aside, briefly, but enough for Georgia Rae to anticipate that the next thing that came out of his mouth would likely be a lie.

"Time for me to confess. I'm here for you."

CHAPTER TWO

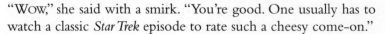

"Wow," she said with a smirk. "You're good. One usually has to watch a classic *Star Trek* episode to rate such a cheesy come-on."

Okay, now he definitely had no idea what she was talking about. From the moment she'd stepped out of the building, Diego had anticipated that the woman barreling toward him on two-inch heels that made more noise than an AK-47 spraying across a tin building would be easy to charm. He was, after all, known in his Little Havana neighborhood for his skills with the ladies. This one, however, despite her big round blue eyes, peachy skin and sweet Southern drawl, wasn't so easy to distract.

Maybe he was losing his touch.

Maybe he just had to kick his *Rico Suave* act up a notch.

He stepped forward, closing in on her personal space. He wasn't sure how she did it, but her perfume—a subtle scent that reminded him of fuzzy, juicy fruits drenched in thick cream—overrode the mingled odors of exhaust, overcooked roast pork from the deli and subway-steamed dust he'd choked on all day. He leaned in closer to score another whiff, but she stepped back and dropped her arm, as if she was prepared to slap him if he made a move she didn't like.

He threw his hands up. "Look, lady…"

"Georgia Rae. Georgia Rae Evans."

"Ms. Evans, then."

She quirked a half grin. "Georgia Rae will do."

He sighed, exasperated, though he wasn't entirely sure why. She was a whirlwind of activity. She walked fast, talked fast, and even standing still, managed to tap her metal-tipped toes on the sidewalk, creating a staccato beat that was slowly driving him crazy. "Fine! Georgia Rae. Georgia Rae Evans of South Carolina or Tennessee or—"

"Duh! Try Georgia, hello? Didn't my first name give it away?"

He shoved his hands back into his pockets and closed his eyes tightly. "Right," he said, expelling the word along with all the frustration this woman created in a split second. Truth be told, for the past few weeks, setting off his temper hadn't been hard. It was a fairly easy task to rattle a man who'd just returned from a war zone to find out that the child he'd been told didn't exist was, in fact, very much alive and living in New York City. And that the little girl, despite her mother's claims to the contrary, was his daughter.

And this woman was going to help him find her, whether she liked it or not.

"Georgia," he continued. "A beautiful name for a beautiful woman."

She arched a brow.

"Not that I'm intentionally trying to charm you with sappy come-on lines," he explained.

"God knows what damage you'd do if you *were* actually trying."

"You don't like my polite conversation?"

She smirked. "Needs work."

"I'll see what I can do. Look, I'm sorry if my watching the studio made you uncomfortable. I thought you wouldn't notice if I stayed across the street."

"So you admit that you were deliberately trying to be secretive? Like a man with something to hide, perhaps?"

"No, I was trying to stay out of the way. But if you're a teacher at the school, you can help me out. I'm looking for…" He dug into his pocket and pulled out the page he'd printed off the Internet with the name of *Groove With Me*'s director. "I didn't want to bother her inside the studio, so I thought I'd catch her on the street and maybe set up an appointment to speak with her."

Georgia's blue eyes narrowed into suspicious slits. Okay, so it wasn't the best cover story he could come up with, but he hadn't exactly planned on being confronted by one of the dance teachers at the school before he could get in and check the place out for himself. He had, however, intended to meet the founder of *Groove With Me,* the program his daughter reportedly danced at twice a week, as casually as possible. He had a great cover story for the program's director—the perfect way to finagle an interview and a tour of the building.

Then he'd return a few times. Gain some trust. Become a familiar face.

And hopefully, over the course of his explorations, he'd find his daughter.

Georgia Rae Evans crossed her arms over her chest, which he promptly noticed was quite nicely endowed. Beneath a pale pink sweater that crisscrossed her cleavage, Georgia's breasts conjured more thoughts about peaches, these exclusively visual.

Unfortunately, she seemed to notice the sudden craving in his eyes.

"I think you'd best get out of here," she warned. "I highly doubt my boss will want to talk to someone who can't look a woman in the eye."

"Hey!" he protested. "You waltz around the city dressed like that and you expect a red-blooded man not to look? Now, if I leered or made some hoochie-hoochie comment, I can understand you being offended, but I'm just admiring." He held out his hands again. "I swear, no harm, no foul."

She slammed her fists on her hips, taking only a split second to realize that the show of annoyance only thrust her breasts out farther.

To her credit, she didn't move.

"The director isn't around today."

"Then I'll wait until tomorrow."

From the way her cheeks sharpened, he could tell she was suck-ing in on the inside of her mouth, a classic sign that she was hold-ing something back. "You'll wait longer than that. She's not expected around here until next week. I'm afraid you should have called first, you know, like polite people do?"

She spun on her heel, marched to the curb, but luckily for him, had to wait for traffic before she could cross. He caught up with her as she leaned slightly forward, trying to decide if she could scoot across with a line of cars shooting by.

"Where is your director?" he asked.

"Do you know her?"

He shook his head. "Not personally. Look, I don't mean to be secretive. I'm just an ex-soldier trying to do something good with my life, okay?"

The words, doused in truth, poured out of him. Before he could call back a single one, she turned slowly, her eyes still narrowed as she assessed his face.

"That might be the first honest thing you've said since we met. What branch were you with, Soldier?"

"Army. The 16th Military Police Brigade."

"Out of Fort Bragg?"

That stopped him. Sure, she was from the South, but he didn't peg her for an Army brat.

"You know Fort Bragg?"

"A bunch of guys from my high school were stationed there. We might know some of the same people."

God, he hoped not.

The traffic cleared, but Georgia made no move to leave. Their eyes locked, and for an instant, he saw a crack in her suspicions.

His stomach dipped.

What the heck? He was trying his best to deceive her, and now he was slightly disappointed that she was starting to buy his line?

The trick to being a good liar meant layering your scam with truth. He had served the 16th at Fort Bragg, with his first tour of overseas duty in Afghanistan and his second in Iraq. After ten years fighting for the United States, he'd finally retired, hoping to settle down, start a family, enjoy the sand that covered beaches instead of deserts.

Then he'd found out about Alexis and his focus changed. He wanted one thing and one thing only—his child. She'd been stolen from him, and damned if some after-school dance teacher was going to keep him from finding her and getting her back.

Georgia opened her mouth to deliver another undoubtedly rapid-fire response when a quartet of young girls counted to three and shouted her name from across the street. They waved vigorously in her direction and his stomach took a nosedive the minute he caught the genuine gleam in her smile.

"Hey, *chicas!* I'll be over there in a minute. You get Miss Marcy to warm you up, okay?"

"*Chicas?*" he said with a grin. "Do you have any idea how cute that sounds when it's said with a Southern accent?"

She smirked. "Actually, I've been told. The girls love to tease me about my horrible Spanish pronunciation."

"You been teaching at *Groove With Me* long?"

She paused and her cheeks slimmed again. She actually had fairly round cheeks, but sleek cheekbones that gave her a blended wholesome and exotic look, especially when paired with her fair skin and enormous blue eyes, which she'd lined in smoky gray. She was a woman who cared about her beauty and made the most of it, even if her afternoon was going to be spent teaching tap class to a collection of teenagers.

"Three years. I started about a year after I moved to New York."

"Where did you live before?"

"Is this twenty questions?"

"Just polite conversation."

"Chicago."

"So that's where you got your taste for the big city."

"What makes you think I'm not from a big city? Atlanta isn't exactly Petticoat Junction."

"You like old television shows."

"You're nosy."

"You're right."

The traffic cleared again, and this time, Georgia Rae started across, with Diego close on her heels. As she tapped her way to the door just beside the ninety-nine-cent store where the stairs to the *Groove With Me* studio began, he figured he'd better make his move now. If the founder of the dance program was truly out of town, then Georgia Rae Evans was his best shot at getting inside.

"Don't you want to know more about me?" he asked.

"No."

He stopped short. Disinterest from a woman was not something he was accustomed to. "Why not?"

She spun, grinning at his easy offense. "Why should I? You came to speak with the director and she's not here. I have a class to teach."

"Can I watch?"

Her eyes widened. "You ask a question like that and yet you don't want to come across as a pervert?"

"I'm not a perv, okay? I'm a veteran who happens to be in possession of a generous grant from a foundation in Miami and I'm looking for a way to spend the money."

"Is that some weird way of asking me out to dinner?"

Diego chuckled. It wasn't, but maybe it should have been. "No, but I will take you out if you promise to tell me everything you know about *Groove With Me,* so I can start a similar organization in Little Havana."

She slid her hands into a sleek fold across her chest. She really did move like a dancer.

"Tempting, but no," she replied. "I don't know anything about you."

"You know I'm patient and persistent."

"So are a lot of serial killers, I'm betting."

"You have my name. The cop looked at my ID. And you did say," he said, his voice deep and teasing, "that you'd looked at me long enough to give a very accurate description. You could check me out."

"Is there a registry for potentially dangerous men?"

"If there is, most of the guys in New York are probably on it."

"If we're talking potential, most of the guys in the United States are probably on it. Where are you staying?"

He dug into his pocket and took out the business card he'd swiped off the front desk of his hotel. "It's near the airport. Less than a mile from here."

She scanned the card, tracing her lips with her tongue, probably completely unaware of how her action was spiking his temperature.

"Good, then I don't have to rush my decision."

She turned to jog up the stairs, but was waylaid when two girls in blue jeans and pigtails "excuse me'd" past both of them.

With a stern glance at her watch, followed by a smile, she acknowledged the girls and then noticed, startled, that he hadn't moved.

"Is there something else, Mr. Diego Paz of Miami, formerly of the 16th Military Police Brigade out of Fort Bragg?"

He couldn't help but smile. She'd listened to every detail he'd told her and probably intended to check him out thoroughly, as promised.

How did a man charm a woman so sure of herself, so confident that she could march across a busy New York street in the middle of a rough neighborhood and confront a stranger without a glimmer of fear? This Georgia Rae Evans was a different sort of woman than he was used to.

"No, nothing else," he said. "Just don't take too long to check me out."

"You forget that you're the one who wants something from me, not the other way around."

He shook his head. "No, ma'am. I'm not forgetting. I'm just figuring that with a little time, that situation might just reverse itself."

CHAPTER THREE

OF ALL THE NERVE.

Georgia Rae rolled her eyes and marched up the stairs. She hated when she sounded like her mother, even when it was just in her thoughts. Not that she didn't love her mother to pieces, but Georgia Rae wanted to sound younger and hipper and more citified, as her grandmother would say. Geez, you'd think four years in Chicago and four in New York would have beat the country girl right out of her. No such luck—especially when she was riled.

But the truth remained that Diego Paz—if that was really his name—definitely had nerve. And a whole lot of other stuff, too, like charm, magnetism and a boatload of cockiness. Worse part was, Georgia Rae wasn't immune to any of the three, particularly when they were so handsomely combined.

She walked into the studio, her ears instantly bombarded with the sound of hip-hop star Usher pounding on the sound system. The girls were doing their warm-up, dancing freestyle in a jagged circle. Miss Marcy, her twenty-two-year-old assistant, undulated in the center, exhibiting a style, grace and oneness with the music that couldn't be taught in any studio. For a moment, Georgia Rae just leaned against the wall and watched.

The minute Marcy caught sight of her standing in the doorway, however, she sashayed over, not missing a single beat. Georgia began unwrapping her sweater and pushing out of her warm-up pants.

"So, what's his story?" Marcy asked, leaning in so she could be heard over the music.

"He says he's interested in *Groove With Me.* Wants to find out what we do here and maybe start his own program in Little Havana."

"Miami? Yeah, he looks sun-kissed."

Georgia smirked. "How could you tell that from a distance?"

Marcy just grinned and Georgia Rae couldn't help but return the smile. Yeah, sun-kissed described Diego Paz with succulent accuracy.

"Did you tell him the big boss was out of town?" Marcy asked.

"Yeah, now he wants to talk to me."

"Are you going to?"

She shrugged. She honestly didn't know. She wasn't entirely sure that Diego Paz was telling her the truth, but what if he was and she brushed him off? Not only might she cost *Groove With Me* the chance to expand into other communities—one of the founder's goals for the year—but she could possibly offend someone with a genuinely good and philanthropic heart. And though she didn't want to admit it to anyone, including herself, she might be passing up a chance to spend a little time with one incredibly hot guy.

In her day job as a Broadway set designer, she had good-looking guys coming out of her ears, but this one—this one didn't seem to want much attention in his direction. His agenda wasn't self-aggrandizing, that much she could tell. And that alone was a refreshing change.

Without another word, Georgia Rae joined her girls in the circle and let the beat infuse into her bloodstream. Amid the laughing, clapping and stomping, she brushed aside all thoughts of Diego Paz. She'd deal with him later. For now, she had to take care of her girls.

"DID YOU FIND HER?"

Diego switched the cell phone to his other ear and checked his watch. His sister could keep him on the line for hours if he let her, and he did not have unlimited minutes. While his claim to Georgia Rae about the grant wasn't entirely a lie, he wasn't made of money, either. Every dime he'd saved over the years—and he'd done quite well with extra combat and hazardous assignment pay—was now going toward finding his child.

"Not yet, but I'm close. Yesterday afternoon, I hooked up with one of the teachers at that dance place."

"Hooked up how?"

The suspicious and slightly lurid tone in his sister's voice caused Diego to shift uncomfortably on the hotel room bed. Maggie, his older sister by just over thirteen months, made it her business to stick her nose in his private life at every opportunity—especially when it came to women. He used to fight her. He used to rail against her interference and tell her in no uncertain terms where to stick her sisterly advice.

Then she'd been right about Callie. From the beginning, she'd pegged his ex as a manipulative, selfish woman with little to no respect for him or the people he loved. Maggie had been so damned right, Diego had learned now to at least listen. As a soldier, his gut instincts had saved lives on more than one occasion. But with women, he'd learned to appreciate the insider's insight his sister doled out.

"We just talked," he admitted. "When I was staking the place out, she actually stomped across the street to tell me to beat it. But I used my natural charm to defuse her."

Maggie barked a laugh. "Natural charm, my *culo*. You're just a good liar."

"I can be convincing, but I don't like to lie. Makes me no better than Callie, *verdad*? And this one, she's a nice woman. I can tell."

"You thought Callie was a nice woman, too."

"No, I thought she was a hot, sexy woman back when that's all that mattered to me. This one is not only hot and sexy, but I can tell she cares about the kids she teaches. You'd like her."

Maggie paused, as if mulling over what Diego had confessed. He wished he hadn't said so much, but it was too late now.

"Tell her the truth, then," Maggie suggested. "Maybe she'll help you get Alexis back."

"Or maybe she'll alert Rita that I'm closing in on her. If Rita gets spooked, she could take Alexis and run again."

"If Alexis is still *with* Rita," Maggie said, her tone tinged with doubt.

He didn't respond, knowing that he and his sister had gone through this conversation a million times, ever since the sordid story of his child's existence and essentially her kidnapping had come to his attention. No use wasting more time hashing out the same old arguments. Instead, he promised to call Maggie when he knew something more, hung up and leaned back on the pillows, wondering how the hell returning to the States could tear him up more than two tours in Afghanistan and Iraq.

It was one thing to face down the bullets and bombs of a sworn enemy—but it was yet another to realize the betrayals and lies of someone he'd once thought he'd loved.

Unable to close his eyes and block out the memories, Diego reached into his duffel bag and extracted the file, brimming with documents and printouts he'd been piecing together for months since Callie's ex-husband, the man who'd soothed Callie's so-called broken heart after Diego kicked her to the curb for cheating on him, crashed his homecoming party after he'd returned from the war.

Diego had never met Mike Jessup before, but he'd known him by reputation. He wasn't a man to lie out of vindictiveness. He wasn't a man to go out looking for trouble, either. Diego had always figured the poor sap had a serious white-knight syndrome, which explained why he'd hooked up with someone as screwed-up as Callie. At the party, he'd taken Diego aside and poured out the entire story of his ex's lies and deceptions, and despite the out-rageousness of his story, Diego knew the man was telling the truth. No one would ever have made up anything so heinous.

Callie had lied to him. Told him the worst lie a woman could utter to a man. Yes, she'd told him when they were breaking up that she might be pregnant, but when he'd insisted on a pregnancy test to make sure she wasn't just manipulating him into staying rather than deploying with his unit, she'd stalled. He'd hounded her relentlessly, even brought over one of those home kits he'd bought at the pharmacy. But she'd refused and told him in no un-certain terms that she never wanted to see him again.

What he hadn't known is that by then she'd found Mike. Good, dependable, reliable, live-in-Miami-until-the-day-he-died Mike. He'd already promised to be there for Callie, so Diego had no longer been needed. He'd gone off to the Middle East thinking he'd escaped the closest call he'd had since the car bomb that killed the soldier walking not fifteen paces in front of him.

If Callie had verified her pregnancy and claimed the baby to be his, Diego would have stayed. He would have moved heaven and earth to make his relationship with Callie work for the sake of the child. Men in his family did not shirk their parental respon-sibilities, which included more than just shelling out child support and visiting their kids every other weekend—or with his military lifestyle, every few months. If you were a father, you acted like a father in every sense of the word.

And Callie had understood that, which was why he suspected her of stretching the truth in the first place. She'd wanted him to stay, even if their relationship had been toxic nearly from the start. Then she'd found another sucker to warm her bed and pay her bills, so Diego had been dismissed with a cold and callous lie.

"I'm not pregnant," Callie had spat. "Thank God! What the hell would I do with some spick kid?"

Diego shook his head to clear away the memory, to calm the clash of emotions. He opened the file and skimmed the pages of documents he'd amassed since meeting with Mike that night. The copy of the marriage certificate for Mike and Callie. The copy of the birth certificate for the baby she'd given birth to not six months after the Jessups' courthouse wedding—and approximately nine months after Diego had walked out. Despite being married at the time her baby was born, Callie had named the baby Alexis Campbell, her maiden name, and left the father line on the baby's birth certificate blank. Why?

Because the baby had been Diego's, that's why. Mike had confessed. Callie had left the line blank so that when she dumped Mike, which she did as soon as she found a man with more money and an even stronger rescue-impulse, she didn't have to give either Mike or Diego access to the child.

Diego later learned that Mike, as Callie's husband at the time of the baby's birth, probably would have had parental rights had he pursued them, but he'd been hurt and angry and had decided to wash himself of Callie entirely. He'd made a grave error in not telling Diego about the baby at that point, but Diego had been overseas and Mike had claimed to have placated his conscience by believing everyone was better off if he didn't get involved.

But then Callie had died. A fatal car wreck with her new husband. She hadn't had the baby with her, and when Mike had learned about the tragedy, he'd checked on the whereabouts of the child. At first, Callie's sister, Rita, had taken good care of Alexis, even promising Mike that he could visit whenever he wanted to. But soon after, things started to deteriorate. Rita started hanging out with shady characters. By the time Mike had finally decided to call social services, Rita had disappeared. And she'd taken Diego's child with her.

A little girl named Alexis Campbell. That's all Diego knew for sure about the baby he'd never known existed.

Not knowing what else to do, Mike had finally tracked Diego down as soon as his unit returned and told him everything he knew, which admittedly hadn't been much.

But luckily for Diego, serving in the military police gave him contacts with guys who knew how to check out things like this. He'd learned that Rita had moved to New York City with friends, but had no permanent address. He'd learned that back in Miami, she preferred calling her niece by her middle name, Amber, and that Amber, four years old when Callie died, loved to dance and had already started classes at the local YMCA. So after running a million Internet searches using various key words, he'd stumbled on the combination that had brought him a clue—*Amber Campbell, New York, dance* and Alexis's age. After searching for hours, he'd finally stumbled onto a Web site sponsored by a dance magazine. After signing in and paying a subscription fee, he'd been allowed to search the archives, where he found a picture of six-year-old Amber Campbell, dancing with an organization called *Groove With Me* out of Spanish Harlem. He slid the picture he'd printed out of the file and scanned the grainy photo again. Was it wishful thinking, or did she really have his dark skin tone? Callie's light eyes? His crooked smile?

A knock on the door sent him straight to his feet, thankful he'd left his service revolver in the possession of the U.S. Army. He'd gotten so jumpy lately. That's what happened, he supposed, when you realized you were willing to break laws and face prison time in order to kidnap your own child. He cursed under his breath, forced himself to calm down and then stalked to the peephole in the door to see who was bothering him.

Golden hair. Peachy skin. Sea-blue eyes.

Could it be?

He opened the door.

"Don't you ask for identification before you go opening your hotel room door? I mean, even I know better, and I was born and raised in a neighborhood where no one used their locks."

He raised an eyebrow. No, he certainly wasn't expecting Georgia Rae Evans to show up at his hotel room, but he somehow wasn't surprised. She seemed like the type to do what she pleased first and think better of it later.

"I could smell your perfume," he replied, emboldened by the way her cheeks rushed with color.

"You're a flirt."

"So I've heard."

She shoved her hands onto her hips, which were no longer

wrapped in baggy, wrinkly dance clothes like the kind his sister used to wear while working out, but in a scooped T-shirt and slim jeans that rode low on her hips and showed off her trim waist and pierced belly button.

"You gonna invite me inside?"

"Now who's being a flirt?"

She shoved a collection of papers at him, which he nearly dropped in his haste to get out of her way before she ran over him. "I'm not flirting. I know what you're really up to, Diego Paz...and I'm here to help."

CHAPTER FOUR

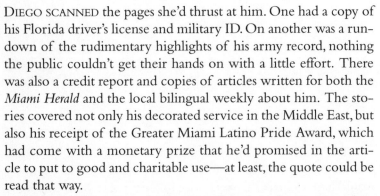

DIEGO SCANNED the pages she'd thrust at him. One had a copy of his Florida driver's license and military ID. On another was a rundown of the rudimentary highlights of his army record, nothing the public couldn't get their hands on with a little effort. There was also a credit report and copies of articles written for both the *Miami Herald* and the local bilingual weekly about him. The stories covered not only his decorated service in the Middle East, but also his receipt of the Greater Miami Latino Pride Award, which had come with a monetary prize that he'd promised in the article to put to good and charitable use—at least, the quote could be read that way.

All the information she'd amassed in less than twenty-four hours supported the story he'd told her on the street. But did she also know about his ulterior motives? About Alexis, the little girl she likely knew as Amber? Did she realize that if she helped him, she could end up being an accomplice to kidnapping—unless, of course, he convinced the right people that Alexis belonged with him and not with the aunt who'd stolen her?

"You a private investigator for your day job?" he asked.

She grinned. "I'm a set designer, actually. And I'm between shows. But I have friends in the right places."

He leafed through the papers one more time, finally convinced she likely didn't know anything he didn't want her to. Yet.

"Of course," he responded. "You work with children. You can't be too careful."

She clapped her hands, as if the matter of who he was and what he wanted was now completely put to rest. "So, what do you say we cruise downstairs, grab some coffee and talk about the program? I spoke with my boss this morning and she said she'd love to meet with you when she gets back."

Her boss? Oh, yeah. The founder of *Groove With Me*. He'd done research about her and her organization after finding Alexis's picture. From what he'd learned, Georgia Rae and her boss had a lot in common. Lots of guts, both of them. A graduate of Brown University, the woman had been twenty-three when she'd lugged her boom box into New York's Lower East Side with a pair of tap shoes and a dream to help the young girls in the neighborhood use dance to bring joy, hope and respect into their lives. She'd worked in the prison system—she'd seen firsthand where misguided childhoods could lead adults, especially women. She'd wanted to make a difference.

But why had Georgia Rae stepped off Broadway to help the children?

And why did he care?

Knowing wouldn't likely aid in his search for Alexis, but he was interested anyway. Before he learned about his daughter, it never would have occurred to him that children had to look to people outside their families for support and love. The Paz clan was extended and involved. His parents had made sure that he and his sisters stayed on the straight and narrow, though when he really thought about it, things hadn't been so easy for other kids he knew. Without the right influences, many of his schoolmates had ended up doing time, doing drugs or both. Like New York, the opportunities in Miami to turn down the wrong road were plentiful.

"That's generous of your boss to agree to see me," Diego said, fighting the urge to crumple the papers in his palm out of frustration for being so close and yet so far from his child. More than anything, he wanted to trust Georgia Rae with the whole story and beg—yes, *beg*—for her help in finding Alexis and getting her back where she belonged, with a father and family who would love her and take care of her and keep her safe. But he wasn't stupid. He had no concrete reason to believe Georgia would be on his side, and he couldn't allow himself to be blinded by beauty yet again. Sure, Georgia seemed to have a good heart, but there was no telling what lies Rita might have filled her head with—and Alexis's. He was, after all, a stranger to his own child.

"Yeah, she's great," Georgia verified. "But I know you don't have unlimited time to stay in the city, so I thought I'd fill you in on the particulars of *Groove With Me* as I know them, then take you over to the studio and give you a tour. We've all really wanted to see the program expanded into other cities. Miami seems like a natural fit."

He nodded and handed Georgia back her dossier. Without drawing too much attention to his actions, he moved to his bed and stashed the file with the information on Alexis back into his duffel and grabbed his jacket. When he turned to move to the door, he found that Georgia Rae had stepped boldly into his personal space. He had to jerk back to keep from running into her—or better yet, running up against her.

She quirked a lopsided grin. "You've got quick reflexes."

Diego couldn't help but lick his teeth beneath his lips, trying to keep himself from responding the way he'd like to. With a tease. A sexy taunt.

"They come in handy."

He slipped his hands into his pockets, knowing that was the only way he was going to keep his hands off her, especially when she perused her way up and down his body, not backing up or pulling away or looking anywhere but longingly from his feet to his hips to his chest to his eyes.

"Do you dance?"

"Excuse me?"

She tilted her head to the left, so that her loose, long golden hair draped sensually across her cheek. "You're obviously in shape. And you're Latin, so you've got rhythm, right?"

He chuckled. "That's a stereotype, like the Southerners talking slow."

She shrugged unapologetically. "Most stereotypes are based in an inkling of truth. Most Southerners talk slower because we have more syllables to pronounce. But I was just wondering if you were going to teach the classes in Miami yourself."

Her outrageous suggestion knocked the tension right out of the air and Diego snorted. When a visual image of him prancing around in front of a bunch of giggling girls flashed in front of his eyes, the humor knocked him in the gut. He doubled over.

Georgia laughed, too, but she was trying hard to be serious. "What? Is that so out of the question?"

He sucked in air to tamp down the laughter. "Yes, actually, it is." He wiped moisture from the corner of his eye. God, it had been a long time since he'd laughed like that. And all at his own expense. This woman was one in a million.

"I'm not looking to get that personally involved, okay? I'll leave the dancing to the professionals. And the children."

"What a shame."

She lingered a moment, and the hungry look in her eyes cut the last of his glee away. There was a feral, feline quality to the way she glanced at him before she turned and moved toward the door with a subtle swing to her hips.

And she thought he had rhythm?

He grabbed his key and his wallet, careful to yank the door closed before he met her at the elevator. They went down two floors and, after a quick walk across the lobby, glanced into the hotel's cookie-cutter restaurant and looked at each other with reluctant frowns.

"Not your cup of tea, either?" she asked.

He smirked. "I don't get to come to New York very often. Sort of hate to waste my time inside a hotel."

She smiled, and the simple process of her lips curling up at the corners and her blue eyes lighting to an iridescent twinkle caught Diego unprepared. He cleared his throat, trying to cover the tightness that suddenly attacked his body from head to toe.

"How about I show you around a little then? Up for some walking?"

He nodded, knowing better than to confess that with her around, he was up for just about anything.

TORTURE. Pure, unadulterated, cruel-to-the-point-of-madness torture, that's what it was. Worse than endless nights in an oven of a desert, baking in the weight of his personal body armor. Worse than basic training. Watching Georgia dance twisted Diego inside and out until he had to use every ounce of self-control not to bolt for the door—or worse, step out onto the studio dance floor, grab her hand and spin her into his arms.

Sitting on a folding chair near the corner, he tore his eyes away from Georgia only after one of the twelve-year-olds in her class twirled out of control and lost her balance. She tripped on his shoe, but he caught her midfall, and with a standing bounce, put her back on her feet.

"Oh, *lo siento, lo siento,*" the girl said, her eyes suddenly dark with wide-eyed terror. Tears brimmed on her eyelids and her mouth trembled.

All for tripping over his big feet?

He released her quickly and put on his biggest smile. "No, no. Don't apologize, *mija.* You dance beautifully, and here I am cramping your space."

He chuckled purposefully, and after a second, he watched her fear slip away.

"I'm clumsy sometimes," she explained.

"Put me out there in a tutu and I'll show you clumsy."

He winked, and with a warm pat on her shoulder, erased the last of the embarrassment from the girl's face. By this point, Georgia danced over and encouraged her student back into the line.

"Keep those toes pointed, *chicas!* That's it. Listen to the music."

Once she was sure the group was completely engaged again,

she turned to Diego. "The classroom is a little crowded. You handled Bibi really well. She's very jumpy around men."

Diego pressed his lips tightly together. He'd seen something in the girl's eyes that he'd seen a few times before—usually in the averted gazes of the young girls who had the misfortune to be born in Afghanistan during the rule of the Taliban.

"She's been abused, hasn't she?"

Georgia nodded sadly, and then shouted another instruction over the rising strains of Tchaikovsky. Diego hadn't listened to much classical music in his life, but when this one surged with a sudden burst of violin, he could feel the underlying eroticism in the rhythm, in the tempo. Georgia responded, swaying side to side, blending into the music and then into the dance as the girls attempted the new steps they'd just learned.

Diego had never seen a ballet. He had no idea how Georgia might compare to the professional dancers who performed on stage night by night, but he was enraptured by what he witnessed. She seemed to grow taller as she danced, her body stretching and elongating into fascinating shapes, her balance flawless, her form sleek. When she twirled, her head snapped with keen precision, but her arms moved with a gentle undulation, like petals in the wind or waves in a breeze. When combined with the sensual dance, the music evoked images at once erotic and mystical. Or maybe Georgia alone was responsible for the sudden wash of images in his mind, ones that had no place in a building full of kids.

Diego sat back in his chair, stunned.

Suddenly, the girls stopped dancing and started clapping. They'd successfully mastered the new combination, and after promising to teach them the rest of the dance next week, Georgia flipped off the music and called the girls into a friendship circle for one last chat before they went home.

Not wanting to intrude, Diego quietly left the rehearsal room, lingering instead inside the cramped office, which, using one of Georgia's endless television and movie references, reminded him of the scene in the first *Star Wars* film where the walls were closing in on a trapped Luke Skywalker and friends. Boxes of costumes and props, file cabinets and desks were squeezed into the tiny space. Bulletin boards dotted the walls, with Post-it squares creating a rainbow of scribbles and notes and reminders. While he waited for Georgia to finish her class, he glanced at the sign-up sheets and announcements pinned above a photo of two teachers with their students and caught sight of a name.

Amber Campbell.

Diego's chest constricted and breath whooshed out of him. He pushed a box out of his way, kicked a stray tap shoe so that it skittered across the floor. With a shaking hand, he traced his fingers over the handwritten name, in big, round, bubbly letters, the *B*s backward. She'd written her name herself, in her tiny, six-year-old hand.

"Hey! Where'd you disappear to?"

Georgia strolled into the room, a white towel rolled around her neck. Yet despite being caught where he shouldn't be, Diego couldn't move.

"Diego?"

With the lightest touch, he traced the name again. She was six, but she could write her whole name. That was something, right? Something special? God, he didn't even know. He had nieces and nephews and cousins in multiples, and yet he had no idea if a six-year-old being able to write her whole name was the sign of a prodigy or something every kid could do.

Georgia stepped near him. He could feel the essence of her body heat, smell the sweet mixture of perspiration and her peachy perfume, but still, he couldn't move.

"Do you know her?"

The edge in her voice, the sharp sound of worry, broke him away.

He shook his head and grinned. "Some kids, they just write so cute, you know? Letters backward, big loopy *E*s. Just caught my eye. What's this sign-up for?"

Georgia leaned over and read the header. "That's a fund-raiser we're doing at a street festival in three weeks. Some dancers I know from the Broadway production of *Wicked* are going to show up, sign autographs, drum up some interest and cash for *Groove With*

Me. The little ones are going to dance. You should see them. They're so full of energy!"

Diego's mouth remained parched. A million questions zoomed around in his brain, but he wasn't sure which one would be the least suspicious, the least likely to set off that honed radar Georgia seemed to have that might peg him as a liar. He'd touched his daughter's name. He'd sat in the same room she danced in twice a week. How much closer could he possibly get without Georgia's help?

"When do they take their lessons?" he asked, hoping he'd chosen the right query, hoping his tone didn't reveal the desperation with which he needed the answer.

"Tomorrow afternoon, actually. At four."

He acknowledged her reply with a curt nod, and then forced himself to walk to the door. Standing near his daughter's signature and not knowing where she was or what kind of life she'd had was like pouring vinegar over an open wound. God, how messed up was he? Did normal fathers act like this over children they'd never met, or was he simply on the edge of losing control?

Despite the music, laughter, giggles and chatter assailing them from all directions, a tense silence stretched between Diego and Georgia until he knew the time had come for him to make a choice. He needed her help. She'd spent all day filling him in on the operations of *Groove With Me,* going over every little detail until he figured he could run the place tomorrow if he was needed. The next step would be for him to talk directly to the founder and director of the program. He'd taken enough of Georgia's time, and yet…

Tomorrow afternoon, actually.

"Georgia, you've been very patient and gracious."

She used the towel to gently pat the sweat off her face. "I'm just doing what I can to help. You can really do a good thing in your neighborhood, Diego, if you decide to go through with this."

He combed his hand through his hair and glanced aside, hating how the lies tasted on his tongue. "Once I make up my mind about something, I'm not one to back down."

"Good for you."

He glanced at Amber's name on the list.

"You've been so helpful, spending your whole day with me. I'd like to repay you."

"That's not necessary."

"Maybe not, but I'd like to take you to dinner. Maybe do a little dancing?"

Her eyes widened. "You'll dance?"

"I actually love to dance, just not in a place that uses tap shoes and tutus."

She licked her lips, her eyes twinkling with humor. "More of a club guy, huh?"

"Like you said, we Latinos do have rhythm."

Georgia turned away as she folded her towel over the back of the office chair. He couldn't see her face, but he could feel the tension as she grappled with her decision to accept or decline. They'd spent the entire day together, but somehow, they'd managed to talk about little other than the dance program and the girls in it. He'd listened raptly, softened by the love in her voice as she spoke about the girls' successes, heartbroken by the sadness when she told him about some of the dire circumstances these little women faced each and every day. He'd waited, ready to grab on to one single offhand comment that would have led him to believe she was talking about his daughter. But she'd been discreet. If the girl she knew as Amber had ever popped into the conversation, he'd been oblivious. And he'd never found a natural way to ask.

And yet, right at this moment, her acceptance of his invitation wasn't entirely about his child. Without much effort, he could cruise by tomorrow and likely be welcomed again with open arms during the four o'clock class. Then once Amber left, he could follow her home, find out where she lived and decide whether or not he would snatch her or go the legal route with DNA tests, petitions and attorneys.

But in the meantime, spending a few hours away from here with Georgia Rae Evans tempted him in ways he hadn't experienced in a long, long time.

"What do you say?" he asked. "I'll make it somewhere nice, I promise. You'll have a great time."

"And if I don't?"

He brought his fist to his chin and pretended to think long and hard, when in reality, he already knew the perfect way to entice her. "If you don't have the time of your life, I pledge to put on a pair of tap shoes and take a lesson in your next class."

Georgia laughed. "Then I hope the night's a bust, because that I have to see!"

CHAPTER FIVE

"Wow."

Georgia turned toward Diego's throaty voice. Pure, unadulterated male hunger gleamed in his eyes, and he punctuated the expression with a wolfish whistle. But since she had spent the last hour coordinating her makeup and clothes and attitude to solicit that exact, passionate response, Georgia didn't fight her own reaction. With a triumphant smile, she shimmied and spun around, giving him a close-up view of the entire sensual package.

He groaned longingly. "You're killing me."

"I'll take that as a compliment," she said, tugging on the hem of her sheer black blouse.

"You should, because I meant it as a compliment." He stepped back and looked some more. "Give me a few seconds to roll my tongue back into my mouth and I'm sure I'll think up something else to say."

She slapped him playfully on the shoulder. "No need to overdo it."

"One *wow* is not overdoing it, not with you."

With a kick in her step that had everything to do with the

surge in her confidence, Georgia moved toward the door. To his credit, Diego reached the handle first and directed her inside with impeccable manners. They'd agreed to meet outside Creole, a New Orleans–themed restaurant just a few blocks away from the dance studio. Georgia's roommate had come to the rescue by delivering her clothes and toiletries so she could shower at *Groove With Me* and not be late for her date, and now Georgia was anticipating a marvelous night of food, drink, music and, hopefully, personal revelation.

A date. *Wow* was right. How long had it been since she had put herself out there last? The dating world, especially in New York, was a scary place. Maybe that's why she'd jumped at the chance for time alone with Diego, even though they'd just met. She had, after all, checked him out pretty thoroughly. And since he was from Miami, she knew he was also going back there soon, which meant pesky little details like keeping her heart safe from being broken again didn't apply tonight. There would be no strings, no entanglements. Just one night of fun and relaxation…and if she got lucky, maybe something more.

While Diego spoke with the hostess about their reservation, Georgia hung back and watched. He spoke quietly and with unshakable politeness, even when he was told the wait would be longer than anticipated. For an instant, images of David flashed in her mind. Flamboyant and dramatic, her ex would have thrown a fit in the face of a restaurant wait. He wasn't a star—yet—but he demanded star treatment everywhere he went. Georgia should have known better than to hang out with a guy like him, but it wasn't as if he was a total loser or anything. He'd been gorgeous and more than ready, willing and able to shower her with attention. An up-and-coming Broadway director, David Marshand had been handsome, talented, driven and generous. After nearly seven years of focusing solely on school, then her career, then her participation in *Groove With Me,* Georgia had been so ready for a relationship a year ago, so primed to find the man of her dreams, her fabled other half. She'd dated off and on, but until David, she hadn't met anyone who had the same interests she did, the same friends and acquaintances. But despite all they'd had in common, they'd had more than their share of differences. She'd ended up with a broken heart and a serious dent in her confidence when it came to her ability to separate the jerks from the princes.

Yet for all his outward appearances, Diego Paz was one of the royal ones. He was a former soldier, a hero, one who cared about not only his country, but his community. He'd listened to her today with rapt attention, as if she was imparting the meaning of life rather than the organizational breakdown of a small, privately-run nonprofit. Despite his dire demeanor the day they'd met on the street, he actually laughed easily and loved to banter. He wasn't college-educated, but he had dreams and goals that he'd already made solid plans to pursue.

And he lived in another state, so whatever came of tonight would soon be a happy memory, with no disappointment attached.

"Want to wait in the bar?" he asked, sliding up close so she could hear him over the raucous zydeco music pumping out of the speakers. "Shouldn't be more than fifteen minutes."

When she nodded, they headed into the lounge area and found a high table in the corner. Diego guided Georgia onto a stool. As he moved around to his own chair, she noticed a slight bounce in his shoulders. The music had infected him, and damned if she didn't find that incredibly appealing.

With a friendly wave to the waiter, they had immediate service.

"What can I get you?" he asked.

Georgia glanced over the drink menu, her taste buds electrified by the wide variety of mixed concoctions, each more exotic and potentially delicious than the next. There were lots of hometown favorites—mint julep, old-fashioned, hurricane. "There's so much to choose from."

"Pick whatever you like," Diego encouraged her. "We live once."

She laughed. "In that case, I'll have a beer."

"A beer? That's it?"

"I'm not a totally cheap date. It should be imported and on draft."

"Make that two."

The waiter ran down a few brands, and after they'd chosen, he disappeared into the crowd.

"You don't seem like the beer type to me," Diego said.

"Really? What kind of woman is a beer type?"

He lifted his hands, as if he wasn't going to touch that statement with a ten-foot pole. "Not going there, but I definitely pegged you for white wine."

"We're not always the people we seem to be. I like my wine red and the drier the better."

"I'll make a mental note."

"No need. Tonight is pretty much all we'll have, right? It's not like we'll see each other again. Your life is in Miami and mine is here in New York."

"This is true, but just because I live in another state doesn't mean I won't want to look you up when I visit. I don't mean to be pushy, Georgia, but I don't know, I feel comfortable with you. Like we are, I don't know…"

"Connected?" The word was out of Georgia's mouth before she could think better of it, not that thinking before she spoke was her forte. She had a very distinct habit of letting her tongue loose when her brain hadn't had a chance to catch up. "Oh, that sounds a little presumptuous, doesn't it?"

"No," he assured her, reaching across the table and laying his hand next to hers, close, but not touching. Diego clearly understood boundaries.

Darn it.

She smiled when his finger tapped closer.

"You just said what I've been wanting to," he told her, "but I didn't want to sound like I was handing you a line. I have to confess that while I was listening to all your information today about *Groove With Me,* what I really wanted to know was more about you."

DIEGO IGNORED the tightening in his chest that accompanied that admission. But when he'd first learned about Alexis months ago, he'd vowed then and there to change his life. That included changing the way he selected his dates and how he treated them, too. Maybe if he'd poked into Callie's background a little more before he'd jumped into bed with her, he wouldn't be in the mess he was in.

Not that he figured he'd have a chance to jump into bed with Georgia anytime soon, but damn, he'd certainly want to explore that option if she showed interest. Becoming a new man didn't include extended celibacy—just more careful planning.

"I told you about me," she said, a shy twinkle in her eye.

Shy, my ass. Coy was more like it.

He grinned, appreciating her technique. "You told me how you got involved with *Groove With Me* and about how much you enjoyed working with the kids. I know you were born and raised outside Atlanta, that you went to college in Chicago and studied set design, and then came to New York to work on Broadway, but really, that's not much."

"That's more than most guys are interested in."

"That's not true."

She raised her eyebrows. "When's the last time you went on a date?"

"With a guy? Can't say I've had the pleasure."

She laughed. "You know what I mean."

"Yeah, I do. I just got out of the army five months ago. I haven't had half a chance to just live a normal life again."

Georgia pursed her lips, leaning forward as she listened. "What's a normal life to you?"

Challenged by the question, Diego stopped to think. He'd been warned that adjusting to civilian life could be hard, but he'd pretty much instantly blended back in with his family, with their concerns and interests and dramas. At the same time, he'd been consumed by thoughts of his daughter, of building a life for her and with her. He hadn't really thought much about himself.

"I'm still working that out."

The waiter arrived with their beer, which he delivered without breaking up their conversation.

"What about work?" she asked.

Diego experienced that stabbing pain between his eyes that usually accompanied this particular topic. He'd had a whole plan in place before he'd learned about Alexis. Now he wasn't so sure.

"At the moment, I'm working at my father's shop. He's a mechanic. Runs his own place. Specializes in foreign sports cars, so he does okay."

"But that's not what you want to do forever?"

He chuckled. He should have known better than to think he could snow her for a second.

"I have an application in with the Miami-Dade police. I was an MP in the service and I enjoyed my assignments."

Only now, he wasn't sure that a single father should work in such a dangerous profession. And yet, his Tio Armando had retired from the force after twenty-two years without ever firing his service revolver. Luckily, Georgia didn't know the details of his life, so she couldn't know how torn he was right now.

Georgia took a healthy swig of her beer, somehow making the action delicate. "Why didn't you stay in? Go career military?"

"I never wanted to be a career soldier. I wanted to serve, learn, then move back home. I love Miami. I love my family, my friends. I wanted to give something back to the country that took us in from Cuba, but now it's time to settle down, make a difference to the people I love."

Georgia's smile was tentative, but sincere. "It's my turn to say, wow."

He shook his head, wondering how big of a fool he looked, pouring out his heart like some poetic sap. "You probably think I'm handing you a line."

"If you are, it's a good one."

For a minute, silence ensued. The music had switched to jazz, which Diego liked, he supposed, but the rhythms didn't pull him, didn't connect with that elemental part of him that would synchronize with his body when the beat was right. The music he'd heard when they first walked in, *that* he liked. Quick and energetic. Sexy, but fun. Reminded him of Georgia. Sultry, but with a bounce that made a man want to dance into a sweat and then cool down with a willing woman.

"What about you?" he asked after taking a long, icy sip from his beer. "How long are you planning to stay in New York and design sets on Broadway?"

"For as long as there is a Broadway."

She curled a lock of hair behind her ear, and for some odd reason, the casual gesture made Diego thirsty again. He downed nearly half his beer in one long gulp and hoped the hostess didn't call them to their table any time soon. Hiding his attraction to Georgia was no longer an easy task, since his body seemed to have a mind of its own.

"Have you been to a show?" she asked.

"Never."

"Oh! You don't know what you're missing!"

Diego hadn't thought Georgia's expression could get any more animated and electric, but the minute the conversation turned to the theatre, she was nearly bouncing in her seat.

"Broadway productions aren't like anything else in the world. I've toured with two companies and I even did a summer in London, but there's just something about a theatre smack-dab in the center of Manhattan with New York all around you that gives off an energy you can't find anywhere else. I love reading the script, working with the design teams, coming up with concepts and then collaborating with the construction crews and the director and the artists until we get it just right. I love being around the music, the performers, the magic. It's unbelievable."

Diego was struck yet again by the enthusiasm with which Georgia attacked life. Because that's what she did—she did more than just live. She grabbed.

"You sound like you'll never leave," he commented.

"Not willingly. I'm starting work on a new show next month. Things will get hectic, but it's the most fabulous hectic. I wouldn't trade my life for anything."

Diego asked her questions about the new musical, which Georgia answered happily, even after they were escorted to their table. She soared off on a million tangents, but Diego didn't mind. Then suddenly, after the waiter delivered the wine Georgia had chosen and served them each a glass, her chatter waned.

"I'm talking too much," she said finally.

"No, you're not. You love what you do. You make me want to go see a…production, you called it? You know, before I leave."

"I can probably get you tickets to just about anything. There are some great new shows."

He shook his head, disbelieving. "Never in my life would I have imagined someone talking me into going to see musical theatre."

She smirked. "Not macho enough for you?"

"I'm just a hardworking guy from Little Havana. I'm not so-phisticated or educated. New York was always a world away."

"Then why'd you come?"

Diego inhaled. Now he had to go back to the lies and half-truths. He liked the conversation better when it was all about her.

"To see *Groove With Me* firsthand."

"You could have called or sent an e-mail."

He shook his head. "It wouldn't have been the same. I needed to meet the girls, see the organization in action. And I had some business in New York anyway, so I just thought I'd drop in and see what it was like for real, not when on display."

"That's understandable. How did you find out about *Groove With Me* anyway? You never told me."

Diego paused, and for an instant, Georgia saw that deer-in-the-headlights look that she hadn't witnessed since they'd first met the day before. "My sister saw an article in a dance magazine," he replied, his tone not as clear as it had been moments before.

"Your sister dances?"

"Yeah, every *mujer* in Little Havana dances."

"Professionally?"

"Maggie? No, she's a legal secretary. But she takes classes to keep in shape."

Whatever she'd thought she'd caught in his voice before—dis-honesty, maybe—was gone now.

"Is she your only sister?"

Diego sipped his wine, and Georgia couldn't help but remember how uncomfortable he'd looked when she'd asked him about his interest in *Groove With Me,* and how his entire mood shifted when he spoke about his family. Pride shone in his eyes and the glow warmed her in a deep, elemental way.

"My parents had three kids back-to-back right after they were married. Marie, Connie and Francie. Ten years later, they had me and Maggie. We're a little over a year apart."

"Five total? Your parents must love children."

"Major understatement. They already have nine grandchildren and can't wait for more. What about you? Do you have brothers and sisters?"

Despite her best efforts, a little bit of the warm feeling slipped away. "No, it's just me. I have lots of cousins, but we're all pretty spread out now. I go home when I can, and luckily for me, my parents love to come to New York, so I see them quite a bit."

The server appeared, ready and able to skillfully describe the night's specials and his personal recommendations, which quickly turned the conversation to food and the endless Cajun and Creole possibilities on the menu. They couldn't decide, so at Diego's suggestion, they ordered an eclectic selection and promised to share. For some reason, Georgia found Diego's suggestion compelling, even though she'd probably done the same thing on other dates before.

Difference was, when she'd met Diego, she'd confronted a macho, intense, driven man with a problem to solve and solutions to find. Over the course of twenty-four hours, she'd discovered there was more to the man than he let on. Yeah, he was still a tough-guy charmer with an eye for beauty, but she'd also found out he was a fascinating man with layers of depth she hungered to explore.

By the time the first course arrived, Georgia made a decision. Diego might be leaving New York soon, but for the duration of his stay, she was going to make sure she stayed in his life. As he'd said earlier, they'd only live once.

"Good choice of restaurants, huh?" he asked, lifting his fork toward her mouth. He'd ordered the fried crawfish salad, but no matter how much she wanted to try the spinach, red onion and warm honey-bacon dressing combination, when he moved the morsel closer to her lips, the only taste she craved was that of Diego's kiss.

She accepted the bite, chewed and allowed the explosion of flavors to play unchecked on her face. "Delicious."

Diego leaned back in his chair, lifted his wineglass, and then, for the first time since they'd arrived at the restaurant, he truly relaxed. She could practically see the tension leave his shoulders and travel down his arms to dissipate through the tips of his fingers, which held the glass with easy confidence, as if sipping wine in a hip New York restaurant was something he did every day.

"You're comfortable just about anywhere, aren't you?" she asked.

"Depends on the company," he said with a grin that warmed her insides with more spice than the crab bisque in front of her.

"You're a real charmer, Diego Paz."

"You keep saying that. Is the charm working?"

She lifted an eyebrow. "Can't you tell?"

He slid the wineglass back onto the table and plucked a golden-brown crawfish from the top of his salad and popped it in his mouth. "I can tell you're a beautiful, generous woman who has been nothing but helpful to me. I'm trying to repay you with dinner, and not surprisingly, the evening doesn't seem like enough."

She sipped a spoonful of soup. "That's because it's not."

"Really?"

Georgia took a long sip from her wine, watching how tightness returned to Diego's body, but this time, the tension was purely sexual, purely in tune with the tautness slipping like molten steel into her veins.

He leaned closer so that she could see the inky blackness of his irises, even in the muted restaurant light. "Then you're going to have to clue me in," he said, "tell me what I'm doing wrong."

With a soft smile, she nodded, ladled a serving of bisque into her spoon and held the utensil aloft so that Diego would have to lean completely forward to receive her offering.

When his mouth was full of the deliciously sweet creamed concoction, Georgia whispered into his ear, "I'm not only going to tell you, I'm going to show you."

CHAPTER SIX

PROVING YET AGAIN how much of a gentleman he was, Diego insisted on riding in the cab from the restaurant to Georgia's apartment on the Upper West Side of Manhattan. Proving yet again how much of a lady she didn't want to be, Georgia tried to think of a way to divert him to his hotel first. No such luck. No matter how many ways she phrased her imaginary suggestions, she knew she'd end up sounding horny.

Which, she supposed, she was.

She sat back in the seat as Diego chitchatted in Spanish with the taxi driver, a Colombian immigrant with a remarkable knowledge of the city and its sights. The man should have been a tour guide. But at least the conversation didn't require her input, giving her a few moments to figure out what she was going to do about Diego Paz.

The attraction was undeniable, and the allure of knowing he wouldn't be around except for a few more days tempted her beyond reason. She was, after all, young and healthy and on birth control. Georgia wasn't one to sleep with any stranger who popped into her life, but Diego, he sparked the part of her femininity that hadn't been lit in a very long time. Georgia had a relatively healthy appreciation for lust, especially when the man in question was clearly as interested in her as she was in him.

Diego leaned back into the seat. "I'm sorry. I'm ignoring you."

She shook her head. "Don't worry. I've driven through the city a million times, and sometimes I hardly notice what's around me."

"I didn't plan on taking you home in order to get a tour of the city."

His confession perked her interest. She turned and leaned closer to him, struck by how the slightly musty cab enhanced the power of his cinnamon-spiced cologne.

"Then why did you insist on taking me home?"

He seemed to gravitate nearer until his breath teased the tendrils of her hair. "I wanted to spend more time with you."

"That's interesting, since here I was trying to figure out how to get us back to your hotel."

Diego's eyes widened, but he didn't back away. Outside, the city flashed by—neon lights and raucous sounds and mass waves of humanity pushing down the crowded sidewalks or driving down the traffic-clogged streets. It was late, but the residents of New York, both permanent and temporary, never seemed to notice.

"You should have just asked."

"And sound sex-starved and easy?"

He shook his head and tentatively reached out and slid his hand over hers. "I would never believe that about you. It's not in your nature to take relationships lightly."

"You don't know that, Diego. You really don't know anything about me other than what I've chosen to tell you—and even all that could be a lie."

"That goes both ways."

The cabbie pulled up to the curb outside Georgia's apartment building. Diego asked the driver to wait, then escorted Georgia to her door. They lingered on the stoop, and despite her best effort, Georgia couldn't manage to look at anything but her Jimmy Choo shoes.

She nearly fainted when Diego crooked a finger beneath her chin and with sensual slowness tilted her head until his eyes met hers.

"I want to kiss you," he admitted.

Her tummy quivered deep inside, and if not for the rumbling of the car engine just a few feet away, she might have heard the rush of blood as it surged through her veins. "So why don't you?"

"We just met," he replied, sounding more reasonable and measured than the incendiary look in his eyes. "I'm leaving soon."

"All the more reason to take what we want, what we deserve," she countered.

The sexual need arcing between them came with a shearing pain. Georgia's throat tightened and her breasts ached. She throbbed with wanting him, wanting what she knew she shouldn't have, not when she sensed he was holding back.

"Maybe I should go inside," she said, but couldn't move an inch.

Diego leaned closer, his lips inches from hers. "Not…quite… yet."

The pressing of his mouth against hers caused an instantaneous explosion of sensations. He tasted of spiced food and fine wine, and the scent of his cologne, mixed intimately with his natural musk, made her dizzy. His kiss was soft, yet powerful, and she didn't think twice when his tongue coaxed her lips open. She willed her body to remain still, but with her mouth alone, she proved just how powerful the two of them could be—together.

Just when she thought she couldn't hold still any longer, Diego broke away. He staggered back a step, and when his gaze cleared from the fog of their overpowering connection, he smiled and smoothed a hand over her hair.

"I want to see you again," he said, smoothing his hand over his mouth in a way that told her he wanted more. Much more. "I plan to stop by *Groove With Me* one more time, tomorrow afternoon. Will you be there?"

She squeezed her eyelids tightly closed, trying to remember

what day it was, what her schedule was...what planet she lived on. God, she couldn't think! The man was like a drug, one that made her forget everything except how long it had been since she'd last had sex. No, more specifically, how long it had been since she'd last had *good* sex.

Too long.

"I'll be there," she answered, "but now, if you're married to some idea about taking it slow, I suggest you go while you still can."

He chuckled, nodding as if she'd nailed his reason for pulling back with perfect accuracy. He stepped toward the waiting taxi, but then turned and intimately, regretfully, touched her cheek. "Thanks for an amazing evening, Georgia Rae Evans."

She turned toward her door and, key in hand, pretended to work the lock, even if she couldn't manage to move until she finally heard the cab drive away. Over her shoulder, she watched the taillights blend into all the others and wondered if she'd just escaped another heartbreak or if she'd lost a chance at something wonderful, even if just for one night.

"OH, GOD, HE'S HERE!"

Marcy shot into the office and nearly brained Georgia with a falling tower of newly purchased tap shoes. At the desk completing paperwork, Georgia screamed as the shoe boxes rained down on her head. When the cardboard and leather stopped clattering, Georgia Rae looked up to see Diego standing in the doorway, his mouth twisted as he attempted not to laugh out loud.

Marcy looked horrified, then giggled. "Oops."

With a snort, Georgia threw up her hands. "You really know how to make an entrance, Marcy."

Her assistant planted her fists on her slim hips, her dark complexion showing the definite signs of a blush. "I was just trying to tell you that your man was here."

"My man? Wow, if I own him, I guess I can put him to work picking up this mess."

Marcy huffed, but started cleaning up while Georgia picked her way through the avalanche of shoes and gestured Diego into the hall. "Sorry about that. I don't know what Marcy was thinking."

"Did you tell her about last night?"

Every last detail. "Would you mind if I did?"

His grin was nothing short of feral. "I'd be honored. It's not every day I kiss a woman like you."

"What kind of woman is that?"

"The kind who knows better than to let me do more than kiss her."

The intimacy was destroyed the moment one of the six-year-olds from Miss Marcy's class tugged on Georgia's jeans.

Georgia fluttered her lashes, fighting to get her life back into focus. Flirting with a hot, dangerous man was not what she should be doing while the children were around.

"What is it, Luisa?"

"Is this your *novio?*"

"Boyfriend? No, honey, he's just here to learn about our classes."

Luisa Marquez, one of the boldest girls in the bunch, wrinkled up her nose. "I think you should date him. He's *muy guapo.*"

Georgia turned and pretended to size Diego up, when in truth, she'd been doing little else for the past two days. She'd come to learn the exact way the light played on his dark hair and across the shadows created by the thick, ebony lashes that surrounded his soulful eyes.

"Yeah, I can see where he's attractive," Georgia conceded, "but I don't think I need to be discussing whether or not a man is handsome with a six-year-old, now, do I?"

Luisa arched a tiny brow. "My *mami* says I have good taste in men."

"Well, I hope you keep that good taste until you're old enough to date, which by the way, isn't anytime soon, okay?"

Luisa rolled her shoulders, and with a practiced, bored expression likely learned from her teenage mother, blew them off and returned to the classroom.

"Sorry about that," Georgia said. "Some of these girls are pretty precocious. They've had to grow up way too fast."

Diego pressed his lips tightly together. "Are they all like that? Talking about men and boys when they're so young?"

Georgia took a deep breath, trying to contain the frustration that sometimes attacked with overwhelming agony. "Some are worse. Some are better. Most of them are being raised in single-parent households with no strong male influence, at least, not one that's worth having. Sometimes I think they know more about sex and drugs than I do."

She watched the girls warming up for their class, sitting on the floor and stretching. Seconds later, Marcy dashed into the room, and immediately the level of energy spiked. She turned on the music, and in seconds, the girls were totally focused on dancing and probably nothing else.

Only after a few minutes had passed did Georgia realize that Diego hadn't said anything. She'd left him a wide opening for a flirtatious comment, and yet when she turned to look at him, he was staring at the girls with a mixture of profound sadness and carefully checked anger—and none of the charming naughtiness she'd come to expect.

"Diego? What's wrong?"

He shook his head, his gaze darting from girl to girl, his expression deeply concerned. She thought she'd been clear with him before about the positive strides most of the children had made, but perhaps seeing the lasting effects of their family lives on girls so young was too real, too difficult for him. He was, after all, a soldier. If he was anything like the military men she'd known in her life, he expected to be able to fix injustices, quickly and efficiently. And with these girls, who lived mainly in East Harlem, the best they could do was a little at a time.

She snagged him by the sleeve of his shirt and led him through the doorway. He followed, but kept his eyes trained on the children as they reviewed their tap routine from the week before.

"You can't take it so personally, Diego. Trust me. It'll eat you up inside."

"I have to take it personally," he replied, his tone flat, but filled with an intensity that had she not known him better, might have frightened her. "Tell me about them."

"I don't think…"

He speared her with a sharp look. "Tell me."

Georgia glanced into the room, then back at Diego. Maybe this was a moment of reckoning for him. Maybe he needed a painful dose of reality to make sure he had the right stuff to take on this project. He couldn't back down or abandon the girls once he started *Groove With Me* in his neighborhood. If there was one thing these children needed, it was adults they could count on. Reliability. Steadiness.

She licked her lips, then started with the girl closest to the window. "That's Nina. Her mother does hair at the salon down the street. Her father is in jail and her mom works long hours to make ends meet. She has five other kids and the oldest girl is pregnant. Her mother loves Nina desperately, but there's only so much attention to go around sometimes. Nina comes here and gets to play with other children and feel important. She's a real leader, too. Catches on to the dancing quick."

Diego nodded, but his gaze never left the children. "What about that one?"

He pointed to the third girl from the end. With her dark hair, dusky complexion and crystal-blue eyes, she was a standout in terms of both beauty and talent. Georgia knew she'd come to them with dance experience, something very rare in a child so young.

"That's Amber."

"What's her story?"

Georgia crossed her arms and rubbed the skin that suddenly prickled over her flesh. "She moved here over a year ago with her aunt, who had a serious drug problem. A neighbor called social services and for a while, Amber was thrown into the system and we didn't know where she was. Some of the teachers here did some checking and found out she'd gone to a group home. Can you imagine? A four—almost five-year-old child with no one to look after her? In a house with older, potentially dangerous kids? Anyway, we tracked down a neighbor who qualified as a foster mother and she took Amber in. She's been with her ever since, and you know, she's finally starting to—"

Diego turned away, nearly knocking Georgia over in his rush to the door. By the time she recovered her equilibrium in order to follow, he'd disappeared down the stairs.

She scurried after him and saw that he hadn't gone out the front to the sidewalk, but had headed under the stairwell and through the door to the alley. Georgia followed, assailed at once by the strong smells from the nearby Dumpster and the wild, unpredictable power of Diego's rage.

Holding the door open, just in case she needed a quick escape, she called out, "Diego, are you all right?"

He kicked the side of the trash container. "Do I look all right?"

She flinched at the anger in his voice. He kicked the metal again and his knuckles were white from the tight fisting of his hands. He let out a long string of curses in Spanish, most of which she'd heard before but couldn't translate. But the words didn't matter. The rage did.

"What's wrong with you? Look, girls like Amber have it tough, but they're survivors. That's why we're here. To give them hope, goals, dreams they can have the courage to pursue."

He spun on her, stalking toward her with such intensity that she nearly retreated behind the door. But despite the ferocity burning in his dark eyes, she knew his rage wasn't for her. But for whom?

"I should have been able to give her those things, Georgia. *Me!* Not some foster parent or social worker or bleeding-heart neighbor. It's my responsibility. Mine! And it was stolen from me. She was stolen from me."

The last words came out strong, with great emotion. Right before her eyes, his heart was breaking, and Georgia had no idea why.

"Diego, who are you talking about?"

"Alexis, my daughter."

"You have a child?"

He closed his eyes and took a succession of deep breaths until he had his emotions under control. "Yes, I do. But you know her as Amber. That *angelita* up there is my daughter. And don't try and stop me because I've come to take her home."

CHAPTER
SEVEN

"DIEGO, what are you talking about?"

Squeezing his eyes shut as tightly as he could, Diego desperately tried to let go of his fury. He thought he'd overcome that emotional backlash a long time ago, after he'd first learned about Alexis. He thought that he'd come to terms with the betrayal and lies, that he'd accepted Callie's death as apt payback for her deceptions. He'd even gone to confession to cleanse that ugliness from his soul. He'd grappled with his guilt and his fear and his temper and had recovered by concentrating solely on recovering Alexis and giving her the life and the love she deserved. With security. A family. A father.

But seeing her in the studio, dancing as if she didn't have a care in the world and yet knowing she'd likely been through hell or worse to get to that safe classroom in the middle of one of the toughest neighborhoods in the city made his blood boil to hazardous levels.

When he finally opened his eyes, his anger tentatively under control, he saw the alarm and confusion in Georgia's eyes. She clutched that door as if she might need to use the steel panel as a protective barrier against him.

"I'm sorry, Georgia. I thought I could handle finding her, but I guess I was wrong. Alexis is my daughter, my child. She was stolen from me before I even knew she existed. I only learned about her five months ago, and since then, I've been searching for her. I found a picture of her in a magazine online and used you and *Groove With Me* to track her here. I thought when I finally saw her in person, I'd feel nothing but joy, but hearing about her life, about how she was abandoned and thrown into a group home and foster care…"

When his voice choked, he stopped talking and turned away. He had to get himself together. He couldn't show Georgia the depth of his anger or he'd ruin everything. Not just because he would need her help at this point, but because he desperately didn't want to lose her friendship, her respect.

Georgia released the door, letting it shut quietly as she walked into the alley and placed her hand softly on his shoulder. "I don't understand what you're talking about."

"There is no grant, Georgia. I mean, I received the money, but I have no plans to start a *Groove With Me* in Miami. That was a lie, an excuse to get in here and find my child. That money is for Alexis, the little girl you call Amber. I'm taking her home with me, Georgia, and when I do, that money will ensure her future. I have to concentrate on her. Can you see that? Can you understand?"

Not surprisingly, Georgia pulled her hand away. "No, Diego, I don't understand. Oh, God." She staggered back a few steps as the truth came into clearer view. "How do you know Amber is your daughter if you've never seen her?"

With as few words as possible, Diego explained the trail that led him here. He told her all he'd learned about Rita and her disappearance in New York, about Mike Jessup's claims and Callie's lies. When he was done, Georgia looked even more horrified than before.

"You plan to steal your daughter back? Diego, I can't let you do that. You don't know that Amber is yours. She could really be Rita's baby. This Mike person could be wrong or misleading you out of spite. And even if she is your child, she has a life here in

New York. Mrs. Baxter took her in when she had no one. She's been uprooted and thrown into a whirlpool of uncertainty and fear. You can't just tear her away because you happen to, maybe, share the same DNA. You need to be careful and work with Mrs. Baxter and the social workers so that Amber isn't traumatized any more than she already has been."

The fire in Diego's blood surged and intensified. "You don't have a say in this, Georgia."

She stood up straighter, her blue eyes narrowed into sapphire slits. "While that little girl is in this building, she's my responsibility. If your story is true, then I feel for you, I really do. You have a long *legal* road ahead of you. But I'm not about to let you take her." She jabbed her finger at his chest. "And if you try to snatch her against her will, I'll kick and scream and fight and protect that child with all I have, do you understand me?"

She spun on her heel and stalked to the door, which didn't respond to her first tug. Or the second. Or the third. She let out a string of curses that snapped Diego out of his rage. Georgia had every right to be furious with him. He'd let his emotions override his good sense. Alexis was no longer in the care of the unstable aunt who'd stolen her. Though the child had traveled a rough road, his baby was now with someone who loved her, someone both Georgia and the state of New York trusted to take good care of her. His child, for the moment, was safe and secure. He didn't have to steal her back, no matter how much his arms ached to hold her.

"Georgia, I'm sorry."

She stopped pounding on the metal long enough to turn around and spear him with an expression that was both incredulous and offended. "Sorry for what, Diego? That you used me? That you lied to me? Or that you were planning on stealing an innocent child from the only home where she's ever known unconditional love and security?"

He swallowed hard. He'd let his strong paternal pull blind him, but he couldn't allow regrets when he'd simply done the best he could to find his child.

"I'm sorry for threatening to take Alexis away without knowing all the facts. But I'm not sorry that I lied or that I used you. How can I be? I had to find my baby. And if I had to run over some people in order to do it, then that's the way it goes. Would you expect a desperate father to do anything less?"

She snared her bottom lip with her teeth. "You could have told me the truth."

He nodded and slipped his hands into his pockets, forcing his palms to flatten and unfist. "When I first met you, I thought Alexis was still with Rita. If I'd told you who I was, I knew you would have gone to Rita to find out if what I claimed was true or if I was some weirdo trying to steal a pretty little girl. In your effort to be fair and responsible, you would have tipped her off and she might have run again. She didn't have legal custody of Alexis. After Callie, Alexis's mother, died, Rita stole her, changed her name to Amber and moved to New York City. It was sheer luck that I found her on what little information I had to work with. You have to understand. Rita wasn't going to let a little thing like the law or doing what's right stand in her way. Hurting Alexis was no big thing to her or she would have brought the baby to me after Callie died instead of running off to New York with a bad drug habit, no job and no way to support a child. You can't blame me for not trusting you. I didn't know you and you didn't know me."

Georgia turned around, slamming her open palms on the door as she leaned back, her anger present, but deflated. "That may be true, but last night, you knew me well enough to kiss me. You could have told me then. I would have listened. Hell, Diego, I would have told you Rita wasn't in the picture anymore."

"I can't change the past, Georgia. But I'm telling you now. What are you going to do?"

She shook her head. The pounding music and clickety-clack of tap shoes from the studio upstairs seeped into the alleyway. In her mind's eye, she could picture little Amber Campbell...actually, Alexis Paz, throwing every ounce of her six-year-old energy into the dance. She could see all the other little girls watching her through the corner of their eyes, knowing they could keep up with the routine if they just watched their friend. She never missed a step. Never missed a beat.

Georgia opened her eyes, but instantly spun around so that Diego wouldn't see the emotional roller coaster playing across her face. She knew and accepted why he'd done what he had—but she also knew the pain of his mistruths hadn't had time to fade. After giving the door one last futile tug, she started down the alleyway. She could slip through the back of the business next to the ninety-nine-cent store and return to her class. To her responsibilities. To her students, like little Amber, who was about to have her world thrown into chaos yet again.

"Where are you going?" Diego shouted after her.

She turned wearily. "I'm going upstairs to call Mrs. Baxter, who's probably going to call social services. In the meantime, I hope you'll contact an attorney, because if you're going to pursue this, and I know you will, then you need to do it right."

"What about Alexis? I want to meet her, Georgia. I have to…"

His voice trailed off and Georgia was sure her stoic glare had something to do with it.

"You'll meet her when the time is right, Diego. And not a moment before."

Juana Baxter was a large woman, the widow of an East Harlem shop owner whose family had railed against him marrying a Puerto Rican, much less a black one. She'd lived through all Harlem's transformations from a predominantly African-American neighborhood to one brimming with Hispanics of various ethnicities and races, and now home to the offices of a former president. But Harlem wasn't gentrified just yet. Juana lived in a small, rent-controlled, spotless apartment five blocks from the dance studio, and while she'd often had more than four or five children in her care at one time, both foster and family, right now, it was just her and Amber.

And for the moment, Georgia and Diego.

"And you believe him?" Juana asked Georgia, her eyes wary as she watched Diego trying to find a comfortable spot on her plastic-covered couch.

Georgia glanced over at Diego and couldn't stop the wash of regret for the way she'd yelled at him two days ago. Though they'd spoken less than ten words to each other since she agreed to set up this meeting with Juana, she had to hope they could someday make right what had gone so wrong. If they could only stay focused on Amber, they'd have a chance.

"He has strong reasons to believe Amber is his daughter, yes. And I believe there's no harm in conducting a DNA test to see if he's right. If Amber is his child, she has a large extended family back in Miami and a father willing to move heaven and earth to have her in his life. She deserves to know them."

Juana started to lift her large body out of the La-Z-Boy chair where she'd been sitting and the task wasn't easy. She wasn't young—hadn't been young for a good long time. Though her hair was still pitch-black and her skin gleamed from perfectly applied makeup, Georgia knew Juana had to be pushing seventy.

"Amber loves me," Juana said. "I'd have adopted her if I wasn't so old. My daughter and her husband were thinking of adopting her for me, so I could make sure that when I pass, she'd have family. She has friends, something she never had with Rita. And a home. She hardly ever talks about Rita anymore, and the nightmares, they stopped. She goes to counseling. She's started kindergarten at a good public school. I can't see where disrupting her life is a good idea. And social services says that I don't have to agree to the DNA test unless he petitions the court."

"I'll do that, if I have to," Diego said. "But we can save the court a whole lot of time and money if you, as her legal guardian, simply sign the papers my attorney will have brought over by tomorrow. I didn't come here to disrupt her life, Mrs. Baxter. I came here to give her the life that was stolen from her when she was just a baby." Diego stood, his hands flush at his side. "I swear, *señora,* if I had known about her, I never would have let anyone take her from me. Never. You have a good heart. You've given her a good home. But she needs to be with her family. Her *real* family."

Georgia folded her hands in her lap, unable to watch as the glossiness in Juana's eyes burgeoned into unshed tears. God, this was so hard on everyone, most especially Amber, who was, luckily, playing upstairs with a neighbor, oblivious to the potential fallout of this adult discussion. When she and Diego had arrived, Amber had skipped out of the apartment with hardly a care in the world.

"Juana, I know you want to do what is best for Amber," Georgia continued. "And I know Diego does, too. He might have gone about things wrong in the beginning, but that was only because he was afraid that Rita would take Amber away again. You and I both knew Rita. His fears were valid."

"She's gone now," Juana said, pointing toward the door. "She left when social services placed Amber with me. She's not coming back. Last I heard, she went to Los Angeles or Vegas or something. We won't hear from her again."

Diego glanced down at the floor and Georgia couldn't help but respect him for the restraint he was exhibiting. She knew his instincts would be to fight until he obtained his objective. He was, after all, a trained soldier. But he was also a good man with a good heart, and she knew he had no desire to hurt the woman who had saved his daughter from the group home.

"You don't know that," he said. "Not for sure. And I mean no disrespect, *señora,* but if Rita showed up here, would you be able to stop her from taking my daughter?"

Juana frowned. "I protect my own."

Diego stepped forward. "But she's not your own. You have children. I have no one but the little baby that no one ever told me about. Her mother didn't give me the chance to be in her life. How can you do that to me, as well? How can you do that to Amber?"

The stone in the pit of Georgia's stomach dropped a few inches. He'd used his child's new name—the only name she'd ever known. He'd pleaded his case with calm and logic. She knew now where her allegiance lay, but Mrs. Baxter had to agree or else a long, ugly legal battle was sure to ensue.

Juana took a deep breath, then made a sign of the cross and said a muttered but desperate prayer.

"Fine. She can take the test. But she's not to know why until we know if you're her father. And if she is your child," she said, stalking toward him with intimidating power, "you're not going to just rip her away, do you understand? I won't let you hurt her."

Georgia watched Diego try desperately to tamp down his excitement, but his smile broke through anyway. "I'll do what's best for Amber, *señora*. I promise."

Juana gave one curt nod. "I'll hold you to that."

CHAPTER
EIGHT

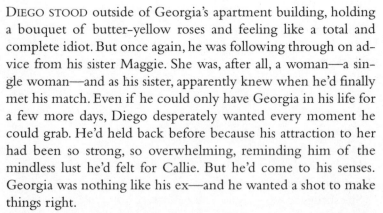

DIEGO STOOD outside of Georgia's apartment building, holding a bouquet of butter-yellow roses and feeling like a total and complete idiot. But once again, he was following through on advice from his sister Maggie. She was, after all, a woman—a single woman—and as his sister, apparently knew when he'd finally met his match. Even if he could only have Georgia in his life for a few more days, Diego desperately wanted every moment he could grab. He'd held back before because his attraction to her had been so strong, so overwhelming, reminding him of the mindless lust he'd felt for Callie. But he'd come to his senses. Georgia was nothing like his ex—and he wanted a shot to make things right.

He was about to press the intercom button to Georgia's apartment when the elevator inside the lobby sliced open and she walked out, her attention on the canvas tote bag she'd slung over her shoulder. Diego stepped away from the glass doors and waited until she looked up.

When she did, her eyes widened and she bit back a smile, but not before Diego experienced a thrill at the unbidden grin. For a second there, she'd been happy to see him. That might go a long way in what he intended to say to her.

She swung open the door. "Did you get my message?"

He glanced down where he'd clipped his cell phone to his waist. "No, I…you called me?"

Her eyes darted to the flowers, and her skin pinkened. "I called about three hours ago. You didn't call me back, so I figured you were still angry."

Diego quietly cursed the unreliability of cell phones as he thrust the flowers toward her. "Do these say angry?"

She chewed her bottom lip, gnawing on the sumptuous peachy lip gloss she'd smoothed over her mouth. God, he'd have paid for an entire hothouse of roses if she'd only allow him a taste of that sweet, luscious fruit.

"Yellow roses are for friendship," she told him.

"I picked them because they were pretty, but if they mean friendship, that's a start."

She took the flowers and held them close, breathing in the sweet, subtle scent and allowing the soft petals to caress her skin. Diego shoved his hands into his pockets, tamping down the insatiable desire to touch her with equal softness. If he wanted the right results, he couldn't rush.

Georgia seemed energized by his gesture and grabbed his arm before she spoke. "You know, you really saved me a whole bunch of drama by coming here. I was all set to head over to your hotel and do a little groveling."

He laughed, ignoring how tight his flesh felt beneath hers. "Groveling? You? What for?"

She shrugged one shoulder. "I really read you the riot act when I first found out about you and Amber. I should have been a little more sensitive to what you'd gone through."

Diego stepped closer and surrendered to his need to touch her by pushing a stray lock of hair away from her cheek. "I lied to you, Georgia. I don't regret that I did what I had to in order to find my daughter, but I do regret hurting you. And I should never have threatened to take Amber. You reacted the only way a woman who cares about children would. I'm glad Amber has you on her side."

A woman from Georgia's building came along the sidewalk, so she and Diego flattened against the call-button panel to give her room to pass. Once they were alone again, Georgia looked at Diego with silent apology. "You want to walk down to the park? Talk about Amber some more? I can tell you more about her, or you can clue me in on what your plans are if things work out the way you hope."

Diego shook his head. "We've taken the DNA tests and now I have about a week to wait until the results. There's nothing more to talk about with Amber. I'm going to learn about her firsthand, when the time is right. If she's not my child, I don't want to disrupt her life any more than it already has been. I've waited six years to be her father. I can wait six more days."

Georgia frowned, glanced down at the flowers, her brow crunched. "Okay, then. Well, I guess I have some errands I need to run, but I should put these upstairs first. Thanks for the roses."

She turned to reenter the building, but Diego's hand shot out and snagged her by the wrist before she could retrieve her key. "Something's lost in the translation. I came here to see you, Georgia. To see *you*. Not to talk about Amber or to plan my future. I'm going to be in New York for at least another week while everything is sorted out, and I thought, maybe…"

"That we could spend time together?"

"Yeah," he said, grinning so much at the spirit in her voice that he was certain he looked like a moron. "You're an amazing woman. I'd like to start over."

She slapped him gently on the shoulders with the flowers. "Sounds like a plan. Let's take care of these beautiful flowers and then I'm going to show you New York like you've never seen it."

WHEN GEORGIA WASN'T teaching or working on the fund-raiser, she and Diego spent afternoons exploring the museums and diverse neighborhoods from Little Italy to Chinatown to the Garment and Diamond Districts. Mornings consisted of sharing coffee and bagels at sidewalk cafés, and evenings were reserved for sampling the vast offerings of New York City restaurants or hot dance clubs. On the night before Diego was scheduled to receive the results of Amber's DNA test, Georgia gifted him with tickets to her favorite Broadway show. They reveled in the music, pageantry and electric excitement of the Great White Way, had espresso and dessert at Sardi's and then walked through Times Square until Georgia's feet ached in her strappy, sexy sandals. Diego hailed a cab, and as they rode back to Georgia's apartment in intimate silence, each wondered where the night would lead. Their days had taken them about as far into friendship as they could possibly go and time was running out.

When the taxi driver parked in front of Georgia's building, she stepped out and turned heavy-lidded eyes on Diego. "Don't ask him to wait," she said with a sultry rhythm, then headed quickly toward her door.

Without a word, Diego paid the fare and followed.

They went up to her apartment without exchanging more than a single stare, locked gazes ripe with fire and longing. As the doors to the elevator swished open on the third floor, Georgia suspected that the tight, enclosed space had echoed with the sound of her heartbeat. She'd arranged theatre tickets for tonight for several reasons, not all of them selfless. Yes, she knew Diego needed a serious distraction to make it through the wait for the DNA test results. And she'd had a clear stroke of luck when her roommate decided to go upstate to visit her fiancé for a few days. She and Diego had the apartment to themselves, and after a long wait for the right moment to take her connection with Diego to the next level, Georgia was ready.

She wanted him, deeply and completely. Nothing could change the fact that once he had the answers to his questions, he'd leave New York. Just two days ago, he'd learned that he'd been accepted into the police academy in Miami. At their lunch dates and in phone conversations, he admitted to her how much he missed his family and friends. And to underscore the reality that his time here was almost done, he'd confessed that he couldn't justify spending any more of what he considered to be Amber's money on a hotel room, hanging around New York, when Mrs. Baxter barely allowed him to see her except for several planned "accidental" meetings in the park where Amber played every day after school.

Once he had the results, he wasn't sticking around. He would stay only long enough for the courts to grant him sole custody, which his attorney assured him wouldn't take long if he proved to be Amber's biological father.

So if Georgia was going to make her move, she'd have to do it now, which was no sacrifice. She'd wanted to make love to him since shortly after they'd met. But throughout all their dates, both casual and formal, he'd held back. That one electric kiss they'd shared still vibrated through both of them, she was sure, but Diego had had his reasons for moving with caution—reasons she didn't need him to explain.

Georgia wanted to say something clever once she shut the door of her apartment behind him. She knew that somewhere in her sophisticated brain, the perfect seductive quip or tease existed, borrowed and blended from all the great dialogue she'd heard both on Broadway and in film. Luckily, the minute she turned around from securing the locks, Diego smashed his mouth against hers, blasting away any need for words at all.

The fire they'd invoked at their first meeting flamed into an inferno. Anticipation had heightened her senses, but it was reality that thrummed instantly to the surface, coating her skin with a warm sheen, making her flesh the perfect conduit for Diego's charged touch.

He untucked her blouse and worked the buttons until the fabric parted. His palms spread over her, sparking an instant wildfire. He explored, learned, aroused. She tore at his clothes with equal need, moaning when her hands met the hard, hot planes of his chest.

He dropped his mouth to her neck and shoulders, peeling away her shirt until she felt a shiver from the cool air, a shiver he immediately countered with his searing kiss. Despite the intimacy, they didn't remain still. Step by stumbling, erotic step, Georgia led

Diego toward her bedroom. Only after they'd crossed the threshold did they come up for air.

Diego stood, dark-eyed and panting, as Georgia reached behind her to unhook her lacy, tinted bra. She'd chosen the apricot color to complement her fair skin and blond hair, and judging by the hungry look in Diego's unmovable gaze, she'd picked correctly. When she let the lingerie fall away, the air around them swelled as fully as her breasts. There was no turning back now.

"Georgia," he said, his voice thick and needful.

She distracted him with a coy smile while she unzipped the back of her skirt and shimmied the material to the ground. She spun slowly while stepping out of her clothes, causing him to groan.

"You're torturing me," he said.

She crooked her finger toward him, beckoning him closer. "That's the idea."

In a second, he was against her, flush and hard, but with his hands hovering around her, instead of on her. The effect was just as arousing. His want simmered off him with so much power, she could feel the coming friction as if his fingers emitted strong, electric currents.

"You're like some rich dessert I'm not allowed to have," he said.

She pressed forward so that her nipples scraped across his bare chest. "Says who?"

"Georgia, I'll be leaving soon."

"I don't care."

He swept a hungry kiss across her lips. "I can't make you any promises."

"I don't care," she said, more forcefully this time, her lips warming his neck with her hot breath. In the light streaming in from outside, she watched his flesh prickle and react. He wouldn't hold out for long.

"I don't want to hurt you. Ever."

Her heart ached at his declaration, but Georgia tightened her chest to press out her emotional reaction. Diego had already infiltrated her defenses like the efficient soldier he was. If she had any chance of making it out of this campaign with her heart intact, she had to maintain a certain distance.

She was probably too late, but she had to try.

"I care about you, Diego," she admitted, loving how the warmth of his body kept their passion stoked, even in this awkward moment. "But to be honest, you've turned me on since the first moment I laid eyes on you. I know you're leaving soon. That's precisely why I won't let this last chance slip away. We may never get another."

Diego licked his lips as he listened, his hands finally skimming over her skin with a lightness that nearly drove her insane. He traced across her shoulders, then dipped his hands lower, across her hips, teasing the sensitive indentation at the base of her spine. Just for an instant. Just enough to jumpstart the thrill skimming through her bloodstream.

"You mean a great deal to me, too, Georgia. More than I ever expected. And *madre di Dios,* you turn me on like no other woman ever has."

She sighed, leaned forward and kissed the hollow at the base of his neck. "Then show me."

Luckily for her, Diego wasn't a man who had to be asked twice.

CHAPTER
NINE

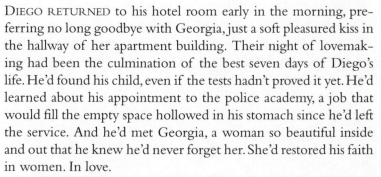

DIEGO RETURNED to his hotel room early in the morning, pre-
ferring no long goodbye with Georgia, just a soft pleasured kiss in
the hallway of her apartment building. Their night of lovemaking had been the culmination of the best seven days of Diego's
life. He'd found his child, even if the tests hadn't proved it yet. He'd
learned about his appointment to the police academy, a job that
would fill the empty space hollowed in his stomach since he'd left
the service. And he'd met Georgia, a woman so beautiful inside
and out that he knew he'd never forget her. She'd restored his faith
in women. In love.

And whatever happened from this point forward couldn't, he
hoped, destroy what he and Georgia had built together, even if the
foundation of their relationship would never house anything more
than a temporary affair and a permanent, long-distance friendship.
They'd always be connected in a way that warmed his soul—and
fired his libido. He had no idea how he'd exist without making
love with Georgia again, but he figured he'd deal with that another day.

Once inside his room, he crashed onto his bed and slept almost immediately, waking around eleven o'clock when the hotel phone rang.

"Mr. Paz? The package you've been expecting just arrived," the clerk announced.

Diego promised to go downstairs soon, but after he hung up, he lingered on the bed for almost half an hour, mentally replaying the many possibilities of what direction his life would go in once he went downstairs and retrieved the report from the lab regarding his DNA and his daughter's.

Images of his first visit with Amber in the park materialized in his mind. He couldn't remember ever shaking so violently, not even the night before he'd gone into his first raid in Kabul to hunt down operatives of the Al Qaeda terrorist network. He'd trained day and night for years for the covert assignment, working with the Army Nightstalkers in a support brigade. But nothing had prepared him to talk informally with the little girl he knew in his heart to be his flesh and blood.

But he couldn't touch her, no matter how his arms ached to hug her or his chest constricted with the need to feel her tiny cheek pressed against him. He'd thought only mothers experienced an inexplicable connection with their children, but he couldn't have been more wrong. When she'd skipped over to him on the park bench while he'd chatted amicably with Mrs. Baxter, her guardian, his smile had nearly cracked his face in two.

"You know Miss Georgia," Amber had announced, cocking her tiny fist on her hip just like she probably saw the big girls do. "You her boyfriend or what?"

He'd cleared his throat, the smile not so hard to tamp down any longer. "Well, I'm a boy and I'm her friend."

The child rolled her eyes. "I saw you at the studio."

Diego decided to turn the conversation. "And I saw you. You're a really great dancer. The best one in the class."

She grinned and shrugged, a telltale blush on her tanned cheeks. "I want to be on Broadway someday. Juana took me to see *Movin' Out* with them Twyla Tharp dancers. It was so cool! They did this one thing—let me show you…"

And she had. Time had slipped away as Diego watched his daughter attempt to recreate the sophisticated dance moves she'd seen on stage. As she danced and tripped and prattled on with words he didn't understand like *plié* and *arabesque,* he searched fruitlessly for signs of the abuse and neglect she'd experienced with Rita, and likely with Callie before that. He saw nothing but animated excitement for dance, and clearly, for her life in New York City. At Mrs. Baxter's suggestion, Amber had shown him around the park, introduced him to her friends and pleaded with him until he bought her a snow cone. He'd left the outing exhausted—and yet never more excited in his entire life.

That energy propelled him to brush his teeth and then head downstairs to retrieve the information from the lab. He'd wanted to wait until he was back in his room before he opened the envelope, but he barely made it to the elevator. He scanned the percentages and graphs and realized he'd learned nothing he didn't already know.

Amber was his child.

The question now was, what was he going to do about it?

He walked to his room in a fog, sliding the card key into the door and then forgetting what to do next. He watched as the little green light flicked back to red and he had to swipe the card again. The room, he noticed, smelled like the coffee he'd left in the in-room carafe since yesterday. He hadn't yet opened the blinds, and the gloomy darkness seemed suited to his mood—which surprisingly wasn't filled with elation or victory.

How could this be so difficult? He knew he had to take Amber to Miami. That's where his family was. That's where his new job was. When he was working, his mother and sisters would be there to take care of her. She'd never go to day care or have any babysitter who didn't share her blood. His father worked for free on the cars of the priests who ran the Catholic school, so Georgia would likely be immediately enrolled there despite the waiting lists. Why then did looking at his duffel bag fill him with dread?

His cell phone rang, and after a disoriented moment, he answered.

"You received your report?"

He wasn't entirely surprised to hear Mrs. Baxter on the other end of the line.

"Yes, ma'am. Just a few minutes ago."

"The social worker called me. Your attorney isn't wasting any time in taking that baby away."

"I don't have time to waste, *señora*. I'm sorry. You've been an amazing foster mother to Amber, but she belongs with me."

The old woman huffed. "The only person who's going to be sorry around here is Amber. You're her father, *verdad,* but she's happy here. She knows people, trusts people."

His heart ached, but he shook his head, silently denying what his daughter's guardian claimed, despite how true her words rang. Amber blended into Spanish Harlem. She loved the city, and through her eyes—and Georgia's—he could see why.

"She'll learn to love and trust in Miami. I promise you, *señora*. Amber will be very happy."

"What about the dance performance coming up? She's been working so hard. She's the star. Miss Georgia made a special place for her to dance by herself. *Por favor,* Diego, let the child stay with me a little longer."

Why wouldn't *no* come out of his mouth?

"I want to see her," he said. "Not like some stranger she knows from the park. She needs to know who I am. If I have to call the social worker—"

Mrs. Baxter interrupted. "God help that she never has to see another social worker her entire life! Come to my house tonight for dinner. We'll explain it all to her together."

Diego released the breath he hadn't realized he was holding. He accepted the generous invitation and then pressed the End button on the phone. Almost instantaneously, he pressed the first three numbers of Georgia's cell phone—then stopped. Yes, she'd want to hear this news from him, but should he call her now? Maybe he should wait until after he'd spoken with Amber. After he'd called his sister and his family and finalized all the arrangements for their move back to Miami.

Then he wouldn't be so tempted to change his mind.

Yet even as he tried to calm his crying mother, who'd shouted the news gleefully to whoever was in earshot, he knew that for all he'd won, thanks to the test results he held in his hand that proved Amber was his child, he was also about to lose something precious.

Georgia.

"FIVE…six…seven…eight."

Georgia half whispered, half shouted the count to the girls from the side of the stage. The music was pounding, loud and intense. The audience, applauding from the first moment the twelve six-year-olds bounded enthusiastically onto the stage to the beat of a Will Smith song, hadn't stopped clapping. Would the noise distract them? Keep them off their count?

Georgia clasped her hands together and prayed. After a few seconds, she peeked one eye open and watched Amber step forward for her solo. The other girls beamed at the crowd while the little girl she'd watched blossom from a scared, unsure foster kid into a confident, talented dancer whipped the collection of parents, neighborhood business owners, residents and charitable donors into a frenzy…none more so than Diego, her father, who stood front and center, his video camera steady in his strong, tanned hand even as his hips rocked to the beat.

Her vision was suddenly clouded by emotions she had no right to have, and Georgia turned away. Since the night they'd made love, she hadn't seen Diego more than twice, once when he'd brought Amber to dance class, and the second time when they'd met for coffee before he went to an appointment with his attorney. Both times, the conversation had been intimate and sweet and awkward. Over the course of the week, she'd hoped their slow separation would ease the pain of knowing that tomorrow morning, he and Amber would be boarding a plane to Miami with only vague promises to return.

Suddenly, the music stopped. Georgia whirled toward the CD player Marcy was manning, but Georgia's assistant had her lips pressed tightly together, grinning as if she'd just won the lottery. Spinning back toward the stage, Georgia gasped as Amber held her hand out to her father, who climbed onto the platform at his daughter's urging. Suddenly, Georgia became aware of a dozen tiny hands pushing her from the sides and behind, propelling her into the middle of the performance area.

"What's going on?"

Marcy had grabbed the microphone.

"Sorry, folks, we didn't want to interrupt our dance, but it seems Amber didn't have the patience to wait until the end for her cue."

Amber and her dance mates giggled and the crowd whispered curiously to each other. Marcy, Georgia's assistant, skittered across the stage and passed the wireless device to Amber, who looked up, wide-eyed and grinning, at her father.

"This is my dad."

A few people in the audience clapped. The rest looked just as perplexed as Georgia felt.

"And he has something he wanted to ask Miss Georgia before we have to leave to go to…Flor'da."

Georgia focused her gaze on Diego. His grin was tilted, his dark eyes twinkling with that bad-boy charm that had so affected her the first day they'd met. God, she'd been so wrong about him then. Yeah, he was still appealing to her on the most elemental, physical levels, but she'd learned that this tough ex-soldier who would have done the unthinkable in order to retrieve his child was also a calm, reasonable man with big dreams and a lot of love to share.

But could they share that love from a distance?

Amber handed the microphone to her father, but not until after he dropped to one knee.

Georgia's heart slammed against her chest.

This couldn't be happening!

Even after Diego pulled a velvet box out of his pocket and the crowd split their reaction between emotional sighs and raucous cheers, Georgia couldn't process what was taking place. All she could think about was her strong feelings for Diego, for Amber…and unfortunately, for her life and career in New York City.

She covered her mouth with her hand.

"Georgia Rae Evans, I know this is a lot to ask, but—"

"Oh, God, Diego! I can't move to Miami! I know how much you love your home and your family, and that Amber here needs to know about her roots and will have lots and lots of relatives to love and look after her all the time and—"

With a groan, Diego stood up and kissed Georgia into submissive silence. The reaction of the crowd was nearly deafening, led by Amber, who'd grabbed the microphone out of his hand and had joined in a chorus of little girls saying, "Ew!" at the top of their lungs.

"Open the box," Diego said, his lips pressed close against her ear.

She did as he asked. Inside, she found two cards—one a laminated New York State driver's license with Diego's picture on it, and the other a business card that said, *Groove With Me,* Miami Chapter, Margarita Paz, instructor.

"What is this?" she asked, partially thankful not to have found jewelry inside the box. She cared about Diego deeply, but as much as jumping into bed or even into a relationship with him felt right, anything more would be too much, too soon.

If he sensed the speck of disappointment lingering in her eyes, however, he didn't let on. He just held her tight, his body molded against hers in ways she knew only his body could.

He pushed her back far enough to be able to see into her eyes. "I've talked a lot with Mrs. Baxter, with the social workers and Amber's teachers at school. They all agree that Amber is just starting to adjust to her home here, and to take her away would set her back. So I established residency here. I mean, I can't think of a better reason to stay in New York…except maybe one."

Their kiss was met with raucous applause. The girls cheered, whooped and danced around until Marcy finally had the sense to turn the music back to the beginning and shoo Diego and Georgia off to the side of the stage. Georgia came up for air to find her world spinning. She hadn't been looking for love. Diego hadn't been looking for love when he'd come to New York on his quest for his child. But they'd found it, and luckily, both of them were smart enough and stubborn enough to hang on tight.

"I can't believe you're going to stay."

Diego pressed his lips together, but nodded confidently. "I know it won't be easy to adjust, but my parents and my sister want to visit. Maggie's going to have to because I've given her a big hunk of the grant money to start another chapter of *Groove With Me,* and the attorney she works for is going to kick in the rest, enough to get them started. New York is where I need to be. Amber loves it here. And honestly, you're here. I couldn't imagine leaving you behind."

Her heart swelled and she wiped an errant tear from her eye. "We haven't known each other for very long."

"I know, but being with you—" he wrapped his hands so tightly around her waist, Georgia wondered if he ever intended to release her "—feels so right. Time isn't going to change my love, Georgia, except to make it stronger."

She slid her palms onto his cheeks. "I feel the same way. You leaving was breaking my heart. And Amber…what about your job?"

"I applied to the New York City police department and one of the guys doing the hiring is an ex-MP like me. It looks good. And Mrs. Baxter wants to keep taking care of Amber when I'm working, so her life won't change that much. I'm looking for a place to live, maybe a house in Brooklyn, close enough for both of us to commute to the city. I don't know. I haven't worked out all the details, but we can do that together."

Georgia kissed Diego soundly, with all the same passion they'd exchanged that night in her apartment, knowing they could fix whatever needed fixing and plan whatever needed planning so long as they worked together.

Diego gave her one last tight squeeze, and then glanced down at the velvet box still in her hand.

"There's something else."

Perplexed and giddy with energy, Georgia moved the cards out of the way and caught the unmistakable glimmer of gold. A delicate heart weaved around a slender, graceful dancer, dangling from a serpentine chain. A lump of emotion formed in her throat, but before she had to choke her way past it to speak, Diego pulled her close and whispered against her ear.

"You danced your way into my heart, Georgia Rae Evans. Now, I'll never let you go."

As he swept her up in another hot, insistent kiss, she had no doubts in her mind and nothing in her heart but love and hope and faith that they'd both finally found the right groove for their love—in each other's arms.